Drifting Fines

Consequences

Consequences

UGO

Toronto

Requests for permission to make copies of any part of this book should be mailed to the following address: Administration Department, Elmira Inc., P.O. Box 80037 Lakeshore Village, Toronto, Ontario, M8V 4A1

Library and Archives Canada Cataloguing in Publication
Ugo (Ugochi Babajide), 1979-, author
Drifting fines : consequences / Ugo.

Issued in print and electronic formats.
ISBN 978-0-9936364-2-4 (bound).--ISBN 978-0-9936364-0-0 (pbk.).--
ISBN 978-0-9936364-1-7 (Kindle).--ISBN -- 978-0-9936364-3-1 (Kobo). --
ISBN 978-0-9936364-4-8 (Nook). --ISBN 978-0-9936364-5-5 (iBook).
I. Title.

PS3621.G6D75 2014   813'.6   C2014-900590-3
                                           C2014-900591-1

Also available in Braille format ISBN 978-0-9936364-6-2

First Edition 2014

Printed in the United States of America

Cover design by Adazing Design
Interior design by Jennifer Zaczek

Dedicated to Boon and Gabby.
Words cannot express how appreciative I am of your patience.

Contents

Fines, noun,
very small particles found in mining, milling, etc.

Consequences

Prologue

MINERS WERE hard at work amid the sound of drills blasting holes in the ground. The enormous tires of the delivery truck maneuvered through the rocky, red earth, halting for its final pickup of the day. With his arms folded across his chest, Juan Gomes watched, entranced by the rhythmic flow. This wasn't exactly the big break he had expected with relocating, but finding work was something to be grateful for.

Most said his family had been too fortunate. As brutal as the civil war had been, not a single Gomes had lost his life in it. When friends and even cousins on the other sides of their family perished, the Gomeses, as those of old would say, *waxed strong*. They had lost friends as well. Some were incarcerated for supporting the Republic, while others sought refuge in France.

According to some, the Gomes family was powerful; to others, they were cowards for never taking a stand for anything. However, minding their business was what the Gomeses knew, and if that kept them alive, so be it. Juan didn't know what to make of it. He just knew that he had to leave Spain because it was in dire straits, and after having survived a war, he was not about to lose his family to starvation.

The truck veered off the grounds, hauling away the final batch of blasted ore for crushing, and leaving dust fumes behind in its trail. Juan covered his mouth and nose with his worn damp rag. Blinking away dust from his eyes, he made out an image of a lanky man approaching through the fumes.

"What are these?" the man asked, pointing to the heap of iron fines the truck had left behind.

"Oh, those are just waste," Juan replied, coughing. "It came from the iron. I see you are new to this."

Ignoring Juan's last statement, the man continued. "*Waste?* It'd be a shame to throw all this away," he said, grabbing a handful of the powdery substance and staring intently at it.

Juan's brows furrowed. "Are you the new guy?"

"I'm sure we can use this for some good." A slight smile crept up on the man's lips as he rubbed the particles together between his fingers.

Juan felt a sudden chill come over him as he watched the mysterious man stroll off without another word. Just then, a mighty wind blew over the entire work site, ruffling through the heap of fines—its particles nearly blinding him.

As he struggled to keep his gaze on the man, he heard someone yell from a distance, "A storm is coming!" Yet his feet remained planted to the ground in sheer fright. There had been something sinister about the man's voice and the fact that he did not make his identity known, let alone, reply to his question.

Although it was difficult to see through the turbulence, he knew he was not imagining what he saw next. The winds had nearly flattened the heap of fines and its particles drifted toward the mystery man.

CHAPTER ONE

Bombshell!

❦

JANUARY, 2013. PRIVATE-I INC., LONDON, UK

DEEP BREATHS, Christian reminded himself. His gaze remained fixed on the growing pile of snow outside the boardroom window as he struggled to recover his train of thought from the snowplow's interruption. For whatever reason, getting back into the flow had begun to hurt physically in the past week. It wasn't just the palpitations anymore, but an aching head and chest. He felt calmer when he didn't have to be alert, but unfortunately, he had used up all the calm allotted for public appearances for that day, barely making it through his last meeting.

"Mr. Cervello, would you like for me to hold your calls for the rest of the day?"

He turned around only to notice everyone had left the boardroom and his assistant was about to close the door behind her.

"Yes, Julia, I would appreciate that."

"Not a problem, sir."

Julia had done such an excellent job at organizing that last-minute Private-I Board meeting and he would certainly miss her. She had come to represent order for him in the past two years and he needed that. Although he'd tried to convince her to relocate with a very handsome salary, he had known that as generous as his offer was, the devoted wife of Tom Banks would decline. He looked up to relationships such as the one Julia and Tom shared, and had thought he and Kathy could live up to that. Yet here he was, having just announced his relocation plans. It was back to Florida for him, a move he never saw coming until a few days ago.

For the past two days, he'd talked himself into believing that it was for the best, as he would oversee Private-I North America and ought to have enough to keep him busy between their various US and Canada locations. Moreover, there was the launch of a Private-I location in Italy by month's end. He was counting on these and more distractions to take his mind away from the bigger revelation he was terrified to acknowledge.

No amount of diversion, however, seemed enough to quench the office buzz that he could only guess started from Kathy. Now that his plan was out in the open, he expected the rumor concerning his decision to take on a life of its own. Why wouldn't it? He was leaving the city of London for good amid plans for a lavish and highly publicized after-wedding party there.

Lost in his thoughts, Christian returned to his office and remained there late into the night. For the most part, he paced the room. Leaning into his leather chair, he stared intently at a picture he shared with Kathy that had been in the same spot for nearly a year. The streetlight that seeped through the large office windows was all the light there was. He needed it that way. It was soothing and very discreet. It created fewer memories.

CASA CERVELLO, KEY BISCAYNE, FLORIDA

Isabella watched as Rachel stormed back into her bedroom and turned up the stereo volume, drowning out her mother's voice. Such was the case whenever the two of them argued about something so minuscule. Apart from Rachel using music as her weapon, it was also her form of release.

More importantly for Isabella, music helped get the two friends out of their shell, and bonded them in more ways than Isabella had ever experienced with anyone else. They rarely ever danced to it—it either just played in the background, or they sang along. Now she just hoped this fight would not dampen Rachel's chipper mood, because with her brother, Christian, getting married in a couple of weeks, there was valid cause to celebrate. Although Isabella had yet to meet Christian, she knew that he and Rachel were extremely close. According to their mother, Christian, an only child, had been thrilled at Rachel's birth. Even though they were just cousins at the time, he referred to her as his little sister, even then. Ultimately, they became siblings when his parents adopted Rachel, soon after she lost hers to a car accident in 1997.

Preparing for a wedding in Spain was exhilarating, and having finally selected their outfits only added to the thrill. Since they had both gotten their fair share of teasing for having such reserved lives, something of this magnitude was sure to spice things up and, until it did, their pastime of daydreaming sufficed.

Rachel talked about how interesting Spanish men were and Isabella found it amusing, *like Rachel would know*. The mere thought of meeting someone on their trip and starting a long-distance relationship terrified Isabella, especially since she would be venturing alone, now that Rachel had started seeing someone. What was more terrifying however, was the fact that ever since meeting him, Rachel's goal had been to get Isabella someone of her own for fear that she'd feel like a third wheel.

Rachel and her mother typically referred to her as *old school,* but so what if her views on relationships were a little traditional. Never one to succumb to pressure, she proudly took on the title of *scaredy cat* that Rachel had given her back in high school. Yes, she was an avid dreamer and proud of it. She was also an extremely picky dater. She was so cautious when it came to dating that her last actual date had been in her sophomore year at Notre Dame.

Isabella typically didn't date men she couldn't see herself with for the long haul, and she wasn't ignorant of the fact that she might remain single for a long time due to her choices—but it was a risk she was willing to take. So she was determined to keep her knight in her dreams until she could find an actual one right there in Florida.

Celebration aside, it was also their routine girls' night, even though they had stopped calling it that since senior high. What *was* routine was the fact that Isabella practically lived in Casa Cervello and Rachel and her mother wondered why she even bothered paying mortgage on her Miami home.

Isabella swung open the double balcony doors, letting in a gentle breeze. She couldn't dare make such noise in her neighborhood, but Rachel's closest neighbor was Biscayne Bay, so . . . she shrugged.

"I don't get how women are expected to meet all these expectations," Rachel said, frowning over a relationship article she had recently edited.

Isabella smiled as she slipped into her pajamas. She was exhausted and wasn't in the mood to start a debate. Besides, it was hard to take Rachel seriously with all that facial paste. Tonight it was the exact match to her hair rollers and toe separators—bright green.

Rachel grunted as she glared at the clock on her nightstand. It was 11:06 p.m. and she still couldn't sleep. It was unlike her to be awake this late. Everyone knew her for falling asleep the minute her head hit the pillow. It couldn't be her argument with her mother because they argued all the time and by morning she knew it would be history. She felt unsettled and had felt that way for the past few days, on and off, but it just hadn't stopped her from sleeping until now. She knew her boyfriend was okay because his last text mentioned he was dozing off.

Hoping that some soft music would help, she reached under Isabella's pillow for the remote. Just as she took hold of it, her phone shrieked—startling Isabella, who had been asleep for nearly two hours.

"Shh . . . I'm so sorry, Isa," she hushed. "Go back to bed."

Rachel whispered into the phone, "Hello."

"Rach?" came a distant voice.

"Who's this?" she frowned, making eye contact with Isabella—now awake, with concern.

"It's me, Christian."

Her heart instantly fell. *Why would Christian be calling at this hour, considering the time difference?* Under normal circumstances, she would have been thrilled to hear his voice, but something didn't seem right.

"Chris! Are you okay?"

"Is this a good time?" he asked.

"Yeah, hold on." She turned to Isabella before getting up from the bed. "Go back to bed, hon. So sorry." Something had to be wrong. Her heart pounded.

Stepping outside the hallway, she closed the door behind her. "Chris . . . " her voice shook. "Is everything okay?"

"Are you alone?"

"I am now, what's wrong?"

"I'm coming home."

"What do you mean—coming home, what happened?"

"It's over. Kathy and I are done."

"What? What happened? We were just—"

"She cheated on me."

"She what? Whoa, whoa, whoa . . . "

"With Kevin."

"*Kevin?*" Rachel's voice went faint. That name had become synonymous with catastrophe. She hadn't seen or heard from Kevin since that night in May 1997, and over the years, her family and friends were careful not to even mention his name around her.

"Listen, I can't say anything more until I come home, okay? I wanted you to be the first to know."

She stared into blank space, dumbfounded.

"Rach, are you still there?"

"Um . . . yeah, I'm here, Chris." *I just wish I didn't have to think of that moron right before bed.* "When are you coming home?"

"Two weeks, I hope. I've got a few things to wrap up first."

She breathed deeply. "Wow! Do you want me to tell Mom?"

"Nah, not yet—she'll flip. I'll tell her myself when I get home."

"Okay. Hey, when did this happen?"

When Christian sighed, she thought she heard a slight chuckle. "Apparently it's been going on for a while . . . I just caught them in action last week."

"Oh no, that's horrible! I'm so sorry, Chris."

"Hmm, right under my nose. Listen, I gotta go, kid."

"Okay, try to keep it together, okay?" Of course, that went without saying. Never one to worry about his personal affairs, it was Christian who took everyone else's worries and turned them into solutions. No one had even seen him shed a tear over her parents' death, and this didn't upset her because she knew how much he adored them. As deeply passionate as he was about people, crying just wasn't his thing. His own parents even dated his last teardrop to preschool age.

"Okay, love you," he said.

"I love you too."

In a daze, Rachel returned to her room. She was surprised to see Isabella still awake. "Oh, Isa, I woke you up." She grimaced.

"Is everything okay?"

"You don't even want to know," Rachel said, pacing the room. "That was Chris."

"Yeah, what happened? Is he all right?" she asked, sitting up on the bed.

"I hope so . . . but the wedding is off. She cheated on him."

Isabella gasped. "What?"

Rachel sat on the bed and stared directly at her. "With his best friend."

CHAPTER TWO

Homecoming

❧

A WEEK had passed since Christian's call dashed their Spanish dreams, and Rachel was back to living vicariously through the lives of the people she wrote about. With Rachel's boyfriend relocating from Manhattan to Miami soon, Isabella was certain that they would discover new and exciting things together, so she was happy for her friend. For Isabella, it had been an arduous week of having to restrain Rachel from opening her big mouth to her mother about her brother's breakup. She wasn't sure why it had to take so much effort to convince Rachel to withhold information that wasn't hers to give. It wasn't as if she was immune to the wrath her mother was sure to bring.

It was cloudy outside—quite dull even for the first week of February. Isabella knew the sun had to be somewhere because of its obvious light, but she hadn't actually seen it for herself for the past two days. Perhaps the absence of its ferocity wasn't such a bad idea, considering the amount of work they had to do in Rachel's mother's garden that day.

Her mother, Pattie, didn't grow little tomato gardens, and although this wasn't as enormous as the one she bragged about growing at the Cervello farms in Calabria, Italy, this was big enough for amateurs like them. Unfortunately, she hadn't attained the same amount of success in South Florida.

As recommended by Isabella's neighbor, Gracie, in order to achieve the perfect tomato garden in Miami, one had to start anywhere from December to mid-February—if at all possible, on a gray day like this—hence, Pattie's urgency. Gracie consistently achieved success with her garden that way. Isabella had introduced the two women, and Pattie's determination to now follow in Gracie's footsteps amused Isabella, since Pattie was hardly ever in town anymore.

Pattie prided herself in being the best at gardening. Only thing was, she didn't spend nearly half the time there as her children did. She also lost sight of the fact that they were no longer kids who she could just pull out and make perform chores on a whim. They had busy lives. Her son, Christian, ran a multinational corporation and, although he lived in another continent, Rachel often joked that even he couldn't escape the clutches of Pattie's garden when he visited. Rachel was a senior editor for a major fashion magazine, yet she was a slave to that garden. Then there was herself—Isabella, the 25-year-old self-employed corporate accountant who wasn't even a Cervello. *Surely, I could say no to Pattie's garden.* The thought alone made Isabella cringe. No one dared get on Pattie's bad side, so they held their peace. *Cowards,* Isabella smiled to herself.

For those who didn't know Patricia Gomes Cervello, she was bossy and stood her ground. To them, she was loud, fun, and meant no harm—most of the time. Perhaps that was why Isabella got along with the family. Her own mom was bossy, and her parents often told her that no matter how successful she became, she still had to fulfill her duties as a member of the Montes household—whether she lived at home or just visited, and no matter the age. The Cervellos ran their home a lot like hers. Even though their children were born and raised in Florida, they had Spanish and Italian parents. Growing up, they had extreme chores because Pattie never considered a maid—having been one herself at a time. Her husband, Tadd, did not share her view and wasn't afraid to voice his opinion.

As much as he had wanted the kids to be self-sufficient, he felt it was unrealistic to force the enormous task of cleaning a house that size on them, and he did not condone it. However, since he was hardly ever home to enforce his rule, it was easier said than done. Thus, the kids quickly accepted their fate, and each time Tadd met them, they were more skilled at working than the last. According to Pattie, if someone couldn't clean all their rooms, they needed a smaller house. So over the years, Isabella witnessed as Pattie cleaned one room at a time—covering the entire house in one week—at times refusing Isabella's help—only to do it all over again the next month.

Late into the afternoon, Isabella started on Pattie's precious edges. From the time on her wrist, she was certain they could still make it out in more than enough time for their basketball game between the Miami Heat and Charlotte Bobcats that night, but convincing Rachel of that was a different story. Considering the amount of time it took Rachel to get ready, and their commute down to the arena, she could understand her concern.

She glanced over at Rachel with a sad smile. They'd recently gotten manipedis to match their jerseys—against Isabella's advice to do it themselves.

Now it was hopeless, especially since they didn't like wearing the oversized gardening gloves Pattie gave them. If Isabella knew Pattie would take advantage of them being home early from work, she would have had Rachel get ready for the game from her house.

"Girls, please don't forget those edges," Pattie reminded for the umpteenth time. "I'll be out in a jiffy—just a quick shower."

"Okay, Aunt Pattie!" Isabella giggled. "She must think we're professional gardeners."

Rachel shook her head. "And to think she's coming back out."

"I heard that!" Pattie yelled, prompting more giggles from Isabella.

"Ugh . . . " Rachel grumbled. "Doesn't it bother you that she's been getting us to do this since we were kids? She's such a bully."

"Hey, I don't know about you but I could use these skills in my garden when I grow up."

"Like you probably won't have some rich dude spoiling you."

"Hey, I'm not the one complaining here with *my attorney* boyfriend."

"Okay," Rachel said, cracking her knuckles. "I'll teach you everything you need to know about gardening and you can knock yourself out. Lord knows, I could open a garden center with all I know. Hmm, a garden center. Are you thinking what I'm thinking?"

"Blog freak!"

"Bingo! 'GardenFab: Practical tips on starting a fabulous nursery.'"

"Yeah, let's see how long that lasts."

"Hey, that's not fair—at least give me some credit for being ambitious."

"Ambition doesn't pay the bills, honey."

Rachel stuck out her tongue and threw dirt at Isabella.

"Dirt fight!" Isabella yelled, as they tossed damp dirt around.

They fought for the garden hose until a black car with tinted windows pulled into the compound.

As the chauffeured vehicle drove by the roundabout, Christian wrapped up an email reply to his father, who was in Italy.

"Here we are, sir," announced the driver, pulling to a stop by the main entrance of the house.

"Just—a—sec . . . there!" Christian exhaled. "Thank you—Julio, yes?"

"Yes sir, Julio Echavez," the driver replied, exiting the car to let him out.

Christian got out and extended his hand. "I'll be in touch if I need your services again. I have your card," he added with a warm smile. If things went his way, it wouldn't be likely, but it was nice to know that he had access to a driver who came highly recommended by his father.

"Thank you, sir," he replied a little too eagerly. "I'll take your bags to the door."

Christian strolled past the water fountain, and around the side of the structure he had called home for most of his life. He didn't have the chance to take a tour the last time he'd visited, and he was pleased with the recent updates to the landscape that had kept his mother busy for the past couple of months. He came upon the recently renovated guesthouse Rachel had raved about—from the look of it, it was more like a rebuild. His wish was that it *was* and that the demons that waited there for his return went along with the old structure.

This was the first major renovation to the two-story Mediterranean-style home on approximately 2.5 acres in a gated estate. His grandfather purchased the property in 1961 as a family heirloom. Having overcome dire poverty, he began the tradition: the home was to belong to all members of the Cervello family worldwide for as long as they lived—whenever they needed a place to stay in Florida. At the age of 23, the next heir was to acquire the property and continue the tradition. Further, that heir must live or have regular access to Florida to be able to care for the home to the best of his or her ability. Casa Cervello was the name he and his wife had coined, and their only son—Christian's father—officially became the first heir to acquire the property in 1980—*his* 23rd birthday. Christian's turn, which he gracefully forfeited, came in 2002. Rather in 2008, he threw an elaborate ceremony marking the day Rachel made history as the first woman to take over the family estate.

As Christian made his way back to the front walkway that led to the vegetable garden, he caught a glimpse of Rachel from afar. He laughed slightly as she came screaming and running toward him, her long black ponytail bouncing in the wind. Seeing the speed in which she approached him, he tried to brace himself for the impact but it was too late. She jumped upon him so fiercely that it sent them both to the grass. The last time they'd seen each other was August, when he couldn't have been happier with all he had going for him. Now there was an unspoken sadness. As they embraced, he considered how much he loved her. Their mothers had shared a special bond—but as twins that was understandable. What the family never expected was for their children, a male and female cousin with a six-year age gap, to have that twin bond. His Aunt Elizabeth used to joke that his and Rachel's connection was much deeper than hers and Pattie's. Some of the things he and Rachel experienced as kids even made his father consider having them professionally evaluated for a research study at the time. Everyone was convinced they could feel each other's pain and read each other's mind.

Christian smiled as he stroked a tear off Rachel's cheek. "Hey, snotty face."

"Hey *you*," she said, playfully beating on his chest. "You said two weeks!"

"I know—I wanted to surprise you."

"Well, you sure did. Gosh, I have missed you."

"You just saw me five months ago, silly."

"*Hey*, five months is a long time," Rachel pouted. "There's been no one to spoil me."

"You forgot you told me about Thomas?" he teased, casually glancing at someone who stood at a distance. He squinted to get a closer look and chills went down his spine. He had a strong sense that this meeting had taken place before, even though he was positive he was looking at this person for the first time.

Nodding in that direction, he asked, "Who's that?"

Rachel whipped around. "Oh, that's Isa. I can't believe you two have never met." She quickly got to her feet and helped him up. Then running up to Isabella she said, "Come meet my brother slash cousin."

As they approached, Christian's brow wrinkled as he attempted to recall where he might have seen her. His heart raced uncomfortably as he struggled to slow his breathing. He couldn't place her face anywhere, but her beauty astounded him from afar. Even in an oversized dirty overall and hair in a tousled bun, she was stunning.

She took a couple more steps toward him.

"This is my best friend, Isabella Montes," Rachel said. "Isa, this is my brother, Chris."

Christian smiled as he extended his hand. "Are you sure we haven't met?"

Isabella shook her head slowly as she placed her small and slender hand in his.

She was even more appealing up close. Underneath the smudge of mud on her cheek, there was a golden-tan to her olive skin tone, and it appeared very soft. There were specks of dirt and grass over her light brown hair. Yet no amount of dirt could conceal a beauty so pure.

"No, but it feels like I've met you already. Rach and Aunt Pattie talk about you quite a bit."

Christian raised his brow. "*Aunt* Pattie . . . hmm." It troubled him that he couldn't recognize her. Could he have been so detached lately that he didn't know someone that was supposed to be close enough to call his own mother "aunt"?

The garden spun around Isabella. From the way Rachel's brother fixed his gaze upon hers, it appeared as though he were analyzing her. It was unsettling and exhilarating at the same time. His hand was warm and dry against its sticky and clammy counterpart. She became very conscious of her appearance. There was a nasty smidgen of mud on her face and under her fingernails. To think that just a few minutes earlier, she and Rachel were having a dirt fight. His prim and proper appearance was a harsh reminder that they had some growing up to do.

Rachel should have at least warned me that she had a cute brother. Come to think of it, she couldn't remember ever seeing any of his pictures around the house—quite strange. Perhaps he was in one of the pictures Rachel had recently placed on the mantel—served her right for never paying attention. Her heart threatened to give her away, and she knew she couldn't afford to sweat with all that grime.

When she couldn't maintain eye contact, her eyes feasted on other areas of him. He was striking in his white, fitted shirt, neatly tucked into gray dress pants. His necktie hung loosely from his collar, and a trench coat draped his left arm. A sophisticated air about him made it difficult for her to think straight. *No one comes off a 10-hour flight looking this good.*

Studying her full lips, Christian expected Isabella to say more—perhaps he could place that remote accent. There was no doubt in his mind that he would have remembered that face if he had ever come across it. She must have been new to the area because Key Biscayne was a small town, and having lived there most his life and having volunteered at the local police department, he knew many of its residents.

He hadn't realized how tight and for how long he'd held her hand until Rachel cleared her throat and looked at their hands with a nervous smile.

Isabella returned a smile, as he released his grip. She enjoyed the feel of his strong handshake, and she hated that he had to let go. "I'm sorry; my hands are dirty," Isabella said sheepishly. "We've been gardening."

"I see." With a tiny smirk, he maintained his stare until she looked away. "That's quite all right," he added in a rich, deep tone.

She felt a connection with him and wondered if he felt the same. *Perhaps that was why he was holding my hand for so long.* She became nervous at the possibility that Rachel noticed it too and would perhaps disapprove. She was one to notice the slightest thing.

"You know, it's odd that you two haven't met—must have kept missing each other with all that traveling you do," Rachel said to Christian. "But you *do* remember me telling you about her, don't you, Chris?"

Keeping his gaze on Isabella, Christian cocked his head, and with one arm folded and his other thumb stroking his chin, he said, "I don't believe so."

"Come on, Chris, I talk about her all the time. Remember . . . my first day at Nautilus? Eighth grade?"

Christian's face lit up. "Oh yeah, I remember. You hadn't spoken to anyone for weeks then this girl . . . that was *you*?"

Isabella shrugged, glancing at Rachel. "I guess."

"Yeah, Isa, I never told you that part." Then, turning back to Christian, Rachel continued, "And remember how you were supposed to go to Notre Dame?"

"Ah, that *was* you. Notre Dame valedictorian."

Isabella nodded. "Class of 2009."

"Fighting Irish."

"All the way." She smiled.

Christian nodded. "Impressive. That *is* something. They have an amazing business school, I hear."

"Yeah, they do," Isabella said.

"What did you study?"

"Accounting."

"Nice. You look like a smart girl."

"She *is*," Rachel said, nudging Isabella. "Tell him how old you were when you got in."

"*No,*" she grumbled, turning away and nibbling on her bottom lip.

"Come on, don't be shy, Isa. She got in when she was sixteen!"

"No kidding." Christian nodded slowly.

"Rachel said you turned down your admission there." Isabella hoped to deflect the attention away from herself. "She never said why."

Christian glanced at Rachel with a warm smile. "It was a tough time for all of us, but hey—you went there, so you get to tell us about the Notre Dame experience. I often wondered what I missed."

"She went on a full scholarship, too!" Rachel blurted.

As Christian's gaze deepened, Isabella felt her face flush, and she had to look away.

"You're making your friend uncomfortable, Rach."

"Oh, come on," Rachel tugged on Isabella's arm. "It's nothing to be shy about, Isa. You earned it."

"It's nice to finally meet you, Isabella, and thanks for being there for my sister."

"It's nice to meet you too. Welcome back."

"Thanks." Christian smiled—bemused as he stared at both women from side to side. "Were you girls rolling in mud?"

"No kidding—ask Mom what's up."

"Ah! You're rebelling! Her slave driving continues, huh?" he chuckled.

"Yup, with her darn garden."

Isabella smiled. "I'm sure you both have some catching up to do. I'll excuse myself."

Christian nodded slowly, his eyes steadfast on her as she made her way into the house. *This ought to be fun,* he thought to himself with a mischievous smirk. "Does she know why I came back?"

"Yeah," Rachel replied. "Why?"

"She probably thinks I'm a loser."

"Oh, stop, Isa's not like that."

"Hey, what happened to Olivia? I thought—"

"Long story," she said, rolling her eyes.

Christian snickered. "Women—just be careful with *best* friends."

"Ha! After what you went through . . . sheesh."

Pattie came out to the hallway in her bathrobe when the front door closed.

"I'm gonna get going now, Aunt Pattie," Isabella announced.

"You girls are done already?"

"Yup." She tried to conceal her smile as she fumbled for her keys in her bag. Knowing how fond of Christian Pattie was, and how just the other day she spoke of missing him terribly, a part of her wanted to announce his return but she restrained herself. It would have been nice to see their reunion, but she didn't want to interfere with their family time.

It was moments like this that she expected to feel left out of the Cervello clan. If Rachel's fear had been of Isabella feeling like a third wheel with Thomas, it was bound to happen either way, now that Christian was home. When he'd looked at her and said, "Thanks for being there for my sister," she wondered if he really meant, *Thanks, but she won't need your services anymore now that I'm back.*

Everyone said the two shared a special bond, and this made Isabella wonder what Christian must have thought of Rachel's introduction of her as *best friend.* She didn't want him to feel as though she was competing with him for Rachel's affection. She couldn't even if she tried. Their bond was something that Pattie told her even *she* had to get accustomed to. They covered for each other, and there was no sacrifice too big for either one of them.

Although he never gave a reason as to why he let go of his Notre Dame dream, she suspected it had something to do with Rachel—especially since he was supposed to enroll in 1997—the same year her parents died. She knew she wasn't going to get the reason out of Rachel, because she rarely spoke about anything that involved what she called her "'97 nightmare." So Isabella chose to stick with her theory, which wasn't farfetched—after all, he *did* let go of his inheritance of Casa Cervello for Rachel.

The more Isabella thought about them, the more envious she became. She couldn't say no one warned her, but she couldn't help thinking—if they were as close as everyone said they were, why hadn't she ever met him? Something didn't add up. Nevertheless, she was bound to get hurt if she wasn't careful. Christian could be jealous of her closeness to Rachel *or* Rachel could disapprove of her liking him.

"Thanks, Nena," Pattie said, slightly hesitating before kissing Isabella on her clean cheek. "What's it with you girls and mud? You'll get people thinking I'm raising pigs here."

Isabella chuckled. "Not nice, Aunt Pattie."

Pattie grumbled, peeking downstairs. "I hope you didn't get dirt all over my brand new marble floor."

"I was *really* careful—I even used the shoe covers!" Isabella whined, stifling a giggle at the sight of Pattie's face, which said she wasn't buying any of it. "Come on, don't be paranoid, Aunt Pattie."

"Where's Rachel?"

"Oh, she'll be in shortly." Isabella winked at Pattie as she crept down each stair in slow motion—both hands raised to avoid the newly polished Cinderella staircase handle.

"Stop making fun of me!" Pattie said.

"Ha, ha! You know I love you." Isabella blew a kiss.

Just as she opened the door to leave, Rachel and Christian walked in, laughing. His laughter died down as soon as his eyes met hers. "I was just leaving," Isabella quickly muttered.

"Christian!" Pattie screamed, racing down the stairs. "Oh, Isa, I'm going to kill you!"

"I wanted it to be a surprise," Isabella said. "I know you'll forgive me."

Christian met his mother halfway up the stairs, and they both embraced.

He kissed her cheek before pulling away to study her face. Like Rachel, she had her silky, jet-black hair gathered in a messy ponytail and aside from the few soft lines around Pattie's eyes that he would be damned to point out, they were a spitting image—right down to the deep-set dimples. At the age of fifty-three, Pattie still got passes when she went out with Rachel. He remembered how some police officers would try to get information out of him about her. With his father away most of the time, it was easy to assume she was single.

"Whoa! You two look more alike every time I see you." Although Rachel simply smiled, he knew her reply to that would be, *she wishes*.

"Which is every light-year," Pattie teased.

"Very funny," Christian said, unamused.

"Have you heard from your father?"

"Yeah, we actually just exchanged emails some minutes ago."

"He's supposed to be home this week. I just saw his missed call and was about to call him back."

Christian made a pained face. "I'm sorry, Mom. He was actually calling to tell you about a change of plans. But it's more complicated than that, so you should talk to him yourself."

"Does it have to do with the Italy office?"

"I'm afraid so."

Pattie sighed. "Did he say how long?"

"No."

"We have so many plans for the spring," Pattie said. "Honestly, I'm sick of traveling."

You don't say, Christian thought. *After what . . . thirty-five years of marriage— and twelve of those spent doing just that.* "I bet. Mom, this has gotta be hard on you. Have you considered just following him and visiting here instead, like he suggested?"

"Yeah, we intend to do that, it's just—" She sighed again. "You're here and I have missed you."

Isabella pulled Rachel to the side. "Hey, I gotta go."

"Why?"

"You have to catch up, silly. He just went through a breakup, coming home must be tough."

"You're right. Thanks so much for understanding."

"That's what friends are for."

Rachel walked Isabella out to her Jeep. "Hey, how about the game?"

"Rain check definitely."

"You don't mind?"

"Come on, my team isn't even playing and we beat you guys last Friday." *Now that was a ticket I could have used.* "Let's give them to Gracie and Frank."

"Ah, good idea—they could use a break."

"Yeah . . . anyway, I'll get going; I'm so sticky. Enjoy your brother."

"So, what do you think of him, cool, huh?" she asked, catching Isabella off guard.

Isabella shrugged, hoping to conceal her stutter. "He's o-okay."

"Miami Heat, baby!" Rachel cheered, throwing both fists in the air.

"Pacers!" Isabella yelled back. She didn't consider herself a sport fanatic but ever since Notre Dame, she supported everything Indiana, even though they weren't even the ones playing tonight.

She certainly didn't take Rachel's question as an invitation to chase her brother. Rachel was simply excited, and when she got that way, she lost all reason in her screams. However, that didn't stop Isabella's heart from doing the chasing. It flipped merely from the thought of him and the breathtaking way he looked into her eyes. He made her feel as though she were in junior high all over again.

When the traffic light turned red, she stared into the mirror, attempting to repeat the faces she must have made while speaking to him. Suddenly a loud honk startled her. She looked ahead to find that the traffic light was green, and the cars ahead of her had long gone. After waving apologetically out the window, she took a deep breath. *Okay, stop it Isa, you need to focus.* With a mischievous smile, she tried her very best not to think of Christian Cervello—at least until she got home.

At the Cervello kitchen table, Rachel smiled as she watched Pattie and Christian. She missed how she ruffled his hair and how he'd made funny faces in return. He was with them for just a day the last time he had visited and, aside from that, they hadn't sat at the table since his brief return from Vancouver five years ago.

"Did you girls finish those edges for me?" Pattie asked, tending to a boiling kettle.

"You just wanted us to remove the turf and add mulch, right? Well, Isa did it."

"Good girl."

"I'm just glad Chris is back because he sure has missed out on his share of gardening."

Closing his eyes, his lips mouthed, "*Shh.*"

Christian wasn't quite ready to tell his mother about his relocation plans, but with Rachel blabbing away, he didn't think he'd have a choice for much longer.

"Mom, don't tell me you're making tea in this weather," Rachel continued.

"Why not? It's not hot out today. Anyway, your brother is English now. I'm sure he would appreciate some tea."

"Not in Florida, he won't," Rachel gibbered on.

"Are you saying we don't drink tea in Florida? You know I've been making tea for him since he was younger."

Rachel rolled her eyes. "Oh yeah, his *special* tea."

Christian expected his mother to drag the truth concerning his return out of him at any moment. He felt the tension creep up and just as he stood up to leave, Rachel grimaced as she mouthed, "Sorry." He flashed her a quick smile and mouthed back, "It's okay."

As he strolled out to the family room nearby, he heard Rachel switch the subject to Thomas—something about his moving truck. His heart rate slowed. It appeared that the wrath of Pattie's decorative fury hadn't gotten to that room yet—still, there was something different about it. *Ah . . . pictures!* Scanning through the frames scattered across the fireplace mantel, his eyes stopped at Rachel's high school graduation picture. She and Isabella were dressed in cap and gowns and stood with his parents and another couple he presumed to be Isabella's folks. He wondered how they could be so close to meeting that day, yet so far. Staring intently at the picture, he fixated over other possible occasions in which their paths might have crossed.

"I bet you find yourself missing Florida weather, huh, Chris?" Pattie yelled from the kitchen. "Your father says this past winter has been brutal in London!"

Apparently, I missed out on a lot, Christian pondered, as his stare burned into a more recent picture of Isabella. He could describe every detail on her face with his eyes closed. Her smooth oval face, delicate chin, and beautiful, luscious lips that curled when she became shy. He particularly loved her big and gentle brown eyes—he could tell that she had a smile in them from the picture, but it wasn't there when they'd met. She was more timid in person—perhaps embarrassed by her untidy appearance. Her warm voice still rang in his ear—soft with that slight accent he still couldn't place.

"Want some sugar or honey?" Pattie's voice was pulling him back.

Breathe, Christian uttered under his breath.

"Chris! Are you still there?" Pattie yelled.

He opened his eyes swiftly. "Yeah, Ma. Some honey will do, please." Then strolling back to the kitchen, he noticed just how extensive the renovations to it were.

"I like what you did to this place."

"I was wondering when you would notice," Pattie replied, placing a tea mug before him.

The marble floors from Christian's last update seemed to be the only thing that remained. The cabinets were now rosewood—he only knew the name because Kathy considered it for his Highland Beach home. The countertops were now glass and marble, and nearly everything else was stainless steel. Though nice, the modern touch left the room feeling quite cold.

"You know what . . . come on," Pattie said motioning to the family room. "Let's relax over here for a bit before you get all settled in. You have a lot to tell me after five years."

"Five years, Mom?" He frowned.

Pattie continued with a threatening gaze. "Because you don't expect me to count that half-day visit in August. Lord knows if *we* never visited you, we probably never would have seen you at all."

Christian and Rachel exchanged a cautious glance as they relaxed into the sofa. Then his gaze drifted back to the mantel. "I see you guys finally decided to put up pictures in this room. It actually feels warm in here for a change."

"That was Rachel. As you can see, it's filled with pictures of her."

Isabella backed into her driveway and reached for her buzzing phone. "Alô!"

"Hey, hon," came a high-pitched voice. "How are ya?" It was her neighbor, Gracie.

"Ahh, just the woman I wanted to see. Are you reading my mind again, Gracie? Or just staring out your window?" Isabella asked, peering in the direction of Gracie's home.

"You know I am. I spoke to your ma earlier, and she wanted me to check on ya. I guess your phone was off when she called. What ya up to, kiddo?"

Gracie was the very sweet but nosy neighbor Isabella inherited when her parents returned to Brazil. Prior to leaving, they had placed their house on the market for sale and Gracie housesat for them when Isabella was at Notre Dame. When the house didn't sell, it ended up being a blessing for Isabella, as she had a place to return to after graduation and internship. Although they ended up losing half the value of the home when some of their neighbors foreclosed during the recent recession, she eventually bought the property off her parents.

Isabella was no longer a child, but convincing her mother of that was another story. Therefore, Gracie's close proximity to her helped ease her mother's worry of having her only child in America. Isabella typically joked about having a life not worthy of monitoring, so she didn't mind the prying. She embraced safety and appreciated having Gracie and her husband close by. Moreover, now that Gracie and Pattie had become garden buddies, she was stuck with Gracie for life.

"Oh, I'm good. Are you guys free tonight?"

"Yup, as a matter of fact, you were on my mind before I heard you drive up. We rented some movies. Wanna come over? We've got pot roast."

"I'd like to relax at home tonight. Thanks for the offer, though. Oh yeah, remember how Rach and I had tickets for tonight's game?"

"Yeah, all my friends are going to that."

"Great. Because neither one of us will be able to attend. So . . . are you coming to get your tickets?"

Gracie screamed so loud that she could hear it from the direction of her house around the cul-de-sac—three homes away.

By the time Isabella reached the top of her staircase, she'd already stripped down her soiled clothes. At this point, she was sweaty and reeked of the outdoors.

As the warm water cascaded over her, the thoughts of Christian that she'd carefully restrained came flooding back. His warm and firm grip had her imagining what his hands would feel like all over her body. *Stop it, Isa,* she muttered, but she didn't mean it. She figured she would cut herself some slack since she'd never felt this way for anyone. His steel-gray eyes bore deeply into hers as if piercing through her very soul. Oh, and that tousled hair—as though someone ran their fingers through it. On anyone else, it would look unkempt, but not him. He was perfect.

As she rinsed the lather from her mid-back-length hair, her mind raced with a multitude of thoughts. *Would he stay here in Florida now that the wedding was off? Would he get back together with his fiancée? Will Rachel hate me if I were to tell her how her brother made me feel? No, I can't possibly tell Rachel.* But how could she possibly keep Rachel in the dark? She was the only one she ever spoke to about such things, and it was the least Rachel would expect, especially since she'd faithfully listened to Isabella's day-dreams of nonexistent men. It was her duty to keep Rachel in the loop. She would do the same.

By day's end, Pattie knew everything. Rachel knew her very well—in fact, better than she did her birth mother. She could sense that Pattie was fum-ing, and that had to explain why she hadn't said a word since Christian wrapped up his story with, "So that's it." She shuddered at the thought of leaving him alone with her right now—even though her intuition told her to do just that in order to avoid hearing the name, Kevin.

"Well, it's no wonder we never got to meet the tramp," Pattie said, fire in her eyes.

That's it, Rachel thought. *Let the sparks fly.*

"Mom—" Christian calmly cautioned.

"What, who cheats on her fiancé weeks to her wedding? Tell me . . . who, but a tramp?"

"Calm down, Mom," Rachel said.

Pattie sat up from her recliner and pointed a finger at Rachel. "Don't you dare tell me to calm down! Did you meet her?"

Rachel remained silent.

"Tell me!"

"No," Rachel muttered, her head bowed.

"Exactly . . . but you go around here excited about some wedding, tell-ing the world, '*My brother's getting married, my brother's getting married,*'" Pattie mocked. "Yet, you never even met the tramp. And you say you love your brother," Pattie scoffed, tossing her hair back.

"Mother." There was a warning in Christian's tone.

Pattie continued. "Oh, oh, then you have the audacity to ask your father and me why we're not excited about the so-called wedding—when we haven't even spoken to her on the phone. You see why now, Rachel?"

Rachel broke down. She was right. It never once dawned on her how ir-rational she'd been in regard to Christian's engagement. Although she had wanted to meet Kathy, she never insisted on it because she felt Kathy didn't really care to meet them. She didn't push the matter for fear that she might end up being the whiny sister-in-law. She wanted Christian's partner to accept her, but in hindsight, she was merely pleasing a woman she'd never met at her brother's expense.

"Leave her alone, Ma, it's not her fault."

"No, Chris, she's right. I failed you," Rachel said, sobbing uncontrollably.

"Now look what you've—" Christian started to say.

"Shush . . . you and Rachel. Just shush! You two always have the perfect words to get yourselves out of a mess. Can you get out of this one now? Hmm, tell me, Eduardo! Who the hell proposes to a woman who doesn't even like his family?"

"Aunt Pattie!" Rachel blurted through tears. "He's been through enough already and he just got back!"

Christian nodded slowly. "Sorry I told you." He got up to leave.

Pattie bowed her head into her hands, and Rachel stood up without a word. The last time she cried that way was the day of her parents' funerals. Then again, she couldn't remember ever feeling this upset. She must have been over the boiling point to refer to Pattie as *Aunt* again. Ever since the adoption was complete, she'd amazed everyone with how quick she had started calling Pattie *Mom*. She never once reverted to calling her *Aunt*. The grief counselor had attributed it to Rachel's emotional state at that time, assuring them that Rachel was in need of a replacement and would most likely revert. However, it never happened for sixteen years—until today. She hadn't meant it, and she hoped that Pattie didn't catch the slip. As upset as she was with her, she never wanted to be the source of her hurt.

Christian stepped into his old room. It was dim from the closed drapes but had a fresh, clean smell. He knew his mother had dusted it regularly because she couldn't stand dust. He had to be about twenty-three when he last called it his room—every other stay after that was brief. It looked peaceful, yet he wasn't sure if he wanted to be there—not if such drama would persist. His brain was one more argument away from an explosion.

There's always the guesthouse, a tiny, sly voice within suggested, as he pulled back the drapes. The thought instantly moistened his palms. He just knew he couldn't go back. With the guesthouse, and his condo some minutes away, his housing possibilities were endless. The problem was that he was certain he couldn't trust himself to live alone in either place, or anywhere else for that matter. Living with Kathy grounded him somehow, and accountability was what he needed the most. Besides, it would be nice to set a better example for Rachel—she had seen too much. *Whatever it takes, I must honor that vow,* he thought as sweat trickled down his temples.

Stepping out into the balcony, he recalled how he would watch the sunset from there. A gentle breeze stroked his face and felt cool against his damp skin—this was a welcome change in contrast to the London chill. Kathy must have been crazy not to have an interest in living in Florida. He tried to convince her that his parents weren't the type to pry into his and Rachel's relationships. With their frequent travels, they were hardly ever around. Yet she didn't budge.

The only times he would have probably seen his family, if married to her, would have been the wedding and perhaps the birth of a child. He couldn't possibly see it working out with his family, as close-knit as they were. The one-hour distance between his future home in Highland Beach and Casa Cervello was great, because it gave him a fresh start from his past while focusing on his future, yet it was close enough for a much-needed Key Biscayne family visit.

He wondered if his mother was right about Kathy disliking them. Perhaps her criticism stemmed from his short and spare visits. He did not want the blame to fall on Kathy. Their relationship started two years ago and before that he'd hardly visited. He couldn't blame anyone else but his demons for keeping him away. As much as he adored Florida, it also terrified him— the familiarity, the women, and the guesthouse. Everything.

Rachel went to him and patted his back. He smiled slightly. "Did you hear her call me, *Eduardo*?"

"She did?" Her eyes widened.

"Yup, the last time she called me that was when she found out that Kevin was the reason your parents left the house that evening. Can you blame her if she's making connections in her head? Our no-good friends."

He hated to remind Rachel of their loss that night, especially since she still blamed herself for the part she played. He knew Rachel hadn't been in contact with Kevin since he had called her in 1997 to convince her to have her parents bail him out of jail, and she'd grown increasingly bitter with him for his lack of concern for her well-being in the aftermath. What Christian didn't understand was how Kevin kept in touch with him over the years, and even worked for him, but still seemed to lack empathy toward Rachel. For the past sixteen years, he'd attributed such ignorance to Kevin's guilt. But after his stint with Kathy last month, the only explanation for Kevin's behavior was total insanity.

CHAPTER THREE

Welcome Distractions

❦

IT HAD been a little over two weeks since Christian returned to Florida, and since that dreadful argument with his mother. They had made peace and vowed never to let an outsider come between them again. Aside from family matters, transitioning hadn't been easy. For one, the recurring nightmare that had haunted him as a child returned. It was of a man bound, gagged, and later brought into a dark room by a group of men. The dream, though never clearly defined, was enough to send chills down his spine every time he woke up from it. He suspected its return had to do with being back in Florida—where it had all began.

In addition to this dream, he experienced occasional flashbacks of that awful day he walked in on Kathy and Kevin. Denial couldn't explain his numbness with reference to Kathy's role because that would contradict the emotional turmoil he felt in regard to Kevin's part. He couldn't wrap his brain around what he and his family did to deserve such treatment from Kevin, when all they ever did was accept him into their home when his own birth parents all but deserted him. Regardless of Kevin's actions, Christian had to admit his own foolishness for offering him a job against Rachel's advice—and even though she wasn't throwing it in his face, he knew what she was thinking.

In an effort to maintain his sanity, he drowned himself in work at the Private-I head office in Miami. His desperation to tame his thoughts caused him to take on every responsibility he could get his hands on. His near constant presence at the office troubled many, and rumors that he wanted to downsize even began to permeate the Atlanta office. The buzz was so prominent that he called a meeting to assure his managers that he was pleased with business, and there was no intention of letting anyone go.

As the tension at work lifted, an intense competition among some of the women vying for his attention ensued. He couldn't blame anyone but himself for that. His close friend in London had mentioned his need for boundaries. He just found it difficult to distance himself from his employees because he loved every aspect of his work. His employees around the world regarded him as *CEO of the people*, in that he liked to interact with his staff, and at times, even attend minor functions with them. It was no secret that he was single, and women made their availability known to him. Therefore, he eventually found it easier to work from home. Besides, he was certain that his recent vow never to have sexual intercourse until marriage wouldn't sit well with them. Who would believe him? *Miami's playboy*. Regardless of what anyone thought, his engagement had taught him the importance of sharing something that special and intimate with one person.

As Christian strolled down the second-floor hallway of Casa Cervello, his and Rachel's childhood friend Olivia came to mind. She'd always come to mind at that particular bend that led up to Rachel's bedroom because, for whatever reason, the two of them would bump into each other at that very spot—even as kids. He smiled. He hadn't seen her since his return, and his calls to her phone went straight to voicemail both times he'd called her.

As he approached Rachel's room, he heard singing coming from inside and paused outside the door. The harmonizing was angelic. He tapped on the door twice and let himself in. Rachel's dimples sunk in when she grinned at him. "Hey you . . . long time no see, I can't believe we're in the same house and rarely see each other."

"I know, I've been working," he said with a quick smile, reaching down to embrace her. As they hugged, his eyes met with Isabella's, and she quickly looked away.

"Don't go overworking yourself now," Rachel said, winking. "You gotta make out time for fun."

"Is that what you girls are doing here?" he said. There was a hint of humor in his voice as his eyes surveyed the room. It was his first time in Rachel's room since his return. It looked different, neater, and organized. Except for the papers scattered across the bed—perhaps music lyrics, and of course, a microphone.

"Doesn't it look like that?" Rachel stared wide-eyed.

Christian's smile turned into a smirk at Isabella. "I should ask your friend. Are you sure she doesn't have you here against your will?"

Isabella laughed. "I actually enjoy it."

"Well it's the calm before my storm of deadlines," Rachel said.

"Ah, work! Sometimes I forget that the rest of the world takes you seriously."

"Ha, ha . . . very funny," Rachel said as she strolled off to gather the papers from her bed.

In the weeks that followed their first meeting, Isabella had only caught sight of him in spurts around Casa Cervello—out the window—as he strolled the compound or paced the hallway while on the phone. Having him there was a treat. As he leaned against Rachel's bedroom door, she assessed his appearance, puzzled. There was something different about him. She was curious and worried it was obvious.

He smiled. "It's the hair."

"Oh," she acknowledged sheepishly.

"Surprised you noticed," he said, raising a brow.

Isabella felt blood instantly rush to her face. She was certain it was an Ivy League haircut, as it was her favorite haircut on a man. It complimented his features—a clean-shaven face that was long and square with a strong, angular jaw line. Shaven or not, he would be alluring either way. Then there was that prominent brow that he raised casually when he was intrigued. She must have interested him because he did that quite a few times with her. Today he was dressed casually in a fitted white polo shirt with a turndown collar and a pair of cargo pants. From the fit of his shirt and exposed arms, she could tell that he had a lean build and was physically fit. Above all else, the gray eyes did it for her. *Like Uncle Tadd's,* she mused.

"It's *Isabella,* yes?" Christian asked, strolling up to her and extending his hand.

How rude of him to interrupt my dreams, she thought, conjuring up an innocent smile. "Yes, it's nice to meet you again," she said softly, extending her hand for a shake. She was going for a quick handshake this time, but he didn't get the drift because he seized her hand firmly and held on to it. It felt much like the first time. Her fingers disappeared into his big grip. He stared into her eyes. She couldn't think straight, and in no time, her mind began to go blank.

Christian loved her facial expressions. He thought he should give them names. This one . . . *a deer caught in headlights.* Her hand was warm and dry and soft to the touch. But as his grip tightened, it quickly became moist.

Upon noticing that, he smiled, aware that she was becoming vulnerable under his gaze and grip. He enjoyed it because it enabled him to get beneath the façade. His overactive brain assessed her from head to toe. He was right about her skin; it was flawless, and this time, nice and clean. He picked up a sweet aroma. It had to be her hair. She still had the poor thing imprisoned in a bun. He tried to gauge the length from the few brave tendrils that managed to escape and drape her tender face.

The one physical attribute he adored most in a woman was hair and the longer it was, the better. The color didn't matter to him, neither did the texture. It could be wavy, straight, loosely or tightly-curled, as long as it could freely roam in the wind. Everyone called it a fetish, but for years, Christian took to hair as if it was a mystical being. He believed that it was alive and could communicate with humans. Now he sensed Isabella's strands were appealing to him to set them free. His mother said it started as a child—that he had cherished hair as a person would a pet.

Pattie's friends often exchanged stories of how the younger Christian would ask if he could touch their hair, and they would watch in wonder as he stroked each person's hair as though he were petting a dog. It stopped being a surprise to Pattie when she witnessed his reaction to her cutting her hair past a certain length—he wept for nearly a day. According to her, all he ever wanted to do was play with her hair and run his chubby little fingers through the strands—at times, making action heroes out of them and tangling Pattie's hair in the process. As he grew older and started buying gifts for Rachel, he would only buy her dolls with extremely long hair. Quite ironically, he had never dated a woman with hair past shoulder length.

She's tiny, Christian thought, estimating Isabella's height to be between five-foot-three to five-foot-four. Next to his six-foot-four frame, he was her Goliath, but unlike David, this was her battle to lose.

Isabella had heard Rachel's phone ring from a distance—so she knew she wasn't totally unaware of her surroundings. She also knew that this man was attempting to read what lay beneath her. Although she never believed in such things, he was starting to convince her that he could see something.

She tried to break away from his gaze, but those beautiful eyes said, *don't*. As her heart raced, in her mind she envisioned numbers increasing in percentages with the words, *almost complete* in bright green. She panicked at the thought that if completed, he would realize that she was falling for him, so she yanked her hand away. The single act was so abrupt that he jerked backward and had to quickly catch his balance. It was the weirdest thing she had ever seen—as though she'd pulled him out of a trance. When she blinked, she saw the numbers again. This time digits were scattered all over, with the words, *incomplete* in red.

So that's it, she thought. *This man is making me hallucinate.* Breathing as though she ran a race, she was curious to know exactly what happened. Of course, she wished he could hold her hand forever, and it seemed as though he wanted the same, but she couldn't let him in—he would know too much.

"Same here," he said.

She was out of it for so long that she had no idea what he was responding to. His dark, penetrating stare intimidated her, but it felt good. She was glad to see that Rachel was still on the phone, and most likely didn't notice the chemistry she was certain they shared.

"I see you make my family happy," he said in a deep and low tone.

"I'm glad to hear that." Isabella smiled nervously as Rachel made her way back to them.

"Yeah, it's rare for them to be comfortable with anyone."

"It's the Private-I in all of us," Rachel interjected.

Christian's stare shifted to Rachel. "We've become very suspicious of people recently, haven't we?"

"You know, I don't think it's that recent," Rachel said. "It's been in the Gomes blood for a while. I guess it has just gotten worse with mom's generation and ours. That's probably why we're old and still single."

Isabella giggled. "Stop."

"Seriously," Rachel said. "Chris, remember our friendship quota? Our moms were very particular about friends. We could only have one best friend each."

"I didn't know that," Isabella said, brows furrowed.

"Yeah, that's how we ended up with Olivia and Kevin. Surprised I never told you, and even now, you know better than anyone I find it hard to make friends. Good thing I found you when we were kids. You snuck in past my limit—maybe it had to do with the way we met. As for Chris, forget it, he attracts people like honey. To him, Kevin was his only true friend but try telling that to all those so-called acquaintances."

Christian explained. "The myth is, our ancestors were very trusting and it got them in deep trouble."

He then went back to staring intensely at Isabella, forcing her to shift her gaze. A small laugh escaped from his lips. He absolutely loved the effect he had on her. She was way too easy to read, and he found it quite entertaining. Fully aware of what had taken place earlier, he wondered if she felt it, too.

His skill as an advanced body-language expert landed him a position as an instructor of the art at Miami PD. Although she had barely spoken the two times they had met, he had gathered plenty from her. He concluded that she was not experienced in terms of relationships. Ever since he was wrong about a junior high crush, who turned out to be the only girl in the entire class without feelings for him, he had stopped making assumptions about women. However, Isabella made it easy for him to make that bold conclusion about her. He was certain and could bet serious money on the fact that not only did she like his attention, but she was also falling for him. Because that was a first, he was intrigued. Most women he assessed were usually interested in his money or sex, and after his experience with women, he had come to believe that was the true way—over his father's flowery Cervello stories about everlasting love.

He worried about Isabella. She probably missed the lesson most women learned from wiser ones on guarding themselves against men knowing such information too soon. Then again, there was an exception—some women did wear their hearts on their sleeve, and even though he saw that as refreshing and brave, he was also slightly troubled by it because these same women ended up as victims of wolves in sheep's clothing. She either never experienced hurt or was just plain naïve about relationships altogether. There perhaps was some childishness—he'd tried to brush it off as nerves the first time. He wondered about her age. She had to be Rachel's age at most. Her reaction to his stare and hand grip, coupled with the strong chemistry they'd shared, was enough for him to know that he could easily have his way with her if he wanted to. She didn't seem like the type who would stalk a man when he was done with her. Her type would simply disappear—brokenhearted.

Rachel laughed. "Why are you scaring the girl?"

"Oh, please," Isabella said hurriedly. Then with a dismissive wave and shrug she said, "I'm okay."

"Listen," Rachel said. "Even if anyone tried anything, Christian's got his eye on them— literally."

Christian made the hand-eye signal for *I'm watching you* to Isabella.

Isabella felt a desperate need to escape. She had never felt more smothered in Rachel's huge bedroom. Christian seemed to take up so much space. "I'm thirsty," Isabella announced. "Anybody want a drink?"

"Ahh! Her defense mechanism," Christian teased. "Someone's got something to hide?"

"No, I don't, I'm just thirsty." She walked out the door.

Rachel gave Christian an evil grin, "You think we scared her?"

"Nah, she should be fine."

Isabella returned to the room with a pitcher of ice water with lemons in one hand and two glasses pinched together in the other. She placed them on Rachel's dresser and poured herself a glass.

"Has anyone heard from Olivia lately?" Christian asked. "Now *that* girl knows how to have fun."

"Oh, give me a break," Rachel said, frowning, as she headed over to pour herself a drink. "That's what you call fun? Have you ever wondered why we grew apart? We have absolutely nothing in common."

Okay . . . maybe it's my cue to leave again, Isabella thought. She tended to feel self-conscious during conversations about or comparing her to Olivia. Ever since she figured she was a replacement for her, she feared she had to live up to certain expectations. She noticed Christian analyze her as Rachel spoke about Olivia.

Just when Isabella was thinking of a new reason to escape, his phone saved her.

"Hello," he said into the phone. "Ah, speak of the devil! Excuse me ladies . . . have a great evening."

When he walked out the door, Isabella asked, "Does he have a thing for Olivia?" She figured she must have caught Rachel off guard because she nearly choked on her drink. "Olivia is an asexual creature," Rachel laughed hysterically. "We don't think she's interested in anyone but herself—oh, and money. You should already know this, Isa. Seriously, she has no feelings in that way for anyone."

Christian continued his call in his study. "It's creepy how you just called, Liv."

Olivia laughed. "I can read your mind, so you better be nice, and tell Rachel to stop talking about me."

"Hmm, I actually believe you."

"So lover boy, how are you holding up? I heard about what happened."

"Nice to see that good news still travels fast in Key Bis."

"Faster than a speeding bullet my love, what's up?"

Christian had been friends with Olivia since grade school at Key Biscayne K-8. Even though she was a couple of years younger than him and Kevin, they both knew she'd always preferred hanging out with older kids, citing that her-age mates were dumb.

Not much was known about Olivia's past, and she chose to keep it that way. What the Cervellos did know was that even as a child, Olivia would frequent their home because she felt she finally belonged somewhere. She even went to school from Casa Cervello for weeks at a time. The Cervellos had never met her parents or siblings, and Pattie had grown tired of asking to meet her mother when her requests repeatedly fell on deaf ears. Christian was aware that Olivia came from a single-parent household and that she had a sibling whom she never met, but every time he tried to get more out of her, she would become defensive and upset, ultimately disappearing for weeks at a time. She would return unkempt and out of it, and for fear that she would run again and be exposed to danger, they all learned to walk on eggshells when it came to Olivia's family history, and chose to embrace her as she was. Eventually, she became an honorary Cervello child with a room of her own.

"*You* tell me. What's good in the Sunshine State?"

"Ahh, you're asking the right person. I'm at your service anytime, you know, just gotta put me on that P-I payroll. Girl's gotta eat."

"Olivia, Olivia, don't tell me you still don't have a job."

"It's the economy, Chris."

"Cut that out, I had George from human resources make up a job for you in the Miami office."

"Chris, you know I don't do the nine-to-five," she whined.

"Then work from home, Olivia. Just do something!"

"All right, I'll think about it, okay?"

"Oh, you're not doing me any favors."

"Who's asking for the favors *now*? When I come home, I'll get back to you about things to do, okay?"

"Come *home*? Where *are* you?"

"Um . . . London?"

Christian grunted. "Oh, don't tell me—"

"I know, I know, she needed me, okay?"

"Is she there with you? Has she been listening the whole time?"

"Listen, we'll talk when I get home, okay?"

"Whatever." What else was he to do anyway? It wasn't as if he could tell her to stop being friends with Kathy. The moment he'd introduced the two of them, they'd instantly hit it off. Olivia told him at the time that Kathy reminded her of herself and felt she was the sister she had never met. At the rate Olivia had called Kathy in London, he suspected that Kathy was taking Rachel's place in Olivia's life. He never thought she clicked with Rachel anyway because they were always at each other's throats. Christian was starting to put things into perspective. Rachel replaced Olivia with Isabella, and Olivia found a match in Kathy.

CHAPTER FOUR

Mind Games

CHRISTIAN PULLED out of his Ocean Drive condominium and headed to the convenience store for gum. Shortly before he'd relocated to Vancouver, he had acquired the 110-residential structure against his father's advice not to for fear surrounding the financial crisis; however, it had turned out to be one of his best business decisions yet.

The building manager had informed him earlier that day that his fully furnished ocean-view penthouse was available for move-in. Although he had briefly considered doing just that shortly after his fight with his mother three weeks ago, he didn't have the peace to go through with it now. Being in the heart of South Beach and its wild nightlife reeked of his past, and having Olivia as his neighbor spelled trouble. In addition to the accountability Casa Cervello gave him, His Mind wanted the close proximity to Isabella to play with her head.

Another tourist . . . great, Christian muttered. *Just what I needed.* With a quick flash at the mirror, he practiced a charming smile. Just as he wound down his window, the traffic light made his day. Cocking his head to the side with a shrug, he waved an apology to the flustered driver. For some reason, tourists knew to come to him for directions. Maybe they could tell he was born and raised in Miami. A place where almost daily, he would meet a tourist who did not hesitate to tell him how lucky he was to live in such paradise.

Yet, he felt like a complete stranger—lost. At least a tourist had a map. He imagined what it would be like to reach for a map when he should know the place like the back of his hand, but a fish out of water had it better because at least it could openly gasp for its final breath shamelessly. He didn't feel he could express himself—not freely at least. Therefore, it was one façade after another.

People appreciated façades. He didn't like them in others, but others seemed to want it from him because they could care less if he was having a bad day. How dare he mention to anyone that he was bored in a place like this? That would be ungrateful. Most people used their hard-earned savings to visit Florida for a week or two out of a year. So, rather than let his feelings show, he would put on the charming smile he'd practiced over the years even though he could barely breathe. It was a wonder how he could still drive.

Lately, the obsessions had spiraled out of control, leading to panic attacks. At least that was what his online research called it. He wouldn't dare go to a shrink, lest they have him committed, but he knew there were three parts of him—*The Madman, The Entrepreneur, and His Body*—or, as he preferred to call them, *His Mind, Genius, and His Shell of a Body*. His Mind was irrational and spontaneous, and this was where his wild side dwelled. Genius, on the other hand, was whom he aspired to be. He was the reasonable one and made it a point to separate himself from the other two by always speaking to him in the second person, '*you*.' His Mind was bossier and always spoke to him in the first person, '*I*.' His Shell was mute—he just followed whoever was the stronger of the two—which of course was His Mind, most of the time. Although the first two had very independent thoughts and seemed like separate components, they were all a part of him. This was enough to confuse any sane person, and this was why it would remain his secret.

Enter *Genius: Christian Cervello* . . . loud applause went off in his head. MIT-bred engineer and CEO of Private-I Secure Systems Inc., an investigative enterprise inspired by his obsessive need to protect his loved ones. Not only did his company have state-of-the-art industrial and home security systems, but they also specialized in personal accessories created to stop crimes before they took place. Thanks to Genius, who managed to make the best out of the mess His Mind created, every single product marketed by the company was born. Right from the University of Miami, he had numerous multimillion-dollar patents and by the time he had graduated from MIT, he'd established his brand internationally. Now, at the age of thirty-three, he had a following that his seasoned competitors couldn't parallel. But what was all that to an insane mind? His wealth and power stemmed from the same brain that drove him mad. Realizing he'd forgotten his next destination, he set the GPS to head home. It was that bad.

Performing music covers was something Rachel and Isabella had picked up since their return from college, after they ditched karaoke. It began with Rachel, who always loved singing. Her voice was magnificent. She just never spoke about how and when she'd started. Isabella, on the other hand, used music to escape. She thought she had a good singing voice, but Rachel would say that because Isabella was inexperienced when it came to romantic relationships, she didn't sound convincing when they sang heartbreak songs. In high school, Rachel had even thought of pairing up with a better singer. But Isabella got better at pretending by daydreaming that her imaginary knight had broken her heart. It worked every time for Rachel.

This time around, Rachel's boyfriend, Thomas Greene, joined them for the first time. He had a good singing voice that complimented the duo. Rachel had met the savvy attorney at the homeless charity event that Isabella helped organize in Manhattan last December, one she'd practically forced Rachel to attend. Now merely two months in, the two of them were inseparable. The girls loved Thomas' quirky sense of humor and referred to him as the serious family attorney by day and "silly goose" by night. This Friday night, they chose to use the entertainment room to unwind from their respective jobs. With Thomas at the piano, Rachel and Isabella harmonized.

Much to their surprise, and Isabella's chagrin, Christian began to applaud at the end of their performance. He'd been standing by the staircase. Rachel clutched her chest, laughing. "You freaked me out!"

"That's the whole idea; you gotta be ready at all times," he said with a half-smile. "You never know who's watching."

Isabella looked down shyly—grateful that Rachel had walked over to Thomas to go over some musical notes with him. She didn't want her to see the effect her brother had on her and possibly continue to add on to what Isabella felt was a growing incriminating list of her unruly emotions. She loved any alone time with him, and she was glad she didn't have to wait another three weeks to see him—just a day this time.

When he began to stroll toward her, she briefly closed her eyes. Taking in the hypnotic scent of his cologne, she couldn't close her eyes for long for fear she imagine anything she dared not entertain. Keeping her eyes open was equally scary because his scorching gaze convinced her that her eyes were the only part of her body that existed to him. So she was trapped with two terrifying options: to turn away and be found guilty of being crazy about him, or give in to temptation and count the black lines around his iris that appeared to grow in number as he stared at her. It was mesmerizing. *How could Kathy possibly let this fish back in the sea?*

Isabella felt sweat begin to form in her palms—it tingled. This was their third face-to-face meeting, and she was darned if they had to shake hands again, especially knowing how wet her hands were getting. She wouldn't survive it. She automatically crossed her arms. "How long have you been watching?"

She noticed him mirror her movement. "Since you took the mic."

With one arm still crossed and the other hand resting under his chin, he gently stroked his chin with his thumb. "I see Rachel finally got the karaoke partner she's been looking for."

Isabella smiled. "Oh, yeah?"

"You see, it was her parents' dream for her to sing because of her angelic voice. Her mom had given her singing lessons as a child. She actually considered attending a performing arts high school before her parents died."

"Really?" she replied, surprised. She seemed to learn something new about Rachel every time she spoke to her brother. She wondered if she really knew her, after all. This was just more proof that she couldn't ever compete with him.

"Yup, I thought you'd know this."

Isabella shook her head. "I just knew she loved music. I've been hearing her own singing voice more and more lately . . . since Thomas."

"Is that so? Because the last time we heard her sing that way was before the accident. Somehow she lost her voice after that and picked up karaoke much later."

"She has a beautiful voice—I always wondered why she never considered a career in singing."

"Tell me about it. Mom says not to push her, though. Hmm, so how about you?"

She laughed. "I can't sing to save any of us."

"Then that makes two of us, but somehow I don't believe you."

"The wonders of karaoke," Isabella said. Then giving him a puzzled look, she asked, "Wait, didn't you say you were listening from the time I took the mic?"

"You got me." He grinned. "Nah, I only heard Rachel's part. You can breathe easy now."

They both glanced over at Thomas and Rachel as they belted out musical notes confidently.

Isabella smiled. "He's good for her."

"I see."

"Do you know he can actually play all the instruments for the songs we perform?" she said excitedly. "I mean, we really don't karaoke anymore—they are more like covers now."

Whatever that means, Christian thought. He didn't know all these fancy terms but was amazed to see just how much interest Isabella had in all this. *Maybe Rachel wasn't holding her against her will, after all.*

"Is that so, now?" he smirked.

"Yes," Isabella said. "He will be performing in our church band with Rachel, too."

"*Our?* You go to our church?"

"Yeah."

"No way, how come I didn't know this?"

"Umm, maybe because you haven't lived here for some time now. Have you been back yet?"

"Nope." He wasn't in the mood to go into details either. "So, Rachel joined the music team, huh?"

"Yeah, I'm so happy for her. I'd tried convincing her for the longest time, but she'd just been so nervous. But it makes sense from what you've said."

As Rachel and Thomas made their way toward them, Isabella sighed in relief, having run out of things to say.

The men shook hands. "It's nice to meet you again," Thomas said.

Now that's a normal handshake, Isabella thought.

"Same here," Christian replied. "So you attend Faith House now?"

"Yeah, I just joined a few weeks ago when I finally relocated."

"Nice. How do you like it so far?"

"It's amazing. I was away from church for a while, so it's good to finally be back home," Thomas said, prompting a back rub from Rachel.

Christian nodded at Rachel. "So Rach, that was amazing."

"Thank you, thank you," Rachel said, bowing.

"Do you girls only sing that one song? I've been hearing it a lot from your bedroom."

"Oh, 'Sending My Love,'" Isabella replied, wondering where the sudden urge to be chatty again came from. "No, we do just about anything duo, but Zhané is our favorite, especially that piece. It's special for Rach."

"Okay, stop." Rachel blushed.

He turned his attention to Isabella, "Do *you* have a special piece?"

She was horrified at the devious gleam in Rachel's eyes, and before she could respond, Rachel said, "Isa's new favorite song is 'La La La,' but she refuses to sing it because it makes her cry. "

Isabella wished the floor would just open and swallow her up. It was bad enough that Christian made her so self-conscious of everything, now she wondered what he would do with this tiny piece of irrelevant information that Rachel felt so obliged to give. It didn't help that Thomas, the great teaser, was grinning.

"Really, Isa?" Thomas tugged on her arm, laughing. "So that's why you—"

"Always." Rachel laughed. "Recently, she's been asking me to perform the whole thing while she just stares into space and listens with tears rolling down her face."

"Stop," Isabella's voice was faint.

Christian smiled as he noticed Isabella's lip curl—he loved it, and would willingly tease her all day just to see it. She covered her face and hurried away from the group. This only caused him to be more intrigued. Thomas and Rachel appeared extremely amused by the whole thing and couldn't seem to get over the fit of giggles that overtook them. "No way," Thomas laughed, holding his belly. "I noticed she did that the last time I watched you sing; this is too funny."

Christian didn't join in on their laughter because he felt for Isabella, but couldn't ignore the two words Rachel had used, *new* and *recently*. It didn't help that she hurried off like some pupil. He was more intrigued than amused because he never knew of a woman who crushed on anyone as a teenager would. He wondered if this was the way he appeared to his junior high crush. The only difference would be that his crush didn't want him back. However, the feelings Isabella had for him were indeed reciprocal.

Maintaining a keen eye on her from across the room, he ventured to ask, "How recent?"

Rachel flashed him a suspicious glance as she struggled to contain her laughter and catch her breath. By now tears were rolling down her face. "For the past couple of weeks, why?"

"Really?" he asked, ignoring her question. "What is it about that song?"

"No idea," she shrugged, as she went to check on Isabella.

Thomas wiped tears from his eyes. "Music can do that; the clue is in the lyrics or melody."

At this point, Christian was one hundred percent certain the clue would reveal some sort of *crush* song. A rush of nostalgia swept over him. "Do you have the CD with you?"

"Yeah, it's right here," Thomas reached into his case.

Christian watched Isabella as she spoke to Rachel. "Can I borrow it?"

"Sure."

He collected the CD and spun it around his finger as his eyes remained on her. Suddenly, he remembered what he was on his way out to get earlier—chewing gum. Somehow, Isabella had the power to clean out his overactive brain, though for a hefty price—replacing the existing memory with just *her*. Something about her didn't quite add up and it was unsettling. He was determined to get into her head somehow, and if music was the key, he was ready to use it.

He walked over to them. "Ladies, I really enjoyed today's karaoke session."

"*Cover*," Rachel corrected with a frown.

With a wicked grin, he said, "Of course, I see these *covers* mean a lot to both of you, and I'm glad. It does look and sound like fun, and now I feel bad for making fun of it earlier. I owe you one. Seriously."

"I'm holding you to that," Rachel said, poking his arm.

"Hey, you're invited to join us anytime." Thomas teased.

"Ah! Thanks, but I think I'll take a rain check on the foursome covers."

Back in his study, Christian busied himself with a patent drawing, as Isabella's song played in the background. Merely focusing on the melody, he soon found himself liking the sound of it. He imagined what she would have said if she caught him. She'd probably scream for him to stop—all the while covering her beautiful face.

A chime came from his computer. It was a face call from his friend in London, David.

"Hey, buddy," Christian greeted.

"I see a good mood, eh. I'm just checking in on the big CEO. How are things in the sunny side of life?"

"Eh, so-so. How are wedding plans coming along?"

"That's actually why I called. I was um . . . wondering if you would still be able to um—"

"Come on, Dave, are you firing me as your best man because I left the city?"

David laughed. "Actually, I'm not, but I was afraid you would have a change of heart."

"So because things don't work out for me, I can't rejoice with others?"

"It's not that. I was just trying to be considerate. But thanks man, it would mean a lot to me and Dee."

"Of course, I understand. How is Dee anyway? Did she go back to Johannesburg yet?"

"Yeah, she left a week after you did. You both left me here in this cold all alone."

"Toughen up, man. You gotta get used to London weather if you wanna bring home the bacon. So what duties am I missing? Rehearsals . . . anything?"

"Okay, yeah, so I was just about to email you guys some details."

"Sure thing." Christian nodded. "Hey Dave, I wanna ask you a question."

"Shoot."

"Do you think it's too soon to—"

David laughed.

"Hey, what's so funny? I didn't even say anything yet."

"I know you, Chris, who is it?"

"I haven't even—"

"Then say it," David insisted.

"It's Rachel's friend."

"Ah! Olivia?"

"No, no, another one. I just met her recently, and she's driving me crazy already."

"Oh, yeah?" David chuckled.

"Totally."

"I don't remember you ever going insane for Kat, so maybe it's a good sign. How long has it been since your breakup?"

"Um, about a month."

David shook his head. "You need time to heal, Chris."

"I know, and Lord knows I'm trying to but—" Christian sighed and ran his fingers through his hair.

David laughed. "I told you, one of these days your hair's gonna fall out if you keep up with that."

"Stop, I'm being serious, Dave."

"Okay, okay, I'm listening; the last thing you said was but. But what?"

"This girl doesn't make it easy to focus on other things, or should I say, she makes it easy to forget Kathy. I don't know. I'm confused."

"So you think its love, eh?"

"Hmm," Christian asked as he squinted at the screen, "What does that look like?"

CHAPTER FIVE

Sowing Seeds

IT WAS nice not having to dress in layers anymore. Even for March, the weather was picture-perfect. The simple acknowledgment of the fact amused Christian, having lived in Florida nearly his entire life. Could it be that he'd actually come to understand what the typical tourist already knew? Yes, his past two years in London made him a better person. Not only did it reinforce his need for stability, but it also made him more appreciative of what he had at home. Now somehow he had to get His Mind to see that and stop looking to London for answers. *Perhaps Isabella could help,* had been Genius' suggestion for weeks, and Christian hadn't ruled that out.

He walked up the path leading to his favorite waterfront restaurant. It looked different in a good way. He'd been away for far too long—how could he ever have thought of living anywhere else. From a distance, he saw Olivia waiting outside for him—her dark hair dancing in the wind. It had been a little over two years since they were here together, and he imagined the strands of her hair were cheering him back to their favorite hangout spot. The place was dear to them, and the staff knew them well. The entire Cervello clan loved seafood and his parents began patronizing the restaurant shortly after they were married, later bringing him and Rachel there as kids.

Yet today, he could hardly recognize the place. It wasn't just this, but almost everything he knew had changed. *Deep breaths,* he muttered as he approached her from behind and whistled.

"Hey, stranger," Olivia smiled, embracing him. "How long have you been back?"

"Well, what do you know . . . exactly a month today. How was London?"

"Don't ask," Olivia said, rolling her eyes.

"Tell me I'm not really at the Rusty Pelican," Christian said, bewildered.

"Oh yeah, you haven't been here for a couple of years. Yup, they spent millions renovating it—I actually like it."

Christian shook his head slowly.

"What, you don't?"

"No, it's not that, it's just that everything's changing. It's kind of scary."

"Come on, playboy, change is good. It used to be your motto. So tell me, what *have* you been up to?"

Christian ran his fingers through his hair. "Drowning myself in work."

"Yeah?" she laughed.

"What's so funny?"

"The hair thingy," Olivia said, motioning. "You still do that—I haven't seen it in years."

"Leave me alone. What's it with my hair anyway? Everyone's pointing it out lately."

Olivia shrugged. "Anyway, I just know it's my cue."

"Your cue for what?"

"To get you someone new," Olivia said, with a crafty gleam in her eyes as she sipped her coffee.

"You're kidding, right?" When she shook her head, he continued, "You hooked me up based on my hair?"

"Nah, the way you . . . forget it, you won't understand."

"Do I do it a lot?" Christian asked, signaling for the waiter.

"Frequently."

He made a face. "You think it's a turnoff?"

"Nah, it's hot. The girls love it."

"I don't do it on purpose, you know. I don't even know when I do it."

Olivia squeezed his hand. "I know you better than you know yourself. You only do that when you're nervous or overwhelmed."

Christian creased his brows, "Anyway, Key Bis seems so different."

"You were in and out the last time you visited. I didn't even get to see you."

"It feels like there's nothing to do."

Olivia chuckled. "That's because you left when you were at your prime. Now you're old and ready to settle down. It's no wonder you can't appreciate the renovation here."

"Wow, thanks, Liv, I see your mean side is still intact, and listen, don't get me wrong and don't go telling them I don't like the new look because I do. It's not about the place, Liv, it's me! I feel like I'm losing control, I'm just—"

"Lonely. It's okay, hon; you can be honest with Liv." She shook her head. "I've always said, the best way to get over old love is with new love."

The waiter arrived and took Christian's order as Olivia powered on her tablet.

"Ha, I don't agree," Christian said.

She shrugged. "You don't have to, but it's true. Besides I don't understand why a fine man like you hasn't been snatched up in a month."

"Oh, believe me, some have tried."

"No one interesting at work?"

"Nope, I don't mix business with pleasure."

"Anymore?" Olivia winked.

"Hey, Kathy and I started out before I offered her the job."

"Hmm, let's see . . . you probably need someone closer to home."

Christian flashed a lopsided grin. "Like you?"

"No, silly, have you considered Isa?"

She threw him off guard with that name, but he found it strange that although he typically had no problem confiding in Olivia, he had a strong urge to protect what he felt for Isabella.

When he didn't respond, Olivia said, "Forget it, Rachel won't let her little puppy out of her sight. Ugh, forget I even suggested it." She shook herself off in disgust. Christian was intrigued.

"Listen, there's a girl I could hook you up with. She has an accent. I know you like that . . . you know, from Kathy and Carla. This one's Russian. She's extremely beautiful and big fun. If I must add, she'll—" clearing her throat, Olivia added with a smile "—satisfy you a hundred percent."

Christian frowned and shook his head. "No, thanks. Besides, I've changed, Liv. I'm not interested in sex right now." *What I am interested in is why Isabella irritates you*, he mused.

Olivia nearly choked on her drink. "What, so you're a monk now because your engagement ended? Get over it, Chris!"

"No, seriously, I have no desire for sex."

Olivia squeezed his hand again. "From what I hear, you have a very healthy appetite." She shrugged. "Also, Kathy sure liked to talk about your escapades. Listen, you're a man and men have needs. You don't need to be ashamed to ask someone to take care of that. It's natural."

"You wouldn't understand—let's just leave it at that, okay?"

Lifting her cup to her lips with a frown, she shot an impatient glance his way. "Don't go turning into those prudes now."

"Who?" Christian asked, amused.

"Your sister and her goodie-two-shoes friend. Don't let them suck you in."

"Listen to yourself, Liv. You're talking about Rach like she's some bad influence. What happened to the two of you anyway? Weren't you besties?"

"First of all, it's apparent that Isa's got more in common with her, but let's talk about influence since you brought that up. It depends on how you look at it. Your sister is a 28-year-old virgin who still acts like a child. Heck, I tried to hook her up, and she was this close to getting laid, but no, little Isa talked her out of it."

"Impressive," Christian nodded. "Sounds like a smart girl." If Olivia thought this would turn him off, she was mistaken. He didn't need negative influences in Rachel's life, and even though Rachel was almost thirty, that didn't mean she needed to become desperate. She had a good head on her shoulders, and he was beginning to see why she and Olivia drifted apart.

"I met her for the first time last month," he said.

Olivia frowned. "No, you *didn't*. She's been coming to your house since she came here from wherever she immigrated from. She might as well pick a room."

"Rachel said the same thing but apparently I don't remember ever meeting her. How come you never talked about her all the times you visited?"

Olivia rolled her eyes. "Seriously, Chris? Anyway, there was a time she wasn't allowed to come to your place."

Christian took a sip of his tea. "Why?"

"How would I know . . . the prude and her family—they're just weird. Perhaps that's why you don't remember her. Then again, you never stayed put in Florida since you graduated. Anyway, it probably worked out for Aunt Pattie because she was on to Rachel's friends like hawks—she might as well have given them background checks."

Christian stifled a chuckle. She was right about his mother, but he couldn't help but smile at the slight disgust in Olivia's eyes as she motioned with her hands.

"Seriously Chris, you need to see them together, they act like children, and Aunt Pattie encourages such silliness. I think she likes it because it makes her feel young herself. If you ask me, she's just lonely because your dad isn't here half the time, and she leans on those girls. I have no time to babysit."

Ouch. Christian grimaced. Olivia had always been blunt, but he knew her to be honest—discreet concerning herself, but honest about her feelings about others. He couldn't help wondering if she was right, "You think so?"

Olivia shrugged. "Sure. I mean, we've always known Rachel acted out with Aunt Pattie but notice how she never addresses it with Rachel? She enables her. The minute she stops, Rachel will grow up and move out."

"Well look at you, Madam Psychology."

"Thanks—I try."

"How old is Isabella?"

"Like 20."

Christian frowned.

"Okay . . . 25, but I gotta give her this, though . . . she's not as childish—except when they get together. But she has no excuse for her immaturity when it comes to relationships. I take Rachel two steps closer to the real world, and Isa takes her a hundred steps back."

"That's not so bad, is it? To wanna save yourself for that special someone?"

"Did you?" Olivia snapped.

"Well . . . "

"Exactly, and you know why? Because we'll all get our little hearts broken regardless. It's inevitable."

Christian nodded at Olivia with concern. "So who broke *your* heart, Liv?"

Olivia looked away. "I'm living my life to the fullest. I'm pretty content that way."

It was April Seventh and Christian was turning thirty-four. He had pretty much confined himself to the Casa Cervello estate for the past month—tormented by the same recurring nightmares. He was also bombarded with recent requests from His Mind to leave Florida, but he agreed with Genius' counter requests to stay because he knew things could have been worse if it hadn't been for Isabella. She somehow eased the brunt of returning to Florida, and seeing her a day to his would-be wedding last month helped tremendously. His days were better when she visited, but with tax season at hand, he didn't expect to see much of her soon.

For his birthday, however, he really just wanted to be alone in his room. Neither Pattie nor Rachel had hinted at anything special, and he was glad—hoping it would be over with quietly. With Rachel away at church and Pattie still fast asleep, he relished his time alone as he waited for sleep to return to his eyes. The background music was soothing. As suggested by Rachel, he'd been using it as a form of therapy last month, and it seemed to help block the hurt. Still, the hurt stemmed from Kevin's betrayal alone, making him wonder whether he ever loved Kathy or if he was just in a rush to get married. His relationship motto was never to look back. Still, even that couldn't explain the numbness he felt over losing her. Although he never looked back at past relationships, he at least had a soft spot for few ex-girlfriends—but with Kathy, a fiancée, nothing.

After church service, Isabella waited in the sanctuary as Rachel wrapped up her music department meeting.

They planned to pick Pattie and the birthday boy up for a surprise trip to a church carnival. According to Rachel, it was her special treat of the day for him and knowing Christian would hate the idea only made her love it more. Her idea was to encourage him to loosen up and be a kid again, but Isabella wasn't keen on that because she didn't want to appear immature to him. Although park rides were her guilty pleasure, she didn't want Christian to know that.

Rachel signaled "five minutes" with her palm and disappeared back into the side room. Just as Isabella went back to her reading, she sensed someone watching her from the corner of her eye. She turned to see. *Elisabeth.*

A chill came over her as the woman stood up and approached her.

"My child," she said in Portuguese.

"Hello, Ms. Elisabeth. Is everything okay?"

"I have a word for you."

"Um . . . Okay." She cringed as Elisabeth looked around. She appeared more nervous than Isabella felt.

"You must remain strong for where the Lord is taking you," she said. "It's not an easy road, but you have been chosen for an assignment, and you will help set many people free."

"Amen," Isabella found herself mumbling. She wondered why she wasn't startled by the message.

"This is for you," Elisabeth said, pressing a tightly rolled piece of paper into Isabella's palm—her hands trembling as she did. Then, giving Isabella a warm smile, she squeezed her hand and walked away.

As Isabella watched her, the chill over her body turned into overwhelming warmth. She didn't have a clue what Elisabeth was referring to, but she had peace that she wouldn't be alone for whatever it was. She breathed deeply as she began to unwrap the paper.

"Boo! You ready?" Rachel asked, startling Isabella.

"Ugh, Rachel!"

"Come on. Let's get going before it gets crowded."

CHAPTER SIX

Decisions

❦

WHEN THE attendant handed Christian tickets, it finally dawned on him that they were at a carnival. *How in the world could I have gotten myself into this mess?* It wasn't exactly what he had in mind when he offered to make it up to the girls. Nevertheless, he was willing to keep his promise.

His lips slowly formed a smile for a giddy Isabella. Things like this made him wonder whether she was indeed twenty-five. He didn't know too many people her age that still went insane for rides and sour gummy worms. Rachel and Pattie said she was a bright corporate accountant. Well, bright she was but he couldn't possibly see her as someone he could take seriously in a corporate setting—especially since he'd only seen her in casual clothing or pajamas. All the same, he couldn't help but notice the countless stares she received from men at the fair.

"Come on, birthday boy." Isabella winked. "Cheer up—you're gonna love it."

The floating overhead sign read, "Crazy Head Loose Moose Bowl Challenge." Apparently, it was a highly coveted game for the locals because he overheard some people mention it was making a return to the fair. They got priority treatment because of his birthday, and Pattie won the spot for captain—she seemed to have mastered the game the last time it was there. The bowling game was unlike any other. It was located outside, and any team could choose who would join them from the bystanders. The bystanders who remained could yell out to the players or cheer them on. Each team player could also swap with any of them. The game seemed very rowdy but it sounded like fun and it involved several movements prompted by a wide screen, some of which were embarrassingly silly.

Watching his mother hop around on one foot, practicing her moves, was hilarious. *Olivia would have a heart attack if she saw her now,* Christian thought. Pattie gathered the team together and explained the game. He saw this as an opportunity to see another side of Isabella and from the sound of the game, he expected her to shy away from it. However, to his surprise, the more Pattie went over the rules, the more Isabella couldn't wait to play. This intrigued him, and he wondered if she became shy around him alone. The game called for six teams, two per team, and as it stood, they only had two teams.

Assessing the bystanders who seemed eager to jump in, Pattie devised the strategy. "Let's choose within ourselves before we open it up to everyone else," she said, grabbing Isabella's hand. "I'm going with Isa."

"I said it first, Mom!" Rachel said, grabbing Isabella's other hand.

"But I'm the captain, I get to choose first."

This is ridiculous. Perhaps if Olivia hadn't pointed out the obvious, he wouldn't have been so critical. He soon smiled as he watched Isabella's hands stretched on both sides as Pattie and Rachel went on a tug of war. She was the cutest thing—in her blue Notre Dame Fighting Irish funnel-neck jersey and a pair of white shorts and high-top converse sneakers. Her hair was up in a high ponytail and with all the commotion, she looked like a teenager, and he was back in junior high. When Isabella began to wince, Christian said, "Okay, hey, hey . . . it's my birthday, and I should get to choose who's on my team first."

"Yeah, Chris is right," Rachel said, letting go of Isabella's hand. "Choose Mom!"

He shook his head, and with a calculating stare, he said, "I want Isabella."

As Pattie finalized players from the group of bystanders, Isabella went off to get more gummy worms at a nearby stand. Christian watched as she interacted with the salesperson and others in the line. He couldn't hear the conversation, but they all laughed in response to something she'd said. Something about her drew people in. He also noticed how men gawked at her as she made her way back to the game—some even looking back. Yet, she seemed oblivious. He considered whether he had been overly confident with his assessment of her. Seeing her outside of Casa Cervello gave him a chance to see a different side of her and learn to appreciate her more. She may have been single and inexperienced, but she wasn't desperate.

Isabella flashed a quick smile at him as she struggled with her bag of gummy worms. He hated to compare her to Kathy, but he missed seeing this carefree side in a woman. As she placed a gummy worm in her mouth, he caught sight of a gold ring on her finger and walked up to her.

"You didn't get married between the last time I saw you and today, did you?"

"*No.*" She giggled, bemused. "Why?"

He gestured at the ring.

"Oh, you haven't seen this?"

"Nope."

"I see. That's probably because I only wear it when I go out."

Curiosity got the best of him. "Why?"

Isabella shrugged. "It helps keep guys at bay."

When he became lost for words, His Mind took over. *She has someone already. Good—no emotional ties!*

Isabella took him by the hand. "Come on."

Christian tried to remain focused as he positioned the bowling ball in his fingertips and waited for the overhead screen to prompt a movement. As he wiggled his hips as prompted, a myriad of thoughts came to mind. Then there were the crazy cheers from women in the crowd as he aimed for the pins while wiggling on one leg. The game was impossible. How was he to focus on striking with so many silly moves? He let go, then turned around nonchalantly with a smirk. The next thing he heard was Isabella's cheer among several others. He'd hit the first strike of the game, but shook his head slowly—pretending not to care that he just impressed her and the entire crowd.

He strolled back to her. "So exactly why would you want to keep men at bay?"

Still excited, she raised her voice above the cheer. "It helps to weed out the bad ones."

He was baffled. "But doesn't a ring on your wedding finger weed out *all* guys?"

Isabella laughed. "You'd be surprised."

"Humor me," he said, leading her to a quieter spot.

"Well, I've found that a ring doesn't seem to mean much nowadays to men or women. Even with this, I have to verbally tell some people I'm taken. Still, what do I get: 'Oh, I can love you better,' or 'so what?'"

"Seriously?" he asked, amazed.

"Yup."

"Wow, I must be old because the last I checked, wedding rings were like 'do not enter' signs."

Isabella patted his arm. "Well, you're in the minority, my friend. Times have changed."

"So exactly how many men do you usually need to keep at bay on a daily basis? Say . . . if you didn't have a ring, how many are we talking?"

"Well, it's not been as bad lately. Just four to five."

"A *day*?"

She nodded.

Just? he mused, nodding slowly. "Isn't it every woman's desire to be approached or found attractive?"

"Isa, your turn!" Pattie yelled.

"I guess I'm not every woman," she replied, running back to the game.

As Isabella took the ball from Pattie, Christian's mind reeled over their conversation. But the whistles from men in the crowd soon interrupted his train of thought. It was then that he knew he wasn't the only one she'd infected with her bug. She definitely had a hold on men. He didn't know what to make of it, but it couldn't possibly be her fault that she was so desirable. She didn't seem to be doing anything to lead them on, but the confidence he had in the shy girl he met in the garden was quickly fading. For the first time, he questioned whether she was even interested in him in *that* way. He watched Isabella cheer Pattie on—drawing more attention to herself as she did. He wished he could just take her back to Casa Cervello and lock her up there—where His Shell of a Body dwelled, keeping a close eye on her, away from all the competition.

The bowling game came to an end with Pattie and Rachel emerging as winners. To Christian's surprise and delight, he learned that the carnival was merely a practical joke on Rachel's part, and she had planned adult-friendly activities for the rest of the day throughout the city.

Before leaving the carnival, the three of them watched Isabella in amusement, as she sat quietly at a corner with her legs folded. With some hair having escaped from her now unruly ponytail, she seriously counted her winnings for the day and she didn't seem a bit bothered. *A woman that accounted for raffle tickets as she would her client's financial accounts—quite impressive,* Christian pondered. Rachel silently stole camera shots of Isabella, and Christian stooped down. "Hey, why don't you take mine—add it to yours and get something nice for yourself."

"You're sure you don't want it?" she asked, eyes twinkling.

Christian shook his head, amused.

She reached up slightly and hugged him, nearly causing him to lose his balance. "Thanks so much, Chris. Wanna come with me?" Christian walked behind her as she strolled casually from store to store. He observed what he instantly coined *the Isabella attraction*—it was magnetic how she drew men in. A group of teenage boys walked past her. He thought he overheard one dare another to make a move. The third kept looking back until he tripped and fell over an erected funnel cake sign. He couldn't help but laugh—all the while, she was unaware. *Is this what it would be like to be with a girl like this?* Even competing with little boys.

Competing with other men for the female heart wasn't a game he played. He was accustomed to getting whatever woman he wanted. He wasn't willing to play this game, but he couldn't deny that she made him feel young again—which wasn't such a bad thing. He stepped up closer to see what being by her side was like. She looked over at him and smiled, melting his heart. Then taking her by the hand, they walked into the next store together. As they looked around, Isabella's smile fell. Scattered across the walls and counters was a mountain of toys. He found her expression quite amusing. His grin was meant to be wicked when their eyes met, but it turned her sad face into giggles.

"Um, I don't see anything I like here. You?"

Christian chuckled. "Hey, I thought you liked kid stuff," he teased.

Isabella smacked him with the tickets and Christian chuckled louder. Though cute, he was glad that there was a limit to her childishness.

"There's a T-shirt store down to your left," the attendant said. "Your tickets should be good there."

"Oh great, thanks," Isabella said, grabbing Christian's hand.

They arrived at a small wooden shed that looked more like an upgraded dog shed. They stared at each other, amused. If not for the makeshift sign that read, *T-shirts for you*, they wouldn't have guessed it was a shop.

Judging from the height of the doorway, he stopped outside the entrance. "You go, I'll wait out here."

"Okay, but I don't know what you want."

"The tickets are yours."

"I know but I'm not a T-shirt girl."

"Oh? I find that hard to believe," he mocked, eyeing her from head to toe.

"Sweatshirts are my thing," she said, tugging her sweatshirt.

Christian shook his head. "How do you do it in Florida?"

"Simple, I'm always freezing."

"You're from Brazil."

"So? I was cold there, too and don't forget I lived in Indiana for five years."

"Indiana weather isn't that bad. It's a far cry from London's."

"It *was* bad. The summers were okay, but I found every other season to be blah . . . then the winters were very cold. We even had snow in April once, you know?"

He looked at her skeptically.

"Seriously . . . "

"Well, pick me something nice."

"Okay, what size do you wear, large?" she asked sheepishly.

"Yes."

She walked in—surprised the T-shirts in that small shed didn't swallow her up. She could barely breathe in there and felt sorry for the lanky teenager she nearly missed huddled among the shirts. She quickly surveyed the collection and finally spotted one with the words, *"you + me"* on the front of it and *"= Sunshine State"* on the back with two teddy bears kissing. She stroked the cotton shirt. The thought that this would be on Christian's skin excited her. She blushed when the attendant looked at her with a puzzled smirk. She then quickly handed the raffle tickets over to him. He neatly folded the shirt and placed it in a bag.

Christian's grin was wide when she made her exit. Giggling, she handed him the shopping bag and covered her face with one hand.

"The first gift you gave me," he said. "It better not be silly, Isabella."

"Hey, I tried." Isabella giggled uncontrollably. "It's the only manly shirt in the store."

He unfolded the shirt and laughed as he held it up. "Manly?"

"You *like?*" she teased.

Christian flashed a crooked smile. "I love it just because you gave it to me."

The next two weeks following Christian's birthday had been remarkably peaceful. Peaceful for Christian meant not obsessing over the norm and not obsessing resulted in not creating anything new. To someone with enough inventions under his belt to last him two life times, this was actually a good thing. His best inventions were born out of unrest, and although perfection was typically the result to his investors and consumers, he was never satisfied unless he had a moment of rest to view his art as an outsider.

Over the years, he had typically achieved this rest in one of three ways: chewing one particular brand of gum in a specific manner, drinking a special tea made the exact way, or being in a committed relationship. Relationships provided the greatest length of rest, which is why he could credit Kathy for the past two years of the most sustained peace he had ever had. That peace allowed him time to continue the discovery into his true self. Although his return to Florida derailed that, the past two weeks had allowed him to put more pieces together.

The biggest discovery yet was that he needed companionship to have more moments of rest. Although he wasn't in one right now, Isabella's near-constant presence on the premises had somehow tricked His Mind into believing that he was in a relationship with her—especially since it had registered that she intrigued him. She hardly ever made eye contact when they crossed paths and he was used to it, but her innocence, smile, and laugh were hypnotic.

She had worked right from Casa Cervello for nearly the entire two weeks. He learned that one of the reasons she loved being there was the private access to the ocean in the backyard, and he never missed an opportunity to watch her at work from his bedroom patio. He'd misjudged her based on her youthful manner, but her long work hours made him seem like the amateur. According to Rachel, it was hectic because it was one of her monthly close periods on the job. As for Rachel, he hardly ever saw her. They worked differently—Isabella, out by the water and Rachel in their father's study. It boggled his mind because he would have imagined the editor by the water and the accountant in the office. What would Olivia say for herself now? It had been so easy for her to find fault in the girls when she didn't even have a job herself.

Coincidentally, with the girl's hectic work schedules culminating around the same time that weekend, they were in the mood for something fun. They had invited him out, but he graciously declined, not because he didn't like their company, but because he liked it too much. He just didn't admit that to them because he felt guilty for indulging in it. It brought out the kid in him; he'd never really had a childhood since his mother and aunt guarded them as children, and Genius kept him in secure mode as an adult. His latest secret was that his thirty-fourth birthday had to be the most fun he'd ever had. Confessing it would encourage more of its kind from Rachel, and Olivia might just have a heart attack.

By Saturday afternoon, he had made up his mind in regard to where he planned to place Isabella in his life. Rarely had they all been in the same room in the past two weeks, but with Pattie back in town briefly to pack for her vacation, and Thomas visiting for the day, everyone but Christian's father, was present for lunch. He couldn't deny the chemistry he shared with Isabella, and he knew it was too thick for the rest of them not to notice. He was certain that Isabella knew—they spoke with their eyes. Hers typically questioned the possibility with apprehension, but his never got a chance to ease her fears because she never looked at him long enough.

That afternoon, her eyes said something different—they were sad and pleaded with him not to go through with his decision. *Things will never be the same*, they said. Overcome with guilt, he hardly touched his meal and politely offered a business excuse. He felt a spiritual connection with Isabella, but the closer he felt to her, the more Olivia's warning about Rachel not approving tormented him. As much as he hated to believe it, Olivia was right. Perhaps Isabella's purpose was to help him move on from the hurt of Kevin's betrayal, and she'd done that nicely.

He needed to find a way to get over her before he fell any deeper. He had good reason—Rachel. Isabella was quite different from the women he dated in the past, and surprisingly, she could very well be the best fit for him, but he had the utmost respect for his sister and her relationships. As much as Rachel put up a good front, she wasn't ignorant of his past escapades with women and she most likely would never approve of him soiling her best friend. Furthermore, Rachel didn't have any friends, and this was her first true friendship since Kevin and Olivia. It wouldn't be easy, but something would have to give. He would only consider Isabella if Rachel approved; apart from that, he had to move on and be far away from her. Olivia was probably right about using a new person to get over someone. She would never know that that someone wasn't Kathy—but Isabella.

Back in his room, he made the call. "Hey, Liv," he greeted.

"Hey, hon."

"I was just thinking of your offer to introduce me to someone."

Olivia laughed. "No one can resist Liv."

"Oh, get over yourself."

"I promise, you'll forget all about Kathy when you meet Sacha. You may even forget she existed."

He was a tad bit disturbed at how quickly Olivia expected to set him up with someone new—showing little to no concern in regard to his fallout with Kathy. She hadn't even asked for his version of the story. Surely, she had to be curious.

"That's her name?"

"Yeah, thought I told you. How's tonight at nineish?" Olivia asked. "I'll call you later with details."

"Sure thing." *Sacha. The possibilities. Sacha.*

Later that evening, with everyone down in the entertainment room, Christian waited in the living room for Julio to arrive. That was when Genius spoke, *why are you so eager to walk away from Isabella? Does it really have to do with Rachel, or are you scared she might be too good for you?*

Christian reached for the remote control as Genius continued. *You've always liked a good challenge. Let me handle her for you.*

"Just stop it!" Christian shouted. He couldn't answer Genius' question, but he vowed to do whatever he could to give himself the peace he desperately craved. The past two years had proved that a relationship didn't have to involve love, so hopefully Sacha would do the trick. In exchange, he hoped for a smooth transition of the peace he presently had to the next companion.

Julio pulled up at an upscale lounge located in Miami Beach, and Olivia had arranged for someone at the door to escort Christian to the special seating area. The atmosphere was surprisingly bright—unlike he pictured it would be, and he was pleasantly surprised that the music was not loud. Any place that involved the possible compromise of safety triggered Genius into protection mode. He'd learned from his time at college that typical nightlife wasn't his thing, so he didn't attend nightclubs.

Olivia rose from her seat as soon as she saw him approach. He nodded a thanks to the escort and embraced Olivia. She wore a dress today, with her hair swept away in a tight bun. She typically wore jumpsuits everywhere—she had casual ones and dressy ones. He guessed the statuesque figure in a skintight blue mini-dress was Sacha. As promised, she was a beauty—about five-foot-nine, he estimated, very slender, with cropped, white-blonde hair. It was as if she walked out of a magazine ad and landed in front of him. He wasn't sure how Olivia did it, but all the girls she introduced to him had an exotic look to them.

Her bright blue eyes and killer smile were no match for her voice—husky with an accent. But, despite her desirable attributes, he'd not been interested in her type for quite some time, and that ought to work out great, considering he wasn't looking for intimacy, but a distraction. At this stage in his life, he was interested in women that looked more normal. One who could eat whatever she wanted from the Rusty Pelican without obsessing over her weight. Again, Isabella came to mind. She wasn't as slim as Sacha, and although he knew many men that would kill for a woman with Sacha's figure, Isabella's petite frame was fine with him. She wasn't as tall as Sacha, and didn't have the model physique that most women he knew coveted, but she was definitely easy on the eyes. Isabella was simple but definitely not plain, and most of all, warm, friendly, and very funny.

His first impression of Sacha didn't include warmth. She was a perfect showpiece for his younger self, but he wanted someone for himself now—a wife. Olivia was right most of the time—she called him old now, and to be honest, he didn't care. He was tired of the games, and he had gotten used to how it felt to have peace of mind. What struck him as interesting was the fact that none of the men seated at the bar looked in their direction since the moment the three of them took their seats. However, Isabella had men gawking at her at a carnival, of all places, and falling for her—even literally. *Why is that?* Isabella couldn't possibly be the most attractive girl in the world, yet something about her attracted men of different ages to her. So much so that she had to pretend to be married to curb the attention. It couldn't be physical beauty alone because Sacha was gorgeous. It had to be a light, and Isabella shone bright.

"Are you always this quiet?" Sacha asked, interrupting his thoughts.

"I'm sorry." He was genuinely so. His internal rant was rude.

"Where did you run off to?" Sacha smiled.

"I just thought of something." He hadn't realized how long he'd been out, but Olivia was gone.

"Or someone?" Now she bit her bottom lip. Isabella did that, but Sacha's was more seducing. "Liv told me about your ex-fiancée, Kathy."

"Oh?"

"It's safe with me."

Her voice was soothing—nice to put him to sleep. "How long have you been friends with Olivia?"

"About a year." Her foot stroked his leg from under the table—he didn't like it and wondered whether Olivia told her about his new boundaries.

"You're a beautiful girl." *Ahh idiot!* he told himself.

Sacha blushed. "Are you always this charming?"

"Would you like another drink?" It was the easiest way to get her off of him.

"That'd be nice."

As he watched the bartender prepare her drink, he pondered what he was doing in a lounge with this stranger, when the woman he was falling in love with was undoubtedly in Casa Cervello wondering if he was okay. Isabella was the nurturing type—he knew it. Before he could finish his train of thought, he felt a tap on his back. When he turned around, Sacha pulled him close and planted a kiss on his lips.

He gently pulled her away. "Let's take this slow, okay?"

"Oh, come on, it's just a little kiss."

"Yes, but I would like to get to know you first. Wouldn't you want to do the same?"

"Of course," she said. "Sorry," she added, rolling her eyes.

It was well after midnight when Christian returned home. Though it was all in his head, he felt guilty for being out with another woman when his heart yearned for Isabella. He wouldn't bear to look in her eyes and was glad that Rachel's text mentioned their spending the night at Isabella's place. Nothing happened with Sacha, yet he felt dirty and his spirits were down because being that close to her brought back flashbacks of the guesthouse. The fact that she could boldly make a move on him reminded him of David's warning of his lack of boundaries with women.

He headed for the entertainment room as he loosened his tie and dropped his keys on the ebony grand piano.

Isabella couldn't sleep. It would be absurd to tell anyone she worried about the safety of a grownup just because he hadn't returned before midnight. Nevertheless, she'd prayed for the Lord to keep him safe. The movie they'd seen earlier involved losing a loved one and to her surprise, it hurt to imagine Christian gone. Perhaps she'd taken for granted all the times that he stayed home. It was wishful thinking that he liked their pastime. But he couldn't possibly—no one but they did. That was why Olivia made fun of them, and that's why he'd mentioned Olivia knew how to have a good time.

She left the room for a glass of water when she heard light playing of the piano from the kitchen, and she peeked down the staircase to see Christian dressed up. She sat on a stair and watched as he played. She applauded when she finished, but quickly realized she'd startled him.

"I didn't know you played." She grinned as she made her way down the stairs.

"I didn't realize anyone was home," he said, reaching for his keys and jacket.

"Oh, um, could you cover the keys? Only so Aunt Pattie won't obsess over dusting them."

He smiled to himself as he closed the fallboard. Everyone knew his mother's shortcoming but they didn't realize she'd generously passed the obsessive trait down to him. "Excuse me," he muttered as he passed her on the staircase. He had mixed emotions, seeing her there in her pajamas with a glass of water. *Now that picture would have been very welcoming if she were mine,* he thought. It was becoming more apparent that she was too comfortable at Casa Cervello, and it would be harder than he thought to let her go.

She stuttered, "I'm sorry I . . . "

"Rachel said you were all spending the night at your place."

"We got busy helping Aunt Pattie plan her vacation and were too tired to drive back downtown. I didn't mean to startle you. It sounded so good. I couldn't possibly interrupt."

He wished he could just hold her close to erase the night he had with Sacha. "Flattery becomes you," he said, walking ahead of her.

"No, seriously it was. No one said you played." She followed him into the kitchen.

He helped himself to a glass of water. "That's because I never did before London."

"It was really good."

Their eyes met, and she bit her bottom lip.

"Are you flirting with me?" he asked, irritated.

"Why would I?" Concern replaced the enthusiasm in her brown eyes.

He held her gaze but when it appeared that she was determined not to look away, he dropped his. It was the first time she held his gaze—as she analyzed his carefully. Perhaps she had become immune to his effect on her. *What did she see?*

"You really should get out more." He walked away then, but from the hallway he yelled out without stopping, "Besides, isn't it past your bedtime?"

His words stung. Did he think she was a child? *Past my bedtime*, she scoffed. She stood in utter disbelief. Could she have said something to annoy him? She thought he had enjoyed her company on his birthday but how could she fool herself that way? He wasn't interested, and he never would be. From Rachel's description of his past girlfriends, she would have to be a toothpick to be considered his type and he didn't have to be courteous or even speak to her just because they had a good time on his birthday. She meant nothing to him apart from being his sister's friend, and he certainly didn't owe her an explanation for his recent awkwardness.

She walked back into Rachel's room and sat at the edge of the bed.

"Isa?" Rachel called out in the dark.

"Rach, do you think we are boring?"

She heard a frown in Rachel's voice. "No, why?"

"Just wondering."

She heard Rachel sit up and reach for the lamp.

"Don't!" She didn't have answers as to why the streams of tears on her lower lids laid waiting to fall.

"Are you okay?"

"Yes."

"You spoke to Chris, didn't you?"

Isabella blinked and the tears fell. She couldn't deny it, but she would be crazy not to admit that, by his suggestion to go out more, he eluded to their being dull. Their peers had teased them for so long, and they thought becoming adults would ease the sting but with people like Olivia constantly throwing it in their face, the nightmare continued. Isabella had learned to build a tough skin, but it didn't mean she couldn't feel the pressure and pain. Rachel took it harder than she did because she'd been bullied in middle and high school for being different. If she suspected her own brother so much as mocked at her pastime, it would kill her spirit.

"You never seemed to care what anyone thought of us. So you tell me, do *you* think we're boring?"

"I think we're safe. I like safe," Isabella replied.

"Atta girl. Well, since you brought it up, I'll have you know that Thomas has been asking for a double date with his best friend."

"Rachel, I—"

"I know what you told me and that's why I never told you till now. Come on Isa, it'll be fun."

Without another word, Isabella got into bed.

CHAPTER SEVEN

Mistake?

❦

BY THE next day, Christian knew that His Mind had waged an all-out war against His Shell of a Body. Perhaps it had expected him to have slept with Sacha. Apparently, Sacha hadn't appeased Genius either, and as punishment—or to some, a blessing—a new invention idea emerged. This time, it involved still images captured on the human iris via a digital contact lens. Perhaps it came about from lying in bed for hours wishing he knew what Isabella had seen in his eyes late last night. He laughed at the concept and hoped it was ridiculous enough not to materialize. But the reality was that his record of turning every stray thought into a masterpiece had yet to be broken.

Following an hour-long workout in the home gym, Christian headed outside for a swim. When he arrived at the entrance to the pool, he scanned the setting. Pattie counted aloud from her lounge chair as Rachel raced through the pool. Stopping short of the back of Pattie's chair, he caught a glimpse of golden brown hair floating in the pool. There was no physical body—just hair. At that moment, it was all that mattered. He had given up on ever seeing her poor hair out of prison; pure gold silk waves floated gracefully in the clear water. She emerged and ran her hands over her face, excitedly taking rapid breaths. He started to back up in the direction from which he came, but it was just his imagination, because he was physically unable to move. Standing a foot behind Pattie's chair, he fixed his eyes on Isabella's hair.

"Sixty-two seconds!" Pattie yelled. "Good job, but she beat you by three seconds."

Christian's lips formed a smile. The girls giggled as they splashed water at each other and Isabella stroked water from her face, panting. His Mind began to make its way through her hair.

"Hey, I thought I heard something," Pattie said, turning to see him.

Christian sighed. "Hey, Mom!" *Deep breaths*, he muttered.

"Are you okay, honey?"

"Yup." His reply was haste.

Isabella and Rachel emerged from the pool and made their way back to their chairs next to Pattie. Christian stuttered, "I – I was just . . . I was just going for a swim, but I see it's occupied. I'll just head back inside."

He turned to leave, but Rachel called out, "Hey!"

"Hello, Rachel." His smile felt awkward, and he feared that Rachel would notice. "I see you're having a great time."

"Yeah, Chris, we know how to live."

"Of course you do." She seemed defensive. He had meant for his statement to come out sarcastic, and it worked. Now he regretted hurting her. Isabella was also distant. Apart from a quick nod to greet him, she lay quietly in her chair with a magazine, as Rachel rubbed sunscreen on Pattie's body.

"So what does everyone have planned for later?" Christian asked.

Pattie replied, "Monopoly."

"Is that fun enough for you?" Rachel snapped.

"What did I say?" This had to do with choosing Olivia's company over theirs last night. He knew it.

"Guys, please! I have a headache," Pattie said. "Baby, didn't you say Thomas wanted to do something with you and Isa—don't let me keep you. Besides I have a ton to do."

"No, not today, Mom, but the good news is she finally agreed to the double date so . . . " Rachel shrugged, throwing a smug look at Christian.

Christian frowned. "Double date?"

"Yup, finally both of us can have your type of fun with real men and perhaps come back really late."

When Pattie snickered, Christian nodded slowly. "So what do we know about these guys?"

Rachel squinted. "I thought you liked Thomas."

"Oh, of course I like Thomas, but I – I don't know this other person."

"Don't worry about it. Besides, you have a contingency plan, don't you?"

"Well, the plan doesn't keep Isabella safe, does it? I mean, she *is* like family, isn't she?"

Christian's eyes followed Isabella as she headed back to the pool. Her hair was down past her back, just as he'd imagined it, but it was her curvaceous figure that surprised him. He could only blame her baggy clothes for it.

"You've never been this protective," Rachel said, forcing his gaze back to her. "Why start when I'm 28?"

"There's never been a reason to, Rach. You hardly ever went out—let alone date."

"Bull!" Rachel yelled.

Pattie interfered. "Rach, he's still your big brother, no matter the age."

"Mom, you know this isn't about me, right?"

Silence lingered for a few seconds before Pattie broke it. "I'm going for a swim. You coming, baby?"

Still glaring at him, Rachel replied, "Yeah."

When she turned to leave, he grabbed her arm. "You never answered my question."

"What question?" She yanked her arm away.

"Isn't Isabella like family?"

"Yeah, she is, and?"

"So what's the big deal if I'm concerned about her safety? How do you suggest we keep her safe?"

"Get her a freaking watch then!"

Rachel stormed off. For the next fifteen minutes, Christian contemplated how acquiring Isabella an accessory worth a quarter of a million dollars might appear to his family, especially since he barely knew her. It had briefly crossed his mind at the fair, but at the time he'd chalked up his concern for her safety to an obsession over her. Now he figured he could blame the extravagant gift on Rachel's idea. He laid back in Pattie's chair, intently watching Isabella until she emerged and made her way back to her chair. He picked up Pattie's magazine. "So are you excited about your date?" he asked, eyes fixed on the print.

"I don't know, I've never been on a double date."

"You don't seem at all thrilled. Have you even met the guy?" he asked, placing the magazine down and carefully observing her.

"No, but hey, you never know, right?"

"You may end up falling for him?"

She squeezed water from her hair with the end of her white towel. "I'll cross that bridge if I ever get there. Why are you so interested anyway?"

Christian shifted uncomfortably. "Well, I'm Rachel's big brother, and I consider you a sister, so you know," he shrugged. "I gotta make sure you both are okay."

"I would think you'd be happy for us. Just earlier, you said I should get out more."

"I did?"

Isabella gathered her belongings. "You know you did. Have a good day, Christian."

It felt more like an eternity, although it had only been a week since Christian had last seen Isabella and the hurt in her eyes. Genius warned him to let it go—since this was what he wanted, it was best to let it play out that way. Surprisingly, he seemed to have reached a nice compromise in regard to Sacha—as long as he kept very busy with her, he could achieve a similar level of peace he got from just watching Isabella from afar. In the past week, he had found confidence in doing things around the village. And he even rode his boat for the first time in two years, all for the wonderful exchange of helping her prepare for a modeling career.

Having returned from the dock in an upbeat mood, he entered the kitchen and right into a land mine.

"Is she stopping by before you girls head out?" Pattie asked.

"Yeah, we're getting ready from here," Rachel replied.

"Now, you girls be careful, and don't go forcing her on him. It's her decision."

Rachel laughed. "Yeah, okay, Mom."

"What's so funny? I know how you get when you're passionate about stuff. I promised her mom I'll—"

"We're like adults." Rachel shrugged.

"You talk to her mother?" Christian asked, pulling out a kitchen chair. He couldn't help himself, everything about Isabella intrigued him still.

"I met her a few times—we actually still communicate . . . Ow!" Pattie winced from the pasta steam.

"Why did they move back to Brazil?" Christian asked, walking over to investigate her burn.

"Why do you care?" Rachel asked. "What are you doing here anyway? You hardly ever spend time with us anymore. We're boring, remember?"

"I never said that," Christian snapped back. "Here Mom, let me run it under cold water."

"Anyway, soon your casa will be ready, and you can have all the fun you want," Rachel grumbled.

"See how she starts on me, Mom?"

Pattie frowned. "Wait . . . why haven't you told me how the building's going?"

"You never asked." He shrugged. "I guessed you didn't care."

"Come on, don't be like that."

"I'm the stepchild," Christian griped, heading back to sit down.

Rachel and Pattie laughed. "Yeah, okay," Rachel said.

There was a knock on the door before he heard the voice that gave him rest. "Hola!" Isabella yelled. She let herself in and came up the stairs holding a brown bag. "Here, I met the grocer at the gate."

"Thanks." Christian took the bag from her, noticing she avoided eye contact.

Isabella went over to kiss Rachel and Pattie on the cheek.

"See? No kiss for me . . . stepchild!"

"Am I missing something?" Isabella's puzzled gaze shifted from Pattie to Rachel.

"Ignore him," Rachel said, laughing and grabbing her hand to leave.

"Wait, I gotta see your mom for a second. Aunt Pattie, you're leaving tonight, right?"

"Uh huh, come on over here and . . . "

"Mmm, I love your hugs," Isabella muffled into her shoulder. "Have a great vacation, okay?"

"You bet I will."

"Make sure you take lots of pictures, relax and eat. No obsessing over your weight."

"Yeah, okay, that'll be a first," Rachel mocked.

"I mean it," Isabella said sternly.

"Yes, Mom," Pattie teased, pinching both her cheeks.

Isabella smiled. "Do you have a ride to the airport?"

"Yeah, Chris is taking me. Go on and get ready; I wanna see you girls before you head out."

The following evening, as Isabella and Rachel lounged by the pool, Isabella rehearsed the conversation she was sure to have with Christian. He would probably want to know all the details about their date, and she didn't plan on sparing any. The possibility that he might be jealous excited her.

A few minutes after they went back to the room, Rachel received a phone call from a colleague.

"Sure, hold on for a minute," Rachel said to the caller. "Um, Isa, I need that magazine for a minute."

"I left it by the pool. I'll grab it."

When Isabella got to the pool entrance, she froze in her tracks when she heard Christian's voice. He had his back to her and spoke into the phone standing outside the hot tub, and in it, was a blonde. She watched as the blonde removed her bikini top and threw it at Christian. Isabella ran back into the house. She thought back to that night by the piano. He'd come home late; perhaps he'd been out with her. This explained his recent attitude change. *He's seeing someone.* Knowing she spent most of her time here, he must have wanted her to know he was off limits. She got the message.

"Oh thanks, Isa," Rachel said, holding out her hand. "Isa, where is it?"

"It's by the pool," Isabella muttered in a withered voice. "Sorry, I couldn't get it, there's someone . . . "

Isabella struggled to breathe and went into the restroom, locking the door behind her.

"Isa, are you okay? Come back!" Then speaking into the phone, Rachel said, "Jason, I'll call you in a few."

She banged on the door, "Isa! What happened, what in the world did you see out there?"

Isabella knew that once Rachel got to the pool and saw the blonde, she would know the truth about her feelings for her brother. First, she needed to find a way to get out of there without having to face her. She needed to pray about this. She was never one to want a man that was involved in another relationship, and God had always been good about removing feelings she had no business having. There really should have been no use crying over this if she'd prayed about Christian the moment she realized she had feelings for him, at least to find out if they were meant to be. Realizing that the coast was clear of Rachel, she grabbed whatever she could find of hers and left Casa Cervello.

Just as Rachel arrived at the entrance to the pool, she bumped into Christian as he made his way into the house.

"Are you okay?" he asked, glaring at a large kitchen knife in her hand with concern.

"I don't know what happened but Isa—" She stopped abruptly. Her apprehension turned to disgust when she saw a naked woman emerging from the hot tub. She turned around to leave and he grabbed her arm.

"Listen, I had no idea she would take her bathing suit off. I don't know what got into her. That's why I'm leaving. What did Isabella see?"

"She saw enough."

CHAPTER EIGHT

Establishing Boundaries

❧

A COUPLE of days later, Christian and Rachel were going over landscape possibilities for his building plan when the doorbell chimed. He opened the door to four young women and found it slightly amusing that each one had a different hair color. From their demeanor, he expected them to be friends of Rachel's, but he knew Rachel didn't have friends aside from Isabella and Olivia. Nevertheless, he called her anyway.

"Oh, we're not here for Rachel," the redhead said boldly.

"No?" Christian asked, confused. He couldn't recognize any of them, but he was afraid to ask. He wondered if he was supposed to know them or if he had an intimate relationship with any of them and could not recall. Then again, they could just be random women. When he returned to Florida from Vancouver, it hadn't taken long for such to come buzzing at the gate as soon as word spread that he was back in town. But this, he realized, was a serious breach of security. Clearing his throat, he said, "Hey, um . . . "

"Jen," the brunette said, waving to get his attention.

"Of course." Christian nodded. "Jen, how did you girls get through the gate?"

"Oh, Kimberly had the code," she replied, staring back at the car, as another brunette exited.

"We tried the guesthouse first, but no one answered."

Rachel came up behind him and whispered, "Hey, you called me?"

"Hold on." He strolled over to his ex-girlfriend, Kimberly. "How many people have access to my home?"

She smiled. "Well, nice to see you too, Christian. Geez. Are you gonna let us in or what?"

Christian sighed before escorting them all to the entertainment room. He thought it was his imagination that he'd lost control in terms of tangible things, but it was apparent he had. *Breached security? I created the security*, he fumed. David was right—he lacked boundaries, not just in relationships, but at home.

Isabella hadn't returned to Casa Cervello since the hot tub incident, and she didn't plan on returning until she felt peace to do so. With Pattie still out of the country, it was easy to avoid the home. Rachel hadn't stopped asking whether she wanted to talk about that day. She managed to elude the issue by citing work. It was always tax season for her anyway.

She was about to make dinner when she received a call from a blocked number. "Hello?"

"Aha!" Rachel said. "I knew you were avoiding me."

Isabella sighed. "No hon, you know I've been extra busy with work."

"If you say so, Isa. Anyway, I just called to tell you that Chris changed the code to the gate."

"Is everything okay?"

"You're not gonna believe this," Rachel chuckled. "A bunch of girls just showed up at our front door looking for him a few hours ago. Talk about awkward."

"Why? He didn't know them?"

"Nope, some ex of his had access. What's even crazier is that she actually came with them, and they were all flirting with him at the same time. I was standing there, but I don't think any of them even noticed me. They were looking at him like he was meat. Listen, I gotta . . . MUST blog about this. Oh, you should have seen how furious he was. Anyway, grab a pen."

"Wait, are you sure he wants me to have it?"

"What he wants isn't important. As soon as his house is finished, he's leaving. Besides you and Olivia are the only ones I ever gave the past codes to. Thomas prefers to ring the bell."

After a good week had gone by, Rachel was finally able to convince Isabella to come over. She needed help preparing for a big editor event at her company. Although Isabella had initially refused, Rachel had assured her that Christian was away in Singapore on a business trip. The fact that Rachel knew to assure her that Christian was away was more confirmation that Rachel was on to her, even though she'd stopped checking in.

After styling Rachel's hair, they spent the next hour catching up until they heard a car pull up to the entrance. Isabella looked through the window. Seeing Julio's black Maybach, her heart began to race. She silently pondered why the prayers to get rid of her feelings for Christian hadn't worked.

"I gotta go," Isabella announced, starting to pack up.

"Why, who's that?"

"I think it's your brother's driver," Isabella said, fumbling in her bag for her keys.

Rachel jumped to the window. "It's her again," she fumed. "Here we go." Appearing visibly disgusted, Rachel ran down the stairs to get the door.

Isabella ran back to the window for a second look. She recognized the blonde from the pool. This time, she was dressed in a bra top and short shorts. She was drop-dead gorgeous—like a model. She was extremely slim; Isabella knew she couldn't possibly pull off dressing like that with the size of her breasts and hips. It looked good on the blonde, but for her it would look obscene. The woman stopped at the door without ringing the doorbell; rather, she appeared to be texting. Isabella remembered the feel of Christian's hand on hers and couldn't imagine . . . she felt a knot in her belly and became nauseated. *Why Lord*, she thought to herself, *I met him first.*

Expecting Rachel to tell her Christian wasn't home, Isabella sat back down and held her stomach tight, as if it would stop the nausea. In a matter of seconds, she heard a door open down the hallway, and before she could gather what was happening, Christian strolled down in a pair of cargo pants and striped oxford shirt. His top two buttons were undone, exposing his chest, and both sleeves were up to his elbows. He appeared equally surprised to see her. He ran his fingers through his hair as he approached. "Hey!"

"Hey," Isabella replied nervously.

"It's been a while. How have you been?"

"Good." She rubbed both her sweaty palms on her jeans. "We didn't realize you were home."

"Yeah, I actually got back in late last night." His laugh was edgy. "I slept through the afternoon."

She nodded. "Oh."

"I guess I'll be seeing you around."

"Yeah." Her reply was nearly inaudible.

He gave her a warm smile and walked down the stairs.

That was when she heard elevated voices. She realized the two women had been arguing. Isabella heard Christian ask Rachel, "What's this about?"

But Rachel stomped back upstairs and went straight into her room, slamming the door. Isabella went in after her. "Are you okay?" she asked. "What happened down there? What did you say to her?"

"I just asked her what she wanted and she gave me an attitude. She didn't believe me when I said he wasn't home. How was I supposed to know he was? That was so embarrassing."

This new side of Rachel never ceased to amaze Isabella. She had become more vocal since either Thomas or Christian arrived in February. "Yeah, he said he got in late. Is that his girlfriend?"

"I don't know. I won't be surprised if she's not. This has happened before. It's all coming back to me now. You know how people turn to the bottle when they're depressed? Well, Chris turns to random girls."

"He's probably just getting to know her. It doesn't seem like him to—"

"Oh, so now you know my brother more than I do?" Rachel snapped. "You know, feel free to tell me anytime what the hell is going on between you two."

"No, I just meant that . . . " Isabella sighed and then continued, "He looks more reserved. That's all."

"Well, I thought so too, especially since he started with Kathy, but he seems to have reverted to his old ways somehow. Who knows, maybe he's trying to get over her with them."

"But you said the other ones came uninvited."

"And? Why would he let them in even after they breached security? Think about it Isa, he's a man."

Isabella's tone was soft with concern. "Where does he find them?"

"I have no idea. I won't be surprised if Olivia has something to do with this. She always has a fix."

"Olivia?"

"Yup. She used to hook him and Kevin up with girls in high school, then after that Christian went off to college—but that didn't stop them all from partying. Goodness, it's like those days all over again. Did you see that girl? I'm surprised he's not caught anything yet."

"Rachel!"

"*What?*" she said, outraged, "Didn't you see her naked in the hot tub the other day? What nerve . . . that's our family tub, Isa, and we don't even know her name!"

A short while later, Christian saw his guest outside and headed up to Rachel's room. He knocked.

"Yes?" Rachel demanded.

"Rachel, may I have a word with you?"

She opened the door.

"In private, please," he said, glancing at Isabella, who stood right behind her.

"I was about to leave," Isabella said.

"Were you now?" Christian's expression was sarcastic.

"No, you *weren't*," Rachel said, pushing Isabella back.

"I'll be downstairs then."

"No, I'll go. You stay. *Please?*"

Rachel walked out to the hallway with him and closed the door behind her. He took slow deep breaths as he stared at her for a few seconds. She looked away from him with her arms crossed.

"I would appreciate if you would respect my guests while I'm still in this house," he said.

She replied without looking at him, "And I'd appreciate if you'd stop making this place into a brothel. Your father would be ashamed of you if he knew you were really a whore."

Christian grimaced. "You have no idea what goes on in my room."

"Yeah, you play Scrabble with those sluts!"

"Listen, I don't give you a problem when you have Thomas over here, and let's not forget Isabella who's here time and time again, all up in my face, I can barely breathe."

"Why should you? You're not screwing her!" Rachel snapped back, finally looking at him.

"Well maybe I should then, huh? Then it'll make you happy to see me with someone you approve."

"Ha! Approve? You wish I would approve of you and Isa. I'll be damned if you touched her."

"Then keep her away from me!" Christian yelled.

Rachel entered her room and slammed the door.

Isabella heard the whole thing. *Well, that's it*, she thought. *Rachel would never support a relationship between Chris and me, even if God said yes.* She felt stuck between a rock and a hard place. By praying for Christian to leave her heart and mind, she'd done all she could to let him go but here she was, still consumed with thoughts of him and what could have been. Rachel's breathing was rapid and she was red. Isabella couldn't remember seeing her this upset. "I'm leaving," Isabella said. "You should take some time to cool off."

"Isa, wait!"

But Isabella left. She came into this family in peace, and she intended to leave with her peace intact.

Christian hadn't spoken to Rachel in a week, and if he had to be honest with himself, he didn't miss her. He became resentful at the mere thought of her, but he knew this feeling would pass. He flipped through pages of sample model headshots when a chime went off on his computer—it was the only drama-free person in his life.

"What's up, buddy?" David asked. "How are you holding up?"

"Please don't ask," Christian said, adjusting his camera settings. "How are things over there?"

"Well, work is fine. My contract is about to end soon, but I'm considering a few options based on Denise's program. I'll keep you posted."

"Please do, and let me know if there's anything I can do to help." David was a gem to have on staff—extremely knowledgeable and bright. They had met when the IT company David worked for in London had contracted him to do some work for Private-I's highly secure network systems. Although the initial assignment was to last for about a month, both companies worked very well together, and David became a regular at Private-I UK for highly sensitive projects. Not only had Christian started to rely on his professional integrity, but he also began to trust him as a friend when their working relationship officially ended.

"Sure. Um, I heard that your friend Kevin resigned."

"Oh?"

"You didn't know?"

"Nope, then again I'm usually the last to know anything."

"Supposedly they're looking for a replacement for him—not that they actually needed his department in the first place, but if they get rid of it now, all those folks working under him lose their jobs."

"Yeah, sounds messy."

"Listen," David said. "I know you gave him that position to help him out, and that was noble of you as a friend, but I suggest you don't fight his resignation. It's for the best, Chris. Let him go if he wants to—he's done enough harm. Just see this as a clean break and move on with your life."

"Oh, I agree with you. I won't fight it. I wish him well."

"Okay, that was easier than I thought." David chuckled. "So, what's up with your sister's friend?"

"Isabella?"

David grinned wide into the camera. "Yeah, the last time we spoke, you had a thing for her."

Christian shook his head. "Ha . . . well, that's not going to work. Besides I have a distraction now."

David raised a brow. "Oh, yeah?"

"Yup, Olivia set me up with someone—Sacha. It's just that I can't seem to get Isabella out of my head long enough to hold a decent conversation with the girl."

"Hmm, that's not good."

"There's nothing serious going on with me and her. She's working on a couple of projects, and I offered to help. I don't mind—in fact, I'm putting more into it to distract myself."

"I don't like the sound of this."

"You don't understand."

"Does she like you?"

"Yeah, but I have zero interest in her in that way; that's why I think it's perfect for both of us. I help her, and she helps keep me busy."

David laughed. "If you need to keep busy, I can send you some work from over here."

"Very funny."

"But seriously, man, didn't you have a location opening up in Italy?"

"It's on hold," Christian said. "We're making our way into Southeast Asia now but my hands are tied because Dad's looking into trade issues with our legal team—it's complicated. Listen, this is good, trust me. Yeah, she needs some refocusing every now and then, but it's okay."

"So what exactly are you doing with her?"

Christian sighed and slightly raising his voice, he said, "I'm helping her get her foot in the door. She always wanted to model, and I'm supporting her."

"How? Vouching for her?" David asked, outraged. "Chris, you don't even know this girl enough to be sticking your neck out for her. Soon you'll be calling these agencies and giving referrals. You gotta be careful; your name is on the line. The press will bury you."

"It hasn't gotten that far." So much for drama-free, David was really getting on his last nerve.

"Okay, listen, if you need to keep reminding her to keep off, she may keep trying until you have to force her out, and then she gets vindictive. Are you using protection?"

Christian turned away from the camera and did not speak. He took slow and deep breaths.

David continued, "Listen, I just want you to be careful. You're a target for many women."

"I'm not a child. Again, I am not sleeping with her."

"I'm sorry, Chris. I overstepped."

"I don't know, Dave. I'm just—"

"What is it you're afraid of?"

"I see the way men stare at her."

"At this Sacha girl?"

"No, Isabella."

"How did we get back to Isabella?"

"It terrifies me because I want her so bad." Christian pulled on his hair with both hands.

"Intimidated, huh?" David asked with a smile.

"I'm not used to it. I never had to compete for anyone."

David clapped. "I like that. You finally met your match. I remember how girls would swarm all around you here when we went out. Man, I couldn't stand you—you were a chick magnet even when you weren't trying."

Christian grinned. "What's your problem, you had Denise."

"And you had Kat—but that didn't stop them."

"I just . . . I don't want this."

"Does she like you?"

"I believe so, but she's just so—clean."

David laughed. "What does that even mean?"

"Wholesome . . . like I would taint her or something. Very pure and innocent."

"Wow, you make her sound like deity."

"I know she's not perfect but—"

"She's not! So it shouldn't be a problem. I don't get it. It sounds to me like you're falling for Isabella, but what I don't understand is why you're so willing to give away what could potentially be yours."

Even if I wanted to pursue a relationship with her, it would be over Rachel's dead body, Christian thought as he wrapped up his conversation with David.

CHAPTER NINE

Mi Casa

THE LOCAL weather forecast called for thunderstorms and having spent all night rolling her hair, it was the last thing Rachel needed. She never had the need for a hairdresser in Florida, but if Isabella kept ignoring her calls, she would need to find one quick. Although there was no rain in sight, Rachel had on a thick shower cap as she waited outside the Miami International Airport. She jumped at the sight of Pattie. "Hey, Mom, how was your flight?" Rachel asked, embracing her.

"It was great for a change. Why in the world do you have that on your head?"

A flash of lightning struck, and Rachel laughed. "That's why."

"I'm glad I dodged it, let's go." Pattie placed her suitcase in the trunk and slammed it shut.

The ladies made a dash for their doors as the first drops came down. "How have you guys been? I hope you're still not fighting with your brother," she said, buckling her seatbelt.

Rachel rolled her eyes. "It's Isa I'm worried about, Mom. I've only seen her a couple of times since you left, and each time she ended up storming out because of him."

"Hmm."

"You know how bad it's gotten? There was a time she stopped by, and he didn't even let her in."

"What?" Pattie exclaimed. "That's unacceptable."

"Ha! Tell me about it. He just collected the box she had and told her I wasn't home, as if she were a salesman." Rachel looked at Pattie suspiciously. "You know something, don't you?"

"Nope . . . but you're glowing. What gives?"

Rachel smiled and made a zip-lip motion.

"Ahh, spill it."

"So you know how Thomas and I have been getting closer? Well, he's been acting strange lately—in a good way—and I think he may have something up his sleeve." Both ladies screamed.

Late that afternoon, Pattie sent for Isabella—and provided Rachel escorted her into the house, Isabella reluctantly complied. She loved Pattie like her own mother and would hate for her predicament to come between them. The past month marked the longest time she had been away from Casa Cervello since her college years. It had been her second home and a place that once brought her joy. But now it was a major pain. She'd been low in spirit for the past two weeks and had no one to confide in but God. It had always been Him *and* Rachel, but with Thomas occupying most of Rachel's time, coupled with Rachel's growing suspicion of Isabella's feelings for her brother, she no longer felt comfortable using her as a sounding board. All she heard from God when she prayed was *wait.* It was His answer for every prayer lately. Even the scriptures she turned to referred to waiting, and the entire message series this past month in church was just that, *Waiting on God.* If she heard one more person ask her to wait, she would tell them off.

With plenty on her mind, her secret struggles had begun to take a toll on her mind and work, so she began seeing a therapist to cope with the stress. She was dealing with plenty of issues with her image and self-worth and, for the first time in her life, she didn't feel beautiful. Seeing Christian's gorgeous blonde girlfriend was a revelation. Isabella had to be at least ten pounds heavier than she was, and much shorter—so that didn't help matters. The boundaries Christian had set were clear to see. They felt more like walls. The past three times she stepped foot on their property, she felt she'd outstayed her welcome. At a time, her heart would race for joy at the mere thought of bumping into Christian there. But today, her heart raced for a different reason—fright. She couldn't believe that his resentment had reached the extent where she was no longer welcome in the home. The worst part was she couldn't think of what she did to upset him.

Pattie grinned as soon as she laid eyes on Isabella. "Hey, Nena, come here and give me some sugar." Isabella climbed onto Pattie's bed, not realizing tears had formed and poured down her face as they hugged. She pushed the thought of everything that had happened in Pattie's absence to the back of her mind. Although she desperately wanted to share her experience, she expected Pattie's loyalty to lie with her son.

Pattie wiped her tears. "Aww, Nena, you look . . . " She stopped herself, frowning.

"You look good," Isabella said, sniffing. "What changed?"

"Stop lying! Can't you see all the weight I've put on? I ate like a pig on that cruise."

"Oh stop, Aunt Pattie," Isabella said, lightly smacking her thigh. "You look relaxed. Tell me, how was it? I've been so jealous."

"Oh, it was great, but I enjoyed the city of *love* more."

Isabella's eyes widened. "You went to Paris?"

"Yeah . . . The cruise was only for two weeks, then my friends and I spent the rest in *Paree*, and boy, did I get you girls some goodies. Grab that carry-on for me. I didn't wanna show Rach anything till you got here."

"Aww, thanks, Aunt Pattie." Isabella giggled as she stole a glance at a sulking Rachel.

"But, seriously, I did gain about seven pounds," Pattie continued as she began to unzip the bag.

"Oh, that's nothing, I have this great DVD by my virtual trainer. I lost four pounds in a week already."

"I knew you looked different." Pattie frowned again. "Why are you dieting? Your body's fine."

"I gotta lose these hips and this . . . " Isabella pointed to her chest.

Pattie and Rachel looked at each other. "You've always liked your body, Isa," Rachel said quietly.

"I'll go get you the DVD. It's actually in the car," Isabella said, heading for the door.

"Oh, it can wait, baby, it's storming out."

"Nope, it stopped as soon as I drove through the gate. What can I say, I'm special," she said with a smile, fighting back tears. She really didn't feel special.

Rachel's eyes lit up. "See? I've missed my sunshine."

"I missed you too, Rach."

"Hey, guess what came in yesterday?"

"That curling iron you ordered from TV?" Isabella rolled her eyes.

"No . . . the birthday pictures."

Pattie cleared her throat.

"Oh," Isabella said with a small smile. The last thing she needed was a sad reminder of how happy they had all been that day. Blondie was taking her place, and soon it would be her in the pictures with the family. The tears resurfaced and it was a perfect time for her escape. She cleared her throat. "Um, I'll go get the video."

As Isabella walked out the door, Rachel called out, "Isa?"

"No, Nena," Pattie said. "She needs a moment. She'll be back."

"What did I say? Was it the pictures?"

"I think so. Don't push her, okay?"

The tears Isabella had carefully held back began to race down her face—and the new batch that formed blurred her vision. She would have to sit in her car to pull herself together before she returned to them. Perhaps she would need to book a session with her therapist. Had she anticipated Pattie's return, they would have discussed it days ago in her last session.

Lost in her thoughts, Isabella didn't realize the front door had opened. Neither did she notice someone walking up the stairs toward her. Before she knew it, they bumped into each other, and a bag filled with beads came flying down the spiral stairs. She frantically apologized to the person she now recognized as the blonde from the hot tub. It was bad enough she was already much taller, but now she towered over Isabella, who stood two steps below her. Her blue eyes were icy with hate. When Isabella turned back to go after the stray beads, she noticed Christian standing by the doorway, with some bags in his hands. She went down each step, picking beads along the way. This was too much; she felt punished. As she picked up beads, more tears flooded her eyes. In a flash, he was by her side, also gathering beads. She didn't dare look at his face and was glad that some of her hair draped her own face.

"I'm so sorry . . . so, so sorry," Isabella said repeatedly.

"You are always here, Isabella," he said.

Isabella was stunned at his cold blatant response. "Sorry?"

"Don't be, but I'm sure it'll be nice to spend some time in your own house for a change."

She heard the blonde giggle.

Wondering what was taking Isabella so long, Rachel went looking for her, and as she feared, she saw Isabella at the foot of the staircase in between Christian and his blonde bombshell. She watched as Isabella walked to the doorway, only for Christian to corner her. Rachel saw that Isabella's head was down and from the heave of her shoulders, she could tell she was furious—breathing fast and hard. Christian just watched her. Isabella took a step toward the door from his left and once again, he blocked her exit.

He then took a step toward her, and bending down with his eyes closed, he took a deep sniff of her hair, his chin gently brushing the top of her forehead. It was hard for Rachel to process the meaning of this, especially since Christian looked as though he was in pain. He finally stepped aside, and Isabella walked out of the house. The blonde stormed off to Christian's room while Rachel ran down the stairs to catch up with Isabella. But by the time she got outside, Isabella's car was gone. Fueled with anger, Rachel ran back into the house to see Christian sitting at the foot of the stairs with his head down. With the envelope in her hand, she repeatedly hit him as she wept aloud, "I hate you . . . I hate you!" As she did this, his birthday pictures fell out of the envelope and all over the floor. Christian held one of Rachel's arms, but she kept fighting him with the other. "Why don't you just go back to London and leave us alone!"

She went straight into her room and slammed the door.

Christian picked up the pictures, and seeing the ones he took with Isabella in happier times, he vowed to put an end to the foolishness by telling Isabella his true feelings and letting the chips fall where they may. He also vowed to end things with Sacha that day. When Christian walked into his room, Sacha was looking out the window with her arms crossed. "You love her, don't you?" she asked, eyes fixed outside the window.

"Yes."

She turned around. "Then what are you doing with me?"

"You know exactly what we are doing, I've never misled you."

"Oh yeah, I'm basically an elevated assistant—someone to ride in your boat and bike with."

"You never had a problem before now."

"That's because—"

"Do you see something more happening here—with us?"

"I thought perhaps you wanted to take things slow."

"Even friendships take time to grow."

Sacha scoffed.

"It's best we stop this charade then," he said. "Call a spade a spade—I needed company, you wanted help for your career. Nothing more."

"Then at least keep your promise. I expect to meet some important connections tonight."

"I intend to keep my promise."

As Sacha paced his room. Genius asked, *Could you ask her to stop that? I'm working here.*

"Will you please stop that," Christian said, pressing his temples.

"Well, I'm going shopping."

He reached for his wallet and handed her a wad of cash. "Julio's out there if you need him."

When Sacha left, Christian relaxed into the recliner and closed his eyes. In his mind's eye, Isabella walked into his room, and he went to hold her close. *I'm so sorry, you have no idea how much I want you.*

Genius convinced him that daydreaming wouldn't bring Isabella back, so he sought Rachel.

"Is she coming back?" Christian asked, tone somber.

"What do *you* think?"

"Can you call her?"

"She's not answering my calls," Rachel said calmly. "Mom drove out to her place to look for her."

"Good," he sighed.

"You *do* know this can't continue, right?"

"I know."

"I miss the both of you."

Christian went to hold her, but she pushed him away. "Don't. Make it up to her, not me."

Back in his room, he opened up the green manila envelope that contained his birthday pictures. They had gone out of their way to make his birthday special, and he'd never even acknowledged how much fun he'd had that day. *Such a hypocrite.* In one particular picture, Isabella grinned wide with frosting smeared all over her nose. He'd taken away that smile in her eyes, and now he felt helpless. He would go to her house if he knew where she lived, but he wouldn't dare ask Rachel for the address. He scoffed at the thought that he once prided himself in knowing Isabella so well. Yet, not having her mere phone number showed how little he knew of her.

CHAPTER TEN

Giving In

❧

IT WAS storming out again and before getting a call from her mother, Isabella had considered taking her emptiness to Crandon Park Beach. She'd spent lots of time there alone recently, on a good day, dreaming of saying her vows to Christian in front of the palm trees. It would be nice to go on a day like this; there was a storm brewing in her. Today's weather reflected the way Christian made her feel—one minute sunny, the next thunderstorms and heavy rain—and it'd been like that all day. Perhaps it was a premonition.

Her mother's request landed her at Aventura Mall for a device she couldn't find back home. While she was tempted to confide in her mother about the recent events, she'd stopped herself because she knew that whatever she told her about Christian could backfire. Besides, she never confided in her about such things. She was the type that was quick to judge, and he could never measure up to her Brazilian expectations.

As the clerk rang up the purchase, he bagged away purpose with it and emptiness returned. *What now?* When Pattie had convinced her to come over, she'd planned on spending the entire evening with her and Rachel. She missed them. *Ah, the Smithson case.* The idea of helping one of her colleagues with an annual audit strangely brought a smile to her face. She would usually welcome such thoughts with dread, and this was why she hadn't given him a straight, "Yes." However, even sorting through financial records was better than returning to an empty house.

As she headed for the nearest mall exit, a window mannequin caught her attention and Christian's blonde girlfriend immediately came to mind. Remembering how provocative she had adorned her perfect figure, she wondered if that was the type of clothing Christian liked to see. *Maybe he thinks I'm too plain.* She allowed her mind to wander as she studied the scantily clad mannequin. Just as she began to walk away, a salesclerk who had been watching her called out. "Can we interest you in our clothing?" she asked.

"Oh, no, thank you," Isabella said. "I was on my way out."

The lady looked at the mannequin. "Actually, I think you have the body for this."

Trying her best not to giggle, Isabella said, "No, that is way too short; I can't possibly go out in that."

"Yeah, but then again, it's not for daytime. It's for a night out."

"My nightlife is nothing to write home about."

The lady smiled. "Then spice it up. Here, come try this on, you're like a four. I'll grab one for you."

"No, I—" But the lady was gone. Isabella hesitantly walked into the store; her head turned from side to side as she stared in amazement at the outfits displayed. *Maybe Chris was right, maybe Rachel and I do need to go out more,* she thought. *No way, this is not our type of life, safe is good.* This struggle over her mind continued as she reluctantly took the black mini-dress from the salesclerk, who was now showing her to the dressing room. After trying on the dress, she bashfully peeked out of the door and beckoned to the salesclerk—who upon seeing her, was speechless.

"Uh, oh, I knew it wouldn't fit right," Isabella said, retreating to the dressing room.

"No, come back. See yourself in the large mirror. Oh my, you are gorgeous."

"I don't feel comfortable wearing something this . . . short." Isabella pulled down the dress.

The stretch, backless mini-dress had a "V" opening extending down to her lower back, with long sleeves, high shoulders and a boat neck. The shoulders and edges of the back slits had pearl embellishments.

"Oh, you'll be fine," the salesclerk replied. "Here, try on these shoes."

Isabella tried the pair of black and gold open-toed stilettos and walked around in them. At this point, it seemed that the entire store was gawking.

"Okay, that's not a good sign. Everyone's staring."

"They're staring because you're beautiful," the salesclerk said.

Isabella blushed. "Thanks." She went back into the dressing room and closed the door.

Back home, Isabella had the dress and shoes spread out on her bed and the struggle within her continued. She was aware of the struggle but was too bitter to listen. Tempted to call Rachel, her irrational voice told her not to. Rachel would try to talk her out of getting used to the kind of fun Christian liked. Before leaving the store, the salesclerk had given her a name for an exclusive club in Miami. She didn't know the area, so she went online for directions. That was when she heard her rational self say, *Don't do it, Isa.*

Isabella replied to her inner voice, *I'm just going for a few minutes—maybe I'll find someone nice that'll finally help me get Christian out of my head, since the prayers didn't work.*

As nighttime drew nearer, and she had showered, she heard the voice again as she was getting dressed. *You are stronger than you think because when you're weak, I am strong.*

I know, she countered. *I just need to clear my head. Lord, please understand.*

She turned up the volume of her bedroom stereo in a desperate attempt to stop the voices. Then she smiled to herself as she remembered how the girls on campus would play music to get in the mood when they prepared to go clubbing. As she slipped into her stilettos, one heel broke. Those were the brand new shoes she'd purchased, and they weren't cheap. Chills came over her when she realized then that even though she wasn't hearing the voices anymore, there were still clear signs not to go out. Her eyes welled up at the thought of how much God loved and wanted to protect her from herself. Nevertheless, she willfully went into her closet and grabbed the pair of leopard print stilettos she'd only worn once—a gift from Rachel. They looked even better, and because they were shorter by an inch, she felt more comfortable in them. Just as she applied her mascara, the stereo instantly stopped playing. Another chill came over her when she discovered that the power on the radio was on but just did not play.

He's giving you a way of escape, her rational voice whispered.

Isabella sighed. *I know.*

Her phone rang, and it was Rachel. "Enough with the signs!" Isabella yelled, ignoring the call.

Christian and Julio sat at the VIP section of the club with some acquaintances of Sacha and Olivia. The club scene had never been his forte and by being there, he was merely keeping his word to Sacha. Every now and then, he would look at his watch or close his eyes to take himself away. The dim atmosphere helped him escape, but it also brought guilt because he envisioned Isabella crying.

Olivia excused herself and stood up. Taking Sacha by the hand, she led her to a corner.

"Hey, are you really expecting people from the modeling agency?"

"Oh please—that was my excuse to get him out and possibly drunk."

Olivia laughed. "I suggest you try another way, Chris doesn't drink."

Sacha rolled her eyes. "I'm not surprised."

"Hey, what's wrong? You've not been yourself," Olivia asked.

"He doesn't want me back in his house."

"Why not?"

"He's just plain weird. He's got no problem spending money on me, but he keeps telling me he doesn't want anything serious. Who does that?"

"Yeah, he made that clear to me, too, but I thought he was kidding. I don't think you're trying hard enough, Sach. He's a man, make him want you."

"Easy for you to say."

"Well, for starters he despises clubs, so avoid taking him to such places. By the way, I hope you know he's not gonna stay here for much longer."

"But didn't you say he likes—"

"Shh, the guesthouse—not here. He's private."

"What exactly happened in that guesthouse?"

"If I tell you, I'd have to eliminate you," Olivia said with a mischievous smile. "Don't be nosy, just try harder. I'll see what I can do to help you buy some time. So you're not going back with him?"

Sacha shook her head. "Before we left the house, he asked me to pack my things but I lied about that."

Olivia smiled. "Atta girl, we'll find a way to stall—don't worry."

As Olivia turned to leave, Sacha pulled her back. "Liv, I'm afraid there's more. There's this girl. I've seen her over there twice already—I think it's his sister's friend."

"Who, Isa?" Olivia frowned.

"Yeah, he called her 'Isabella.'"

"Oh please . . . that's child's play. Chris isn't interested in such nonsense."

"But he loves her."

"You're delusional. He just met her. Besides, I need him available." Olivia left for the bar while Sacha walked back to Christian. "Hey, hon, you don't look too well."

"I'll be all right," Christian said with a flat tone. "Do you think we could cut this short?"

Sacha pouted. "Come on . . . I'm having fun."

"But I'm not. The music is too loud, and I have a splitting headache. Listen, why don't you just stay with Olivia? She can probably take you home afterward. I'll just head home."

"No, you promised, and the agents are not here yet. Don't do this. Okay, listen. Give me fifteen minutes to find out where they are, and I'll be ready, okay?" Sacha kissed him on the cheek and walked away.

Christian opened his eyes when he heard a sudden loud chatter around him. Three men had walked into the club and had instantly drawn the attention of the women at his table. He watched Olivia walk over from the bar to greet one of the men. She then returned to her seat shortly after with a devious smile.

Christian knew that look. "Who's that guy?"

Olivia smiled with her eyes. "A man with the power and means to make me a very wealthy woman."

Even at a younger age, Olivia had been street–smart, and now at the age of thirty-one, she had a dark side that Christian believed stemmed from years of hidden family secrets. It usually manifested in her occasional nonchalance for others, or narcissistic views of herself. Olivia was a go-getter with a severe thirst for the finest things in life. The problem he had with this was that she never worked a day in her life and had to support this lifestyle somehow. The answer to the how was one that no one dared ask her for the longest time.

Rachel and Pattie had grown less patient with Olivia's entitled nature. But it seemed to Christian that as those closest to Olivia became more vocal, she had become more brash and brazen. *A man with the power and the means?* Intriguing. He was certain that Olivia had business dealings she never talked about. Now he was determined to hear about some of her ventures. It would help pass time as he waited for Sacha's return.

He noticed Olivia's slight mischievous grin as she stirred her drink. She was in deep thought. Christian's gaze shifted to the three women at his corner as they arose in unison and made their way to the mystery man's VIP corner. When Olivia saw this, she threw her head back, laughing and shaking her head as she watched them swarm around him like bees. Then nudging Christian's arm, Olivia said, "That hottie just renewed a challenge he had for me about a year ago."

Christian lifted a brow.

"Wait for it . . . " Olivia took a sip of her martini. "To hook him up with a lady in this city who . . . check this out . . . he's never been intimate with."

Christian made a face. "What? That's absurd, for how much?"

"Does a cool million sound absurd to you?"

Christian sat up in his seat as Genius screamed to get out. "What does he do for a living?"

Olivia shrugged. "Who knows, who cares, he's got it, and I want it. Now if only I can find a woman he hasn't been with in this damn city."

"This probably won't be the place," Christian said sarcastically. There was a possibility that he was still daydreaming because this talk was bizarre. He was even more dumbfounded at Olivia's frantic search through her phone list. Perhaps she'd had too much to drink.

"I still can't believe I was this close to getting that million a year ago," Olivia griped.

He knew Genius was *this* close to solving a bizarre mystery. "How close?" Christian asked Olivia.

Olivia continued to search through her phone list.

Christian breathed deeply. "Um, Olivia, by being close, you don't happen to mean—"

Olivia grinned. "Oh, out with it Chris . . . yeah, it was her."

"You mean to tell me that you tried to set my sister up with a man you hardly know?"

"Stop overreacting."

"Wait, you just said it yourself, that you have no idea what he does for a living. For all we know, he could be a serial killer."

"Oh, come off it, Chris. Look at him." Olivia nodded to the man. "Rachel is an adult. My job wasn't to make sure he slept with her. All I had to do was introduce them to each other. He was gonna do the rest. At least, that's what I think—work his charm on her—which shouldn't be hard because he is very good-looking."

He looked in the direction of the mystery man. The two members of his entourage were speaking to the three women from Christian's VIP section, but the man himself drank his champagne and nodded to the music.

Olivia yelled over the music. "Listen, it never happened, okay? So let's just drop it. Knowing you, you'd probably fixate over this forever."

"So how about you, Liv?" Christian nodded to her. "Have you been with him?"

"Goodness, no!" she said, disgusted. "I'm off the table." She walked back to the bar.

Christian looked at Julio in disbelief. He then looked at the man again—now seated alone, before glancing at his watch. "Time's up."

"I'll get the car," Julio replied.

"Thanks, Julio."

Isabella looked out the window, and seeing the cab parked out front, she grabbed her purse and jacket and headed downstairs. As she locked her door, she noticed a note outside her mailbox and took it with her. Once in the cab, she prayed for protection, but felt a strong sense of hypocrisy as she did. She had ignored the signs and promptings, and the note in her hand, from Aunt Pattie, was yet another escape that she had chosen to ignore.

Julio had only been away for about five minutes, but Christian was already antsy. He started to put on his suit when he felt Olivia's stare. "Have you seen Sacha?" Christian asked. "It's been like twenty-five minutes since she left."

"Nope, she's probably on the dance floor or something."

"Well, I'm leaving. Can you please see to it that she gets home okay? I can have Julio transfer her bags to your car if that's okay with you."

"Um, I was kind of hoping I could join you guys because I didn't bring my car."

"Well, I guess you girls are gonna have to take a cab home then," he said, dialing Julio.

Just then, Julio walked in and announced that the car was outside.

"Thanks, Julio," Christian said, bending over to kiss Olivia goodnight.

"Listen, let me look for her on the dance floor," Olivia pleaded.

"And I can check the back rooms real quick," Julio added.

As they both left, Christian grudgingly sat back down. He occupied himself with memories of better times with Isabella. She calmed him down, even if it was her who riled him up in the first place.

Isabella walked through the door of the club with her head held high. Surely that would help conceal her nerves. Her legs felt like jelly, and she feared she would trip on her three-inch stilettos. It was her first time in a nightclub and walking through the doors by herself felt awkward. As soon as she checked in her jacket, she headed straight for the bar because she remembered how the girls in college said they did that to loosen up. It was dimmer in the club than she'd imagined it would be, and she was shaking inside from fear. *What would I say if someone offered to buy me a drink?*

In Christian's daydream, he was about to take Isabella's hand in his when he was interrupted by a whistle. He opened his eyes to see someone who resembled her in a black mini-dress that must have come with a promise only to conceal the underwear. His eyes followed the long honey-toned legs down to a pair of animal-print heels with gold chains at the ankle. Her mid-back length hair hung low and thanks to its density, provided a decent covering for her bare back. His Mind nearly convinced him that the long, rich tresses were, in fact, part of the dress's design. It had to be, because there was no way a dress that bare could be legal. Not only did this person catch his attention, but the attention of all the men that set eyes on her. Christian watched as she walked across the bar, followed by a trail of hungry-looking men. Just when he concluded it was part of his dream, Olivia surfaced in it and walked toward her. The two women exchanged a casual hug and in seconds, Olivia took her by the hand and walked her to his section.

"Hey, look what the cat brought in," Olivia teased. "Beautiful Isabella . . . ooh la la."

Christian glared at Isabella. "What are you doing here?"

"Hey, hey, easy," Olivia interjected. "A girl's got a right to party. Isabella here could make me a huge chunk of change with all these men salivating over her."

Staring directly at Christian, Isabella said, "Why not, Olivia, I hear you're a fixer-upper."

Olivia grinned. "Wow, Isa's not playing around; keep this up and you'll lose your title."

Christian and Isabella glared at each other the entire time Olivia spoke.

"Antonio!" Olivia called out, motioning the mystery man over.

Christian watched as he strolled over with a crooked smile. He was clean-shaven with a buzz cut. He was about the same height as Christian and, like him, he dressed in a suit and tie.

Olivia proceeded, "Tony, this is Isabella, Isabella . . . Tony."

Antonio took Isabella's hand and kissed it. "The pleasure is mine. Would you like to sit with me?"

"I would love to," Isabella responded, her cold gaze on Christian.

I should punch him for putting his dirty lips on her. He fumed. *Relax, it's a greeting,* Genius reasoned.

Christian noticed her ring was absent, and he assumed she must have been ready to mingle. He kept watch on Antonio as he walked her to his section. Shortly after she sat down, Antonio went off to the bar. Christian calmly strolled up behind Isabella and grabbed the back of her arm.

"Ow! that hurts," Isabella shrieked, as she twisted around and stood to face him, suddenly glad she had on the stilettos for some height advantage.

"What in the world are you doing here?" he asked, breathing deeply into her ear. There was passion in his voice, and her knees felt weak again. If he hadn't held on to her arm, she would have certainly tumbled. She saw repulsion in his eyes, but there was something more. *Jealousy. It was about time.*

"Let go of me; this isn't Casa Cervello," Isabella said sarcastically. "Just leave me alone; I'm not bothering you or your family."

"Do you realize how many men in here want to get you into bed? Look around you."

Isabella looked around with a half-smile. "That wouldn't be such a bad thing, would it?"

Antonio walked up to the table and frowned. "Excuse me, is this man bothering you?"

Christian remained silent and kept his eye on Isabella.

She sighed. "No, I'm fine. He's my friend's brother, just give us a minute."

"You don't belong here," Christian said through his teeth. "I'm taking you home."

Antonio confronted Christian. "Hey, hey . . . "

Julio stepped in between the two men, towering over them. "Is there a problem?" he asked, his tone daunting.

Antonio backed away with both hands up.

Christian walked away and out of the club with Isabella; Julio followed closely behind.

Christian and Isabella got into the back of the vehicle.

"Did you drive?" Christian asked flatly.

"No," she replied.

An awkward silence lingered in the car. Christian's stare had made her feel unclean. He'd been rude lately, but that stare was new. Almost like he was only protecting her for Rachel's sake.

"Casa Cervello?" Julio asked.

"No," Christian said. "Take her home."

"May I have your address, Ms.?" Julio asked. "Excuse me, Ms.?"

"Isabella!" Christian called. "What's your address?"

"Oh . . . It's 82 Bayston Terrace," Isabella replied.

During the drive, Christian noticed Isabella shiver. "Julio, could you turn off the AC?"

"Thanks," Isabella mumbled. "My jacket is at the club."

"Oh?" Julio replied, "I can pick it up for you later, do you have the tag?"

She reached into her purse and pulled out the tag. As she did, Christian stole a glance at her legs. His dreams did them no justice. They were smooth like glass, and in the heels, they went on forever. Her beauty in baggy clothes and a ponytail was enough to attract a man, but this was a crime. He continued to glance at her from the corner of his eyes. The bold curls in her hair begged to be touched, and the urge to run his fingers through them was so strong that he sat on one hand to avoid any mishaps.

"Dresses don't come any longer than that, huh?" Christian grumbled. *That was mean*, Genius said.

He took off his suit jacket and covered her thighs.

Back in the nightclub, Sacha met Olivia at the bar. "Have you seen Chris?"

"Nope, he was gone before I came back from looking for you. He probably took Isa home—your loss." Olivia shrugged. "Where *were* you anyway?"

Sacha frowned. "Wait, what? She was here?"

"Oh, you should have seen her. I think you're right. Those two got more than chemistry going on."

"Do I need to hear this?"

"Listen, if you can't sit your butt still, you can't expect me to work any miracles for you. Chris probably won't be back. So I suggest you plan a date elsewhere next time if you wanna keep him interested." She gave Sacha a pat on her arm before heading back to her seat.

To Olivia's surprise, Antonio was sitting in Christian's spot.

"Olivia, Olivia," he said with a smile as he poured her a glass of Cristal.

She let out a big sigh and sat down next to him, smiling.

He winked as he handed her the glass. "I've just been sitting here thinking . . . I must have lost touch with this beautiful city because I'd concluded that I knew every woman worth knowing."

Olivia took a sip of her champagne. "I still have a few *tricks* up my sleeve, Tony."

"No pun intended, I hope," he said with a raised brow.

Olivia laughed. "Ah, good one—but no, not her. She's cream of the crop—if you know what I mean."

"Crème de la crème is okay with me."

"Don't ever underestimate me again."

"Oh, I won't," he said, bowing to her.

"So tell me, Antonio, just how serious are you?"

Antonio sat up with a serious look. "I want Isabella," he said, enunciating her name with a strong Spanish accent. "Get her to me and I'll double the price. Is that serious enough for you, my dear Olivia?"

Olivia violently coughed from her drink. Antonio patted her back.

Isabella's lawn security lights came on as Julio pulled up into her driveway.

"Nice place," Christian said, looking around the neighborhood.

"Thank you," she replied, without making eye contact.

"Hey, I won't tell Rachel if you don't want me to."

Still avoiding his stare, she handed his suit jacket back to him. "Thank you."

Christian seized her arm, forcing her to make eye contact. "You didn't drink earlier, did you?"

"No," she said, looking away.

"What exactly got into you?"

"I don't know."

"That wasn't like you."

Isabella scoffed. "Funny, you've never taken the time to know what *is* like me. Goodnight, Christian. Thank you for the ride, Julio." With her stilettos in hand, she walked barefoot out of the car and into her house.

When Julio started to drive off, Christian cried out, "Julio, please wait!"

As soon as Isabella closed the door, she dropped her shoes and stooped down to the floor, weeping for a few minutes. She got up and headed straight to the bathroom to run her bathwater. She didn't dare look at her reflection in the mirror—she felt sleazy and cheap. She turned on the stereo and stripped off her clothes before getting into the tub—only to start crying all over again as soon as her song started to play.

CHAPTER ELEVEN

Trigger Me

OUT IN the driveway, Julio and Christian both sat in silence. Christian's mind was unsettled and he was breathing heavily.

"Is everything okay, Mr. Cervello?" Julio asked, looking at the rearview mirror.

"I don't know," Christian panted.

Christian didn't know how to express his current emotional state. He was at peace outside Isabella's house, and he longed to hold her, but there was the frightening thought of what could have happened if he and Julio weren't at the club. He felt overwhelming love and peace around Isabella's light. Yet, he was confused as to how this light that could instantly lift him out of a depressive state would want to be in the dark.

He clutched his chest. His breathing had begun to slow down.

"What's the matter?" Julio asked, concerned.

"Tell me, Julio, what is it with people nowadays? Did you see what happened in that club?"

"Yeah, tell me about it, especially that guy. You heard what Olivia said about him, shocking stuff."

"I knew I wasn't going paranoid when I heard that. Can you imagine what could have happened if we weren't there? What's it with these girls today . . . my goodness . . . and Olivia!"

Julio shook his head. "Yup, that's how a good girl goes bad."

"The guy had so much charm; Isabella would never have known about his reputation. He was so close, Julio, if you hadn't delayed by looking for Sacha—"

"You know what scares me the most?" Julio asked.

"What?" Christian asked, making eye contact with Julio in the rearview mirror.

"I saw two of the guys he came with, dealing drugs in the restroom."

Christian panted again. How could he convince someone whom he hurt many times before that the charming young man she met in the club wasn't what he seemed? What could have happened if he decided not to honor his promise to accompany Sacha tonight, or if she had been ready to leave when he nagged her, or if Olivia and Julio hadn't made that final plea to search for her, or if he hadn't had that conversation about Antonio with Olivia? *Okay, stop!* Genius said. Sweat trickled down Christian's temples. Rather than be grateful that he helped Isabella dodge a bullet, he dwelled on the what-ifs and the worst-case scenarios.

Although his trusty Genius turned such obsessions into a multimillion-dollar enterprise, no matter how good his devices were, he had little peace. No one knew about the secret battles he faced—the doubts and insecurities. All they saw was His Shell of a Body. Christian felt Julio's gaze on him from the rearview mirror.

"It's okay," Julio said. "We were there and nothing happened, okay?"

Christian closed his eyes and envisioned Isabella in bed with Antonio against her will. Perhaps that was how he managed to sleep with so many women—a sick challenge. He opened his eyes again panted even more as sweat trickled down his palms. He loosened his tie to help relieve the choking sensation he felt.

"Hey, what's going on?" Julio asked, fearful.

Christian's voice was strained. "I'm okay, Julio."

"No, you're not," Julio said, opening the door, "I know a panic attack when I see one."

"No, don't come out. I'm fine," Christian said, winding down his window.

Julio closed the door and raised his voice. "Listen, she's okay. We just dropped her home; you hear me? I doubt she'll be out there again after the way you spoke to her. Now try to relax. Deep breaths . . . "

Christian breathed in through his nose and exhaled through his mouth.

"That's it . . . " Julio guided. "Keep going."

He continued the breathing exercises until his heart rate slowed down.

"You think I was too hard on her?" Christian asked.

"No, but I do think you are too hard on yourself. Your mind seems to be playing games on you. You have to get it under control."

"Yeah, I do tend to worry a lot."

"I think it's more than that," Julio said, making eye contact with Christian. "You can try to hide it from her all you want, but I think you're in love with that girl."

"Is it that obvious?"

"It doesn't make you less of a man to admit it."

"What should I do?"

"Go in there."

"What? Are you crazy? Do you have any idea what time it is? I can't just walk in now."

"But we just dropped her off."

"So what? So, let's say for argument sake, she lets me in, and I don't think she will—"

"Um . . . just—" Julio stuttered.

A phone rang. Both men looked at each other. On the third ring, Julio asked, "Is that you?"

"No, I thought it was you. Where is it coming from?" Christian traced the sound to the back seat floor—under the front passenger seat. It stopped ringing by the time he reached it. There were twelve missed calls from the same number.

"Rachel?" Christian muttered.

"Ah, she must have forgotten her phone," Julio smiled. "You thinking what I'm thinking?"

Christian shook his head.

"Start by saying, 'You forgot this.'"

It had to be a clear sign. Christian's heart raced, this time for excitement.

"Go on," Julio urged.

"How about the girls? I meant to go back because Sacha's belongings are still in the car."

"I'll go back and make sure they get home safe, and I'll pick up the lady's jacket."

"Great, thanks, Julio. Listen, please tell Sacha I tried waiting but—"

"Just go. Will I be taking her back to your place?"

"Goodness no . . . her stuff is in the trunk already, just ask for her address and take her home."

Julio nodded. "Okay, would you like for me to wait until she opens the door?"

"Even if she doesn't, Lord knows I'll sleep out here."

Julio laughed. "Okay, Romeo." He drove off, while Christian rang Isabella's doorbell.

There was a bit of a chill in the air, and Christian was glad he had his suit. He rang Isabella's doorbell for a third time before he came to the conclusion that she was sleeping or in the bathroom. So he got comfortable on the front porch steps and fought the temptation to look through her phone. He had to admit that fate had a charm. Just earlier today, he didn't have her address or phone number. Now he was sitting at her doorstep, holding her phone, and he didn't even need Rachel's help for this.

Inside, Isabella had cried herself to sleep and was awakening to what sounded like the doorbell. She'd heard that sound earlier but thinking it was the music, she drifted right back to sleep. No one in their right mind would come to see her at that hour except . . . Rachel? Oh shoot! She got out of the bathtub and fastened her robe as she crept down the stairs slowly.

"Who is it?" she asked, grabbing her intruder pole from the corner of the door. She looked in the peephole and saw no one.

"It's me, Christian," he said, coming into view.

When Isabella opened the door, Christian was pleased to see that she hadn't put her hair back in prison. The curls were still in place, but water dripped from the tips onto her cotton robe, with some drops finding their way to her neck and down her cleavage.

"Hey," Christian said sheepishly. "I guessed you'd be bathing or sleeping."

Isabella smiled. "Both. Are you okay?"

"Um, yeah, you forgot this."

Isabella took the phone. "Wow . . . I didn't even notice. Thanks."

"Yeah, it was on the floor," Christian added.

She looked past Christian to the driveway.

"He left," Christian said.

"Oh, is he coming back for you?"

"No."

"Um . . . do you need a ride home?" she asked, avoiding eye contact.

"I guess it's too late to let me in, huh?"

Isabella cleared her throat, "Oh, no. I'm sorry, come in."

"Are you sure?" Christian asked skeptically, eyeing the pole in her hand. "Anyway, I see you've got a weapon just in case you need to use it."

They both laughed as they headed up the stairs.

"I can only guess you're here to apologize for snapping at me in your house earlier," Isabella said.

Christian remained quiet as they reached the top of the stairs. He recognized the music that blared as the *new* and *recent* one, and he smiled. "No wonder you didn't hear the doorbell."

"Oh, yeah, I know it's loud."

As Christian looked around her home, he heard humming and knew that Genius was taking notes. He hardly did that unless he had a challenge, so it felt good to know he wasn't the only one that she intrigued. The lights were dim—a clear indication that she had retired for the night. Yet he studied everything carefully—the pictures, decorations – storing them in his hard drive. Hopefully he would take the same images under daylight.

Isabella stood behind him, observing how he stroked pieces of her furniture as he walked by. She didn't know what to make of it, but was more thrilled that he was in her home. She'd played the moment in her mind many times, but it was never this profound, and it was always daylight when she saw him there. Although she'd vowed in the tub never to ignore the Lord the way she had, she still couldn't help seeing His loving hand in the end result. Of all the clubs in Miami, the salesclerk sent her straight to Christian.

"Have you been crying?" Christian asked, looking at the pictures on her bookshelf.

She scoffed. "Me?"

"Yes, you," he said, turning to stare intently at her.

"Why are you here?" Isabella managed to ask, her heart galloping.

He strolled to a bookshelf on the opposite end of the wall. "*Battlefield of the Mind*, Hmm . . . Joyce Meyer."

"You know her?" Isabella asked, approaching him.

"Rachel's mom introduced us to her teaching."

"Really? I love my mama Joyce."

"I'm slowly getting to know what you like."

They held each other's gaze. "Can I borrow this?" Christian asked.

"Definitely."

"Thanks," he said, collecting the book from the shelf. "So, when did you accept Christ?"

"July 18, 2003—it was a Friday night prayer service at Faith House."

"You know the exact date." He nodded.

"It means a lot to me; besides, I'm into dates."

"Hmm . . . "

"Would you like something to drink?" she asked.

"Some water will do."

"Okay," she said, heading to the fridge.

"So, when did *you* get saved?" She handed the glass to him.

"Thanks. I was much younger. Aunt Liz invited us to the church—same church by the way. At the time, she was the only one in the family that attended. I'm sure it's a much deeper experience when you do it as an adult. Lord knows my relationship with him could be better."

Isabella nodded.

"Listen, this is going to sound awkward, but I was wondering if I could spend the night here."

Obviously caught off guard, she didn't know what to think or say. No man had ever spent the night in her house. The idea was nerve-racking, and she wondered what Gracie would think or say if she even saw him around her house at this ungodly hour.

He continued. "I know it's weird, it's just that there's something about this place. I feel comfortable here, and I would hate to call Julio back."

"Um . . . sure, why not. I hope you can manage; I mean, it doesn't exactly have the amenities Casa Cervello has but—" *What's the worst that could happen? He's Aunt Pattie's son and Rachel's brother.*

"Don't be silly, this place is . . . peaceful is the word. Thanks. I can sleep on the couch if it's okay. I promise I won't be a bother."

"Now why would you sleep on the couch?" She frowned. "I've got a guest room on the main floor."

"You sure it's okay?"

"Of course, come on, I'll show you to the room."

They walked downstairs to the guest room, and she opened the door.

"Good to see you relaxed," Isabella said, flicking on the lights, glad she cleaned the room yesterday.

"Yeah, I guess it's something about this place. I'm really sorry about earlier; it was uncalled for."

"Thanks, I appreciate that. Would you care for something to eat?"

"Nah, I'm about ready to crash. Thanks, anyway."

"Okay, the bathroom is through the closet door. Have a good night," she said, turning to leave.

"Oh . . . um, Isabella?"

She turned around. "Yes?"

"I noticed you didn't have on your ring earlier."

From her facial expression, Christian figured he'd surprised her.

"You noticed. I actually left it at home."

"Oh?" he asked, raising a challenging brow.

"Yes."

"I couldn't possibly see that club as a place to deliberately meet someone for a serious relationship."

Isabella shrugged. "Who said anything about a serious relationship?"

This time, she caught him off guard by her response. "I think you should call my sister and let her know you're okay, she's worried about you."

He wanted to imagine Isabella as the perfect picture he had drawn up in his head even though reason screamed for him to wake up. Perhaps she didn't want a rescue. *Could it be the reason she was crying? Could she have really wanted to meet Antonio?* He was probably barking up the wrong tree because he couldn't understand how a young woman, who he presumed had never been to a nightclub, could confidently take a taxi and show up on her own with no support from a friend—not to mention barely dressed.

Her actions showed little discretion for her own safety, and he worried that she was either very naive or promiscuous. Whatever the case was, he was beginning to find that this visit to her home, although therapeutic, had created more doubts in his mind about the woman he was falling for. *Who is Isabella Montes and how much does Rachel think she knows about her?* Christian continued looking around her guest room, sniffing the pillows. Genius had called this an obsession, but he believed he was madly in love with Isabella Montes, and as he lay in bed later that night, he wondered if she was in love with him, too.

CHAPTER TWELVE

Deception

❦

THE NEXT morning, Isabella dreaded having to leave a beautiful creature behind in her home, but she was coming to terms with the unpredictability of life. Just yesterday, she was looking forward to a booked-solid Saturday when she'd eventually called her colleague and agreed to help with the Smithson audit. If she knew Christian would be spending the night, she'd still be dreaming in bed. She might as well start believing in these dreams since it looked like they were coming true, one fate-driven moment after another.

She headed downstairs to invite Christian for breakfast. The guest room door was slightly open, so she peeped in, only to see him still fast asleep. She leaned her head against the doorpost, studying him. He looked peaceful, and she could probably watch him forever, but she had to get going. Back upstairs, she poured the green tea that Pattie had taught her to make into a flask. It felt silly having to do that, but she'd already gone through the trouble of making it and it wasn't as if she was at the liberty to share the recipe with him anyway. Pattie made her swear never to reveal it to him for fear that he would stop drinking. "He's weird like that," she would say. Pattie had been making the tea for him since he was a child and, according to her, it calmed him down.

Too scared to ask what that meant and even more frightened to know the response, she held her peace. For whatever reason, it was Christian's *special* tea, and she had become an expert at making it. Why wouldn't she— she'd made it so many times in her house for herself, all the while daydreaming that one day she would be making it for him here. The moment had arrived . . . life. She knew precisely how many slices of lemon it took to make a 34-ounce jar, and the right amount of ginseng, ginger, and honey. Pattie had warned that if she were off by even the diameter of the slice of lemon, Christian would know, as he was very observant. True to Pattie's claim, Isabella had witnessed his brilliance for herself when she purposefully left a small detail out. She noticed that Christian took one sip of the tea and without a word or facial expression, he briefly glanced at the mug and never lifted it to his lips again. He didn't comment about it either; he simply went back to reading his paper like nothing happened.

She tightened the lid of the flask and quickly scribbled on a note and tacked it onto it.

> *Good Morning, Chris,*
>   *Here is your special tea. I am off to work. Your breakfast is in the fridge. I hope you enjoyed your stay.*
> *—Isa*

Christian opened his eyes, slightly disoriented until the flowery decorations in the room reminded him of where he was. It was nearly ten in the morning, and he hadn't slept that long in ages. He headed upstairs to the kitchen. It wasn't long before he spotted a note that read:

He smiled to himself, imagining what she looked like in her work clothes. He grabbed the flask along with the teacup she'd placed next to it and headed to the living room. He had made it through to the third chapter of the *Mind* book before sleep caught up with him and, so far, it had helped him deal with the obsessive and negative thoughts that crept up concerning Isabella's nightclub motives. Besides, now that he could see her home décor in the daylight, he couldn't picture her in any other way apart from wholesome.

Just as he relaxed into Isabella's recliner, his phone rang. *Sacha*. He allowed it to go to voicemail and checked the message soon after:

> Hey, what happened to you last night? Well listen, I'm stuck in this hotel without my stuff, so can you come get me, please?

Christian immediately dialed Julio's number.

"Good morning, sir," Julio greeted.

"Hello, Julio."

"I trust you were able to get into the house last night."

"Yes, thanks. Hey, um, I just got a voicemail from Sacha. Weren't you able to take her home?"

"She decided to go to a hotel instead so I put her in one, sir."

"Hmm . . . why is that?"

"She mentioned that her belongings were at your place . . . including her keys."

Christian frowned. "But she said she'd packed her stuff in the trunk."

"I know you did say so, sir, but I checked, and it appears she never packed."

Learning that Sacha had lied, Christian stood up and paced up and down the small living room.

"Will you be able to pick her up? I believe she's ready."

"Not a problem, sir."

"Oh wait, I don't have my car and I have a meeting with the builders today. Perhaps you can come for me first. I'll figure something out when you get here."

"When do you need me, sir?"

"If you can be here in an hour . . . "

"Will do."

Christian took a shower and headed back upstairs to heat up his breakfast. As he sat drinking the remainder of his tea, it struck him that it tasted just like the one his mother made. Then remembering Isabella's *special tea* comment, he figured she must have watched his mother make it. His eyes scanned her living and dining room thoroughly—taking in every inch to store in his overloaded brain to dissect later.

He glanced down the hallway and thought of taking a quick peek into her bedroom, but the thought left as quickly as it came. He didn't dare walk past the area in which she'd welcomed him last night, and he was content with that because even though he didn't have strong boundaries for himself, he respected the boundaries of others. From the rooms he had seen, it wasn't hard to tell that she had an obsession with flowers. Some were real and still fresh, a few were withering away, and others were silk. He snapped pictures of them with his phone.

Julio arrived about fifteen minutes later, and as he saw Christian approach, he exited the car and smiled. "Good morning, Mr. Cervello; don't you look like a brand new man."

Christian blushed. "Come on, Julio, I can get my own door . . . and please call me *Chris*."

"Oh no, sir, I can't possibly . . . "

"Then *Christian*, if it makes you feel better."

"Okay sir, I mean . . . Christian."

Christian laughed as he sat in the back seat. "It'll get easier."

"I pray everything went well?" Julio asked.

"Well is an understatement. Um, do you know what kind of flower this is?" He handed over his phone.

"Those are definitely orchids," Julio said, returning the phone. "I know because my wife is a florist."

"Oh, is she? I didn't know that." Christian's phone rang. "Excuse me, Julio."

Christian wrapped up his call. "Okay, change of plans. That was Rachel—I forgot she was coming."

"So, head over to your place first?"

"Yes, please, thank you. Then, I think it's best Rach and I head off to Highland Beach from there while you get Sacha. Where is the hotel? In Miami?"

"No, sir, Coral Gables."

"Okay, perfect. It's close to home. I'll text her that you'll be there in a few but drop me off first so I can have her stuff ready for pickup. Oh, no . . . I forgot to leave a thank-you note for Isabella, and I forgot to get her number too."

Julio laughed. "That girl has got you forgetting all sorts of things. Not to worry, we've got some notepads in the back console; why don't you write one now?"

"You're amazing, Julio. I'd do that, but I locked the door and she's not home. But if you could drop it off at her office, I'd appreciate that."

"Sure thing, sir, I can take it along with her jacket. Do you know her work address?"

"I'll look it up. *What's that name again?*" Christian muttered, browsing through his phone. "I remember seeing it on the fridge. I – M – Something . . . C . . . Accounting. Found it."

Christian grabbed a notepad and after writing on a sheet, he folded it and wrote her name on the back of it. Then on a separate sheet, he wrote down her work address. He caught a glimpse of her jacket and sniffed it. It had her smell—it calmed the nerves that Sacha worked up.

Julio pulled up in front of the house, and Christian jumped out. "Okay, don't wait for us. Get Sacha. I'll have her stuff out in the foyer. I'll leave the front door open for you to get her stuff. Don't let her into the house alone. Please don't forget Isabella's note—it's with her jacket. The work address is on a separate sheet."

"No problem, sir."

Julio pulled up at the front entrance of the hotel a little while later, and seeing Sacha and Olivia approach, he exited.

"Good morning, ladies. Ms. Olivia, will you be joining us?"

"Yeah, Julio—I hope it's okay. I decided to spend the night with her."

"I do hope you both enjoyed your stay."

"Could you not speak unless spoken to?" Sacha snapped.

"Yes, ma'am."

Olivia whispered, "That was cruel, Sach." Then to Julio, she said, "She had a rough night, Julio; pay her no mind. I'm actually glad I'm here because, with an attitude like hers, you're gonna need all the protection you can get."

Sacha plugged in her headphones, closing her eyes as she relaxed into the backseat.

Olivia's eye caught a red jacket pushed to Sacha's extreme end and recognized it as Isabella's. As she picked it up, two neatly folded pieces of paper fell out.

She nudged Sacha's shoulder. "Hey, lookie, lookie," she whispered, holding up the note.

Sacha removed her headphones and frowned. "What?"

"To Ms. *Montes*," Olivia whispered teasingly.

Sacha grabbed the note and they silently read it:

> Isabella,
>
> Thanks for letting me stay over. I needed a change of scenery and your place was very warm. Please forgive me for acting strange last night. My mind was all over the place. I'm probably still not making sense. Enjoy your workday. I look forward to seeing you soon.
> Thanks again,
> -Chris

With a cunning smile, Olivia whispered, "I guess now we know where he was last night."

"I knew he was with that stupid!"

Olivia nudged her, "Shh . . . no no, don't panic when you're with Liv. This is nothing—I specialize in making lemonade out of lemons."

"Is everything okay back there?" Julio asked, looking through the rearview mirror.

"Yeah, Julio, we're just fine," Olivia replied. She then unplugged the headphone from Sacha's iPod, and set the music to play out.

"Are you thinking what I'm thinking?" Sacha whispered, biting on her bottom lip.

"Go first."

"Get rid of it."

"Oh my dear," Olivia said shaking her head. "You have a whole lot to learn, don't you? No, let her get a note from Chris. That's fine . . . and let *him* get a reply. Got a piece of paper?"

"Now what in the world would I be doing with paper?" Sacha snapped.

"Okay, okay, sheesh—Grouch. Here we go . . . there's a lot of space left here," Olivia said, ripping out the blank section of the note.

Sacha whispered, "What are you doing?"

"Watch and learn."

A few minutes later, Olivia looked up in time to see Julio turn into the street that led up to the estate.

"Oh, no," Olivia whispered.

"What?" Sacha asked.

"You're coming to my place,"

"I am?"

"Shh . . . can't you see we need time for this?"

Sacha nodded hastily.

"Julio, darling," Olivia pouted. "I am so sorry. I forgot to tell you—I need to head over to my place to pick up Chris' camera. He wants it back. I'm sorry that I completely forgot. I live around the corner anyway."

"Oh, that's not a problem," Julio replied. "I'll need your address."

"Oh, it's right on Ocean Drive."

Julio's phone rang as he parked in front of Olivia's condominium. As he spoke into the phone, Sacha and Olivia prepared to exit the vehicle.

"Wow, this is hot," Sacha said, lifting the red jacket from Olivia's lap. "Where did you get it and how come I'm just seeing it?"

"Oh, it's not mine," Olivia said, tossing it back in the same spot she found it. "It's Isa's. I guess she forgot it. It *is* hot. I convinced her to get it when we went shopping with Rachel. I've got great taste, you know."

Sacha scowled at Olivia. "Oh, spare me. Listen, if she forgot her jacket here, don't you think it'll give him an excuse to see her again?"

"Nice, I'm glad to see I'm rubbing off on you, but that shouldn't be a problem because I think it's being delivered with the note."

"You can't be certain."

"Well, that's where I found the note, along with her office address. Still, you're right—anything can happen. Who's to say Julio's supposed to deliver it, and if he is, what if he forgets? We can't afford to take chances. Give it to me. Although I gotta tell you, when I'm done writing this reply, I don't think a jacket dipped in gold will make him wanna see her again."

Sacha gasped. "You're the spawn of the devil. I owe you one."

"You sure do. I don't work for free," Olivia said, carefully positioning the note between the console.

Julio got off the phone. "Okay," he said, looking at Olivia through the rearview mirror. "I'll wait for you to bring the camera."

Olivia stuttered, "Oh, um . . . I would like to take Sacha with me, only because I wanna make her breakfast before she goes back."

Julio nodded.

"Can you come back for her in like an hour." Olivia asked.

"Okay, I need to get to downtown Miami anyway. I figure with the traffic back and forth—"

"I bet," she said. "These tourists mean business, and we still have a week to Memorial Day weekend."

Aside from landscaping and inspections, Christian's Highland Beach home was just about complete. While he spoke to the lead architect, Rachel strolled through the compound. She hadn't seen so many palm trees on one site, but she wasn't surprised because Christian loved them—something about the way they swayed in the breeze, he had said. She was pleased with the project and the thought of decorating the entire house quickly led her to thinking of whom her brother would be sharing the beautiful home. She stole a glance at him; he now stood alone and appeared to be in deep thought.

"I can't believe it's done," Rachel said, strolling over to meet him.

Christian smiled. "It's turned out nicely."

"So um . . . the other guy—the one with a ponytail . . . "

"The landscape architect?"

"Yeah . . . he said you changed your mind about the area to the side. Didn't you want a golf course?"

Christian started to stroll away. "Yeah, I'm still not so sure."

"Not sure?" Rachel laughed, running to keep up with him. "He's actually taking notes on which plants to work around a tropical landscape with an orchid garden. Sounds pretty specific to me."

She noticed his jaw clench. "I mean, there's nothing wrong with that. I actually prefer it to the golf thingy. I was just wondering if that girl you're seeing was the reason for this softer side."

"There's nothing going on between us."

Rachel threw her hands up. "You know what, I had no right. Listen, you don't owe me an explanation. Your place is just about done, and I'm sure you'll be thrilled to have your privacy back."

Rachel noticed that Christian had stopped walking. She turned around to see his brows drawn in.

"Has it ever occurred to you that if I wanted privacy so bad, I'd be in the guesthouse? And just in case you forgot, I do own the building Olivia lives in."

Rachel shrugged. "Why *do you* stay with us?"

"Good question," he said, beginning to walk again.

She ran up to catch up with him. "Hey, what was that about with you and Isa yesterday?"

"I was hoping you weren't gonna ask."

"Chris, I know you're the rightful owner of Casa Cervello."

Christian stopped walking again. This time he frowned. "What?"

"I don't—"

"Seriously, Rach? Are we back to this again?"

She began to stutter.

"Have I ever made you feel like you weren't the rightful custodian of that house since 2008?"

"No, but . . . " she stopped, feeling the tears creep up.

"But what?"

"I can't help feeling I have no control."

"That's ridiculous, the entire thing is in your name!"

"You changed the security code!"

"With your permission and for our safety."

"You don't let Isa in, and when she makes it in, you chase her out."

"I told you I—"

"Listen, the least I expect is simple courtesy because she's been nothing but respectful to us."

Christian rubbed his face. "I crossed the line and I'm extremely sorry. It won't happen again—expect a change from me."

"I appreciate that, but you really gotta tell her that. You know if I didn't know any better, I would swear there were some kind of sexual tension between you two."

"No, nothing like that."

Olivia handed Sacha the note and received a high five in return. "Oh, where have you been all my life?"

Olivia laughed. "Stop!"

"This ought to give him a change of scenery all right." Sacha frowned. "You sealed it?"

Olivia grabbed both her shoulders. "You seriously don't trust me by now? Hey, it's a surprise—just hand it to him and watch the fireworks. Besides, not knowing what's in it will give you a more authentic reaction—you know too much already."

"Where do I tell him it's from?"

"Just say Julio asked you to give it to him. That's why it has to be sealed—if Isa's letting him down, she'd do it privately—in a sealed letter. Julio will be wondering about the camera, so I'll give you that."

"I was wondering, didn't you say you lied about not having your car at the club?"

"I wondered when you were gonna ask," Olivia said. "It *is* there. I just had to buy time somehow. If Chris knew I had my car, Julio would never be running around for us this way."

"You think of everything." Sacha smiled. "I promise never to get on your bad side."

"It's my full time job to think of my next move and believe me, I have a lot riding on this working in your favor . . . at the moment."

Olivia and Sacha were waiting in the lobby by the time Julio walked through the main entrance. Both women simultaneously stood up. "Now do as I said," Olivia whispered. "Make sure you hand it to him when Julio is gone."

"Okay," Sacha said, walking away.

"Sacha, wait! The camera." Olivia ran up to her and hung the strap over her neck. "Make sure you bring this back because I'm using it for a project."

"Before I forget," Julio said to Sacha, "I was wondering if any of you ladies had mistakenly collected a red jacket from the car."

Sacha stuttered. "Um, I didn't, I'll ask Olivia." Sacha turned back to find Olivia just as she was about to head into the elevator. "Liv, he's asking about the jacket, what do I say?"

Olivia walked up to Julio. "Oh, yeah, Julio, I took it because I recognized it was Isa's. I'll make sure she gets it. Not to worry, she's my friend."

"Thanks, I appreciate that," Julio replied.

Julio parked outside Casa Cervello and before exiting the car, he announced, "I'll get your belongings."

Sacha rushed out and caught up with him. "Thanks, but I don't need your help. I'll be fine."

"I'm just following instructions, Ms.," Julio said as he laid hold of the doorknob. "Strange, the door was supposed to be unlocked," he muttered.

"No problem. I always just text him anyway. He doesn't like for me to ring the doorbell."

"I'll wait by the car."

"Suit yourself," Sacha said, rolling her eyes at him as she sent a text to Christian.

Christian was in his study when he received a text message from Sacha. When he opened the door, he waved at Julio at a distance.

"Hey," he said to Sacha.

"I just wanna get my stuff."

"Sure, come in."

Sacha stayed silent as she climbed up the stairs. "You told me you packed your stuff last night," Christian said. "In fact, you said it was in the trunk."

"I know," she replied, letting herself into his bedroom. "I didn't want us to be late for the club."

"I didn't realize there was a time restriction for entry to the club."

Her icy, blue eyes narrowed at him. "Very funny."

Christian responded with a half-smile.

"Couldn't wait to get rid of me, huh?" she said, eyeing her satchel bags, which leaned against the wall.

"It's not that. I wasn't home earlier, and I didn't want you to stress about who might have been home. I asked Julio to pick up your stuff from the foyer for your convenience. It was still here by the time I returned, so I took it back upstairs."

"How thoughtful." Her tone was sarcastic. "Oh, by the way, this is from Julio."

"What's this?" The sealed envelope had "Chris," written on it. It couldn't be from Julio because he wasn't comfortable using that name. Besides he would talk to him . . . if anything.

Sacha shrugged. "How would I know."

He took the note into the restroom and ripped it open.

> Christian,
>
> I received your note. Thanks, but I really wish you hadn't come last night. It was a big mistake. I'm somewhat interested in someone at the moment, and I can't have you stopping by like you did last night—it could cause

problems. I hope you understand what I mean. Thanks in advance.

–Isa

Christian froze. The negative thoughts he'd carefully tucked away came flooding back. He could barely breathe. After some time, Sacha yelled out from the bedroom, "Christian, are you okay?"

I knew it, he thought. *It's him.* The feeling of rejection from advancements to a woman was rare for him. It stung. Genius spoke, *You should ask Julio about the note.* Christian snapped back, *There you go again trying to rationalize things, can't you see it in black and white?*

Sacha banged on the restroom door, interrupting Christian's internal dialogue. "Chris, if you don't open up, I'll call your family in here!"

He opened the door, and Sacha pulled him close.

"Was it the note?" she asked. "What was in it—did someone die?"

He was speechless. She ran to the restroom and retrieved the note from the floor. She then ran back out to Christian yelling, "That stupid girl, how dare she? You don't need stupid little girls in your life; you need a real woman. You know what? I'll be right back. I'll tell Julio to go. I'm not leaving you alone tonight."

CHAPTER THIRTEEN

Brokenness

THE FIRST week of June had come to an uneventful end. Likewise was the fate of the last week of May for Christian. Ever since he read that note three weeks ago, he hadn't left the Casa Cervello grounds. He could not remember ever feeling this way. He knew obsessions, panic, and anxiety very well, but this feeling had him content with just lying in bed for hours on end. He wasn't used to being idle this way, and as hard as he tried to stay on his feet, his body always seemed to find its way back to the bed.

He could barely move, but His Mind—as always—roamed. There in his bed, with his eyes closed, came three new invention ideas, courtesy of Genius. Now, he would have to rely on his memory to store the details for later, since he lacked the strength to write. In addition to the inability to move, was the emptiness—more like self-pity and shame. He had that similar feeling on his birthday, but he'd managed to pull through that episode in just a day. This, on the other hand, was brutal. The last meal he could remember having was lobster with Rachel and his mother before their departure for Italy that Tuesday after Memorial Day. Apart from water and the obsessive amount of Big Red gum he'd consumed—that most likely kept him alive—he had no appetite.

Rachel's text last night announced they had arrived at the airport and would be taking a taxi home. His response to the text was to use all his might to stand up and lock his door. However, he soon regretted that move when he figured it would be rude to avoid them after two weeks of absence—especially since he ignored their long-distance calls the entire time. He had to be careful not to raise any red flags. How he wished the world would get to know and accept the real him. *Christian Eduardo Cervello* was a figment with no allowance for a bad season because too much depended on him—his family, friends, the board, his employees, investors and even the tourists. So yet again, a good front was imperative.

For the rest of that night, Christian found himself slightly resenting Rachel for sending a text and not following up with the annoyance he anticipated would come within the same hour. It had also taken supernatural intervention to get him to stand back up to unlock the door when he still couldn't find the door remote. He made a mental note to see about inventing a tracker for that too. Rachel's text quickly became his new focus for that night, putting him through anticipation, fear, anger, and vulnerability. The text had him scrambling for a brand new façade. All the while, His Shell of a Body lay in bed, hoping to savor the last few minutes of freedom.

Any moment they would walk in with all that merriment which should ideally prompt a smile or cheer. Those smiles hurt because they strained his worn-out facial muscles. What was more punishing than a fake smile was them never barging in. The anticipation the text stirred carried on through the night. He wished for tears, but his heart threatened to find its way out from his mouth if he dared open it to cry. It didn't help when the sleep that eluded him for days finally came soon after the stupid text. Hence, his new fixation—the fear of sleep due to a possible interruption. Genius stayed silent through it all. He just hummed like he did whenever he felt ignored or was hard at work.

By dawn, Christian heard footsteps. His heart raced again when His mind alerted, *any minute now*. He looked at the time. He'd slept for fifteen minutes but if felt like an entire day. This brought a genuine smile to his weary face. They should barge in soon and start their happy tales of Rachel's engagement in romantic Sicily. He already knew about it because Thomas informed him of his intentions to propose in a helicopter over Mount Etna. Christian loved Rachel more than life itself, and knew Thomas would make a perfect husband. However, at this moment, he lacked the energy and patience needed to deal with people. He just wanted peace and quiet. *Any minute now,* he thought. The footsteps died down, and he drifted back to sleep.

Isabella walked into Christian's room unannounced. She was holding a brown mug in her hand with the Acronym I.M.C. *It must be my tea,* he thought. He was excited to see her, but was too tired to show it. He lay in the middle of a pile of dirty clothes and dishes and in the background—music. Isabella looked over at the stereo, then back at Christian, as she cautiously sat on the bed. She placed the mug down and took his hand in hers. She then placed her other hand on his face, stroking it lightly with her slender fingers, brushing the overgrown hair into place.

"What do you want from me?" he asked with his eyes closed, enjoying the feel of her fingers over his face. "Tell me, name anything and I'll give it to you."

Still holding his hand, she placed her other hand over his chest. "I want your heart."

"What do you want from it?"

She looked into his eyes. "I want to take care of it so you won't hurt anymore."

He moved both her hands away from him. "I can't do that, Isabella, there's gotta be something else."

He watched as tears began to well up in her eyes, and then turned his back to her.

Christian opened his eyes and looked around for Isabella, only to see his mother standing by the door. She walked over and sat down on his bed. He knew his hair must be an overgrown shag by now, but his room was meticulous, so he hoped to play off the fear and concern he saw in her eyes. Rachel stood by his door. He sat up and managed a smile. "Come here and give me a hug, our wife-to-be."

Rachel brightened up. "How did you know?"

"Why, my brother-in-law told me about his plans. Let me see the ring."

Rachel smiled through tears as she cuddled up next to him in the bed, extending her hand.

"Very *nice* . . . he has very good taste. Congrats, kid. You beat me to it too, huh?"

When no one replied, he said, "What time is it anyway? I'm so sleepy."

Pattie and Rachel exchanged a cautious glance. "But you've been sleeping all day, hon," his mother said. "I mean, we wanna give you privacy, but my goodness Chris, I think you may need some help."

"I need help because I slept all day?"

"Chris, it's more than that," Rachel said. "You ignored all our calls while we were away. Your staff is concerned about you too. Apparently, you missed some important meetings, Erica Steinberg just—"

"Oh, yeah, my assistant. She left me a message on my cell."

"Well, do you plan to call her back? She's worried about you; we all are."

He closed his eyes. "Don't, Rach, I'll be fine. It is probably just the flu or something. I just feel weak."

"It may do some good for you to leave the house," Pattie said.

"Yeah, you're probably right," Christian reached for his phone. "I'll call Julio—I need to be somewhere anyway."

"Oh, nice," Rachel said with a sly smirk, grabbing the phone from his hand. "I'll call him right now."

"I can do it myself," he grunted.

"Oh no, I've got this."

Pattie stood up. "Son, Rachel and I are heading to the salon to get ready for a gala tonight. I was supposed to go with your father, but something came up, and he won't be back for another three weeks. It's bad enough he couldn't attend his own niece's wedding."

Christian frowned. "Oh, yeah? When I visited last month, he was just about done."

"I know." Pattie sighed.

"How was the wedding? I shudder to think of what Bianca was like leading up to it."

"Tell me about it, we were all walking on eggshells, but she was okay; I guess. It was actually lovely. We got to see most of the family, and everyone sends their greetings."

"Why don't you skip the gala and get some rest? You gotta be exhausted."

"I know. We're jetlagged like you wouldn't believe. We've been sleeping since we came in last night. I actually just woke up like an hour ago—half the day is gone. The thing is, we already RSVP'd last month, and your dad is a special guest. I need to be there to represent him—It won't look good if none of us show up. Listen, we'll be out late but it'll make us feel better to see you out of the house today, even for a few minutes."

Christian smiled.

Rachel wrapped up her call to Julio. "Okay, he'll be here in a few."

Christian's eyes narrowed at her, and she winked at him. "You can't con a con artist," she said. "Besides, you're a horrible liar."

He glanced at his watch. "Aren't you guys coming back to get ready?"

Rachel replied, "We're dressing up at Olivia's. We owe her a visit."

As soon as Pattie and Rachel left, Christian put on some music and closed his eyes, hoping the music would lure Isabella back into his dreams. He may not be able to have her in real life, but in his dreams, she was all his. He didn't realize when he drifted off to sleep until the shrill sound of the phone woke him up.

"Hey, Julio," Christian greeted, attempting to sound cheerful.

"Hello, sir, I'm glad to hear you're okay. I just called to let you know I'm in the compound and ready when you are."

Just then, there was a ring at the gate, and from his room surveillance screen, he could see Sacha standing there. He sighed deeply as he pressed the ignore button. Sacha's attempts to gain entry into Casa Cervello for the past two weeks had been so persistent that he considered a restraining order.

"I'm so sorry, I meant to call you back to cancel but I forgot. Rachel just wasn't having it."

"It's not a problem, sir. I'll be back whenever you need me."

Christian was brushing his teeth when he heard a knock. He assumed that Rachel or Pattie had forgotten something. When he walked back into his bedroom, his heart nearly stopped when he saw Sacha sitting at the edge of his bed.

"How the hell did you get in here? Who let you in?"

"I'm concerned about you, Chris," Sacha said, walking toward him.

"I'm fine, just leave, please . . . now! I won't tolerate this intrusion."

She snapped back, "I'm not leaving you!"

Christian walked up very close to her face, closing the gap between them. "With all due respect, Sacha, we're not in a relationship and I don't owe you an explanation. When I say I do not want your company, I mean it. Now get out!" Sacha stormed out of the room and closed the door.

About fifteen minutes later, Olivia walked up the stairs of the Cervello residence and by habit, went straight to the kitchen. She saw Sacha sitting there with her head in her hands. She dropped her purse on the table and pulled up a chair.

"Hey, I came as soon as I got your message," Olivia said. "What's going on?"

"How in the world did you get through that gate?"

Olivia shrugged. "I'm family, what can I say?"

Sacha rolled her eyes. "Okay, we know the note was really good but I'm afraid it backfired. He has totally shut down, Liv. It's been nearly a month, and she still has some kind of hold on him. Heck, he won't even return my calls or let me in."

"How *did* you get in?"

"I snuck in like a rat when the driver drove out."

"Oh, wow, so I guess it's true. Rachel just told me some minutes ago about how they suspect he's depressed." Olivia shrugged. "Well, if he is, why blame yourself? Perhaps he needs a shrink."

"Nah," Sacha said, shaking her head. "It's the plan, Liv, it backfired. He's in love with that girl and wants nothing to do with me."

Olivia stood up and walked to the fridge. "Well, don't blame me if you can't keep your man—I did my part. You gotta take control of the situation. Do I have to do everything for you guys? Nurse him back to health. You don't need me for this."

Sacha went to Olivia and grabbed her arm, pleading, "Actually I do need you, Liv. It's been too long. If I could do it, it would have been done by now. I need this man badly; I don't think you understand."

"Listen, I took the horse to the lake, Sach, I can't make it drink the water. Get creative."

"I know, but can you convince him that there is, in fact, a guy in her life, and they're going strong? At least so he can forget her for good."

Olivia placed her glass in the sink. "I'll see what I can cook up. Where is he now?"

"In his bedroom."

As Olivia made her way to Christian's room, she asked, "Is anyone else home?"

"I don't think so. Didn't you say they were in Italy?"

"Yeah, but they came back last night," Olivia said. "Oh shoot! They're probably at the hair salon already, they'll be heading to my place later."

Olivia walked into Christian's room and made a face. "Damn, it reeks in here."

Christian ignored Olivia and scowled at Sacha, who was cowering behind her. "I thought I told you I didn't want company."

"I'm sorry, Chris," Sacha stuttered. "I had to call someone."

Olivia opened up the blinds. "Oh, so now I'm company, Chris? Listen, I won't even take offense to that. I need you to get yourself together. We're all worried about you. I don't know what's going on, but you have a business to run and you, my friend, don't look like a CEO. You sure don't smell like one."

Sacha frowned. "Liv, that's unnecessary."

"Oh, cut it out. I'm just messing with him. Listen, I'll make him lunch. See to it he gets a shower."

"I'm sorry, Chris," Sacha pleaded.

Christian walked into the restroom without a word. Olivia had been there for him through thick and thin. Sometimes he felt like her surrogate father but this time around, he was grateful that she was the one looking out for him. He needed this sort of tough love to move forward.

Olivia got off the phone and turned to see Sacha standing at the kitchen entrance with a grin on her face.

"I don't know what or how you do it, but he's in the shower," Sacha said.

"Good."

"So, what are you cooking up?"

"Literally or figuratively?" Olivia smiled.

Sacha rubbed her hands together. "Oh, I'm scared."

"Don't be." Olivia sorted through dishes. "You said he was in the shower?"

"Yeah, why?"

"I gotta make sure." She headed off in the direction of Christian's room.

In a few minutes, Olivia was back in the kitchen, and Sacha took a seat. "Um, Liv, I've been meaning to ask you . . . Is Christian like . . . can he like . . . you know . . . perform?"

Olivia nearly dropped the dish in her hand. "*What? Who? Chris?* You gotta be out of your mind. That man has the sexual appetite of a horse." She laughed until she had to catch her breath.

Sacha frowned. "I don't see what's so funny about that. First off, I don't really think he is because I've seen how he gets around her but—"

"He's attracted to her, that's why." Olivia said. "Listen, Chris doesn't sleep around when he has someone of interest. He's gotta fall for you, Sach. Find a way to make that happen, no more excuses, and no more Olivia after today, you hear me?"

"I don't have that kind of patience."

Olivia shrugged. "Well, that's up to you. It's *your* problem."

"How come you know so much about his sexual appetite anyway?"

Olivia smiled. "I've got my sources."

"And a horse? You never cease to amaze me."

"Oh stop," Olivia dismissed. "I was speaking figuratively."

"Do you always have to do that? It's annoying. You and the damn horses."

"What? I've known the man for nearly my entire life and most of the girls he's ever been with came from me. And you know what, Sach, girls talk. So I know."

Sacha muttered something as she frantically looked through her purse. "I don't know—no one ever hears about *your* sex life so who knows? Maybe the horses do. As for your Christian, I've got something for him," Sacha dropped a pill into his glass.

Olivia frowned. "Hey, what's that? Don't tell me you . . . "

"He may be able to resist me but he can't possibly resist the power of this pill."

"Where did you get it from?"

"You've got your sources; I've got mine. I bought it from some dealer at the club that night. There are a couple of kinds in here. They use some for the chicks; I forgot which one he said could work on him the best—I have all night to try them all out."

"That's insane, Sacha. What if it messes him up?"

"Oh, just stop it. It won't. Men do it to women all the time." Sacha stirred the drink with a fork and then placed the glass next the plate of food Olivia dished out for Christian. Olivia shook her head and smiled.

A short while later, Christian walked into the kitchen and sat to eat Olivia's chicken alfredo.

"That was Rachel texting me," Olivia told Sacha. "They should be heading over to my place in a bit and it looks like Isa is still waiting on a ride—her Jeep is being serviced." Olivia kissed Christian on the cheek as he ate. "Gotta run."

"Thanks, Liv," he said.

"Anything for you, mi amor."

Nearly twenty minutes after Olivia left, Christian wrapped up his meal. As he washed out his dish, he could feel Sacha's burning gaze on him and was uncomfortable having her there.

"How do you feel?" she asked.

"Fine," he said, taking a last sip of his drink. Without another word, he headed to the fridge for a refill.

The doorbell rang.

"Can you get that?" he asked, pouring his drink.

"Um, I think you should—since it's your place, and all."

"It's probably Olivia—she just left."

Sacha cleared her throat. "Olivia texted me over fifteen minutes ago when she got to the salon. Besides, would Olivia ring the doorbell?"

"You're right." *Who could ring the doorbell without getting through the gate,* Genius pondered. Christian replied Genius, *Finally, something we both agree on.*

Christian was still processing how someone could get through the gate without being let in when he opened the door to a man about his height.

"Hello, I'm here to pick up Isabella," the man announced. At least he was polite.

Upon hearing the distinctive voice and accent, Christian frowned. "I remember you."

"Oh yeah, you're her brother. I'm sorry. My name is Antonio." He extended his hand.

Christian looked down at his hand but did not accept it.

"Oh, it looks like she already got a ride from a friend." His voice was shaky as he looked through his phone. "I'm sorry for the mix-up; I'll be on my way."

Antonio hurried into a white convertible Jaguar.

You're shutting down, get to your room now, Genius said. His body froze as he watched Antonio's convertible roof come down. *The nerve—her brother? He knows darn well I'm not her brother.*

"Who was it?" Sacha asked, running down the stairs.

"No one of significance." He went up to his bedroom and was about to close the door when Sacha held it open. He went straight to his surveillance screen, only to find that the gate surveillance was disabled. He must have mistakenly shut it off when he ignored Sacha at the gate.

He became dizzy, and his knees went weak as sweat trickled down his temples and palms. When he became nauseated, he ran to the bathroom and splashed cold water on his face. He looked into the mirror, but his vision was blurry. He panted, and his hands shook uncontrollably as he shut off the faucet. *It must be the food,* he thought. *You have no allergies,* he heard Genius say. He closed his eyes and saw Isabella's hair caught in the wind from Antonio's open convertible roof. He could even hear her laughter and music. *Pull yourself together, Chris,* Genius said. *The music is coming from your bedroom.*

He hopped into the shower, and as the cold water came over him, he heard David's warning about Sacha. Her type was capable of framing a man, so he stayed put, hoping that she wasn't crazy enough to break down his door. He hated how he had let this go on for this long. The lack of boundaries in his life and home was embarrassing. No matter how many times he'd asked Sacha to leave, she found her way back, and no matter how many times he changed the security code, he still had intruders.

Christian heard banging on the door. It was so loud that he thought either he was delusional or Sacha was insane.

"If you don't open this door, I'll kick it down," Sacha screamed. "And you know I'll do it because your mom and sister aren't home!"

Christian never felt more helpless when it came to his safety. He considered escaping but there was only one way out of his restroom—unless he considered the window and from her persistent rant, the window was beginning to look quite welcoming. If only he had his phone, he would call the police.

The banging stopped. He took deep breaths with his eyes closed, only to open them back up to the sound of Sacha attempting to pry open the door with an instrument.

With his hair and body still dripping, Christian donned his robe and opened the door. "Have you lost your mind?" he yelled, hardly making out her image.

"Oh baby, I get worried about you when you lock yourself in the bathroom like that."

"Like what? What can I possibly do to harm myself in my own bathroom and why would I?"

She tugged at his robe—he held on tight to it. "You need to leave my house, Sacha. I won't say it again!" he screamed. "I need my privacy, for goodness sake!"

"Nope, I'm not leaving. Look at you." She grabbed his hand, pulling him to the mirror.

"Look at yourself, Chris!" she yelled. "Look what she's done to you. You haven't shaved in ages, your eyes are bloodshot, you've lost weight, and now it looks like you've gone paranoid. How can I possibly leave you like this—and you think I'm the one hurting you? No, it's that girl."

Christian looked into the mirror. It was no use.

"She doesn't deserve you. I'm not saying that I do, but I've been here for you through so much of her drama. You just have to learn to love the one you're with, Chris."

When Sacha cradled his face in her hands, he felt himself go in and out of consciousness.

"Stop fighting it, Chris," she said. "I know you want me. Be free."

She took him by the hand and walked him to the bed.

Just before Olivia drifted off to sleep, her phone rang.

"Hey Liv," Sacha greeted.

"Hey, sex kitten, how did it go?"

"You were right."

"I usually am, but what about?"

"Oh, Liv, that man is a monster. You should have seen him. He had no idea what hit him; it was scary. I thought I'd have to do all the work, but he was half there and half dead."

"That's creepy."

"His body was alive, but he was a mental vegetable, but it didn't stop him from reaching for his protection. Like a part of his brain was thinking through stuff. Seriously, he was talking to himself—at one point he yelled, 'I will, damn it!' but when I spoke to him, it was like I wasn't there. As long as I had him, who cares if he spoke to me. I'm such an idiot because I have no idea which one I put in his drink."

"That's deceptive, Sacha."

"Wait, isn't that your middle name?"

Olivia giggled. "Where's he now?"

"Sleeping like a baby."

"And you?"

"In the kitchen."

"So I guess they're not back yet."

"Nope, he said they're coming home late, and I'm glad, because I can't stand them."

"Hey, hey . . . that's my family you're talking about. Well, I'm going to bed. I'm glad you got what you wanted, but I'm just curious about something, Sach."

"What?"

"This can't be all you want, is it? I mean, it's gotta be more than just landing the guy in bed."

"What do you mean?"

"Well, let's put it this way. Some people work for a living, and some, if they are wise enough, can make little Cervellos work for them."

"Huh? There you go again with your metaphors."

"No metaphors, dear. I'm hoping that the seeds I'm planting right now are falling on fertile ground."

"Wait . . . Ahh."

"Aha."

"Oh, Olivia, I never thought about that!"

"Shh, you're gonna wake him up."

"Oh, my, why didn't you . . . "

"Now get going. You've got all night."

"But how, he wouldn't touch me without protection."

"Get creative."

Christian opened his eyes just as Sacha climbed on top of him. Seeing her naked was confirmation that something had, in fact, happened. He still had no idea what came over him. It all happened so fast and now he had a splitting headache.

"Hey, sunshine," Sacha said, interrupting his thoughts. "Thanks for last night. It was explosive."

"I'm sorry, Sacha, I don't know what got over me and I can't remember anything."

"Oh, don't apologize for anything; it was meant to be and you, my stallion, were superb." She rolled her hips over his. "I want another round of that."

"I can't, I'm sleepy—maybe later."

CHAPTER FOURTEEN

Temptation

❦

AS CHRISTIAN prepared to shave for the first time in three weeks, Sacha mapped out their day. Up until his three-week downward spiral, he had her to thank for his fixation on tennis and cycling and today she promised he would find new things to preoccupy himself with. In just one night, he'd developed a soft spot for her, and it had seemed he had jumped to conclusions about her. Besides, she was hard to get rid of and perhaps for a good reason. She was there for him both times something concerning Isabella had gotten him down.

She was right about one thing—Isabella didn't want him and had made it very clear in her note. If only he hadn't heard that little detail about Antonio at the club; he just didn't seem right for Isabella, but then again, he didn't really know her so perhaps he was exactly her type. Perhaps he had misjudged him as he had Sacha and Isabella. He seemed to be doing a lot of that lately. If he had known Isabella was that easy, he wouldn't have made Olivia feel so bad about making such connections—she could use the million. *This is what you wanted*, Genius reminded. Christian agreed. He couldn't blame Isabella or Antonio. *He* pushed Isabella away.

Sacha had assured him that he appeared more relaxed this morning, but he'd really been fighting with inner demons since their night together. For one, he faced intense guilt for going against his promise on celibacy, but what was more troubling was the fact that he craved to be with her again—at least to know what it was like. His Mind had been telling him it wouldn't hurt since he'd already broken his vow, and he decided that he would go ahead with it.

"*Hey,*" he said, stroking the back of her cropped hair.

"Mmm, that feels good, don't stop," she said, her eyes closed.

"Have you ever considered growing it out?"

"It's grown since I met you, didn't you notice? Olivia told me you like long hair."

"Is that why you're growing it out?"

"Yup."

"Don't do that. Anyway, it suits you short."

Sacha opened her eyes. "You think so?"

"I can't imagine it any different."

"Wanna see a picture of me with longer hair? I'm naturally brunette."

"No way."

"I'll show you," she said, going through her tablet.

He took it from her and placed it on the desk. "Perhaps later."

"Look at that—you want me. That's a first. Weren't you gonna shave?"

"It can wait." He started to pick her up.

"Give me a minute, I'm thirsty."

"Can't it wait?" he grumbled, nibbling on her neck.

"No, silly, you want anything?"

"No." Sacha started toward the door in her underwear. "Hey! You do realize I don't live alone, right?"

"Duh."

"Well, do you mind?" he said, stepping into the restroom.

Out in the kitchen, Rachel and Isabella were busy at the kitchen table as Pattie made breakfast.

"You should at least stay for breakfast, Nena," Pattie urged.

"Yeah, Isa, your meeting doesn't start for another couple of hours."

"Okay, but I still have to leave early to set up," Isabella said, placing the projector on the floor.

Between pancakes, Pattie glanced at Isabella's PowerPoint slides. "How many are you expecting?"

"About fifteen," Isabella said. "Um . . . have you guys heard from Chris?" The words came out of her mouth before she knew it, and once they did, she avoided eye contact.

"Yeah, we finally spoke to him yesterday," Rachel said.

"Oh nice, when is he coming back to Florida?"

Pattie frowned. "Coming *back*?" she asked, looking at an equally puzzled Rachel.

Before anyone could reply, the infamous blonde strolled into the kitchen wearing a large T-shirt. Isabella guessed she probably resided with them because it was the only explanation for her strolling into the kitchen so casually with barely any clothes on. Isabella shifted uncomfortably in her seat as she became nauseated from recognizing the shirt she'd given Christian on his birthday. She couldn't mistake the contempt she saw in her blue eyes when their eyes met.

Offering a blanket "Hey," she headed straight for the fridge.

"*Hey?*" Rachel asked in disbelief.

Ignoring Rachel, she grabbed the orange juice.

"And who are you, young lady?" Pattie asked calmly.

"Yeah, please tell us," Rachel said. "Since you lack the decency to introduce yourself to my mother."

"You again?" the blonde replied. "Just leave me the hell alone!"

"I thought Chris was still out of the country," Isabella muttered, but no one seemed to be listening.

Rachel stood up, scowling at the blonde, as though daring her to speak, and without breaking her stare, she said, "Isabella, love, I think you need to get going, things are about to get fiery."

"Yeah, I think I should," Isabella said, packing up the projector and heading downstairs.

"Christian!" Pattie screamed.

Christian arrived at the kitchen entrance. "Where is she? I can smell her." He sniffed as he looked around the hallway and family room. "Is she hiding? Isabella!" he cried. "Now if only I could follow that trail."

The women stared in amazement.

"Christian!"

"Ma?"

"Get in here!"

He strolled up to his mother and planted a kiss on her cheek. "Hey, Ma."

"What's wrong with you?" Pattie asked. "And who is this young lady that came barging into my kitchen half-naked—forget about introducing herself."

Christian turned to her. "I thought I told you to put on some clothes, Sacha."

"Ah, she has a name!" Rachel screamed.

"I did put on something!" Sacha yelled, tugging at the shirt. "You know what"—she slammed the open juice bottle on the table, sending a big splash all over—"forget the stupid juice!"

"Ahh . . . feisty one, huh?" Rachel teased, catching up with Sacha in the hallway. "You better come back here and clean up your mess!"

Christian stood between them, holding Rachel back.

Pattie confronted Sacha. "Please leave our home; you're not welcome here."

Sacha stormed downstairs. Christian followed her. When he cradled her face, he noticed she was breathing fast. "Listen, I'm sorry about this. Wait for me at the hotel. I'll get your stuff and meet you there."

She nodded.

"Where are the clothes you had on from yesterday?"

"They're somewhere in the room . . . please grab my phone under the pillow."

He returned with her phone and a pair of shorts and waited as she slipped into them before escorting her to Julio's waiting car. "Are you both ready?" Julio asked.

"I'm afraid not, change of plans. Could you please take her to the Westin Hotel at Coral Gables?"

"Not a problem, sir," Julio replied.

Turning to Sacha, he handed a black card to her. "Take this in case you need anything. Wait for me there; don't leave. Julio will make sure you get a room under my name. I'll be there soon."

When he got back into the house, he went right into the kitchen. "I'm very sorry, Mom."

"My goodness, Christian, your choice of women confounds me!" Pattie yelled.

Christian walked away without a word.

"He's never been disrespectful to me, but when it comes to women, he loses his head."

"You know what, Mom, I think the way you handled his breakup with Kathy drove him to this."

"The way I handled his breakup?"

"Yes you, can't you just talk to him about being careful and let go of the criticism? Remember how you took the news? You drove him over the edge, and now this happens over and over again."

Overhearing the end of Rachel's statement, Christian returned. "What, are you jealous?"

"Jealous?" Rachel scoffed. "Give me a break. Let me remind you that I'm engaged to be married."

"Oh, that's nice; throw it in my face."

"Stop it, both of you!" Pattie yelled.

"You need help!" Rachel screamed at Christian.

"And you need to mind your business, Rachel, you're far from perfect."

"I said stop it!" Pattie said. "Chris, your sister was actually supporting you—you heard her all wrong."

"I'll be out of the house by the end of the day," Christian muttered.

Rachel broke down.

"And where are you gonna go?" Pattie asked Christian.

"Ocean Drive. It's about time. It's best for all of us."

"Chris, this is totally unnecessary," Pattie replied.

"Is it?"

Rachel ran out of the kitchen, sobbing. Christian walked out, while Pattie turned off the stove and threw the pancakes in the trash.

Christian fumed in his room. He felt like a stranger—misunderstood lately by everyone but Sacha, it seemed. He didn't want to remain there for another minute, so he decided to freshen up in the hotel. There was nothing keeping him at the house—nothing left to protect. Rachel obviously didn't need him, now that she had Thomas. Isabella was history, so was his vow. Leaving was good because there were too many reminders of Isabella. She would always be part of Casa Cervello.

He packed a small bag for himself. As he slipped Sacha's tablet into its case, a small plastic bag fell out. It contained pills of different colors; some were small, round and white, others were greenish-gray and a few were multi-toned—orange and red and white and blue. Concluding they were just vitamins, he placed the bag in his pocket and headed for the hotel. *You should check what those are*, Genius said, breaking the silence in his head as he drove. "No, I refuse to be paranoid!" Christian said to himself aloud.

Christian walked up to the attendant at the hotel lobby and flashed a special card.

The attendant appeared skeptical. "Mr. Cervello?"

"Somewhere under all this," Christian said, pointing to his face. "Need ID?"

The man shook his head and provided him with a room key.

When Christian turned to leave, he chuckled. *It can't be.* Her back was to him, and she appeared to be looking for someone. Christian snuck up behind her. "Boo! Looking for him?"

Isabella clutched her chest. "Ugh, don't do that. You scared me. Goodness, Christian! I almost didn't recognize you. When did you get back?"

With a half-smile, Christian leaned toward her and sniffed her hair. "Hmm, ahh . . . you were in our house earlier, weren't you?"

She raised an inquisitive brow. "Yes . . . "

"I knew it!"

"Is that a problem again? I thought we—"

"Oh, no, I just knew I wasn't going crazy. So, where is he?" he asked, looking around.

"Who?" She followed his stare.

"Your lover."

"Excuse me?"

"You know, I never saw you as the type to meet up with strange men at a hotel . . . maybe your comfy place, but a *hotel*?"

"Okay, now you're really starting to scare me."

"Scare you?" Christian scoffed. "So you're gonna pretend like you don't know what I'm talking about? What, did he break your little heart already?"

A woman approached Isabella. "Ah . . . there you are! Excuse me, Ms. Montes; the boardroom is now ready. Thanks for your patience."

"You're most welcome, thank you," Isabella replied.

Christian rubbed his face, embarrassed, as the woman walked away. "Meeting, huh?"

"Yeah," Isabella said. "Our boardroom had some water damage from that storm three weeks ago, and it's taking the building management forever to fix it."

"That must suck."

"Yeah, it's an old building. Our lease is up by the end of the year and, we don't plan on renewing it."

"I don't blame you."

"I was over earlier to borrow Rachel's projector, but it looks like they've got everything here."

He smiled. "I could have told you that."

"And here I was thinking I was just booking a room with chairs and a screen."

"Listen, Isabella, I'm sorry for—"

"Are you okay, Chris?"

He looked away.

"Because your family is concerned about you."

"I know."

"And so am I. I'm here if you need to talk about it, but I must go now—the meeting starts in a bit."

Christian nodded and watched as she disappeared into the crowd of shuttle passengers who appeared to have gathered in the lobby for a city tour. He started to make his way to the elevator when he spotted someone who resembled Sacha at the lower rotunda. He looked closer and saw that it was, in fact, her and that she chatted with a man at The 1862 Room restaurant. She giggled and tugged at the man as one would a friend. She then whispered into his ear and walked out to the corner. Christian hid further and saw her pull out her phone from her pocket.

In seconds, his phone rang.

"Hey, sexy," Sacha crooned.

"Hey."

"Are you still home?"

"Yup."

"Okay. How long do you think it'll take you to get here?"

"About an hour. Is that okay? I was hoping to speak to my mother after that episode."

"Of course. I actually just bumped into an old friend, so take your time. Can you just text me before you leave? I wanna be ready for you."

"Sure."

Sacha walked back into the restaurant. She whispered into the man's ear again, and they kissed.

Christian quickly headed for the elevator, and once in his room, he sat on a sofa directly facing the door. *Any moment now,* he said to himself, shaking his crossed leg. In a matter of minutes, the key unlocked. The doorknob turned amid the sound of heavy panting. With her back to Christian, Sacha made her way into the room. Her male companion made eye contact with Christian and froze. Sacha turned around slowly.

"What's going on here?" the man asked, keeping his gaze on a paper-white Sacha.

"That's what I wanna know," Christian said with a side smile.

Facing the man, Sacha stuttered. "I'm so sorry. This is my boyfriend."

Christian got up and walked toward them. "Come on in—make yourselves comfortable."

"No, I'll be on my way out." The man stammered as he shook his head. "So sorry, man, I had no idea."

"Come on . . . I'm not her boyfriend, but it seems that she must have mixed up her busy schedule."

Sacha bowed her head as Christian approached her. "My card, please."

She handed him the black card.

"This room is booked in my name," Christian said to the man. "I should go downstairs and check out, but for your trouble, I'll see to it that they give you at least an hour. That was the amount of time she allotted for you—anticipating my arrival, of course."

Christian turned to Sacha and asked, "Is an hour enough or should I extend it to two?"

Sacha remained silent. Christian spoke into her ear. "And to think I was starting to fall for you."

Christian fought the temptation to get into his car and head back home to pack for his condo move, but he figured the least he could have at the hotel was peace of mind, especially since Sacha was gone for good. Seeing Isabella at the hotel kept him sane. Somehow she lifted his spirits and appeased Genius. Something about her helped him move on even if she was the one who got him down in the first place. He was addicted to her presence and was now coming to the realization that it was her absence that made him depressed for three weeks. She wasn't good for him, yet he needed her in order to get better.

In his new room, he finally had the chance to shower and shave. He also spoke to a frantic Olivia, who had called on Sacha's behalf. He warned Olivia to keep Sacha away or have her face legal consequences, but agreed to a visit from Olivia, who sounded genuinely sorry. As he waited for room service to deliver his meal, he read the book he borrowed from Isabella until his phone rang.

"Well if it isn't London's finest groom-to-be."

David laughed. "Hey, how did you know it was me?"

"You're the only one that calls me from weird numbers. What's up?"

"No, *you* tell me what's up. I've been worried about you."

"It's been hard, Dave. You're so far away, and I could really use a friend in this town."

"Well, that's gonna change real soon."

"Why, you visiting?"

"Nope—moving."

"Get out! Florida?"

"Miami, baby!"

"Wait . . . what? How about Dee? Her residency program."

"Well, remember how you convinced her to apply to University of Miami's medical school program?"

"I didn't think she took me seriously."

"That's just it. She figured she had nothing to lose and boom! Miller School of Medicine has this global observership program. Man, I gotta tell you, it's gotta be a God setup because back then we didn't know you would relocate to Florida."

"Neither did I!"

"Wait, but that's not why we are moving—check this out. Just when I was wrapping up my last contract, an external position came up in your Florida office for a senior project manager for the engineering department. I called you a week ago to tell you I was in town for the interview, but I couldn't get through."

"Come on, Dave, you know you don't need to go through human resources to get a job."

"I know, but I rather do it the right way. They're working with immigration now."

"I can't believe I missed all this. This is insane."

"I know." David's tone grew somber. "That's why I'm so worried. Does this have to do with the women?"

"You were right about Sacha—so much for company."

"I still don't understand. If you just wanted company, why not hang out with your sister?"

"Well, for one, she's all about Thomas—they are engaged now. Then if it isn't him, it's Isabella. I'm still trying my hardest to get her out of my system."

"Why? Why don't you just tell her how you feel?"

"It's too late. She's seeing someone now. Listen, Olivia's connections haven't gotten me far over the years. The actual relationships I've ever been in were with women I met myself, so I'm done with her setups."

"Hallelujah!"

Christian laughed. "I was thinking, maybe Denise can introduce me to someone nice, like herself?" Lightning couldn't possibly strike twice. What were the chances he would find another Denise Baruti? The black South African beauty was literally a former beauty pageant turned aspiring doctor. "Okay, I'm not being picky—they don't have to be . . . "

"Listen, Chris, if I didn't think you and Isabella had potential, trust me, I would have introduced you to someone. Denise has a ton of lovely single friends."

"Okay, then . . . what are we waiting for?"

"But Isabella—"

"Stop it, I told you she is taken."

"That's what you told yourself. I don't know the girl, but there's something about her that brings out this side of you that feels like, I don't know. I never saw you this way with Kathy. You usually have this confidence with women but with Isabella, she just has this hold over you."

"She drives me insane."

"See? No one's ever driven you insane but yourself. That's how I know it's real. She's got you . . . "

"Humbled?"

"Exactly. Listen, I gotta go. Denise is waiting."

"Okay, say hey to her and take it easy. And thanks for calling, I needed that boost."

"Sure, one more thing, be careful with strange women, they see you for what you are—a CEO."

"Why, thanks Dave."

"Be careful, Christian, I mean it. Guard your home and your heart."

"I will."

There was a knock on the door. Finally, room service with his food. He was starved. Christian opened the door. It must have been a dream. *No, it can't be her,* he thought, *she had on something else earlier.* A beautiful brunette stood at the door dressed in a short, beige skirt and a green, long-sleeved blouse. Her dark brown hair went down to her back, and her big, brown eyes held him captive. Her resemblance to Isabella was striking, right down to their height. She smelled good—perfume—but it was still good.

"Hello," she greeted with a captivating smile.

"Hey," Christian replied. For whatever reason, she made him nervous.

"Um, Olivia sent me."

"Olivia?"

"Our mutual friend."

"Oh yeah, Liv," Chris said, extending his hand. "I'm Chris." How else would she have known his room number if it wasn't for Liv. She looked smitten, yet she maintained solid eye contact as she took his hand.

"Hello, Chris," she said. Isabella would have looked away—she wasn't as bold.

"Come in, have a seat." Christian said. *Why in the world would you do that?* Genius asked.

She looked around the room, apparently impressed.

"Would you like a drink?" he asked.

"Yes, thank you. What do you have?"

Good question, Christian mumbled as he headed to the bar. "Chardonnay?" She nodded. He handed her a glass and took his seat across from her.

"Don't you drink?" she asked.

Christian smiled. "No."

"So, you're just gonna watch me?"

"Well, I actually have a drink right here."

She laughed. "Perrier?"

"Is something wrong with it?"

"No, you just don't look like . . . " she stopped.

"Like what?" Christian asked, puzzled.

"A man who doesn't drink."

Christian's puzzled look turned into a smile. "What does a guy who doesn't drink look like? Or should I say, what do I look like?"

"A bad boy." She placed her glass down and unbuttoned her blouse—maintaining solid eye contact.

Christian held up both his hands in the air and exclaimed, "Whoa, whoa, whoa."

She lifted a brow. "What?"

"I don't even know your name."

"My name is Rana."

Christian's brows creased as he nodded slowly. "Rana."

"What?"

He cocked his head to the side. "You don't look like a *Rana*."

"What do I look like?"

"An *Isabella*. Can I call you that?" If she were less aggressive with lighter hair, she'd be her.

She smiled. "Hmm, you role play—I like. Call me whatever you want, honey. I'll be your *Isabella*."

He watched her undress fully and stand before him, but he didn't expect her next move toward him.

"Hold up," he said, reaching into his bag. "I've got something for you."

Rana grinned. "What's that?"

He waved a flat case in the air. "Guess."

"Candy?"

"Well, you can call it that too, no wrong answers."

He handed the case to her. Upon opening it, she frowned. "These are condoms."

"Ah."

She handed the case back to him. "I don't use these."

What did David tell you? Genius asked. *I've got this,* Christian replied to Genius.

"Um okay . . . what *do* you use?"

"Birth control pills."

"That's nice, but the pill doesn't protect you, and you don't even know me."

"Well, I'm clean and I'm sure you are too because I trust Olivia's connections."

"Connections? Didn't you say you were her friend?"

"Well, we *are* friendly."

"Okay . . . um, you know what . . . " he said, picking up pieces of her clothing from the floor and handing them to her. "Here's what's going to happen. You're going to go back to Olivia, and I guess she's paying you, so I want you to request full price, but nothing will be happening between us, okay?"

Rana rolled her eyes. "Okay, okay . . . I'll use it. She did say you were a tough one."

Christian shook his head. "Don't worry, sweetie. Just take your time and dress—no rush. Can I just ask . . . what is it you actually do?"

"If I tell you, you'll have to sleep with me."

"Okay, I'm not that curious."

Moving into his Ocean Drive condo early didn't seem like such a bad idea, after all, since it was clear he wasn't going to get peace of mind at the hotel.

"Would you like another room, sir?" the attendant asked.

Christian shook his head. "Oh, please, no. Just close out all rooms under my name and put it on my tab."

"Have a good day, sir."

As he headed for the exit, his phone rang.

"Well if it isn't Florida's finest madam."

"Rana just told me what happened," Olivia said. "She's hysterical—said you embarrassed her."

"Where do you get these women from?"

"Don't worry about that!"

"Don't? For one, a girl I've never met in my life stripped naked in front of me and wanted unprotected sex. Doesn't that disturb you?"

Olivia sighed. "Oh yeah, about that—I'm sorry. She's a nymph with little reason."

Christian laughed. "Listen to yourself. She said you were friends."

"But in her defense, she did say she offered to wear something later."

"Are these hookers, Liv?"

"I told you to let it go, Chris; stop being nosey! You had a good time with Sacha, didn't you?"

Christian scoffed. "I'm sure the other guy could say the same."

"Listen, I told you Sacha really likes you, but she's had it with Rachel. She's really kicking herself for what she did to you."

"She can join a growing list."

"Stop being so cynical, Christian; learn to forgive."

"Listen Olivia, I already warned you about Sacha over the phone. Now I'll say this just once. Don't you ever send any more women my way. I'm no piece of meat."

Olivia laughed. "Who said you were?"

"Then why did you send Isabella?" Christian snapped.

"Who?"

Christian stuttered. "I mean the last girl, what's her name again?"

"Rana; she was my gift to you to make up for Sacha."

"Gift?" Christian scoffed. "I told you I just wanted company and all these girls want something more. Well, you know what, I don't need the company anymore. I'm fine by myself, thank you." God forbid he told Olivia he was moving into the Ocean Drive building; she would probably make the entire building a brothel, knowing he was her neighbor.

"Come on, you don't mean that," Olivia said. "You never seemed to mind in the past, you and Kevin."

"I told you I've changed. Please respect that and stop with the temptations. Lord knows I don't need it. Besides, those girls you introduced to Kevin and me over the years were supposed to be your friends."

"They were!"

"Then why do I get a sense you're actually doing this for a living? What's so hard to understand when I say I'm not looking for a sexual relationship?"

"Because I know you, Chris. See what happened with Sacha? You couldn't resist in the end."

"Stop it, just stop!" Christian hated that he was causing a scene at the hotel lobby. They probably were afraid to warn him about it, as their valued customer, so he lowered his tone. "You know nothing about me now. My peers are settling down, and I want more for myself."

"But Chris—"

"I'm serious, Liv. If you send anyone my way or if I see anyone on my property, I'll have them arrested."

"Calm down, you're overreacting."

"I'm done; have a great day, Olivia."

Christian hung up. *A gift,* he scoffed again. *You did well,* Genius said. This shocked Christian.

He recalled Isabella's last words to him: "Your family is concerned about you and so am I." He scoffed again. *Women*. At that moment, an epiphany had him hurrying back to the front desk.

"Hello again, Mr. Cervello, did you forget something?"

"Yes," Christian panted. "I forgot something in that room."

"Not a problem, sir. You had two rooms; do you remember which one it might be in?"

"Um, I believe it was the second. Yes, the second, for sure."

"Fine. Give me a moment, sir. Okay, here you go." The man handed Christian the card.

"Oh, and can the valet have my car ready?"

"Yes, sir."

"Thanks." When Christian got back into the room, he was glad to see that the Isabella lookalike had left. He figured they missed each other in separate elevators because he hadn't seen her while he was in the lobby. He grabbed the book from the recliner and immediately turned to the back of the front cover that read:

If found, please return to Isabella Montes
at Faith House Church Lost and Found Dept.

His heart raced, and his fingers trembled slightly as he pulled out her note from the middle of the book. He closed his eyes and breathed in deeply, counting backward from five to one. He then compared the two hand-writings side by side. The writing in the note looked closer to print with the lettering clean and straight, whereas the message in the book had more of a cursive look to it with a slant. Genius was right. He reached for his phone and dialed Julio.

A few moments later, Julio arrived at the lobby and approached a pacing Christian.

"You wanted to see me, sir," Julio greeted.

"Do you remember the note you gave me from Ms. Montes?"

Julio frowned. "Um . . . no sir. You mean the note *you* gave me to give her."

Christian felt blood drain from his face as he handed the note to Julio in what felt like slow motion. Julio appeared hesitant to take it.

Julio read the note. "Who gave this to you?"

"You. Well, Sacha said you gave it to her to give to me. It's been three weeks."

"That's not true, sir. You can ask Ms. Montes herself. I never even expected a reply from her. I didn't give that lady anything to give to you."

"Oh my . . . " Christian muttered, running his fingers through his hair and pacing around Julio.

"The blonde must have written that. You got it the same day you wrote to Ms. Montes?"

Christian nodded slowly.

"Strange coincidence, huh?"

Sacha must have known about his note somehow. "I'll get to the bottom of this. Thanks, Julio."

"Do you need a ride, sir?"

"No, thanks, I have my car with me, and I won't need any services for the rest of the day."

"Okay, sir."

"Hey, Julio! Didn't you say your wife was a florist?"

"Yes, sir."

"How soon do you think she can arrange for three dozen of those flowers I showed you?"

"You mean the orchids?"

"Yeah."

"I'll give her a call. Where do you want them delivered?"

"To her office—Ms. Montes—anonymously please."

CHAPTER FIFTEEN

Second Chances

❦

THE GROWING tension at Casa Cervello had Rachel wishing she were still in Italy. With all that was going on, she hadn't had the opportunity to bask in the beauty of her engagement to Thomas. The drama seemed to stem from Christian's relationships. She wondered if she would ever get along with anyone he was with. She hadn't spoken to Pattie since the breakfast blowup, and Christian was probably settling into his Ocean Drive pad. She distinctively remembered the three of them promising each other months earlier never to let anyone come between them. Yet here they were, not speaking, and there lied the problem—Blondie. For someone whose name she just got to know—and forget—she sure was causing a lot of trouble.

Just when Rachel had found a way to get Isabella back in the house, Christian had given her another reason to run. For sure, his feelings for Isabella had to figure into all this. Rachel was determined to get to the bottom of it today. She refused to let her sixteen-year relationship with Isabella fizzle.

Later that afternoon, when Rachel's call to Isabella went straight to voicemail, she headed to her workplace. Upon arriving, Isabella's assistant informed her that she might catch her in the parking lot—having just left minutes earlier. Rachel ran out to find Isabella's Jeep exiting the premises and her attempts to flag her down went unnoticed. *That's it Isa; you leave me no other choice.* She turned the key in her ignition and followed Isabella close enough not to lose her but far enough not to draw her suspicion. Two minutes into the drive, she realized that Isabella was not going home—having passed her exit. She continued for another five minutes until Isabella pulled into a single office building. *What the . . .* she muttered, squinting at the overhead sign. Tears crept up as she watched her friend park and walk through the door. As soon as Isabella was out of sight, Rachel wept aloud in her car.

She tried to convince herself that Isabella could have gone to a therapist's office to discuss financial accounts, but something told her it was worse. They had gone through so much together, but now Isabella was so far away. Rachel cried for nearly the entire hour and as soon as she saw Isabella walk out, she exited the car and ran to her, yelling out her name.

"What are you doing here?" Isabella said, frowning and looking around.

A red-eyed Rachel blurted out, "Busted! So this is it?" she asked, pointing at the building.

"This is nothing," Isabella dismissed.

"I don't know, please tell me what I'm doing wrong. First, it's Chris . . . now you. My goodness, two of the most important people in my life weren't even there for my engagement. I've lost you both, and it hurts."

"Who told you I was here?"

Rachel sniffed. "I followed you. Tracy said you had just left. I tried to wave you down but—"

"Stalker!" Isabella smiled. "I should have you arrested."

Rachel smiled through her tears, whispering, "What are you doing seeing a shrink, Isa?"

"You see? This is exactly why I didn't tell you. I knew you'd panic."

"Of course, I'd panic! You must have no one to talk to, to resort to this. What happened to us? We told each other everything."

"I've just been down lately. My family hasn't been much help—talking to them is pointless. Their response to everything is *come home and marry*— as if they're giving away free men over there. So yeah, I've missed having someone to talk to."

"How about me? I was only in Italy for two weeks, and I even called you from there."

"I know, hon. It's just that you haven't exactly been as accessible as you used to be, and of course, it's understandable. I mean, we knew it would happen eventually, right? It's life."

"Let me make it up to you. Anything but this, please."

"This?" Isabella laughed. "This is nothing to be ashamed of. My mental health is important. I have a young business to grow. I need peace of mind to run it effectively, and my therapist is very good."

"If you say so." Rachel rolled her eyes, smiling. Her nerves multiplied, but as she promised herself she would, she ventured on. "Um, I have a question. I think I already know the answer, but I don't wanna assume."

"Okay," Isabella said. It sounded more like a question and her countenance seemed slightly defensive.

"I don't wanna make you uncomfortable. I'm already uncomfortable, so to make it easy for both of us, just answer yes or no to the question and then an okay if you understand. Is that all right?"

"Sure," Isabella sighed.

"What you haven't told me . . . does it have to do with a guy you're interested in?"

Isabella looked away and folded her arms. "Yeah."

Thanks to Christian, Rachel knew a thing or two about body language. Isabella had already answered the questions she was yet to ask, without her knowing it. Nevertheless, she continued. "If this guy is my brother, I want you to know that I'm okay with it, and you have my blessings, okay?"

Isabella was silent.

"I'm not asking for a confession, Isa. Just say 'okay' if you understand me."

"Okay."

"Good." When Rachel embraced Isabella, she noticed that she let out a deep sigh, and she hoped it was one of relief and not irritation. She couldn't imagine what it must have felt like to be in Isabella's shoes. How exactly would she have reacted if Isabella had a brother she was interested in? Would she take the humble road or just shove it in her face and tell her to deal with it? The way Isabella had handled the situation was confirmation to Rachel that she would make an honorable sister-in-law if it ever came to that.

Following their embrace, there was an awkward silence. She watched as Isabella fidgeted with her car keys and smiled as she imagined Isabella as her sister-in-law—a Cervello.

Isabella was grateful when her phone rang. Her assistant, Tracy, informed her that dozens of orchids were delivered to the office and wasn't sure if she wanted them sent to her home since she'd left for the weekend.

"I'm on my way," Isabella said.

"Is everything okay?" Rachel asked.

"I guess. That was Tracy. You didn't happen to . . . Nah. I gotta head back to the office."

"Call me?" Rachel asked.

"I promise," Isabella said, squeezing her hand.

Late that evening, Christian spotted Rachel and his mother in the flower garden as he pulled up front. "Hey, guys," he said, walking up to them.

Pattie nodded while Rachel said, "Hey," without looking up.

"I was wondering if I could speak to both of you. Do you have a minute?"

Rachel and Pattie looked at each other.

"Perhaps we could talk here," Pattie said. "We're gonna be out here for a while."

Christian nodded. "Mom, words can't express how very sorry I am for disrespecting you in your home." He turned to Rachel. "I'm especially sorry for how I've treated you, Rach. I know you love me, and I'm sorry that I hurt you for so long. Things aren't the same without you in my life as my friend first."

They remained silent as Christian continued.

"I wasn't willing to listen to what anyone had to say but I can tell you now that I've been depressed for the past month. Yes, even before you traveled to Italy. I was afraid to admit it, but I'm no longer in denial. I'm asking you to consider forgiving me. It would help me to move on."

Christian began to walk away when Rachel reached out and pulled him close, weeping into his chest. Pattie joined in on the embrace. Rachel pulled away and wiped her eyes with the back of her hand. "I forgive you. We had a feeling you were depressed, but we didn't wanna push it. I'm glad that you've come clean."

Pattie spoke, "Honey, I forgive you too, but we're not the only ones you owe an apology to."

"Yeah," Rachel added. "You already know you owe Isa an apology for the way you've treated her."

Christian nodded. "I don't even know where to start with that."

Pattie and Rachel exchanged a look, and Rachel frowned and shook her head swiftly.

"Why don't you start by telling us what's going on between the two of you," Pattie sounded careful. "I mean, it's intense watching the both of you together."

Christian ran his fingers through his hair as Pattie continued. "At first, it was cute and all, but then everything went terribly wrong, and it all seemed to happen around the time that other girl started coming here. At least that's what Rachel says, because I was away at the time, but hon, please tell us how you feel—don't fight this alone. What's going on? Do you have feelings for Isa?"

Christian sighed. "Yes."

Rachel exclaimed. "I knew it! Mom, didn't I . . . wait, why haven't you said anything?"

"Well, I didn't wanna mess things up for the two of you. I know what you've been through with friends—especially with Olivia. I know what friendships mean to you. Besides, Olivia didn't think it was a good idea either. I thought I'd give it a go only if you approved. I've been trying so hard to get her out of my head, but it's obvious that she isn't going anywhere. I don't even know how she feels about me." He looked at Rachel, hopeful.

"I don't know," Rachel said defensively. "She's never talked to me about her feelings for you, so I don't know. What do you think, Mom?"

Pattie frowned at Rachel. "How do I know? I think she likes you, but you should ask Rachel . . . Nena?"

Rachel relented. "Okay, okay . . . I see it, all right? I'm a woman—I know. I just didn't want to push her or assume, but I've been able to put the little things that have happened together."

"Like what?" Christian asked.

"You know . . . the way she looks at you—she gets excited. Then she never talks about other guys anymore. Then she asks if you're gonna hang out with us. When I try to probe, she changes the subject. Who knows, maybe she's uncomfortable liking you because of me."

"Yeah, I could see that," Pattie said, nodding. "Isa isn't disrespectful. She cares too much about us, so if she has a thing for you, I bet you she's fighting it all alone."

"Tell me about it. I busted her outside a shrink's office earlier," Rachel said to Christian.

"Shh," Pattie warned.

"What?" Christian asked, brows furrowed.

Rachel realized she said too much. "Hey, why don't you just start by telling her you're sorry and go from there. If you're worried about me, you don't have to be. Just don't hurt her."

His face lit up as he lifted Rachel off the ground. "You don't understand what this means to me."

"Whoa, whoa, I'm not saying she's interested. Heck, she might not even like you after all the hell you put her through," she said as he put her down. "Isa's a very beautiful girl and many guys have been checking her out, especially lately." Rachel flashed Pattie a grin.

"What do you mean, lately?" Christian raised a brow.

Pattie frowned at Rachel.

"Well, apparently someone delivered dozens of flowers to her office."

Christian smiled. "She deserved it."

"Well, you certainly don't seem a bit bothered by it," Pattie said.

"All I am saying is, you have my blessings," Rachel said. "I would love it, but it's up to you two."

"Well, I thank you both for your forgiveness. I promise you'll see a change in me."

"Heard that before," Rachel said, playfully jabbing him as he walked away. "Hey, Chris, does this mean you're not leaving anymore?"

"Stop begging me to stay, snotty face!" he said, walking away.

"Ha! He's not leaving . . . just watch."

"And you are sure because?" Pattie asked.

"I'm his snotty face," Rachel said. "My Chris is back."

"That was sweet of you, Rach; God knows I won't miss seeing blondie in this house. Christian needs a decent woman in his life. How I wish it would be Isa."

"I know, Mom, me too."

Olivia sat in line at the gas station when a familiar face exited the car in front of her.

What? No, it can't be, she said to herself.

In seconds, she realized it was Kevin.

"Well, I'll be damned." she said in a controlled tone as she got out of her car. "Kevin!" she yelled.

He turned around, appearing surprised to see her.

"Yeah, Liv," he said, smiling. "It's not a ghost, it's me."

"Please tell me this is some practical joke," Olivia said, staring at his car in disgust.

"Nope. I left London after the scandal with Kathy."

"Did he fire you?"

"Nah . . . I wish he had, though."

"So what are you doing here?"

"I quit."

"You what—are you insane? You walked out on a hundred-K salary with no experience? You fool, don't you know Chris did you a favor?"

"So says the GED holder," Kevin said, seething.

"Call me whatever you want, like dropping out of a two-year program accounts for anything."

"At least I started!" Kevin yelled, starting to cause a scene. "Listen, I don't need this right now, okay? If this is your idea of support, it's shitty. So drop it."

Olivia looked around. "Okay, I'm sorry, but goodness, Kevin."

Kevin bowed his head and noticed the pump had stopped. "Oh shoot, I wasn't supposed to fill that up. Ugh, *Olivia*!" he yelled, turning red.

"What, so you can't afford gas either?"

"Things are tight, okay? I'm looking for work."

"Don't tell me you had no savings," Olivia screamed. "Oh my, damn Kevin!"

She reached into her purse and handed him some cash.

"No, I don't need your money."

"Shut up and take it. You can't live like this, look at this piece of . . . " nodding at his car.

"It's called a modest living, Liv; learn how to do that sometime."

The line behind Olivia started to honk. She handed him her card. "Listen, call me. I mean it. I can help you. You can't live like this. My goodness, even Christian would die if he saw you living like this."

A few days later, Christian and some security experts from Private-I wrapped up installations of the latest home security. As he headed halfway back up the stairs, he heard Isabella's contagious laugh and froze there.

"You should have seen him, Mom," Rachel said. "He was gawking at her."

"No, he wasn't," Isabella said, giggling.

"Do tell," Pattie said. "Who's this one now? I can't keep up with them anymore."

"He's been stalking her forever. He's probably the one that sent the flowers."

"Nah, it can't be him," Isabella said. "We hardly speak. There's no way he knew I liked orchids."

"And Mom, check this out, she and her so-called firm are heading to Cancun for *vacation*."

"*Hmm* . . . " Pattie teased.

Isabella giggled. "Stop it you guys; it's for work."

Christian's eavesdropping was short-lived when the security experts closed the front door.

Isabella tensed when she heard the front door close, then footsteps up the staircase. "You heard that?"

"What, the door?" Pattie asked.

Isabella muttered, "It's probably Christian." She gathered her things together.

Pattie grabbed her arm. "Listen, you can't go running out of this house every time he comes around."

Christian walked into the family room, and it grew silent. Isabella clutched her handbag and without making eye contact she told him, "I'm sorry, I didn't realize you were home; I'll be on my way."

Christian cornered her with a look of concern. "There's nothing to apologize for. I was just updating the security system. Please carry on."

Rachel tried hard to contain her laughter as she took Pattie by the hand and whisked her off to the kitchen. "What did I tell you, Mom, feel that chemistry?"

Back in the family room, Christian and Isabella, rooted in the same spot, faced each other in intense silence. His eyes caught the orchids sitting on the table. He wasn't surprised that some of the flowers would end up in Casa Cervello—she was selfless.

"In fact, you know what," he said, breaking the silence. "I do think we need to clear the air." He took her by the hand and walked to the kitchen. "Do you ladies mind if I steal Isabella for a minute?"

Pattie smirked. "Oh, not a problem." Rachel struggled to contain her giggle.

Christian walked Isabella down the end of the hallway and up the stairs to his study. Years ago, he had converted the large den into a multipurpose unit of study-lounge-sitting room-bar with the study being his primary purpose. After years of taking women in and out of his bedroom, he considered this his sanctuary.

Christian smiled. "Please feel free to have a seat."

"Whoa." Isabella stared in excitement at the rotating furniture that transformed before her eyes.

"You've never been in this room?" he asked with a half-smile.

"*No,*" she looked at him in disbelief.

"I thought Rachel would have shown it to you by now since you practically live here. Feel free to look around. In fact, I'll be glad to give you a personal tour of it."

She looked away as soon as their eyes met. Her eyes roamed to a frame on the wall. In it, Christian held up a plaque; the mayor stood by his side.

"You have the key to the city?" she asked.

"Yup."

"Impressive," she nodded. "That's a really nice picture of the mayor."

"Yeah, I love it. I think someone said something funny right before it was taken."

"Wait, I remember this. Rachel mentioned something about it. It was last year, right?"

"Yeah, where *were* you?" he asked, squinting.

"I was in Brazil visiting my parents."

"Would you have come?"

She shrugged. "Yeah, Rach and I usually attend events together."

He chuckled.

"What's so funny? This isn't about us being boring again, is it?"

"Oh no, it's just that we seem to have kept missing each other in the past, and now, we can't stop bumping into each other."

Christian pressed a button that collapsed half the study, transforming it into a sitting area with a rotating bar. Isabella's eyes widened even more. "Hmm, no wonder."

"No wonder what?"

"The ladies love your room."

"If you mean my mom and sister, yeah, they actually love it. They're the only ladies who have ever been in here. Do you care for a drink?"

"I didn't know you drank." Isabella casually crossed her arms.

"Oh, I don't—apart from a celebratory glass. I'm having some lemon Perrier, care for some?"

"Yes, please, thank you."

"You're welcome, Isabella."

For some reason, the sound of ice clinking in the background made Isabella very nervous. The reality that they were spending some quality time in Casa Cervello for the first time, without Pattie or Rachel, was finally setting in.

He handed her the glass and continued to stare intensely at her.

"Thanks." She took the glass and looked away. He was doing it again with his eyes. His deep, gray eyes were like the lens of a professional camera, zooming in on its prey.

"You are dressed very nice today."

"Today?" Isabella laughed. "Thanks. You're used to seeing me in rough or casual clothes."

"Or pajamas," he laughed. "Robe, or a barely-there dress."

"Not nice," Isabella said. "I see you're nicely shaved now."

He stepped closer and assessed her as one would a lab test. "Do you find me intimidating, Isabella?"

"Why would I?" she scoffed, standing up straight. "So, um, you wanted to see me?"

His gaze remained steadfast. "Then why are you fidgeting?"

"I am not," she blurted.

He looked down at her hands, "Yeah, you are."

Isabella realized her hands had been trembling, and the new clinking sound was coming from the ice in her glass. She placed her drink down and looked away, straightening her chiffon skirt.

"I wanted to apologize," he said.

"You already did, remember?"

"Well, for starters, I'm sorry for making your life miserable for the past month."

She shook her head. "No, it hasn't been. I've been fine."

"Then why have you kept your distance from us? How come no one has seen or heard from you in nearly a month—even after we made up at your house."

"I've been busy."

"I bet." His mouth formed a smirk as he began to pace around her. "Let's see . . . working, planting a new garden, visiting your shrink . . . "

Isabella frowned. "Are you having me followed?"

"Now why would I do that?" he asked. "Thing is, you somehow have my entire family taken by you. Everything you do seems to affect them. My father is even concerned about you from across the world."

"Listen, if you're concerned about me hurting your family, you can rest assured, I've known them nearly my entire life. I love them like my very own."

"Oh, I'm not worried about you and them. Trust me, my mother has me convinced you're the biological daughter she never had. Heck, with the way you and Rach run around here, I'm starting to wonder if you're my little sister."

She scoffed. "Yeah, I remember *that* part, *little sister*. Oh, I got your message loud and clear."

Christian frowned as she continued. "So what then is your concern?"

He quietly studied her when a gust of wind blew through the open sliding doors, sending some papers from the counter to the floor behind Isabella. She moved to help.

"Thanks, I've got it," he said. Then speaking into her ear from behind her, he said, "My concern, my dear, is that you're extremely distracting. Not exactly what a man needs around when he hopes to move on—if you understand what I mean." He walked out to the balcony.

Isabella stood frozen at the possibility that Christian had feelings for her. Her emotions were a combination of shock, fear, and pleasure. She wanted to scream out for joy but resorted to going out to the balcony for some fresh air. She opted for the opposite end. His study had an impressive waterfront view and the strong winds sent waves rippling through it. The sound was soothing to her puzzled mind. Memories of the moments she'd shared with him and all the subtle hints came flooding back. The lingering handshakes and stares—not to mention, the hair sniffs. As she reminisced, she played with a lock of her hair and sniffed on it. Whatever got him on to her hair— she didn't know, but she found herself wearing it down more, even when she wasn't at Casa Cervello. She'd also even stuck to the same shampoo she used since the first day he sniffed it.

Every now and then, the wind tousled her straightened hair and ruffled through her chiffon skirt. Between pulling her skirt into place and taming her hair, it was fruitless. Christian cleared his throat, bringing her back to reality. She wondered how long he'd been watching her and figured she break the unbearable silence. "Listen, I'm sorry that I'm causing a distraction. I respect what you said about wanting to move on and all, but I need you to understand that it's hard to stop seeing your mom and your sister just like that. We've known each other for too long. I tried to keep my distance for over a month, and I'm still answering questions from them about that. Rachel, I can handle, but Aunt Pattie is a pit bull when it comes to these things. I'm in a bind; I don't know what else to do or say, and I hate lying to them."

He frowned. "Listen, no one's asking you to lie and no one's asking you to keep your distance. Wait a minute, what's going on? You've said a mouthful already. What did you say I told you about moving on? And exactly what did you mean earlier when you said you got *my* message loud and clear?"

"I'm talking about your note."

"What note?" he asked, approaching her.

She stuttered as he stepped closer. "The um, the—the note, the one you gave to my assistant, Tracy, through Julio."

"Do you still have it?"

Isabella scoffed. "What, you forgot what you wrote already?"

"Please!"

"Well, yeah, I think it's in my purse." *Of course it's in my purse, It's what helps me move on from you between sessions.*

"Well . . . do you mind? I need to know what it said."

She proceeded to read from memory:

Isabella,

Coming over last night was a mistake. I've had unresolved feelings for Kathy for quite some time now, and I'm trying my best to make things work with someone new. I'll be in London for about a month to finalize things with Kathy. I hope I didn't send you mixed signals last night. I care about you like I would my own little sister. You're a beautiful girl, and I know you will meet someone special one day. Take care of yourself.

-Christian

"There, I memorized it," Isabella said.

"I didn't write that."

"*Okay . . .*"

He held both her arms. "I swear."

"Don't swear."

"Okay, I promise you. I didn't write that. Now can I see the actual note, please?" He looked desperate.

She nodded, and they both headed downstairs to the family room, where she retrieved the slightly worn, neatly folded note from her purse and handed it over to him.

His eyes widened. "You *did* memorize it, but it's not me, and that's not even my handwriting."

"If you didn't write it, who did? Are you implying Tracy made this whole thing up? For crying out loud, she doesn't even know Julio."

"I'm not saying I didn't write you *a* note, I did . . . but wait right here, I wanna show you something."

Christian went into his bedroom and seconds later, handed her a note. "Look, this was supposed to be *from* you. In fact, I thought it was from you until some days ago."

She read the note. "My goodness . . . the only note I ever left you was in my house about your breakfast. I mean, you could've known my writing from that."

"Oh, I forgot about that, but this is how I figured it out," he showed her the section of the book with lost and found instructions. "Come to think of it, both those notes have the same writing."

Isabella gawked at him with her hands over her mouth.

Christian nodded. "Yup—Julio and I suspect it's Sacha. He picked her up that day."

"So this Sacha . . . is she *juice girl?*" Isabella said. "Rachel told me what happened after I left."

"You and Rachel are too much with these names."

Isabella laughed.

"Good to see you laugh again."

"So . . . you didn't write that." She pointed to the note.

Christian's smile was warm. "No, and for the record, I never had any plans to visit Kathy."

"No wonder Rach and Aunt Pattie looked at me as if I'd lost it when I asked when you were returning."

"You asked a similar question at the hotel—I wondered about that."

"So what did you do with yourself when Rachel and Pattie were in Italy? Why were they concerned?"

Christian walked over to the family room window. "Well, since we're being honest, I was depressed."

She gasped. "Oh no . . . Chris."

"No, please don't feel sorry for me."

Christian was desperate to change the subject because he wasn't ready to tell her that she was the reason why he was depressed in the first place. He didn't want to hear about her fling with Antonio either. He knew the notes were fake now, but her and him having some kind of fling had to have happened. Unfortunately, he couldn't blame Sacha for him mysteriously showing up at his place, because he was still speaking with her when the doorbell rang. He knew that Sacha didn't even have the code because she had told him the story of how she snuck through the gate. He couldn't blame Olivia either. She was long gone before he arrived. It didn't help matters that the gate surveillance camera was off—now he would never know exactly how the creep got in. For all he knew, with all Antonio's money, he could have broken the code. With the new security in place, it should take care of any future nuisance for good.

Perhaps it was just a fling or perhaps there was nothing at all. It wouldn't be a stretch to see Antonio's stunt as his revenge for taking Isabella away from him that night. *Stop driving yourself insane, and ask her about it,* Genius said. However, Christian was frightened to hear her response. He didn't want to see her any different than he had initially pictured. He just needed to block the nightmare from his head and move on.

"Now that we've gotten that under control, would you like to head back upstairs?"

Isabella nodded.

They walked back to his study and headed straight for the balcony.

Isabella shook her head. "Wow."

"I know, it's crazy—I'm so sorry."

She smiled. "I'm sorry, too. Hmm, no wonder I never got the 'thanks for your hospitality' note."

Christian grinned. "And at the hotel, when I asked about this so-called guy you were interested in . . . hey wait, there may be some truth to that." *Okay, Chris . . . easy,* Genius said. *If you won't ask her, lay off the topic.*

"Don't start," Isabella chuckled.

Hmm, did she hear Genius? Christian thought. "I overheard you ladies downstairs."

"What do you *think* you heard?" she asked with a smile in her eyes.

"Some flowers, some stalking, and a vacation?"

"It's *not* a vacation—its work, but try telling that to your mom and sister when it's Cancun."

"Hmm, sounds like you need a chaperone," he said with a half-smile.

"Why?"

"Men stalk you and you get flowers from secret admirers. Isn't that enough reason?" He leaned on the opposite end of the wall, observing her. Her hair was a huge distraction with his assessment of her facial expression, and for the first time he wished it were up in a bun.

There was a knock on the door. "Chris! Isa?" Rachel called.

"It's open!" Christian yelled.

Rachel entered into the room, excited. "Guess what? Dad's coming home in less than two hours. His assistant let it slip, Mom wasn't supposed to know."

"Great," Christian said nonchalantly.

"Wow, that's amazing," Isabella said. "Hey, Christian, you haven't seen your dad since . . . "

"Last month. Second week of May to be exact."

"Oh."

Rachel replied, "Yeah, they work together a lot overseas."

"Oh, like when you traveled to Singapore?"

He nodded.

"Well, Isa, Mom needs you for a quick makeover."

Isabella turned to Christian. "Perhaps we can finish later?"

"You promise?" he asked in a husky tone.

Isabella moistened her lips. "Promise."

Rachel raised a brow.

"I'll hold you to that," Christian replied.

Isabella walked out the door, and Rachel nudged Christian's arm. "Aha!"

Christian smiled back and shook his head.

Rachel caught up with Isabella in the hallway. "Are you okay, hon?"

"I think your brother likes me," Isabella said bashfully.

"You think?"

Isabella twisted Rachel's arm. "You knew?"

"Ouch! Who didn't? Oh yeah . . . just you. Let's go."

Christian's father, Tadd, was home in less than two hours, and after every-one had welcomed him home, he disappeared with Pattie while Rachel went off to see a movie with Thomas. Isabella was straightening the makeup room when Christian walked up behind her. "Can I help you clean up?"

"I'm just about done, but that's sweet of you."

"Good, then we can finish up our conversation."

"Sure, I'll just wash my hands."

"Do you usually get yourself covered in makeup this way when you give them makeovers?"

Isabella chuckled, staring into the mirror at his reflection with mischief. He looked amused. She had replaced her elegant, white blouse for a stained T-shirt and an apron, and her arms and cheeks had different shades and smudges of makeup. She used a cloth to wipe down her face. When it came to getting prettied up, she wasn't keen on makeup. If she absolutely had to wear some, she preferred a natural makeup palette, favoring earth tones. She usually did everyone's makeup—including hers, although Rachel and Pattie teased her for what she considered makeup. For her, makeup was simple—enough to highlight her features, so something as simple as tinted lip-gloss was makeup.

"What would they do without you?" he said, smiling.

She returned the smile as she replaced the apron and took off the T-shirt that was over her blouse.

He pointed to her hair.

"Oh," she replied, letting it back down.

Back in his study, Isabella had no idea what they would talk about. Still, she never wanted to leave.

"So, where were we?"

"I need a chaperone?" Isabella giggled.

"Ah yes, you're a good student. You know, I was thinking . . . I actually feel bad for what I put you through—even before the fake notes. I treated you badly."

"Yeah, you were a pretty shitty host," she nodded.

"It isn't fair to punish you or anyone for my misfortune with Kathy."

"It's okay, I understand better now."

Christian walked up to her and held her arm lightly. "Then, let me make it up to you."

It was another moment she'd dreamt of—yet he still caught her off guard. She relished the feel of his strong hand over her bare arm.

He took both her hands in his. "I noticed the kitchen calendar has June 22 marked for your birthday. Allow me to throw you a party here."

Isabella gasped. "What?"

"Please, it's the only way I can forgive myself for what I've done to you."

"Are you always this hard on yourself?"

"Don't deny me this opportunity."

She smiled at him.

CHAPTER SIXTEEN

New Beginnings

⤜❧⤛

WITH PATTIE and Tadd out of the country, Christian diligently planned Isabella's birthday party with Rachel's help. It did not take much to get Rachel excited, and although her enthusiasm should have been contagious, he struggled internally by the minute. She probably was too preoccupied with her list to notice that his hadn't grown since she last checked it. Christian's tension grew as he assessed each male guest against Isabella. Although they weren't officially an item, he hoped he'd made his intentions known to her, albeit indirectly. *Will this party be a mistake, or an opportunity to face my fears head on?* he pondered.

"I think we should invite as many single men as possible," Christian blurted, not realizing he had made his thoughts audible until Rachel replied.

"Why?" Rachel asked. "And why in the world are you sweating?"

Christian looked down at his hands. The sweat from his temples and palms had rubbed off some of the ink on his page. "I can't stand cheap pens; where did you get this from?"

"No clue. I need help for my pen-thieving ways. I don't even know when I do it. Here, use this—I think it's yours."

He took the pen from her. It *was* his, and he'd given up looking for it. He sat up and squared his shoulders. "I don't know, maybe she could get hooked up."

"And why would you wanna do that?"

"I guess to face my fears in a nonthreatening environment."

"Yeah . . . you're nuts."

He flipped the pen obsessively in his hand. He didn't think he was crazy. He'd seen how men reacted around Isabella. Even if he had faith in her, he couldn't trust men. He also couldn't trust himself for fear that all the attention she received would turn him off again. It was hard to come to terms with the fact that Isabella was still single. He wondered whether she would find someone interesting if given a larger variety in a place she felt comfortable. It did seem as though she went from a sheltered life to Notre Dame to a guarded life. *Then how do I explain the club and Antonio? Could she be rebelling? No, she's not me. I used to get excited with a variety of women, but that doesn't mean Isabella is the same way.* He marveled at the conceived thought. It wasn't Genius. He was positive because Genius's voice always came in the second person. This was Christian's thought, and it was positive for once. He had Isabella's book to thank for that.

"I'm gonna call Isa to make sure we're not missing anyone," Rachel said.

There were close to a hundred people by the time Julio pulled up to Casa Cervello and Rachel and Isabella stared in shock—hardly recognizing the place. Isabella had heard that the party planners had worked tirelessly for a day, but it looked like it took a week to pull off. Christian had put in so much into making her party a success and Isabella felt guilty for not helping with the preparations. Rather, he had asked Rachel to keep her away from the house two days before the event, so the girls had spent that time rehearsing their cover songs for the party.

The theme, suggested by Christian in homage to Isabella's birth era was the '80s and despite the short notice, most guests came dressed to impress. Nearly all the women had big hair and leotards while the men—and there were lots—went either for the rock star look or Hawaiian T-shirts. There were some *Miami Vice* rejects too. *This ought to be fun,* Isabella thought. Even the female waiters who served hors d'oeuvres were in costumes— fishnet gloves and bright-colored leotards. Isabella was glad she opted for the classic *Palmer girl* look and hoped no one else would show up dressed that way.

She had planned to do her own makeup, but Rachel was adamant against it, which was probably best because, given the opportunity, she would skip it entirely, tuck her hair in a bun, and hold up a sign that read, *Palmer girl.* However, Christian had paid a hefty fee to ensure she had the right look by hiring a professional artist from New York renowned for her '80s-themed makeovers. By the time Isabella stared into the mirror, a pale-faced woman with dark eye shadow and bright red lipstick stared back at her. The artist knew her job well because Isabella had no recognizable trait left. When she slicked her long hair effortlessly into a neat shiny bun, and fitted her in a long-sleeved, skin-tight black mini-dress, complete with sheer black stockings and pumps, Isabella realized she was more than just a makeup artist—she was three-in-one.

For Rachel's look, the stylist frowned upon the store-bought wig the girls had enthusiastically picked up from the Halloween costume shop. Opting for a more natural look, she braided the sides of Rachel's hair. Color, gel, and tons of hairspray later, Isabella's best friend disappeared into thin air, and Cyndi Lauper stared back at her with an off-shoulder blouse, a crinoline skirt over a colorful pair of leggings, and a myriad of beads.

Rachel successfully made her way past the guests and into the house, but Isabella wasn't as fortunate. Somehow the guests had figured out she was the celebrant and went out of their way to greet her. As special as this made her feel, all she really yearned for was to see Christian. He didn't strike her as someone who would play dress-up so she leaned toward betting that he wouldn't.

It looked to her like Christian had kept true to his promise of inviting his classmates because she couldn't recognize anyone. As she progressed through the boisterous crowd, a familiar voice called out to her, and a closer look revealed her colleagues under the Blues Brothers disguise. They would be all spending the entire week in Mexico together, and this was a good opportunity to see what they were like outside of work. However, with Tracy absent, it only meant more men. Apart from Rachel and Gracie, the only women Isabella recognized at her own party were two female acquaintances from her downtown homeless shelter volunteer site, and even they must have felt out of place in their regular clothes.

The search for the man she loved led her past Pattie's rose garden and right to an elegant white gazebo. She had never noticed it before on the property and wondered whether it was just for the party. A slight wind blew through the sheer white curtains invitingly and just as she approached it, she heard slight chatter. Some guests were heading back to the party from the direction of the dock. As soon as they cleared from her view, she saw him. With his back to her, he helped a pretty blonde dressed like Paula Abdul off the boat. The blonde giggled at something he'd said, and Isabella felt a tinge of jealousy as she watched her smack his arm.

She wanted to run to him but decided to play it cool, wishing he would just turn around and notice her. *Come on Chris, I'm right here—turn,* she muttered. She nearly fainted when, at that exact moment, he turned around and quickly excused himself. As he approached her, her heart did somersaults. She was right; he didn't follow the theme—a button-down dress shirt, black tie, and black slacks. *Such a party pooper.*

"Well, if it isn't my very own sidekick. Just so you know, I'll be performing with you guys—the glorious foursome at last."

Isabella covered her mouth. "You're Robert Palmer?"

"Why yes, of course, and your outfit isn't complete without your guitar. White or red?"

"White."

"Good," he smiled. "Because that's all we've got." When Isabella's laughter died down, he said, "You don't quite look like yourself with all that makeup and I'm glad."

Isabella's brows creased. "I don't know whether to take that as a compliment."

"She did a great job."

"I know, and I can't begin to—"

"Then don't. Just promise me you'll have a great time, okay?"

"Okay."

"And try not to laugh so much if you wanna win the costume contest. Palmer girls keep a straight face. It's actually part of the costume."

"I'll try to remember that." She stifled a giggle. "Which reminds me, how come the guests knew I was the birthday girl?"

"Oh, well, your look was the only one prohibited in the invitation. What can I say, you're special."

Rumor had it that Christian hired the best-known DJ in Miami, and it should have been hard to keep even the most bashful seated. Yet, Isabella found it hard to lose her inhibitions with Christian around and, as good as the music was, it didn't take long for some men to gripe about the party's obvious shortcoming. When Christian's trainer offered to invite more women, Isabella noticed Christian frown at the idea. Nonetheless, he agreed to comply as long as Isabella consented, and not wanting to be a killjoy, she welcomed the proposition. Besides, it was true—apart from the two volunteers, who kept themselves hidden away in the house—the few female guests who were present had arrived with dates.

Christian's eyes said something and Isabella wondered if he expected her to read it. He hadn't said much to her since their initial meeting by the dock, but he had a genuine smile whenever their eyes met. He appeared to be in deep thought, and she wondered whether he feared running into someone from his past. She had seen how even ladies with dates flirted with him, so it should be no surprise what the single ones would do when they arrived. Even stranger than his mood was the fact that he periodically retreated to that mysterious gazebo. She had asked Rachel about it, but she simply shrugged—something about Christian not liking noise. Isabella was more curious than upset because his retreats didn't stop him from socializing with the guests. In fact, he was the perfect host—ensuring that everyone was comfortable and even giving some a personal tour of the mansion.

Isabella joined a group who had formed a line around the water fountain, dancing to "Funky Town." As soon as the coast was clear, she broke from the crowd. Allowing her curiosity to guide her, she strolled casually back to the rose garden. When she pulled back the sheer curtains, the spectacular Tuscan-style design took her by surprise. There was a luxurious, white sofa with red-and-white striped pillows. The white guitar that rested on it must have been the one he mentioned. Two weaved coffee tables with white cushioned tops surrounded two smaller white sofas and a near-empty lemon Perrier sat on the table next to a *Sky Mall* magazine and, surprisingly, her *Battlefield of the Mind* book. He had used colorful tabs on multiple pages. A fan stood in the corner. White noise—Rachel was right. She heard classical music but couldn't locate where the sound came from. White sheers formed a ceiling canopy and in the center hung a large outdoor chandelier. The party was so close, yet with this sanctuary, it was so far away. Absolute peace.

Isabella hurried back to the party, right in time for Christian to introduce her to his cousin visiting from Naples. It felt awkward that in all his introductions of her, he referred to her simply as "Rachel's friend." *Perhaps that's all I am,* she thought, shaking his cousin's hand. Before he could speak, there was a loud cheer followed by an influx of women in two separate limos. None wore costumes, and some were practically naked in what were supposed to be bathing suits. Isabella noticed Christian's quick reaction—a slight frown, right before he excused himself and headed into the house, passing by Rachel without a word.

"Why was everyone yelling?" Rachel asked, joining her cousin and Isabella. She nodded in the direction of the women. "Where did *they* come from?"

"The guys thought we needed more women."

"So what . . . they brought a busload?"

"Fifteen, I counted. They came in limos." Isabella smirked.

"Are you okay with that?"

"I guess."

"Okay. Well, listen. We're going live in less than an hour, and I was wondering if your volunteers wanna be Palmer girls too. Can you ask them?"

"Sure, they probably would, since they have no costumes. Where's Thomas?"

"The makeup artist is making him into a Robert Palmer as we speak." Rachel winked.

"But Chris—"

"Can't sing! He'll do drums. Besides, you gotta admit, with Thomas's hair, he makes a better Robert."

"But you're not even dressed like a Palmer girl."

"That's because I'm supposed to be Cyndi Lauper—duh. You guys are featuring me as a guest."

After their performance and following the contest for best '80s costume– which Rachel won, the guests gathered outside for the birthday song. A fresh-faced Isabella stood in a white, two-piece bikini, mesh sarong, and side ponytail, as the crowd serenaded her.

"Make a wish!" the guests chanted.

"Okay, okay," she said bashfully, as the caterers wheeled in an enormous cake in the shape of a Rubik's Cube. Upon seeing the cake, her heart began to pound. "Whose idea was this?" Her smile was nervous.

Rachel smiled hesitantly at Christian, who stood with his arms folded. "Make a wish," he prompted.

Isabella closed her eyes briefly, and when she blew out the candles, fireworks went off, surprising her and the crowd. She cut the cake and marveled at the inside, which also bore patterns of the cube.

As the music blasted on, some guests went off to dance, while some took pictures of the cake and others stopped to chat with Isabella. When the crowd cleared, she felt Christian's presence behind her.

"So what did you wish for?" he asked. His tone made her weak in the knees.

Turning around, she smiled. "It's private."

"You like your cake?"

"A Rubik's Cube . . . seriously?"

"What better than the favorite '80s toy?"

"They terrify me. How did you . . . Rachel doesn't even know that. No one knows that."

Christian smirked. "Interesting, it actually reminds me of you."

"Why? You think I'm hard to figure out?"

"Are you?"

"I'm an open book."

"Yeah? Well, actually I used to be able to solve them, but I can't any-more, unless blindfolded."

"Wait, what?" She didn't know whether to be intrigued by this man or petrified.

She watched as he crossed his arms over his chest. From his smug expres-sion, she took it that he enjoyed catching her off guard.

"Long story." Christian said. "So you've never solved a Rubik's Cube?"

"No," Isabella replied, bemused.

"You wanna learn?"

"Not really."

"If you change your mind, just know the trick is in the sides. Start there, and it'll line up eventually."

"Then how come you can't solve it anymore?"

He winked. "I told you . . . long story."

"I've been meaning to ask you, how do you like that book you bor-rowed?"

"Oh, it's amazing. I've been practicing plenty. It looks like I'll have to get you a new one."

"Oh, don't worry about it," she said airily. "I'm just glad it's working for you."

"Extremely. It's good to have a shut-off switch. It's a work in progress, but I'm sleeping better."

"Well, I can't thank you enough for all this. This party is unbelievable. Even fireworks . . . wow."

"We had to make it special for you—you're family," Christian said, his gaze piercing.

"It's an honor to be considered that."

"The honor is ours. I guess I was the last one to catch the Isa bug."

She giggled.

"Well, since you're like family, there's something you should have," Christian added.

"Oh?" She couldn't imagine what could top the party.

"Come with me." He walked her into the house, and once they arrived at his study, he closed the door and handed her a box wrapped in blue, me-tallic paper and a white bow.

Her body froze at the sight of it, but her heart raced.

Christian said, "Don't worry, it's not what you think."

"Oh," she smiled.

She unwrapped the gift box to a white and silver designer watch. "Oh no, I can't," she said, handing it back to him with trembling fingers.

Christian insisted. "Yes, you can, and you will."

She shook her head. "No, this is too much. I can't."

He pressed the box into her hand, "You must. It was made for you." *Made*? she thought. This must be *the* watch. She'd always wanted to borrow Rachel's but couldn't. Her heart raced the more.

"Oh my . . . I love huge watches, how did you know?"

Christian winked. "You do know it's a security watch, don't you?"

Isabella nodded enthusiastically. "Rachel told me. Oh, thank you so much, Christian. This is the best party and gift ever." She pulled the watch from the box and hugged him tightly. When she noticed that he held back his embrace, she pulled back sheepishly. *Perhaps that was too much,* she thought.

"Is it?" he asked with a crooked grin. "I'm glad."

"I'm afraid to ask how much this is."

"Then don't."

She nodded.

"Have you heard from your parents yet?"

"Yeah, they called very early and sang to me. That's their special way since they're so far away."

"Sweet; that reminds me, my folks called earlier for you. Mom said your phone was off."

"Oh, no! I turned it off because I kept getting calls while I was getting my makeup done."

"It's okay. She thought you'd be here. They hate to be missing all the fun. They love the '80s."

"I bet. Aunt Pattie got me listening to some of those songs."

He smiled as his eyes traveled into the distance. "I've been . . . 'Waiting for a Girl Like You.'"

"You what?" She asked, astonishment.

"My favorite '80s song. Shouldn't be surprising though—Mom used to have it on repeat back then. If you don't know *Foreigner*, you know nothing about the '80s."

"Hey, I was born in the '80s," Isabella defended, hoping to hide her sudden disillusionment. "I spent the rest of the '80s and most of my '90s exposed to Brazilian music—that's all my mom played."

"Until we corrupted you," he said, lips drawn into a side smirk.

"'80s music is actually quite clean."

"Do you have a favorite?"

"Yeah . . . it's funny you asked. Because my favorite reminds me of this house for some reason."

"What's the name?"

He seemed genuinely interested.

"Don't laugh," She said, frowning slightly.

When Christian laughed, she pouted.

"Okay, I won't. I promise." He crossed his heart.

"'Please Don't Go Girl.'"

"No way! New Kids?"

"Uh, huh. It reminds me of this house and I don't remember your mom ever playing it."

Christian ducked to whisper in her ear. "Don't tell anyone, but that was one of my favorites, too."

"*No!*" She grinned, delighted to have something in common with him.

Christian's stare was calculating. "I noticed you didn't cause any distractions until you changed out of your costume. I'm considering sending you back to that era."

She cleared her throat, pointing to the watch. "So um, with this, you can tell where I am at all times?"

"Is that what you want?" Christian asked, his lips slowly curving into an enigmatic smile.

"Just wondering," she shrugged, feeling a sudden heat on her face.

"Is it what you want?" he repeated. Isabella focused on releasing the buckles on the watchstraps.

He took a step closer and reached for the watch. "Here, I'll help you with that." He secured the straps around her wrist. The feel of his hands against hers sent ripples through her skin.

"Are you cold?" he asked.

The instant she shook her head, she realized she admitted something else.

"I could, but I won't," he continued. "I don't track anyone. It's my sworn policy. The device activates in case of emergency. The GPS technology works with your body temperature and pulse."

Isabella nodded. "Cool. Is it available in stores? I noticed the designer name."

"Unfortunately, it isn't. I designed this specifically for members of my family. I contract with different designers to use their shells as my cover, so just about anyone could have this same design and no one would know it's actually more than a watch. This is confidential stuff, so Rachel must really trust you."

Isabella smiled. "Well, she didn't tell me that much, so thanks."

"Don't be scared by it, just live your life and watch what the watch can do for you. No pun intended."

Isabella smiled. "Good one, and thanks again." She didn't know when her arms moved to hug him again, but this time he hugged her back. She thought she heard him catch a breath against her hair before pulling away. In a flash, he was by the door.

"Come on, let's head back before anyone misses you." He held the door for her with a mischievous smile. "So when do you leave for your *vacation*?"

"Don't say it like that." Isabella chuckled as they headed out.

When the last traces of the sun made an exit, the outdoor lights came on, and it was clear to see that the guests weren't prepared to let nighttime faze them. In fact, some guests were just arriving. Apart from the fact that the amount of women had doubled to nearly sixty since Isabella's last count, not much else had changed. The waiters still served up drinks and finger foods outside, professional caterers served up main courses inside, and Isabella was yet to hear a single '80s hit repeated. Some guests had gathered in the pool to join her and Rachel for a game of water volleyball, and although she had every reason to smile, her mind kept wandering back to the gazebo and its purpose.

"Hmm . . . I see someone gave you a gift," Rachel teased.

Isabella stroked the watch, observing the screen's change to swim mode. "You like?"

"Mmhmm, now you can stop begging to borrow mine."

"How could something this complicated be water-resistant?"

"My brother is a genius," Rachel replied.

Christian was leaning over the patio rail, watching Isabella and Rachel, when Olivia joined him.

"Great party," Olivia said. "You've outdone yourself, Mr. C."

"Thanks for finally making it," Christian said, without looking at her. "Now it's just a pool party."

"For *Isabella*," she sneered.

"Yes, for Isabella," Christian said sternly. "Rachel's friend."

"I was Rachel's friend first. You never threw *me* a party."

Christian turned to face her. "Seriously, Liv?"

She smiled. "Ah, truth hurts, huh. What—you just use me to hook you up with the fine ladies? All along you had this one over here—little Miss Perfect."

Glancing impatiently at his watch, Christian said, "Do I sense some jealousy in your tone?"

"Me? Jealous?" Olivia scoffed. "Please don't insult me. So what's going on with you two anyway?"

Christian kept his gaze on the pool. "Zilch. She's Rachel's friend. I rather it stays that way."

"I see the way you look at her."

"You're delusional."

"What happened to us, Chris? You don't tell me anything anymore. We used to be close."

"I'm sorry, Liv, I've not exactly been in *Kumbaya* mode recently. I've been out of it for a while."

"*Okay.*" She walked away, and a short time later returned with two drinks. "Look at them."

"What's wrong, grouch?" Christian accepted the drink. "What have they done to you now?"

"For starters, Rachel used to play around with me that way. Now she can't even find time for me."

Christian flashed a sarcastic grin. "That's funny, I don't remember a playful side to you, Liv. You know what I remember? I remember you making fun of Rachel and calling her a little *wuss*." He looked into Olivia's eyes. "In fact, I don't remember you being there when her parents died."

Olivia looked away. "That's not fair."

"But it's true, isn't it?" Christian asked softly.

"Well, that's beside the point. We've known each other since grade school, for goodness sake."

"Grade school," Christian said in a carefully controlled tone as he turned back to face the pool.

Olivia snapped. "So the fuck what? What does that even mean?" She walked up close.

"It means people change, Liv. I learned that recently—and please watch your language around me!"

"Oh, excuse me!" she yelled, starting to cause a scene. "I see where your loyalty goes up to."

Christian seethed. "Don't you tell me about loyalty. I wasn't the one who climbed into his best friend's bed and screwed his fiancée. And don't you forget he was my grade school friend too."

Christian walked away. Thomas went after him and asked, "Are you okay, man?"

"I will be in a minute."

Olivia casually strolled up to the pool and stooped down. "Hey, girls."

Rachel flashed a wide grin. "Hey, I was looking for you."

"You were?" Olivia's tone was sarcastic.

"Yeah, some hottie was asking if you were single."

"Get out," Olivia said in a flat tone.

Isabella giggled. "Yeah, seriously . . . "

Olivia tossed her hair, responding directly to Rachel. "Is he still here?"

"Yup, don't look now, but that's him with Frank."

"It's okay," Olivia said with a dismissive wave. "I have a headache anyway. I'm going inside."

"Oh, we'll go in with you; Isa was just saying she was tired."

Rachel tugged at her tangled hair.

"You should have covered it like I told you," Isabella said.

"But I rinsed out all the stuff she put in."

"You didn't condition it before you got into the pool. Anyway, it's a small price you had to pay for winning the contest."

"Why, you're jealous?" Rachel teased.

Meanwhile, Olivia sat quietly at the foot of the bed, fiddling with the settings on a video camera.

"Ah, good thing someone had a camera to record," Rachel said. "That's one thing we didn't plan for."

"But I saw them outside," Olivia said.

"Photographers," Rachel corrected.

"Oh, don't they do both?" Olivia asked with a slight frown.

"That one apparently doesn't. How long have you been recording?"

"Half an hour. I came late. Hopefully someone got some earlier from a personal camera."

"Nah, it's okay," Isabella said. "I'll never forget this day anyway."

"I bet," Olivia snickered. "Might as well get some now, huh? Testing, testing. Here's the birthday girl."

"That's a really nice camera, Olivia," Isabella said.

Rachel whipped around. "Hey, Chris has one just like that."

"I know . . . it's his. He let me borrow it for a project I'm working on."

"Yeah?" Rachel asked. "What project?"

"I'll tell you later; this is rolling."

"Now or never," Rachel said, frowning.

"Okay, it's for a makeup ad," Olivia said bashfully.

Isabella became excited. "Really?"

There was a knock on the door and Rachel went to get it. "Hey, hon," she said, embracing Thomas.

"I was wondering where you girls were. Are you okay?" he asked, trying to peek through the door.

"Yeah, we were just relaxing for a bit. Too much fun for one day. Are guests starting to leave?"

Thomas scoffed. "You're kidding, right? I don't think anyone's thinking of leaving. Chris has the caterers working overtime. Love connections are going on."

Rachel wrapped her arms around his neck. "I'm not surprised. This *is* the house of love, after all."

"Is it now?"

"Mmhmm."

"Then how come I'm the only one without love?"

"You and Chris. Was he looking for us?"

"Nah, he was catching up with some new guys the last time I checked."

"He must be exhausted. I'll be back out as soon as I'm done with my hair to help him, but I think the birthday girl's done for the night."

"Your hair's fine."

"You'll say anything to have me," Rachel said, kissing him.

"Hey, is that Olivia's voice I just heard?" Thomas asked. He stretched past Rachel to peek through the door. "I thought she left."

"Don't start, babe . . . she's behaving."

"All right, just hurry back, okay?"

The party continued with some guests breaking into a dance contest while Christian joined Thomas for a game of pool. "You think this gig will go on till tomorrow?" Thomas asked.

"Not on my watch. I had the DJ announce closing time at midnight. It started at noon, and I'm beat."

"I hear you. Hey, Chris, I wanted to tell you that it's okay to be creeped out by Olivia's behavior. I know she's an old friend, but it may be a good idea to keep your distance as Rachel has started to."

Even for someone who barely knew Olivia, Christian knew Thomas was on to something. *What was it about Olivia that seemed to rub people the wrong way?* "I never heard you sound so—"

"Serious?" Thomas asked with a wicked laugh as he positioned his pool stick. "Yeah, I can be goofy, but I do have a serious side. I could never understand Olivia since Rachel introduced me to her. There's something about her—I can't quite put my hands on it, but I've been advising your sister to slowly break off the remaining ties she has with her."

"Ha! That's gonna be tough," Christian said with a half-smile as he walked over to the other end of the pool table. "The roots run deep."

"But it's necessary."

"Speaking of the girls, have you seen them?"

"Rachel's with Isa and Olivia."

Christian frowned. "Excuse me."

Back in Rachel's room, Isabella had started to nod off when Olivia stood up to leave. "Okay, ladies," Olivia said. "It was lovely, but I need to retire for the night."

"Are you okay to drive?"

"Yup . . . and let me guess, Isa's sleeping over, huh?"

"Nope," Rachel replied. "She's actually traveling tomorrow and needs to pack. Why, you're jealous?"

"Should I be?" Olivia kissed both ladies and left, bumping into Christian down the hallway.

"Hey, lover boy," she teased. "Thanks for the invite."

"Anytime, Olivia."

"Hey, does she know?" she asked, pointing to Rachel's door.

"Know what?"

Olivia's lips curled into a devious smile. "Does she know about you? I bet you haven't told her."

"What are you getting at?"

"The wild parties . . . the women . . . ouch."

"That's my past and you seem very interested in it."

"Ooh," she said shaking her head. "Tsk, tsk, you're a bad boy, Christian Cervello. You know this isn't gonna work, right? The two of you . . . Uh uh, she's too clean for you. We're soiled, Chris—you and I. Besides, you don't settle—I know you."

"You know nothing. Need I remind you I was engaged to be married?"

With a sly grin, she whispered. "And now you're not. Aww." She cocked her head to the side as she circled him. "Could this . . . past of yours possibly be coming back to haunt you? You know, Sacha said the same thing the other girls said about you. Heck, if you weren't like my brother I'd wanna see for myself."

"Shut up, Olivia, you're drunk."

"*Oh?* But all I had was iced tea. With you, remember? I guess we're both drunk," she said with a laugh that gave him the chills. "You're insatiable, my friend. That little girl can't possibly measure up to those women I know you want. So I trust you'll need my services again, very soon."

"Tell me, Olivia, what exactly *are* your services?"

Olivia smiled. "I'm sure you'll remember just how valuable I am when you're in need again."

He watched her walk past the hallway bend until she was out of sight. *What if she tells Isabella about me?* Christian thought. *Don't let her intimidate you,* Genius replied. Christian smiled to himself, glad to know that Genius hadn't neglected him after all; he needed the support. He tapped on Rachel's door. He would have to warn her to be careful around Olivia.

Isabella jumped at the sound of Julio's midnight wake-up call. She quickly showered and put on a pair of Rachel's pajamas before grabbing her bag. She couldn't see any guests in the house, but the chef greeted her as he packed up to leave. She marveled at how professional cleaners diligently erased whatever evidence was left of the greatest party ever. She hesitated slightly in the hallway before heading to Christian's room.

By the third knock, she assumed he was asleep, but when she turned to leave, she heard the door open. Goosebumps ravished her skin as her favorite '80s song, "Please Don't Go Girl," played in the background. She figured he must have had company. *Of course, why else would it take him so long to answer the door, and why would he just stick his head out like he was hiding something or someone. Perhaps she was the one he spent time with in the gazebo.* Nausea quickly crept up.

"You're awake," he said, raising a brow.

"Um, I just wanted to thank you for everything."

"How many times are you gonna do that?"

"I um . . . I'm heading back home now. Julio's waiting."

"Do you have to leave now? It's late."

"I haven't packed and my flight leaves tomorrow; well, it's today now."

"There's no one in here, you know," he said, opening the door slightly. He was in a bathrobe.

"Of course," she shrugged, pretending not to be relieved that she was wrong.

"When does your flight leave?"

"At noon."

Christian slowly nodded. "Text me when you get home."

When Isabella nodded, he said, "I still don't have your number, by the way."

"I don't have yours either."

"Do you want it?"

She nodded.

"Let me have your phone."

Christian typed into her phone. "I'll have yours when you text me."

CHAPTER SEVENTEEN

A Knowing

❧

THE NEXT day, Christian woke up from sleep in a cold sweat and with a pounding heart. He couldn't recall much of the dream, only that it had that same man in a dark room with his hands, feet, and mouth bound. Long after he woke up, he could still hear the muffled sound of the man's attempts to cry out ringing in his head. Since the age of thirteen, he'd walk over to Rachel's room after such a dream. Even as a child, Rachel was extremely good at interpreting dreams. However, this dream was one she could never wrap her head around. She had once told him that she needed more information to interpret it. He hoped to have more before he sought her again for help, but he couldn't resist walking over to her room. Seeing her fast asleep, he headed back to his bedroom and soon found himself desperately craving his home church. He hadn't attended since he left for London, and he felt a strong pull to go now.

It felt as though he'd never left Faith House and Pastor Bernard looked and sounded better than ever. Growing up, he had always remembered the tall, and now elderly, African American man as having an aura of overwhelming peace. His aunt Liz had trusted the pastor with her many dark secrets and every time Christian stepped foot in the church since her death, he found himself wondering the same thing—why he ever stopped regularly attending in the first place. Before he could ever answer the question, he would grow cold again the minute he left the church.

Service was just about over when the pastor announced: "Before I dismiss you, I have one more announcement. As you probably know, our precious Elisabeth Suares Santos from our Life prayer ministry department went to be with the Lord this past Friday. If you wish to attend the wake, the ushers will be handing out the flyers for details."

Christian's heart skipped. The name was familiar, and a facial image flashed in his head to match it, but he quickly pushed away the possibility. An usher approached him, and he reached out in what felt like slow motion to take a flyer. He held the flyer in shaky hands and took in a deep breath before reluctantly looking at the picture. He felt his head begin to swell as blurry flashbacks of him and Rachel as kids in the church came to mind. He could see Elisabeth and his aunt Liz working around the church. Pastor Bernard gave the benediction, his strong commanding voice partially drowned in the background of Christian's memories.

After the service, Christian walked over to the pastor. "Long time no see," Pastor Bernard said, grinning. "How is life in Vancouver?"

Christian smiled as they shook hands, "Oh pastor, it's been a long time since I was in Canada. I actually relocated to London two years ago, but I'm here again now—to stay."

"Ah, a busy man. Good to have you back, son," he said, patting Christian on the back.

"Thank you, sir, it's good to be home."

"I can't thank you enough for the security system you donated to the church, but what we'd love more is having you reconnected to the fold."

"I know, pastor. I feel so lost."

"It doesn't have to be that way."

Christian nodded. "I'm working on it. Um, pastor, how exactly did Elisabeth die?"

"I heard she passed away in her sleep."

"Wow," Christian said, rubbing the back of his neck.

A member of the church staff walked over to Pastor Bernard, and he excused himself.

Christian remained in his vehicle for close to two hours—deep in thought. He hadn't realized how much time had passed until nearly all the cars in the church parking lot were gone. He picked up his phone and called Rachel.

"Hola!" she said cheerfully.

"What's up?" He considered telling her the news, hating to ruin her chipper mood.

"At Isa's, helping her pack."

"Oh? Shouldn't she be at the airport by now?"

"Actually, when she called to confirm her flight, they told her it was delayed due to a storm in Mexico, so she's leaving tomorrow instead. You home?"

"Nah . . . sitting in the car outside church."

"How was service? Shoot! I was supposed to meet with Elisabeth today."

"So you *do* remember her."

Rachel laughed. "Of course, silly—*creepy church lady*, remember?"

"Yeah." Christian laughed. "Wait, you were supposed to be meeting with her today?"

"Yeah, after service. Did you see her?"

He focused on the chilling sensation down his spine.

"Chris?"

"Rachel, I don't know how to say this."

"To say what?" she demanded. "Stop with the suspense, Chris. What happened?"

"Elisabeth is dead. Apparently, she died in her sleep on Friday." The phone went silent.

"Rach! You still there?"

"Don't say that," she said in a low shaky voice. "That's so weird. I just spoke to her last weekend when I invited her to Isa's party."

"That *is* creepy," Christian said in a near whisper.

"I feel so bad."

"Why?"

"Because the last time I saw her, it looked like she could use the company. But I was in a hurry, and I promised her we would hang out today, after church. Why didn't you take me to church with you?"

"I came to your room, but you were sleeping and I didn't wanna wake you or be late. But that's beside the point, she didn't die today. She died on Friday."

As Rachel wept, Christian could hear Isabella consoling her in the background.

"There's nothing you could have done to stop it," Christian continued.

"Hey, Chris," Isabella said into the phone. "How are you holding up?"

"I'm hanging in there." His sigh was heavy.

"I had no idea you guys were that close to Elisabeth. It seems like she meant a lot to you both."

"It's a long story. I can't even explain the connection. It had been a while since I had seen her but—"

"But what?"

"I feel connected to her and I don't know why."

"Well, Rachel can't talk anymore. Wanna come over to my place? I'll make you guys lunch."

"That would be nice."

The three of them were up for nearly the entire night sharing stories. The conversations had turned so dark that they felt more comfortable spending the night together at Isabella's house. At a certain point, the lights in Isabella's living room went out when Rachel shared a story about their family that her mother had told them before her death. The three of them ended up crashing on the living room floor.

The next morning, Christian and Rachel accompanied Isabella to the airport. With Rachel in the front seat and Isabella in the back, Christian drove in silence until Rachel turned on the radio. To Isabella and Rachel's delight, their favorite song, "Sending My Love" came on the radio and, without warning, the girls belted out the lyrics. This went on until her eyes met Christian's in the rearview mirror. Isabella blushed and stopped singing.

Christian's Range Rover pulled up at the terminal, and they all got out. He brought out Isabella's luggage while the two girls embraced. He then walked over to Isabella and hugged her. With her head on his chest, she could hear his heartbeat—strong and fast.

"Call us when you get there, okay?" Christian asked.

"Okay," Isabella replied quietly.

He then reached down and brushed his lips across her forehead.

Isabella waved to them and walked away.

Back in the car, Christian was silent.

"Aww, you miss her already, don't you? So do I. That was nice what you did for her."

When Christian gave her a puzzled look, she said, "The watch."

"Oh, don't tell me you didn't know about it all along."

Rachel nudged his arm. "Yeah, but I didn't think you'd go through with it; it's a lot."

"Not when you have to protect someone you—"

"What?"

He fumbled with the stereo.

"Finish the sentence, Chris. Someone you what? Love? Come on, it's me. Tell me, when did you know?"

Christian sighed. "You're never gonna let this go, are you?"

"Nope."

"That first day I met her—in the garden."

"Ha! I knew it. Speaking of the garden, what's up with the gazebo?"

"Mom wanted it—I thought you knew."

"Didn't we used to have one? I saw pictures."

"Yeah, you were younger then. I think there was a termite problem."

"So, you were saying . . . "

"My feelings got deeper when she called Mom 'Aunt Pattie.'"

Rachel laughed. "Why?"

"Because it reminded me of how Mom said she used to call Nonni 'Auntie Maria' when she met her. And, remember how close Mom was to Aunt Mona?"

"Oh yeah . . . " Rachel smiled.

"Reminds me of you and Isabella."

"I never thought of that. Perhaps that's why Mom likes her so much."

Christian started the car, and Rachel nudged him, teasing, "Chris loves Isa."

"You were on to me the whole time," he said, blushing.

"So what are you guys like now, going together?"

Christian shook his head. "I'm not playing those games anymore."

"So . . . "

"So what?"

"Don't you wanna be exclusive?"

"Of course I do. I'm just going about Isabella differently; that's all."

"Well, she's gonna wanna be exclusive, so whatever you're thinking—"

"Is unique," Christian concluded. "I'm going to marry that girl."

"Whoa, whoa, whoa, wait a minute. You guys haven't even been on one date. What makes you think she even wants to marry you? Because she's single? I mean, with all due respect, Chris."

Christian laughed. "Okay."

Rachel stared at him suspiciously. "Okay what? Do you know something that I don't?"

"You'll be the first to know, I promise. Can I at least trust you not to tell her how I feel or my plans?"

"My lips are sealed. Good thing you asked me first, I would have told her everything."

CHAPTER EIGHTEEN

Regrets

❦

ISABELLA AND her colleagues had wrapped up the main business events two days earlier than expected, and while her colleagues opted to stay back, she gladly returned to Miami. Not a single day had gone by without her thinking of Christian. It hadn't been hard to do with the watch in her face. She had even found herself wishing he would track her just to feel close to him. She couldn't contain her excitement from the thought of seeing him again. He was scheduled to leave tomorrow evening for David's wedding, so she figured her early arrival was God's doing.

Isabella's enthusiasm died when Rachel arrived to pick her up. It took everything in her not to break down when Rachel mentioned Christian had chosen to leave for London on a commercial flight earlier than planned—a few minutes ago, in fact. She faintly took in details of Rachel's plans with Thomas as she held on to the last strand of hope that she might at least catch a glimpse of him before his check-in— *British Airways? No, I think Delta. Just ask Rach,* she mumbled to herself as her eyes glanced over the overhead signs. Then, finding herself alone, she looked back, and saw that Rachel had stopped a few feet behind her, just staring.

Blood rushed to her face as she walked back to her. "I'm sorry, Rach."

Rachel rested her hand on her shoulder. "He's not here, Isa. I didn't drop him off. Julio did. His team is setting up security in the new house, and he's leaving from the Palm Beach airport soon after. We didn't know you were coming in today. I wish you had called. I could tell he missed you. Perhaps he would have stayed if you had called last night."

Isabella nodded, wishing Rachel would shut up. She felt worse knowing that her planned surprise return backfired. Now a stupid hour's distance kept her from seeing him. She took deep breaths and prayed.

It's just for a weekend, she told herself. *Okay, maybe a week—but you'll live.*

Later that evening at Casa Cervello, Isabella helped Rachel get ready for her date while she taste-tested Gracie's homemade lollipops. Gracie had provided them with a basket full of wine-flavored treats, and Isabella was grateful for the perfect timing because her sweet tooth helped take her mind off Christian. She still wasn't comfortable opening up to Rachel about him—it was awkward. So when Rachel asked if she was okay, she played off her fears as flight fatigue. The truth was she wondered if Christian would bump into Kathy in London and reconsider their relationship.

"Suck in," Isabella told Rachel.

Rachel inhaled as Isabella zipped up her blue cocktail dress.

Isabella smiled at her from the mirror. "Good girl."

Rachel grinned as she admired her hair and makeup. "You know, you're getting really good at this. You should consider—"

"Just shut it! That was the gate—I'll let him in. Are you ready?" Isabella coughed.

"Are you okay?"

Isabella slammed down on her chest, coughing violently. "Yeah . . . I just choked on my spit."

"Nah, it's you and that candy," Rachel said, smacking her back. "Exactly how much *did* you have?"

"Why? I'm still on the first one. These are good. She's gonna sell out." She coughed. "Just watch."

"Which flavor is that?" Rachel asked.

"Hmm, don't know. I think Strawberry Rum." She grabbed the wrapper. "Close, Cherry Chardonnay."

"That's it," Rachel said, giggling. "You're probably drunk off the candy."

"Stop! But, seriously, check out these wrappers. Did you know there's a message behind them?"

"Really?" Rachel asked, reaching for her shoes.

"'Romance is closer than you think,'" Isabella read.

"Oh please, that's probably for me. You're the one stuck in this house."

Isabella handed her the basket. "Here, try one."

"Nah . . . can't mess up my lipstick."

"At least just read it."

Rachel opened a wrapper. "'Make up your mind.' Okay, that's silly."

Isabella laughed uncontrollably.

"Whatever," Rachel said. "It's silly anyway. Try again and see."

Isabella grabbed another lollipop and grinned. "Look! 'Romance is closer than you think.' Ha-ha!"

"No fair!" Rachel pouted.

"Oh, stop it. It's just silly candy. Gracie was probably drunk when she came up with the words."

Rachel held up two shoes. "Help me choose one."

Isabella started to giggle again.

Rachel frowned. "What's so funny?"

"The candy wrapper was right about you."

Rachel's fit of giggles had Isabella on damage control for her smudging mascara. The doorbell rang. "Go. The black pair's fine." She kissed Rachel on the cheek. "Have fun, babe."

"I would say the same for you, but . . . "

Isabella stuck out her tongue.

When Rachel walked out the door, Isabella ran to the window and watched as the car drove off. She imagined what her first date with Christian might be like. The thoughts only reminded her of her fears of losing him. She went back to Rachel's room and cleaned up as she blasted music to drown her fears.

Christian walked out of the airport limo and into Palm Beach International Airport.

"I'm sorry, sir," the attendant announced. "Flight number 5699 was delayed again due to poor weather conditions in Detroit. I apologize for the inconvenience."

"Do you know how much longer it'll be delayed? Perhaps I can just wait here if it isn't a long wait."

"Unfortunately, we just found out it will be delayed until tomorrow. I understand some of the passengers have opted to fly out of Miami International. The next available one with extra seats left is flight number 8823 at 11:30 a.m., leaving from Miami to Atlanta. If you decide to take that, your estimated arrival time should be the following morning."

"Ouch." Christian grimaced. "I guess it won't make much of a difference. I'll wait it out."

"We can lodge you in a hotel until then."

"No, thank you," Christian smiled. "I've got one already."

"I apologize again for the inconvenience."

He winked. "Better safe than sorry, right?"

"Right." She smiled.

Back in his hotel room, Christian's cell phone rang just as he was about to walk out to the balcony. *Private.*

"Hello?"

"*Hey,* hon," Olivia said. "I just saw you walk in."

"You always seem to know when I'm in a hotel. When did you even start blocking your number?"

"Don't be paranoid. I was at the lobby restaurant."

"Of all the hotels—I won't even ask why you're in Palm Beach."

"Good. So, what room are you in?"

"Nah, I'll come right down. I need some fresh air anyway."

"Suit yourself."

Christian walked out the elevator and sent Olivia a text. She immediately called his phone. "We're at the lobby restaurant. Table seven."

"*We?*" Christian asked curiously. The phone was dead.

"Good evening, sir," the waiter greeted. "Welcome to *Casa Lontano Da Casa.*"

"Good evening. Someone at table seven is expecting me."

"Right this way, sir."

Olivia met him halfway as she went to greet him with a kiss. "Don't you look dashing."

"Aren't we supposed to be mad at each other?"

"Don't be silly, Chris. Siblings fight. I didn't mean all that stuff I said, and I won't tell Isa anything."

They both walked up to the table, and Christian stiffened as soon as he saw his ex-fiancée, Kathy.

Christian glared at Olivia in outrage. "What's this about?"

Kathy stood up and approached him. "Baby, let me ex—"

"What are you doing here?" Christian demanded in a controlled voice as his eyes scanned the room.

Kathy stuttered. "I . . . I was visiting a friend."

He looked at her. "You don't have any friends in the Palm Beach area, remember?"

Olivia stepped in between them. "Guys, please don't cause a scene; this place is way too fancy."

Christian kept his gaze on Kathy. "I'm sure it is, Liv. I'm sure you had it all planned out."

"You know what, I'm leaving," Olivia said, grabbing her purse.

Christian turned to her. "Of course, leave. Make a mess and leave; that's your motto."

When Olivia walked away, Kathy said, "I didn't come here to cause you trouble. I was actually flying back to London today, but my flight was delayed. Listen, things didn't end well with us. There was no closure. I know how you feel about closure."

"Closure?" Christian laughed aloud, beginning to draw the attention of some of the guests. "Oh, yeah, you're right about that. Then again, you were too busy screwing my best friend to get closure, right?"

"That's not fair," Kathy snapped, fighting back tears.

"But it happened, didn't it, Kat?"

"Can you at least sit down, so we don't cause a scene," Kathy pleaded. Christian reluctantly sat.

"Listen, the truth about that night is that I wasn't there of my own free will. Kevin, he . . . he raped me."

An expressionless Christian began to clap—again, causing the guests to look their way. "I've known Kevin Hendricks to be a lot of things, but a rapist?" Christian said, shaking his headed swiftly. "Not quite one of them."

Kathy continued, "You don't know—"

The manager walked up to the table. "Sir, madam, I'm sorry but I will have to ask you to leave."

"I apologize for the trouble, sir," Christian said, before retrieving his wallet and placing two hundred-dollar bills on the table. "Good evening, Ms. Giles."

Olivia was in the main lobby when Christian walked out of the restaurant. She started to follow him, but stopped short and headed back into the restaurant to see Kathy crying. "Did you tell him?" Olivia asked.

"Yes, and it was stupid," Kathy blurted. "We should have just stuck with the original plan."

Olivia sat down. "No, it wasn't stupid. You see, growing up, when I got upset that my efforts weren't showing fast enough, Christian always told me, 'When you plant a seed in the ground, you can't expect it to grow overnight.' You have no idea what you did, Kat. You can't see it now, but you've won. Call *that* Plan A."

Olivia grinned at the cash on the table. She picked it up and sniffed it. "I love getting paid in advance."

Christian cringed at the idea of being on the same flight as Kathy the next day. He had never missed his jet as much as he did now. With no desire to remain in the same hotel with the women, he packed up his belongings and called for a driver. The driver pulled up to Casa Cervello nearly an hour later. Seeing the lights inside the home on, Christian figured Rachel must have changed her plans for the evening with Thomas. He had hoped to make it to his bed without a series of questions. He would eventually tell her what happened, but not tonight. Between the flight delay, Olivia, and Kathy, he had his fill of drama for one day.

Rachel's door was slightly open, and he held his breath as he continued on to the other end of the hallway, sighing as soon as he made it into his room uninterrupted. She probably wouldn't have heard him with all that noise—he swore his sister was going deaf. Soon after he walked in, the song "Careless Whisper" started to play. It was loud enough to hear the words, and he hated it—only because it was his and Kathy's song. He contemplated countering the noise with some sound of his own, but he had a horrible headache and just wanted peace. However, when His Mind took the liberty of digging up memories of their first date, he was ready to risk Rachel's nagging if it meant he didn't have to hear the song. He texted:

> I'm home because of a flight delay, but I need to get some sleep. Can you please turn your music down?

The music continued, so did the flashbacks. This time Kathy was in bed with Kevin.

Christian breathed in deeply, kicking off his shoes and slipping on his room slippers. There was a time he and Kathy would listen to it on repeat to make it last longer. Now, it was the longest, and most irritating five minutes. He wondered why the music had such an effect on him still. Was he really over Kathy, or did this feeling have to do with just seeing her? *Deep breaths*, he said to himself, walking calmly to Rachel's room. A mass of golden-brown hair draped the pillow. *No way,* he thought. His heart raced. Unless Rachel had dyed her hair between that morning and now, it had to be Isabella. He stood, mesmerized at the mere sight of her.

The resentment lifted, and the background music meant absolutely nothing, other than the fact that it was recording new memories with the beautiful creature sleeping peacefully on his sister's bed. *That's how she sleeps.* On her side, in a fetal position, her right arm cradled a basket of candy. When the song finished and another started, he reached for the stereo volume—trying hard not to take his eyes off her. Her hair covered her entire face, but he recognized the clothes she wore as Rachel's off-shoulder Cyndi Lauper blouse, paired with shorts. He reached over and covered her bare legs with a blanket. As he brushed the hair away from her face, he saw a lollipop in her mouth. He had started to remove it when she woke up.

Startled, Isabella immediately sat up in the bed, pushing her tousled hair out of her face—some strands entangled around the stick. She appeared embarrassed. "Oops."

"That could be a hazard, you know?"

"What?" she giggled.

"Sleeping with a lollipop in your mouth."

"I bet."

Glad he had an excuse to touch her hair, he sat next to her and helped detangle it. "Where's this from anyway?" he asked, motioning to the basket.

"My neighbor, Gracie's new business. You gotta try it; they're so good." As she spoke, he studied her lips—stained red from the candy. Any moment now, that fascinating curl should surface—if he stared at her long enough. With his eyes still on her lips, he mechanically reached out for a lollipop and unwrapped one.

She caught him off guard by standing to her feet and swiftly tossing her hair down toward her waist, gathering the voluminous waves in both hands and twisting it.

"When did you get in?" he asked.

"Right before noon. Rachel picked me up."

"Why so soon?"

"We finished sooner than expected. How about you? Shouldn't you be on a plane to London?" she asked, eyes skimming the floor.

"My flight was delayed. What are you looking for?"

"My rubber band . . . ah, there it is."

"Your hair looked fine the way it was," he said. "Leave it down . . . I like it."

As she released her hair, her mind went blank until a text message alert brought her back. It was probably from Rachel. She froze again when he stood up, keeping his gaze on her. She managed to look away—fiddling with her headband, she ensured she snapped it hard enough against her wrist to ensure she wasn't dreaming.

"Now about that candy," he said—his voice thick.

"Oh yeah, they have messages inside them. Check it out."

He glanced at his candy wrapper and nodded to her. "What did yours say?"

Isabella pulled both wrappers from her shorts in excitement. "Hey, I asked first."

"You just asked me to check and I did."

"Ugh," she grunted.

He moistened his lips. "I love messing with you."

"Why?"

"Because you make it so easy," he said, staring at her mouth. "Come on, spit it out—it's probably the same generic words for everyone anyway, and here . . . take this—I'm not a sweet tooth."

She took the lollipop from him. "But Rachel had something different and hers was right on."

"I'm guessing she is on her date with Thomas."

Isabella nodded. "Okay, it says, '*Romance is closer than you think.*'"

"Aha! Told you it's all generic stuff."

"Why?" she asked.

He handed over his wrapper. "That's why."

"You got the same thing! That's creepy."

"Oh, stop it." He scoffed.

"No, seriously, I got it twice. I'll grab another and see. You're probably right. Maybe it's just two different messages." He smiled as he watched her place his lollipop in her mouth and eagerly unwrap another.

"'The time is now.' Okay . . . " she made a face.

"That's what it said?".

"Yup, silly I know." Isabella gathered the fallen wrappers from the ground.

"Why?" His brows creased. "They may be on to something."

She stood back up, bemused, and removed the candy from her mouth. "On to what?"

Christian took her face in both his hands and, with his thumbs, he traced the corners of her lips slowly before kissing them and pulling away.

"Mmm, this *is* good," he said, licking his lips. "Let me have mine back."

Still reeling from what just happened, she was mute. *Our first kiss*, she thought. She didn't think it would happen this way. She had rehearsed it differently. Her fingers reached for her lips in shock.

With a side smile, he pulled the lollipop from her lifeless hand and put it in his mouth.

"Hmm . . . very nice, but I prefer the way it tastes on your mouth—come here."

He pulled her face close. This time, she was a more prepared participant; thus it lasted longer. His hand roamed freely through the back of her hair—massaging her scalp. They mutually pulled away and silently stood holding each other. She closed her eyes as she rested against his chest. After what seemed like several minutes, he pulled away, then holding both sides of her face, he looked directly into her eyes and then kissed her forehead. She noticed a small smirk before he placed the lollipop back into his mouth and walked away. She stood in that spot until she heard Rachel come through the front door some minutes later.

"I knew you couldn't resist," Olivia said, embracing Kevin after he entered her condo.

"I'm only here to tell you I've decided to apologize to Chris for all I've put him through."

"You'll do no such thing!" Olivia raged.

"*Excuse me?*"

Olivia took his hand and walked him over to the couch, "Listen, it's been hard on you—I know. You had it all . . . born into money, Chris wasn't. Now he has this empire and endless money and here you are, living like a rat—getting jobs from him and now crawling back to him, like all those girls do. It's time to man up. I tried to connect you with some of Miami's hottest girls, but no, they wanted Chris. I tried setting you up with Kathy, and you almost had her, but now all she wants is him. Can't you see the pattern?"

"It wasn't his fault. He didn't take anything from me. I spent all my inheritance money myself. All he ever did was give me good advice, which I never took. He didn't borrow a dime of my money, and he worked hard for what he has. As for the girls, he minded his business, and they wanted him. I can't compete with him anymore, Liv. I'm tired, so just drop it."

"Don't you see? He doesn't even have to try, but he gets his way. I've been true to you, haven't I?"

Kevin sighed. "Where's this going?"

"Answer the question, Kev!"

"A huge pain, but yes, and?"

"You wanted Kathy and I made it happen."

"Made what happen? She's not with me."

With a bemused smile, Olivia said, "I can take a dog to the bowl, but I can't make it eat, can I?"

"So now I'm a dog, Liv?"

Olivia laughed. "See how slow you are? No, silly, all I'm saying is you gotta learn how to keep 'em."

"Well, I never got her. Let me remind you that she wasn't one of your girls to give away. Chris met her first, on his own—from school." Kevin paced the room. "And all she wanted was money. Why in the world she would think I owned a majority of Private-I shares is beyond me."

"How *did* it go down anyway?" Olivia asked, her tone somber.

Kevin sat down. "It all started shortly after he introduced me to her. Remember how we all had dinner that night at the top of his condo, and shortly after, you told me she had these feelings for me and not him?"

Olivia nodded.

"Well, I believed you because she started showing up at my condo in her spare time. We would meet a couple of nights a week when Chris was away." Kevin shook his head and continued with a deep sigh. "She said she wanted me and then one thing led to another. She told me she didn't really love him, you know, the same thing you'd said. Well anyway, in a few weeks, things started to change. It was like she was in a hurry or something. She would make excuses about how she couldn't come because she was busy. Then she kept asking me the same questions about shares that I knew nothing about. I kept telling her that, but she thought I was faking. She said I was too humble. I mean, maybe I led her on in the end because that was the only way I could get her to sleep with me. I told her I'd tell her all about my shares. Next thing, Chris walks in and boom . . . I messed up his life. Maybe it's a good thing it happened because he doesn't need such a woman."

"Oh, so now you care about what's good for him?" Olivia sneered.

"Forgive me for caring, Liv, but let me remind you that Chris is our friend and our loyalty is to him and not Kathy. We failed him. You knew he was engaged to be married, but you were pulling strings for Kathy to be with me. We all failed him, all three of us. Your conscience may be dead, but mine is still intact."

Kevin stood up to leave. "I'm going to find him and do what's right."

"No." Olivia pushed him back onto the couch. "Stop pretending like you never wanted Kathy."

"Yeah, I wanted her, so what? Maybe that's because you told me she was single when you showed me her picture before I even met her, remember? I never should have listened to you. Then you tell me you didn't know they were in a relationship. Come on, Liv, you know you did—with all those trips you made to visit them? You know what, forget it. The point is, she was never interested in me in that way, and you know what, she had a right not to be. So what if she wanted Chris, he met her first. Stop butting heads!"

Again, Kevin stood up to leave but Olivia pushed him back down. "Now listen," Olivia said through clenched teeth. "You have one more try at this, are you in?"

"Try at what? What scheme do you have up your sleeve this time?"

Olivia laughed. "You make me sound so evil."

"That's because you are."

"Either you're in or out—I'm not gonna force you."

"I'm done hurting my best friend," Kevin said, standing up to leave and walking toward the door. This time Olivia didn't stop him but simply laughed. "You are so delusional. When will you ever learn? Haven't you heard that David Crenshaw is his *new* best friend? Remember him? The Private-I contractor that was supposed to be his best man?"

Kevin stopped, and without looking back, he said, "No, he wasn't," his voice, shaky.

Olivia shrugged. "Do I think it's fair? No . . . and get this, that was before you even betrayed him—meaning, he didn't think you two were as close as you thought. Come on, you've been brothers since grade school." She walked up to him and laid her hand on the back of his shoulder. "Listen, there's no way I'm gonna let you crawl back to Christian. No way. You're better than that, and you know it."

Isabella could not contain her excitement when Rachel announced that Christian would be home in time for the Fourth of July festival and Elisabeth's funeral that weekend. The last time she'd seen him was the night he kissed her and walked away. As mysteriously as he had shown up in Rachel's room that night, he mysteriously left the next day—so fast that Isabella wondered whether she dreamt the whole thing. Her assurance that it had happened was the feel of his lips on her mouth. He branded them as his very own property, and she loved it.

With both her mother, Ana, and her father, Felix, on speakerphone, Isabella decided it was a good time to mention her interest in someone, especially since they had stressed her so much lately about settling down.

"Alô Mamae, Alô Papai," she greeted cheerfully.

"Filha," Ana said. "When are you coming home?"

Isabella sighed. "I'm doing fine, Mom, thank you for asking."

Felix laughed. "Pay your mother no mind. How are you, honey? How was the party and your trip?"

"Oh Dad, the party was amazing, and I was in Mexico only for three days, but enough about me . . . how are you two? Did you ever get that shipment?"

"Oh, we must have forgotten to tell her, Ana," Felix said. "Yes, we got it a long time ago, Obrigado."

"You're welcome, I'm glad."

Ana asked, "Filha, do you remember Gloria's son, Eduardo?"

Isabella knew where this was going. "No, Mom."

"You know . . . home-school Edu?"

"Oh, yeah, how is he doing?"

"Oh, baby, he's doing just fine. He's a doctor now—one of the most re-spected new doctors in Brazil. He's appearing on all the talk shows. You need to see how the ladies here are vying for his hand in marriage. I wish we had made you return to Brazil with us."

"Wow. Good for him," Isabella said, ignoring her last statement.

"No, baby—good for you because he still asks about you. Remember how crazy he used to be about you? He's never forgotten."

Perhaps today isn't the day to tell them about Chris, Isabella thought.

CHAPTER NINETEEN

Meet Pandora

❦

ELISABETH SUARES Santos was laid to rest at a well-attended ceremony. As guests began to head to the reception, set to take place at the home of Elisabeth's sister, the three of them made their way back to the car. No one uttered a word the entire drive. Rachel's guilt tore at her. Elisabeth was her mother's closest friend and had remained a good friend to her mom until the very end. She and Christian had always seen Elisabeth as odd; perhaps it had to do with her old eccentric ways. However, her mother never forced them to embrace her.

Rachel's guilt had to do with the way she and Christian had mocked her when they were children, even coining the name *creepy church lady* for her—when all she was to her mother was a faithful friend. They never mocked her to her face, but they had cringed when she embraced them, and that was bad enough. It had been sixteen years since her mother had died, and Elisabeth still loved and cared for Rachel from a distance. Of course, she was closer to her than Christian was, but that was because Christian stopped attending church altogether after her mother died and only returned to visit sparingly before he left for Vancouver. Even then, Rachel remembered how Elisabeth had tried opening up to her a number of times, but Rachel never seemed to have time.

Rachel looked over at Christian, wondering whether he thought along the same lines. "Penny for your thoughts." She smiled.

Christian smiled back. "Just wondering what we're still doing sitting here." It had been ten minutes since they pulled up to the sister's house, but they sat in silence, each observing the other.

"Okay, guys," Isabella said. "People are staring through the window. Let's go in."

They knocked on the partially open front door and walked into a crowd full of mourners at the main floor, and some standing all around the top of the staircase. The aroma of Portuguese food filled the room, and they had a clear view of the kitchen upstairs. There stood a woman in her late 50s dressed in all black, with a long, black hair scarf. Rachel was the first to notice her, and when they both made eye contact, Rachel released a long wail. Her cries attracted the attention of all the guests. The woman ran from the kitchen and down the steps toward them, mumbling words in a foreign language.

Upon seeing her, Christian gasped, holding Rachel tight. Isabella also appeared frightened, but listened intently to what the woman, who was now smiling, said. She opened her arms. "Children, I'm not a ghost. My name is Rosa. Elisabeth was my identical twin sister. I've gotten this a lot since she passed away. Please come in."

Isabella heaved a sigh and started to giggle, as did some of the guests.

"What did she say?" Christian asked, cradling Rachel's head against his chest.

"She's Elisabeth's identical twin," Isabella said. "She gets it all the time." Christian and Rachel sighed.

"We didn't see you at the funeral," Isabella said.

"Oh dear, I couldn't handle it. My son and his wife were there to assist Elisabeth's kids."

Then pointing to Christian and Rachel, Rosa continued in Portuguese, "Let me guess, you two were Elizabeth's kids?"

"Yes," Isabella replied. "Well, Rachel is her daughter and Christian is her nephew."

"Yes," Rosa nodded. "I remember, she referred to both of them as her kids. They won't remember me, but she used to bring them back here after church to play with the other kids when they were little."

Isabella lifted a brow as she glanced at them. "Is that so?" Seeing Christian's and Rachel's curious gazes, Isabella whispered to them. "I'll tell you later."

"I take it you're their friend," Rosa said.

"Yes, my name is Isabella," she said, extending her hand.

Rosa's gaze burned into hers as she took her hand, nodding slowly. "Hmm."

Isabella and Christian shared a quick side-glance as his brow lifted.

Rosa ushered the three of them up the stairs and began to introduce them in Portuguese to some of the guests. "Their mom was my sister's best friend," Isabella would hear and translate. "Ah, I see," was the response she heard.

Rosa asked if they were ready to have something to eat. Isabella agreed to a drink for the three of them.

"What language is she speaking?" Christian asked Isabella.

"Portuguese."

"Oh, I always thought Spanish was the main language in Brazil."

"We predominantly speak Portuguese."

"Hmm," Christian said, eyebrows furrowed. "Why did I think Elisabeth was Spanish?" he muttered.

"Perhaps because your aunt was Spanish, and she was close to her."

"My mom knew Portuguese," Rachel told Isabella. "My dad was from Portugal, he met Elisabeth first."

"How come you never learned?" Christian teased, nudging Rachel's elbow.

"The same reason you didn't. Besides, you knew them longer than I did."

"Okay, guys, cut it out," Isabella said. "I'll tell you what they say or if anyone talks about us."

"You do that," Christian replied with a wink.

Rosa returned with drinks. "I hope you kids are settling in okay. Sorry, I can't speak English too well."

"No problem," Isabella said. "I've been translating for them."

"Oh dear, my sister was always so afraid to come to the mansion to visit because of their scary dogs."

"Oh, the dogs died a long time ago," Isabella replied. "They never got new ones."

Excusing herself, Isabella translated what she'd said so far.

"If you don't mind, I'll be translating for them as we talk."

"Oh, not a problem, honey," Rosa smiled. "You are a good friend to them. I see it." She then spoke directly to Christian and Rachel in Portuguese, "Actually, I've been waiting for you kids to come back here."

"Why?" Isabella asked, translating back and forth.

"I need to speak to you about something very important. I believe that now is the time to let you know."

Rachel and Christian exchanged a frightful stare.

"Where would you like to speak to them?" Isabella asked.

"Back downstairs. The family room is more private." Rosa led them to the family room on the main level. Four kids were playing video games there, and Rosa snapped at them in Portuguese. The kids, now grumpy, walked off.

"Grandkids," she said, shaking her head. She then turned off the TV and invited them in.

"Please make yourselves comfortable, I'll be right back."

The three of them exchanged apprehensive looks as they stood in the middle of the room. The room had windows on both sides of the wall—one blocked with storage. Isabella reached for a nearby light switch. The light bulb was quite dull, but enough to see visible black stitching on a red love seat and a larger sofa covered in plastic wrap. "What are you afraid of, Rachel?" Isabella asked.

"I don't know," Rachel said in a shaky tone. "I always had this feeling Elisabeth wanted to tell me something but felt I wasn't ready to take it."

Christian nodded. "That same eerie feeling I had when I heard she died."

"Okay, let's take a deep breath in," Isabella said. They complied. "And out." She would wait to tell them about the note Elisabeth gave her on Christian's birthday. It had to be related, and she was certain that whatever Rosa had for them was going to change their lives forever.

Rosa walked into the room with a rolled-up poster board. She placed the poster board on a wooden coffee table and invited them to sit. When they did, she looked at Christian and Rachel almost fearfully. Then turning to Isabella, she said, "Okay, don't tell them what I'm about to say." Isabella struggled to maintain her calm.

"Their family is cursed," Rosa announced.

Isabella gasped.

"Yes, it's well-known but their parents have kept it from them," Rosa said, looking directly at Isabella.

Christian demanded, "What is she saying?"

Isabella managed a smile. "Hold on, I'll tell you everything, I promise." Then turning to Rosa, Isabella said, "You *do* know they will have to know this, right?"

"Oh, of course," Rosa said. "But you must find a way to say it where they won't panic. They must know there's hope. Many families are cursed; it's just that the magnitude of this one happens to be more than I've seen in my experience."

"What can you tell me about the magnitude?" Isabella asked.

Rosa shifted in her seat. "Well, for one, there appears to be many strange but consistent patterns. Just when Elisabeth thought she was on to one, another would appear."

"Excuse me," Isabella said. "Can I take notes, or better yet, record you? I'd hate to forget anything."

"Sure, it's not a problem."

Isabella retrieved her cell phone and began to record. She noticed Christian pace the room, and Rachel had her head down in her lap.

"Okay, you were talking about a pattern," Isabella prompted.

"Yes," Rosa said, opening the poster board and tacking the four corners down with paperweights. "My sister, Elisabeth and her friend, Elizabeth, with a "Z", were very close. Listen, I would hate to confuse you, so how about we refer to the girl's mother as *Liz*?" Isabella nodded.

"Liz confided in my sister about some fears she had about her family and some recurrent dreams she had of dying. From what she knew of her family, many of the deaths they suffered were untimely and tragic—like car accidents; some involved more than one family member from different generations and some had died young."

Isabella held her chest. "What family in particular?"

"The Gomes family, which I believe is Rachel and Christian's maternal family. Here is the family tree."

Isabella reviewed the large map. "It's so thorough."

"Yes, Liz started it and my sister continued it after Liz passed away in 1997. You will see that Liz had been gaining insight about her family as led by the Holy Spirit. She was just careful not to involve her husband or children for fear that she would create fear and alienation. She wanted them to have a family that was as normal as possible. She tried to get her sister involved, but her sister had told her numerous times that she wanted nothing to do with it and accused her of being paranoid. Therefore, she confided mostly in my sister, and they grew close in the process. It's interesting; they were both identical twins, with the same name, and both worked in the prayer ministry."

"That *is* interesting." Isabella nodded. "Where you also involved in the process?"

"Not that much. They consulted me from time to time with concerns, but I knew about the map."

"How many other people know about the map?"

"No one. It was just the three of us and both of them are gone now."

Isabella muttered, "Rachel said she had this feeling that your sister wanted to tell her something."

"I wouldn't be surprised if it was about this," Rosa said.

"Why do you think she didn't tell her all this time?"

"Well, for one, Liz made my sister promise never to tell the kids even after she died—at least, not until Elisabeth had the complete picture. She didn't want her to instill unnecessary fear with no concrete answers."

"Why does it sound like Liz knew she would die before Elisabeth?" Isabella asked, terrified.

Rosa shook her head with a sad smile. "Liz always spoke of her death. She was a troubled soul. She just didn't know when it was coming. But if you ask me, she lived in fear her whole life."

"But she was saved, wasn't she?" Isabella asked. "Why so much fear?"

"My child, you have no idea how many Christians live in fear and hold on to some kind of plan, just in case their faith fails them."

"Really? But the Bible says—"

"I know what the Bible says, dear, and it's right, but try telling that to someone who's been hurting for decades and had no prior foundation in Christ."

"Is that what happened with Rachel's mom? Did she have a Plan B?"

"Yes, my child. I'm sorry to say that she did. No, let me correct myself, at first, she did. That was around the time we met her. We told her that Jesus Christ was the only way to end this mess." Rosa sighed. "She said there was a charm their father gave them to ward off evil spirits. According to her, it worked for her father for a while. He believed it saved his life from the car crash that claimed his wife. Apparently, he was upset that his wife didn't have hers on the day of the accident and made all the kids swear to wear it forever."

"What?" This was all absurd to Isabella.

"Yes."

"So, how did he end up dying?" Isabella asked, "I mean . . . Rachel's grandfather?"

"Well, according to this chart, he died of a broken heart."

Isabella covered her mouth. Tears formed in her eyes. "Did Liz have it on at the time of her death?"

"No, she didn't, and listen to me—that has absolutely nothing to do with her death. Only God knows why. You know, I had my doubts that she was totally committed to Christ up until the day she died."

"What makes you believe she was committed in the end?"

"Because she didn't have it on. She did away with it and began to put her trust in the Lord. I must say, I'm proud of her. It couldn't have been easy letting go of that necklace—especially with no Christian foundation. I know she loved the Lord, and now she's in Heaven. But if you ask me, it was a matter of time."

"Why do you say that?"

"Because she was an excessive worrier, and eventually she succumbed to the very thing she was afraid of. Fear is a curse all on its own, and it affects even the strongest Christians; each individual must face it. Apart from the fact that her family was facing a curse that someone else pronounced, she was facing her own self-inflicted curse—fear, and it is sad that she had to face it alone. Although I was proud that she stood up for her beliefs, her sister, on the other hand, blamed her for her own death."

"Aunt Pattie?" Isabella asked. "Why?"

"Well, after the viewing, when she was alone with Liz's casket, we overheard her screaming at her body. She was extremely upset that the necklace wasn't on her body at the time of death because apparently their brother had made them renew their vow never to remove it after their father died."

"Their brother?"

"Oh, you didn't know Liz and Patricia had a brother?"

Isabella shook her head, glancing at Rachel, who appeared to have fallen asleep. "No, I didn't."

"Well, they had a brother who died protecting Patricia."

Isabella nearly lost her balance, causing Christian to walk over to hold her.

"Listen," he said. "I don't know what she's telling you, but it's time for us to leave."

"No," Isabella said, her voice faint. "She's not upsetting me. I'll tell you everything. It's just a lot now."

Isabella turned back to Rosa. "I'm sorry, Rosa, please continue."

"Listen, my child, you'll have to be stronger than this because it gets deeper. You must be strong and of good courage; don't be afraid or dismayed for God—"

"Will be with me wherever I go," Isabella finished. It was the scripture Elisabeth had given her in the note. Chills ran down her back as she remembered how Elisabeth walked up to her and encouraged her. "Yes, I'm strong. I can do this," Isabella said, taking in deep breaths. She had learned the art from her therapist. Now she used it anytime she could and it worked every time.

"Good, because I believe you were the one chosen to assist this family," Rosa said, pointing to a stick drawing with Isabella's name circled. Next to her name was the year 1997, along with the scripture Elisabeth had given to her in the tightly rolled paper. That delivery was listed as fulfilled on 4/7/13—Christian's birthday of all days.

Isabella's eyes widened. "Liz knew of me before she even met me? I hadn't even met Rachel before her mother died."

Rosa smiled. "Our God is mysterious. Your name appeared in her dream." Rosa pointed to the chart.

"That's how you knew . . . downstairs." Tears were running down Isabella's face now.

"Yes, dear. All we knew from Liz's dream was your name—no description. But I felt it when I saw you."

"Their brother . . . what was his name?"

"Eduardo," Rosa said, pointing to the chart.

"Did he have on the necklace when he got killed?"

Rosa smiled. "Aha! You are reasoning the way the women would want you to. The answer to your question is *yes*. He had on the necklace the day he got killed," she said, pointing to the symbol for the necklace on the chart. "I believe knowing this is what helped strengthen Liz's decision to let the damn thing go. As you can see, we can't credit that necklace for anything. Having it on didn't protect Eduardo, so we can confidently say that not having it on didn't take Liz's life. My question is, does any surviving Gomes have it on?"

"I'll ask them," Isabella said. She walked over to Christian. "Chris, do you know about a necklace that your mother and Aunt Liz wore for protection?"

Christian rubbed the back of his neck. "There's some strange one my mother has been wearing for the longest time. I don't know about Aunt Liz, but my mom definitely still wears one. In fact, she got one for Rachel and I when she returned from Spain after the funeral. Come on, we weren't gonna wear that crap."

Isabella nodded.

"Wait," Christian said. "Is that what this is about? Are we supposed to be wearing some necklace?"

"Oh, no," Isabella laughed. "Goodness no. Hold on, I'll fill you in on everything shortly."

Isabella walked back to Rosa and translated what he had said. Rosa nodded. "Good, some kids today are proving to be smarter than their parents. Liz told me that her twin was not interested in her suspicions, so she made several trips to Spain alone to research. It was challenging because the Gomeses back home were gone."

"And when you mentioned that someone pronounced the curse, how could you be so sure?"

"It's the rumor. We can't be sure about anything, dear, only God knows."

"Oh my, so where do we stand now? What do we do?"

"We start by turning to the cross. I never told you how the two of them met. Liz was in a desperate search for a way to break the curse, and her husband's friend invited her to the church. It just so happened that the same day, the preaching was on generational curses.

"After service, there was an altar call and as my sister prayed for Liz, she could tell that several demonic spirits tormented her. Threats from strange voices came out of Liz as she lay on the ground. There were certain things the Lord revealed to my sister that I can't get into right now, but it convinced her of their family's bondage.

"After that, Liz tried to get her sister to see that there was another way, but her sister wasn't hearing it. She made Liz feel like she was crazy—telling her all she had to do was wear some jewelry. Eventually, Liz stopped pressing her and was just grateful that she'd allowed her to take her son to church with her little girl. This was how they eventually got saved. With time, they discovered their spiritual gifts."

"Gifts, really?" Isabella asked, intrigued.

Rosa glanced proudly at Christian. "I don't quite know because it's not on the chart, but one of them has the gift of knowledge and the other the gift of wisdom, one manifesting through dreams. If I'm not mistaken, one dreams and the other interprets." Rosa stared at Isabella long and hard before asking, "How strong are the two of them in their faith?"

Isabella shrugged. "They've both admitted that their relationship with Christ could be better."

Rosa grinned, pointing a finger. "Aha! Start there. The good news is that they still have those gifts. I can't say if he was the dreamer and she was the interpreter, but they used to be very active in church as kids."

Isabella shook her head in disbelief. "What happened?"

Rosa smiled sadly. "Your guess is as good as mine. As soon as Liz died, they stopped attending church regularly, and then stopped altogether. Well, according to my sister, at least. She hardly spoke of them until recently, when the girl came back to church."

Pointing to the poster, Rosa said, "These are all the clues we have left."

Isabella stroked the poster. "It looks so neat after all these years. Has it been here since?"

Rosa smiled proudly. "Yes, up until now. I am giving it to you all today. My job is done."

Isabella was surprised. "Are you sure? I mean . . . "

"Yes, Elisabeth fulfilled her promise to Liz by keeping it to herself and diligently working on it. However, she couldn't complete the project without involving them somehow because they may all have a part to play in solving the puzzle. She tried to find a way to expose it to them without disrespecting Patricia, but at times she became timid. So, she asked me to promise that if she died before me, I was to expose it without further delay, and this is what I am doing, keeping my promise to my sister. I prayed for them to come here, and they came."

"It's probably what she wanted to tell Rachel."

"I believe so too. It was hard for her to keep that promise to Liz for all those years. I wonder if . . . "

"If what?" Isabella asked.

Rosa sighed. "I wonder if that was what ate at her heart. You know she died in her sleep, don't you?"

"Yeah, I heard. Do you think Elisabeth may have even wanted to die just to be free from the promise?"

Rosa shrugged. "Who knows? There were close—even closer than *I* was with Elisabeth, my *own* twin. They shared a special connection that we didn't share. I'm just happy that they can reconnect now—under better circumstances—and I'm happy because I'm not bound to a promise to keep a secret. I couldn't live like that. Seriously, Isabella, I think it's right. They need to know. Use wisdom. That's your gift."

Isabella's eyes widened. "Really? I heard that before; my mom and aunt told me. How did you know?"

Rosa smiled. "The Lord revealed it to me just now." She grabbed her shoulders. "Don't worry, my child, it's a good thing. You're in this family for a reason."

"Is the Lord telling you anything else right now?" Isabella asked, hopeful.

"No, but take this sealed envelope. You are not to open it until after three months from today."

When Isabella nodded, Rosa scribbled the current date, July 5, 2013, and said, "Liz's final dream. Promise me."

"I promise I won't open it until after three months from today. I'll put it away and mark my calendar."

There were sounds of footsteps coming down the stairs; then a voice called out, "Ms. Rosa?"

Rosa went to the doorway. "Yes?"

The woman said, "I hate to interrupt, but some of the guests are leaving and wanted to say good-bye."

"Okay, I'll be right there."

Rosa turned to Isabella. "I'll be back in a little while. Let me mingle with some of the other guests. It'll be rude if I don't. You can use this time to update them on what I've told you so far."

After Rosa went upstairs, Isabella sighed heavily as she rested into the small lumpy couch. Rachel sat up and looked over at her with a tired smile.

Isabella started. "Okay, so which of you is the dreamer, and who's the interpreter?"

Sometime later, after Isabella had brought them up to speed, Rosa came back downstairs. "How are you kids doing?" she asked—this time in Spanish.

"We are doing fine," Christian replied eagerly in Spanish.

Rosa smiled and said in broken English, "Ah, you speaking Español?"

Christian smiled. "Yes ma'am," he continued in Spanish. "I wish you spoke it earlier; perhaps we could have spared you both the translation—it must be a strain."

Rosa shook her head. "Unfortunately, I don't speak Spanish well. I understand more than I can speak."

Then she smiled at Isabella and continued in Portuguese. "Have you told them?"

"Yes—also I found out that he's the dreamer, and she's the interpreter."

Rosa looked at Christian, "Good, do you remember the dream you had of your auntie's car accident?"

After Isabella had translated, she noticed him swallow hard. "Yes," he replied, "it's in my old journal."

Rosa said to Isabella, "Yes, that was the last time I saw him."

"You no longer attend Faith House?" Isabella asked Rosa.

"No, dear, I never did. I go to a Portuguese church down the road. I visited their church on special occasions. It's hard because they only have Spanish translation and not Portuguese. You're doing a great job translating; if your pastor ever wants to expand that way, you should look into it."

Isabella smiled. "Sure." She had never quite given translating a thought.

Rosa looked at Christian and asked in broken English, "Still you dreaming today?"

"Yes, I still dream but it's all jumbled up now," Christian said, motioning with his hands as his gaze shifted from Rosa to Isabella.

"Tell him that his dreams are rusty because he has strayed far from the Lord. All he has to do is return to Him, and the dreams will start to get clearer again."

Rosa then turned to Rachel. "You interpreted the dream he had of your mother, didn't you?"

"Yes," Rachel said, "Christian told me about a dream involving Kevin, and I remember immediately knowing Kevin wasn't the victim. We were both frightened. We tried to stop Mom from going out two weeks in advance, but then I ended up being the reason she went to get Kevin that night. How could I have forgotten?"

Rachel burst into tears and Christian went to hold her.

Rosa also went to hold Rachel. "No, no, my child, how can you try to stop your mother from going out? That would be fear-motivated. When you have such dreams, you should learn to rebuke them with prayer. The gift is good. But as a child, you may have needed some guidance."

"It's my fault," Rachel said. "If I hadn't urged her to go, both of them would have probably been alive today."

Christian looked at Isabella as he cradled Rachel's head. "Ask her where we go from here?"

"Pray, fast, get closer to the vine, and you'll solve this mystery. Most of this map came from both women's revelations. There's still a huge chunk missing, but only through the blood can you piece it together."

Isabella nodded slowly as she stared blankly into space.

"Let us pray," Rosa announced. Gathering them together in a circle, she prayed in Portuguese as Isabella translated. Afterward, Rosa seemed to fall into a trancelike state. "Record this—don't interrupt me when I start."

Isabella rushed to grab her phone and fumbled with it as Rosa blurted, "There is a multi-pattern involving the curse that was pronounced. It started at least two generations ago. The people closest to them are hurting them. There is something huge about trust. This is a recurring pattern. Look to the past to help you deal with the future. Try your best to get their mother involved because she holds a big piece to the puzzle. She knew much more than her sister Elizabeth did. You will need to use all your gifts. According to the map, there will be other people along the way to help you all. Do whatever the Lord tells you to do—if he does not lead you, wait. Be obedient, and finally, pray without ceasing."

For the first time, Isabella sat for dinner with the entire Cervello clan and Thomas. Eating at the dining table was rare for them because they were hardly ever around at the same time to do that. Tadd's work as an international trade lawyer had him overseas most of the time, and if he had his way, he would have Pattie with him on all his trips. Traveling did not seem to bother her until recently, and to date his Asian business venture had been the longest he'd been away at a stretch. Apparently, it shouldn't have been that long, and this was why Pattie hadn't traveled with him.

Pattie had always considered Isabella as her child, but Isabella didn't feel the love that night, and hadn't felt it since the day Rachel confronted Pattie with the taboo issue—a secret that Pattie hoped she had buried years ago along with her sister's body. Pattie took the fireworks out on Christian and Rachel, but with Isabella, she hadn't uttered a single word. Still, Isabella couldn't mistake the cold stares she flashed her way and wondered what she had done wrong—could it have been translating the information for them and now knowing too much as an outsider? Whatever it was, the tension had become unbearable, and she knew she wasn't the only one walking on eggshells.

As they sat, silently passing dishes to one another, Isabella recalled that last conversation the day after they returned from Rosa's home. Rachel had gone against Christian's advice to wait for Tadd, and it resulted in dozens of broken china dishware. Isabella had never seen that side of Pattie, and she didn't know whether to be frightened or just ignore it—perhaps blame it on stress or fear. She'd ultimately decided to give Pattie the benefit of the doubt, even if she wasn't speaking to her.

Christian reached for a second serving of pot roast. *Well, at least someone has an appetite,* Isabella thought. She didn't dare look in Pattie's direction. She hated being afraid of Pattie, and she wished she could snap out of it, but she couldn't shake the memory of her fit of rage that day. With each dish she threw, she cursed in Spanish, referring to *Eduardo*—a name Isabella now knew belonged to her deceased brother. She also had words for her deceased sister. She couldn't shake the sight of Rachel—stooped in a corner, weeping the entire time. Christian had warned Isabella not to intervene—ensuring Pattie's rage would pass.

However, it didn't—and when all the china she could reach was gone, the only words she uttered to Isabella came with fire in her eyes—a demand to see Rosa. Isabella complied, afraid of what she might do to the woman when they got there. However, they were not prepared for what happened next. Rosa's only son met them at the door and informed them that his mother had passed away a day earlier—merely a day after her sister was buried. Pattie's expression—a mixture of fright and sincere regret—caught Isabella by surprise, and Isabella wound up holding a distraught Pattie as she wept in the car for half an hour outside Rosa's house. Being unable to reach Rosa regarding the matter must have been eerie for Pattie. Rosa had come to mean so much to them, and her death only added to the already crippling suspense.

"Patkey, did you give some thought to what the children said about this curse?" Tadd asked, as he helped himself to a glass of red wine.

Isabella froze. Straightforward but sweet was the best way to describe Taddeo Cervello. Respected in his home and by his peers, he was clearly the voice of reason in Casa Cervello. He did not speak much, but when he did, people listened. He was a powerful and very kind and understanding family man who was very much devoted to his Patkey—a gentle giant to her boisterous spitfire. They certainly balanced each other out.

Christian, watching his mother's expression closely, said cautiously, "Dad."

"It's okay," Pattie said to Christian, putting down her cutlery. "As a matter of fact, I did."

Thomas' stare at Isabella asked whether the both of them should leave, but Isabella was too scared to even nod or move.

Pattie continued, "She, um . . . God bless her soul. Rosa was right—we all need to get closer to God."

"So, what's this thing I'm hearing about a family curse?" Tadd persisted, his voice commanding.

Pattie rolled her eyes. "What family doesn't have problems, huh? Oh, forgive me—I forgot, yours does not. Yeah kids, your father here has the perfect family. Every single sibling of his is alive and well. Heck, even his parents and grandparents are alive and kicking. What do I have? Nothing."

"Come on, Mom," Rachel said. "You have *all* of us."

Pattie let out a frustrated laugh. "Us? Gomes? Yeah, I've got you and Christian, that's it."

"And we have Dad," Christian chimed in.

Pattie scoffed. "Yeah, good thing we have Dad because maybe his luck could rub off on us."

"There's no such thing as luck," Isabella mumbled, biting her tongue as soon as she spoke.

Pattie turned to Isabella with fire in her eyes and Christian must have seen what she saw because he deflected it to himself. "Mom, calm down."

Pattie's gaze turned to Christian. "Why don't you ask your little girl-friend here what she really thinks about us after all this?"

Christian wiped his mouth with his napkin and placed it down.

"Aunt Pattie, I'm part of this now because the women made it clear that I could help," Isabella said. "You're the only family I have in Florida, and I don't intend to go anywhere unless you tell me to leave." Isabella wasn't sure where the sudden boldness came from, but she was sick of being afraid. "So I'm asking all of you now, if anyone wants me to leave, I promise I will, and you'll never hear a word of this outside this house from me; I'll take it to my grave. Just say the word." She didn't realize how shaken she was until Tadd went to hold her. Everyone else reached out except for Pattie, who sat with her arms folded, rapidly jiggling her feet. Isabella stood up and headed for the door and just as she opened it, Pattie yelled, "Nena, don't leave!"

Isabella ran back, and they both embraced. Pattie held both sides of her face and repeatedly kissed her as she wiped her tears away. "You are part of this family, do you hear me?"

"Yes, Aunt Pattie."

"Go ahead, I know there's something you have been meaning to tell me since last week, so just say it."

"No," Isabella said, shaking her head.

"Say it!"

"Okay, I believe you know more about what's going on in your family than you're telling us, and I'm not asking you to admit it right now, but I just want you to know that in order for us to get to the bottom of this, we're gonna need you to tell us what you know. Rosa said that we can only do this together."

After what seemed like several minutes and many held breaths, Pattie asked, "What do I do?"

"Start by removing that thing on your neck," Isabella said.

CHAPTER TWENTY

Courtship

❧

CHRISTIAN APPRECIATED having his father, Tadd, around. He balanced things out, and they both shared a quiet resolve. Some had said he was the spitting image of Tadd, while those who had known his aunt Elizabeth believed he was a lot like her. Although he saw comparisons to his aunt as flattering, as they were both avid thinkers, he also saw it as a concern, because they both shared a tormented side. His aunt understood him better than his own mother did, and he had her to thank for helping Pattie accept him as he was.

Christian preferred to work things through on his own, but that usually caused problems for him, especially when his conclusions were wrong—his obsessions eagerly took over before he could reach out for help. His aunt, on the other hand, always seemed to him as someone who would first reach out for help and, if she did not get it, go forward on her own. Pattie and Rachel were very similar, and there was a lot to admire with their type. For one, they were never ashamed to ask for help and to keep asking until they got it. Also, they were never afraid to express themselves and often spoke without thinking—a nightmare for Christian to conceive. However, he could admit there was something gutsy and liberating about it.

Christian hesitated outside the family room doorway when he saw Tadd relaxing with a glass of wine—watching the evening news. Tadd was in a league of his own when it came to personality types—he hadn't a care in the world, and for many years, Christian had idealized him.

"Hey, Dad," Christian said, waving.

"Hey, son, come sit with your old man for a minute," Tadd said, patting the seat next to him. "I meant to tell you that I went to see the new house with your mom and sister the other day. I like what you did with the place; I'm proud of you, son."

Christian smiled. "That means a lot to me, Dad."

"If you think about it, you are the first Cervello to build a house from the ground up in this country. This house has been in our family for over 50 years, but with a brand new home, you have a new beginning."

"You're not mad?" Christian asked.

"Why would I be? Handing Casa Cervello over to Rachel was our best alternative. That was noble, what you did. You know, she told me that it was what actually convinced her that she was a Cervello."

"She said that?"

"Yeah, that was an amazing sacrifice. She understands you didn't have to do that."

Tadd turned off the TV. "Now son, I want you to be straight with me."

"Sure, Dad," Christian's brow creased.

"What are your plans with Isabella?"

Christian stood up and walked to the fireplace mantel, staring at Isabella's picture in a frame.

"It's a simple question, son."

"I know, Dad, it's just—"

"Do you have feelings for her?"

"I'm in love with her, Dad."

"So what's the holdup?"

"She's just . . . I don't know; she just seems so put together. Perfect. As if my dreams suddenly materialized. I keep expecting to wake up."

Tadd stood up and went to Christian. "Listen son, you got it! Same thing happened to my dad and me."

"Really?" he asked, wide-eyed.

"I was hoping you'd say she seemed too good to be true because that has been the Cervello way."

"No way. So what I feel is normal?"

"Our family is blessed. Cervellos mate extremely well, and you know what we believe is the secret to our success?" Tadd asked with a cheeky grin. "We are faithful, and the women we marry are also."

Christian had nearly broken a well-known tradition with his choice of Kathy. Since February, his father had been very gracious not to bring up the subject, other than to advise him to be careful with the next relationship.

"I never understood why my mom and dad stayed very close to one another," Tadd continued. "They still travel together; they keep no secrets." The lines in the corner of his eyes creased as he smiled. "Look at your mom and me, we never complain about where we want to be. She knew how homesick I was, and it just so happened that she was, too. We're finished with the house back home, and before you know it, we'll be back where we started, Calabria. The key is togetherness. Whatever you do, do it together."

Tadd searched Christian's face long and hard. "No one is perfect, son, but the trickiest part to finding your bride is recognizing she is yours despite how perfect you think she is, and making the move before someone smarter than you does. If you think she's so good that you fail to make the move, you'll lose her. So decide quickly."

"What do you think of Isabella, Dad?"

Tadd waved. "Oh, please—that girl was born to be a Cervello. See you later, son." Tadd patted him on the back. "*My* girl is waiting."

Christian stood looking at Isabella's picture with a smile long after his father walked out.

Nearly a month had gone by since Isabella courageously confronted Pattie. Since then, she had helped the family in their journey back to God— inviting Tadd and Pattie to church and initiating a weekly Bible study, of which Thomas was now in charge. Inasmuch as she loved how they considered her family, she wondered whether the bombshell news affected the dynamic of her and Christian's relationship for good. They had remained courteous with one another, and she knew she shouldn't complain, but it wasn't exactly what she had hoped for at this stage—especially after their kiss. He seemed quite distant now, and the idea that he may have taken the brotherly love to a whole other level terrified her. She was not his sister, and as much as she loved seeing him at Casa Cervello, she considered laying low for a while to remind him of that fact. She couldn't doubt their chemistry, but she wasn't ready to assume anything more. One thing was certain—not knowing where they stood was nerve-wracking.

Isabella was lying on her living room sofa watching a Saturday movie special when her doorbell rang.

"It's open, Gracie!" she called out.

The door squeaked open, followed by heavier than normal footsteps up the stairs. "Now what's a vivacious lady doing at home on a Saturday after- noon?" came the husky voice to which she had grown accustomed. She had expected Gracie to join her in between commercials because they had both grown weary of calling each other on the phone to discuss the movie.

Isabella greeted Christian with a side hug, partially lifting herself from the couch. "Please, have a seat," she urged. She needed to ensure he didn't know how badly she wanted to see him and was glad that the movie was interesting enough to help conceal her excitement.

"Thanks," Christian said, relaxing into the couch.

"Would you like anything to drink?" she asked.

"No, thanks."

"Good, I was hoping you would say that—commercial's over." Isabella winked.

Christian threw a throw pillow at her. "Lazy!"

"Shh, I can't miss this."

"What's the name?"

"No clue, I missed the opening credits."

"Oh, wait, I've seen this," Christian said, leaning forward in his seat, "It's really good."

"Shh, don't tell me!"

Christian laughed. "You know, I can just get you the DVD."

"Not necessary," she said, with eyes glued on the screen. "It's almost done."

"If you say so." Christian stood to leave. "I'll just come back another time when you're less busy."

"No, please don't go," she said, searching his face for an expression. She couldn't read one, but she was certain she sounded desperate now, and she didn't care.

"But your movie isn't even halfway through yet; you probably won't notice with all the commercials. I really don't mind coming back. Besides, I should have called you first."

"Don't you wanna watch it again?" she asked.

"Nah, I need to be somewhere." He glanced at his watch. "I came to speak to you, but it can wait."

Like hell it can, Isabella turned off the TV. "I was rude; please speak." She sat up, pulled her legs up to her chest, and hugged her knees.

Christian sat back down, this time at the edge of the couch. "So, I was wondering if you—would—like—to—um . . ."

Isabella giggled. "Why are you talking like that?"

"Like what?" Christian grinned.

"Robotic . . . if—you—would—like . . ."

A faint smile crept to his lips. "Stop, Isabella, I'm trying here."

"Okay, I'm sorry," she said, attempting to appear serious, but certain there was humor in her eyes.

"I wanna take you out for dinner."

The humor instantly left when her heart surely stopped. She had anticipated growing old waiting to hear those words. *At least Rachel can stop teasing me already,* she mused.

"Well?" Christian asked, apprehensive.

"Of course, I would love to," she said, blushing.

Christian smiled. "Great!"

"So, is this like a date?"

"I would rather not call it that."

He must have seen her face fall in disappointment.

"How about we call it a non-date date?" he added.

Isabella laughed. "Okay, you lost me."

"Just tell me you'll come—we'll have a good time; I promise."

"I usually love surprises, but can I know what to expect?"

"Okay, do you remember when you stood up to my mom?"

"Oh my goodness, don't remind me." She covered her face with the pillow.

"No, that was actually good," he said, walking over and sitting next to
her. "I saw another side of you, this no-nonsense side. I knew you had to
have a serious side."

"You think your mom was . . . you think I—" Isabella grimaced, hug-
ging the pillow tight.

"No, you weren't disrespectful at all. She actually loved it. You were polite, but told her what she needed to hear. I would like if you brought that
side of you to the dinner."

Isabella bit down on her bottom lip. "That's kind of scary."

"Listen, just leave the nice and charming Isa at home."

"Aha! So I *wasn't* nice to your mother."

"You were serious. I can't tell you how many times I've played this dating game, where everyone comes perfectly packaged and well-rehearsed. I'm
sure you know what I mean."

"Yeah, with the stuff you aren't supposed to do or say?"

"Exactly—it hasn't gotten either one of us far, has it?"

She shook her head.

He stared at her intensely, as though reading her. Isabella could never
get used to that stare. It had the power to either freeze or melt her. "I have
some serious questions for you," Christian said. "I don't want to have to
wait to ask them, and I would love for you to ask me whatever your heart
desires."

Isabella lifted a brow, but she remained tight-lipped.

"So if you're up for it, it may be a good idea to brainstorm the questions
you may have for me between now and then—nothing is off-limits. It will

be a 'no questions barred' date. Ask anything, the past, present, future, me, habits, anything."

Isabella's heart raced with a thrill. There were so many things she had wondered about him, but she had been too chicken to ask Rachel. Now she could do that personally. When Christian cleared his throat, she looked at him and stiffened at the realization that the questioning would go both ways.

"There's nothing to be afraid of," Christian said with a warm smile, as though reading her mind. "There's nothing you can tell me that will change how I feel about you—as long as you're honest."

"No questions barred, huh?" Isabella asked quietly, biting her lower lip again.

"No questions barred," he said, reaching for her hand. Her eyes fell to his hand. His touch soothed her nerves so much that she hadn't realized when her eyes started to close.

Christian squeezed her hand and her eyes flew open. She cleared her throat. "How many questions?"

"As many as your little heart desires." He flashed a crooked grin. "So, do we have a non-date date?"

"Yes," she smiled.

"Great." He stood up. "I'll call you with the details as soon as I book the restaurant."

"Sure." She stood up and followed closely behind him as he made his way down the stairs.

"Where to?" she asked.

"The mall—wanna come? My treat," he asked grinning.

"No, thanks."

He stopped and raised a speculative brow. "What woman doesn't like shopping?"

"Don't get me wrong; I love shopping. I just don't have the patience for malls unless I know—"

"Exactly what you want," Christian finished. "Ah, I know your type."

"Oh, yeah?" Isabella asked, crossing her arms. "What's my type?"

Christian studied her face carefully. "You need a personal shopper."

A few days later, Christian walked into the kitchen to find Rachel eating a fruit salad.

"Hey," he greeted cheerfully.

She cleared her throat. "I've been meaning to talk to you. About this date—"

"Cool, huh?" Christian said flashing a proud grin as he poured some juice in a glass.

"Cool? Are you out of your mind? That's like premarital therapy."

"That's the whole idea. I want to find out who she is before I put a ring on her finger, and she might wanna do the same before she says yes."

"But it's too soon to get that deep."

"So, when do you suggest we have the talk?" He asked, pausing halfway with his juice in hand. "Oh yeah, after we're married."

"Well, no, but perhaps you should date for a while."

"How old am I, Rach?"

Rachel frowned. "What's that supposed to mean?"

"How old?" he persisted.

"Thirty-four."

"I'm done with dating games. Dad has always said a man is supposed to know who his wife is within six months to a year. He was right."

"That was Dad's time." Rachel argued. "Things have changed."

"And did Dad say that to his dad too? Come on, you of all people know; you blog about it all the time. For crying out loud, you're engaged to be married to a man you started dating in December. Looks like Thomas thinks like a Cervello."

"But we dated the entire time. You and Isa have known each other almost as long, but you haven't even told her how you feel."

"That's why we're having this nonconventional date, and I intend to catch up with one dinner date."

Rachel's smile was condescending. "One date? What can you possibly learn about each other in a maximum of two hours?"

Christian's grin was mischievous. "Well, that's where you come in. Your job will be to make sure your friend gets a lot of sleep because the restaurant is booked for six hours."

When Rachel's mouth fell open, Christian ruffled her hair. "Hey, it'll be intense, but I know your Isa can take it. She's a trouper."

"Okay, but are you sure you wanna do it this way?" Rachel said, standing up. "You know. . .any questions."

"Why not?" Christian shrugged. "What do we have to hide that won't eventually surface?"

Rachel's countenance fell. "What if she asks about our family?"

"What about our family?" he asked, brows creasing.

"You know . . . the curse," Rachel mumbled.

"She already knows what we know, remember? She translated the entire thing."

"But what if it gets deeper, and she finds she can't continue?"

"What are you implying?" His tone grew somber. "Neither one of us will marry because of a curse?"

Rachel shook her head. "No, it's just that—"

"Listen," he said, embracing her. "I'll tell her what I know. That's the best I can do, okay?"

Rachel nodded.

"Stop worrying so much; we're gonna be okay, you and me, all right?"

Rachel nodded again. "Okay. Can I just ask this . . . ?"

"Shoot!" He released her and took a sip of his juice.

"Is there any question you have for Isa that might disqualify her if you couldn't take the answer?"

"Why?" He flashed a grin. "Did she want you to ask me that?"

"No, silly."

Christian nodded slowly. "That's actually a good question."

"Well?"

"Yeah."

Rachel sighed, throwing her hands up. "Then why do this?"

"For one, any such issue would be based on the present and future, never the past."

When Rachel frowned, he said, "Okay, for instance, if she were to tell me that she was extremely promiscuous in her past, I wouldn't judge her based on that because people change. However, I would like to know that she presently isn't. You know, trust is important to me."

Rachel nodded and Christian smiled. "Good. Well, I would like to know that she is completely available, as in not interested in anyone else. I refuse to play games. I don't share my woman."

Rachel raised her hand for a high five. "You've spoken like a true Cervello."

"Well, I don't know about that," he said, clasping his hand into hers. "I almost missed it with Kathy. Dad and Grandpa seemed to have it easier with women. Maybe it's just our generation."

Rachel sighed. "Well, if that's all there is, sounds like I don't have to worry about Isa."

CHAPTER TWENTY-ONE

Non-Date Date

IT WAS the most anticipated Friday in Isabella's memory. A few minutes past seven, she sat in front of the mirror in the red, chiffon mini-dress that Rachel had helped her pick out. They settled for something comfortable enough to last the duration of the date, yet elegant enough to mark a first date. The above-the-knee dress had a layered, A-line skirt, a bateau neckline, and a fitted bodice, embellished with handmade flowers that floated away from the bodice. Since Christian loved her hair down, she had it that way for the night, with a middle part.

As Rachel set Isabella's hair with some styling wax, their eyes met in the mirror. "I've never seen anyone getting ready for a date look so miserable." Rachel said. "Hon, are you sure this is a good idea?"

"I think so. It'll work out in the end. Like bad-tasting medicine that cures you."

Rachel frowned. "Hmm . . . if you say so, babe. So, I don't need to do your makeup?"

When Isabella shook her head, Rachel threw a fist in the air. "Yes!"

Isabella rolled her eyes. "Lazy."

When Christian had called Isabella to confirm their date, he'd specifically asked she not wear makeup because he anticipated that their sharing might lead to tears, and he did not want them to worry about her looking pretty.

"It's kind of embarrassing that I haven't been on a date for years," Isabella said. "He's probably gonna ask about that. What will I say?"

"Well, you did go on one with Thomas and I some months ago, remember?"

"Does that count?" Isabella asked, her gaze hopeful.

"Of course it counts," Rachel said with a slight frown. "I mean, it wasn't like the two of you had enough chemistry to even start a smoke, but Christian doesn't have to know that. Besides, picky is good. Ah! I keep listening for the doorbell, but he's walking down the hallway to get you."

They both giggled. Isabella shook her head. "That's why it doesn't feel like a real date . . . ugh, my life."

"It's okay," Rachel's smile was reassuring. "You guys are just practicing how to be a married couple."

Isabella stiffened. This could go either way—she might impress him or totally turn him off. He seemed so established and focused. For him to request she bring her serious side, she wondered if he thought she was immature. She never fared well with past dates, so only God could keep this one from being a complete disaster. According to Rachel's suspicions, her brother's goal was to ensure that her façade would crumble after so many hours together. Whether this was true or not, it only added to her nerves.

"Listen," Rachel said, interrupting her thoughts. "Chris is a body language expert. You may end up telling him stuff without even opening your mouth. So, keep the fidgeting in check."

There was a knock at Rachel's bedroom door. "Got your list?" she whispered.

Isabella nodded.

"Go get 'em."

Isabella was still processing the body language tip by the time Rachel opened the door. Her lips parted at the sight of Christian in a fitted, black suit. The top button of his black dress shirt was unbuttoned, slightly exposing his chest. The contrast against his skin was astonishing. Even though she noticed his sly smirk, she couldn't take her eyes off him.

"Hey, handsome," Rachel said, embracing him. "Mmm . . . you smell good."

Christian glanced at Isabella with a smile that showed in his eyes. "Isabella?" He extended his arm to her, and she placed hers in his as they walked down the hallway, Rachel following closely behind. He did smell good, and that messed with her senses.

When they got to the front door, Rachel placed Isabella's platform sandals before her and fastened the buckles. As soon as she stood up to hug them, Isabella noticed tears beginning to form in Rachel's eyes, and she scowled at her—prompting a hasty apology from Rachel as she backed away.

The ride to the restaurant was a quiet one—reminiscent of their journey home from the nightclub a few months earlier. Julio drove, while they each sat in the same spot in the back seat of the Maybach. Christian could feel Isabella's mood—she was tense. He reached for her hand over the arm rest and squeezed it. She exhaled and so did he. He had reserved a section of the brand new, posh Italian restaurant, *Sogno Stravagante*, and paid a hefty price to ensure management kept his reservation confidential. He knew Rachel was thrilled at the opportunity to be the first to cover the pre-launch, and he could just see her at her computer editing away right this minute. After midnight, her article would be published—fresh with information from the horse's mouth to her readers. By this time tomorrow, he expected the press to hound the location.

There was no better place to take the woman he saw as *his* dream come true. To him, Isabella looked like someone who could use a good pampering. He had never come across any woman this self-sufficient. He had heard and seen for himself just how responsible she was with money—perhaps it was the accountant in her, but it gave him more reason to want to reward her for her independence. She intrigued him—having lived alone for so long with her family overseas; she had extreme discipline.

Upon exiting the car, Isabella gulped at the sight of the restaurant. There were no words to describe it apart from *rich people territory*. She just hoped she wouldn't throw up on her dress. She didn't know whether to be intimidated or amused by the host dressed in a tuxedo and white gloves—eagerly waiting to greet them at the front entrance. It must have taken everything in him to stop himself from ushering them out of the car all by himself. The handsome middle-aged man grinned as he bowed, before guiding them inside.

He then introduced them to three waiters who stood in line, also in tuxedos. She had never been to a restaurant where waiters dressed up . . . only in movies did she see such extravagance. *Yeah . . . more like intimidated,* she pondered. Christian squeezed her hand and offered a warm smile. She loved how he knew when to calm her nerves. She smiled back and finally relaxed when he muttered something about the waiters dressing nicer than *they* had.

The host stepped aside as Christian opted to pull out Isabella's seat—he then whispered something to the man, who quickly walked away. Christian stared intently at her as he reached into his inner suit pocket and retrieved a small notepad. He then took off his suit jacket, and just as he began to drape it over his seat, one of the many waiters arrived to rescue him from the dire task. *This ought to be an interesting night*, she thought, stifling a chuckle. Even though Christian was filthy rich, she never saw him that way because he was so down to earth. Whatever the case, he seemed just as awestruck with the experience, and she was glad she was not alone.

"You look stunning," Christian said, breaking the silence with his steady, camera-lens gaze. "I just wish you hadn't worn makeup."

"I didn't," she said, grabbing a napkin from the table and stroking her face. *Could I have passed out and not known when Rachel . . .*

"You gotta be kidding me," Christian marveled.

"See?" she said, showing him the clean napkin.

"You're so beautiful," he said with an admiring gaze. Isabella blushed.

Before she could thank him, the host returned with a box of tissue encased in a gold canister. As her brow slowly lifted, the reality of her night dawned on her once more—and Rachel was not there to support her.

Christian held her hand as it rested on the table. "Relax." She exhaled as she attempted to smile through the tears she fought back. She nodded repeatedly and slowly, casting a wishful gaze at the exit. *Then he'll really think I'm immature.* His stare was deep and constant, and it didn't help that there were no other guests in the room to distract him. In fact, their table—lit with a single lamp, exuded more light than the entire room.

"Are we starting now?" Isabella asked, without looking at his face.

"Well, I was hoping we could eat first. I'm starving . . . you?"

"I just want to get it over with," Isabella said, sighing.

The waiter came over to review the menu they had selected days earlier, and as soon as he walked away, Christian's brows creased. "Wow, I wanted you to bring your serious side but not *this* serious. I promise it won't be as bad as you think—just let it flow naturally."

"I'm sorry, it's just my nerves."

He placed his pad on the table. She reached into her purse and pulled out a sheet, her hands trembling.

"Did you write a book?" he teased.

"Hey, stop making fun of me," She scowled. "You said there wasn't a limit. Besides, I just have six."

"Nah, there's no limit—just messing with you. We have all night. Besides, six is nothing. Just so you know, you can add other questions as we go on, okay?"

"Good to know. So, while we wait for our drinks, can you tell me what happens now?"

"Be yourself," Christian said, casting a quick glance at the live band.

"Can I ask regular questions?"

"Of course. I'll repeat the rules—ask whatever you wish. All questions must be answered to the best of your ability, and no questions are barred."

"Feels like I'm back in school." *Geez*, she muttered under her breath, sitting on both her hands to help control the trembling.

He continued, "You may answer a question as briefly as you wish, but be prepared to elaborate if asked for details."

Isabella nodded. "Hmm. So how many do you have?"

Christian held up two fingers.

"Just two?"

"Well, unless I come up with more along the way."

The waiter arrived with their drinks—two bottles of lemon Perrier and a bottle of red Zinfandel. Isabella's stare was speculative, and he responded with a mischievous, crooked grin. They both remained silent as the waiter worked the wine bottle and poured them each a glass before he asked if they would like the live music to continue. Christian looked at her, and she nodded to the waiter. He promised to return briefly.

"How does it taste?" she asked, feeling giddy all of a sudden—perhaps grateful for the distraction.

"Will you believe me if I said I had no idea? I should have asked my dad; he's the wine guru."

"It smells sweet." She sniffed.

"Good. I hope it's spicy. I asked for something peppery and fruity, and they suggested this."

"Didn't you say you weren't a sweet tooth?"

"I'm not—I'll take spicy over sweet any day. By the way, please don't feel obliged to—I just wanted this day to feel extra special."

Isabella smiled. Apparently, he had thought the entire night through. She was touched. Rachel had mentioned the grand opening for the restaurant was set for tomorrow, so this meant they were the very first guests to grace it, apart from the cooks, waiters, and live performers, all of whom seemed suspiciously eager to cater to their every need.

The waiter arrived with their hors d'oeuvres, which looked more like a work of art to her rather than food. She knew the names she had selected from the menu he sent her, but now she struggled to match them with the variety before her. He must have ordered the entire menu to decide what he wanted. She only recognized the *Caviar Canapés*, because she and Rachel made such a poor attempt at them last year.

"Ladies first?" he asked, catching her off guard.

"What's your full name?"

"Christian Eduardo Cervello."

Isabella drew a sharp breath. "Eduardo?"

Christian smiled. "Yeah, I know."

With a quick smile, she imagined shooting the elephant in the room, before blowing out her gun and pulling herself together. "So . . . a Spanish middle name, huh?"

"As you know, my mother is Spanish. Here's a little trivia for you: my great-grandfather, grandfather and dad are all married to Spanish women."

"No way!"

Christian nodded slowly. "All three. It *is* strange."

"Was Kathy Spanish?"

"Nah, British."

"Hmm, that's interesting. You went against the grain, huh?"

"I tend to do that." His lips curved into a wicked grin. "Perhaps that's why it didn't work out for me."

"Are you superstitious? I mean, is that the reason you wanted to marry her in Spain?"

"Not superstitious actually, I should clarify it wasn't a rule that the men in my family marry Spanish women—it just happened that way. In regards to the location . . . strangely, Kathy and her parents didn't have a preference. So, since it was important for Rachel and I to get in touch with that side of us, we chose Spain. We know so much about our dad's side, and we're not even that close to our paternal cousins—mainly because they mostly live in Italy. There *is* a big Cervello presence back home."

"I heard," she nodded. "It's probably why your parents can't wait to leave."

"You sense that, too? Yeah, they're hardly ever here anymore. Who knows . . . but Aunt Mona is helping them with arrangements over there."

Isabella's brows creased.

"My father's sister," Christian explained.

"Oh." Isabella nodded.

"She lives in Sicily. Casa Cervello is home to her when she visits the US, which she hasn't since Aunt Liz died, by the way. But we still love her. Dad has two other sisters—all with adult children. They visit at times. You actually met one of them at your party."

"Oh, yeah, I remember," Isabella said, taking a sip of her water. "The one visiting from Naples." When he nodded, she said, "Hmm, Uncle Tadd seemed to have made great use of the house."

Christian nodded. "Since law school, he's taken great care of it. My grandfather is extremely proud of him."

"You were next in line, weren't you? I guess you didn't want it."

"Casa Cervello has and will always be home to all Cervellos. Whoever's name is on paper is merely the custodian for the period from age twenty-three till their heir turns twenty-three. He did it that way to share the responsibility. It's actually a huge responsibility. The guardian just gets to make major decisions and pay taxes, but on the plus side, live there as long as they please—passing it on to the next generation. Rachel understands its original purpose and vows to honor it. Besides, she's better suited for it than I ever would have been. I've never seen anyone more protective and respectful of a home. I hardly deserve it after . . . "

As his voice faded, Isabella noticed his quick cautious gaze before he reached for his water. He had definitely said too much, it seemed.

"I would have never guessed you guys had other cousins until Rachel mentioned going back for your cousin's wedding. She never talks about them."

From his facial expression, she could tell he was grateful for her rescue.

"Check this out," he said enthusiastically, but the waiters arrived to present the next course.

They soon disappeared back into the dimly lit room. "So you were saying . . . check this out."

Christian grinned. "Ah yes, that cousin that got married—Bianca—is actually the daughter of the aunt who was best friends with my mother—Aunt Mona . . . kind of like you and Rachel."

"They're no longer close?"

Christian shrugged. "Somewhat . . . my aunt blames herself for my Uncle Eduardo's death . . . that is, whenever my mom isn't blaming herself for it." He sighed impatiently. "Listen, I was wrong to bring it up because it's a long story, and I know I set the rules for this no-questions-barred thing, but if I get into this now, we'll never be able to talk about us. So tell me, would you like for me to talk about it now?"

Isabella shook her head. "As curious as I am, all this will probably come out with our research."

"I agree," Christian smiled.

She smiled back. Proud to be hitting all the right points in the mature department with the way she handled things so far. "But it *is* interesting that you know so little about your Spanish side. No other cousins from there? Aunts . . . uncles?"

"Nothing. Rachel's my only cousin from that end." He shrugged. "That I know of . . . at least. Our parents never had the desire to indulge us. I feel like somehow our family has lost touch of the importance of culture in that respect."

"That *is* sad."

Christian shrugged. "Well, at least they could care less who either one of us marry."

Isabella laughed. "That's a relief."

"Yeah, I have much respect for them for that."

"Have you ever dated someone outside of your race?" she asked.

"Yup," Christian grinned. "The very first girl I can say I loved was actually African—Carla."

"Yeah?"

He nodded. "In undergrad." He stared at a distance, perhaps recalling the memories. "UM, end of junior year. Sometimes I wonder if she really loved me or if she loved me just for being part-Italian."

"Why would you think that?" she giggled.

"Because she had bragged to her friends that I was Italian before she knew I couldn't even speak it."

Isabella's laughter was so contagious that Christian joined in. "You couldn't?" she asked.

Christian struggled to contain his laughter. "At the time? No. It was funny, all her introductions of me started that way, 'He's Italian,' and she would try to get me to speak the language because she thought it was hot. It was embarrassing; I tell you. She eventually got the message."

"That is hilarious," Isabella said.

"It wasn't then, but now I look back I can actually laugh at it. My goodness, I was so smitten with that girl, it was nuts. I actually owe it to her for finally learning Italian in undergrad. It helped to have parents that were fluent in it. They never forced it on us—which was good."

"Thanks for sharing that with me."

Christian replied with a penetrating gaze, "You are welcome. I doubt we would've been talking about family or even exes on a conventional first date."

"I bet."

"By the way, I'm glad to see you're finally relaxed."

She took another sip of her water. "I'm actually enjoying getting to know you. So, what happened to Carla?"

"She went back to Ivory Coast after graduation," Christian said, becoming serious. "Her parents didn't approve of her marrying outside her race." He shrugged. "She was a mama's girl, so she didn't fight for us."

"Aww, Chris."

"No worries, that was ages ago. How about you, have *you* dated outside your race?"

Isabella nodded, "In fact, I dated this exchange student from Paris for half a semester at Notre Dame. He was from the Philippines."

"Oh yeah? Wow, we're all over the map now."

"Yeah, unfortunately, I don't think my parents are as enlightened as yours when it comes to dating outside of my race, but I believe I would be the fighter for relationships—call me stubborn."

Christian became serious again. "Do you think your parents will like me?"

"I think so. But deep down inside, they'll probably wish you were a good Brazilian boy."

Christian smiled. "Well, then I'm glad you are a fighter—I would hate for you to be another Carla."

Isabella blushed, wondering if this meant they were officially an item.

"So? What happened to the guy?"

Isabella smiled. "Tony? That was his name, by the way. You really wanna know?"

"I wouldn't have asked . . . " There was a mischievous twinkle in his eye.

Isabella looked away as she giggled silently. "He dumped me."

They both burst into laughter. "I can't even imagine anyone dumping you," he said incredulously as Isabella continued to chuckle. "Why?" he pressed. "Now, I'm really curious."

Her laugh died down and with a shrug she said, "He wanted something I couldn't give him."

Christian quietly studied her. The waiter's timely interruption was more than welcome for her. They silently watched as one waiter cleared their table and another waiter placed the next course before them. Apart from the pleasantries surrounding the meal and music, they quietly ate their steak dinner as the live saxophone blared, but she could tell that Christian was eager to return to their conversation.

During dessert, Isabella finally broke the silence. "It must really mean a lot to you—to have the restaurant stay open for us this way."

"I take relationships very seriously," he said, his eyes full of passion.

"So," Isabella said, looking to her wrist by habit.

"I noticed you didn't wear your watch."

"Should I have?" she asked, raising a brow.

"You trust me, I guess,"

Isabella shrugged. "To some extent, yeah. After all, you *were* the one that got it for me. What time is it?"

Christian's lips formed into a side smirk as he glanced at his Rolex. "A little after ten."

"So, two hours later, we know so much more about each other—even some of our past relationships."

"See? Can you get that from any other kind of date?"

"No, you were right. It was a bright idea . . . somewhat freeing."

He picked up his pad with a dark gaze. "Let's hope you still feel that way after we're done with this."

She dropped her fork inadvertently.

"Relax, Bella."

A warm rush came over her. "You sounded just like my father."

"He calls you *Bella*?"

Isabella nodded. "When I was younger."

"Why did he stop?"

"I don't know," she said. "He and the rest of the world call me *Isa* now."

"So I can call you Bella?" Christian asked with a cheeky grin.

She smiled. "I actually like it. I hated it when he stopped calling me that. I noticed something about you; you never refer to me as *Isa*—you always use my full name. Why is that?"

He looked into her eyes as he grabbed hold of both her hands. "Relax."

Isabella stuttered. "I know I should; I'm so sorry my palms are sweaty." Then pulling her hands away, she asked, "So you prefer to call me Bella?"

Christian leaned back in his chair. "If you don't mind . . . yes. I want a name that only I could call you."

This time she felt a hot flash over her face and neck.

"Do you have a middle name?"

"Marie."

"Pretty," he nodded.

"When my mom gets upset she goes, *Isabella Marie Montes*," Isabella demonstrated, pointing her fingers in a warning gesture, with her other hand on her waist.

"Feisty." He smiled. "I would love to meet her."

"Yeah, Mom's a firecracker."

"Ladies first," his tone was deep and low.

Isabella straightened out her paper. "Okay, the first one has many parts. Where do you currently stand with Kathy? Do you still have feelings for her, and . . . Rach mentioned she was here some weeks ago . . . why?"

"That was loaded. I stand nowhere with Kathy. I have no feelings for her whatsoever, and she was here to visit a friend."

She nodded. "Hmm, okay. The orchids?"

"Yes."

"Ha. It wasn't until recently I put it together. How did you know I like orchids?"

"They were all over your house."

"You are very observant."

"Comes with my profession," he said, his grin lopsided. "Did you like them?"

"I loved them—thank you so much."

"My pleasure."

"What did your original note to me say?"

"Well, I can't remember verbatim like *you* but it basically thanked you for your hospitality."

"Have you ever tracked me with the watch?"

Christian grinned. "Is that part of your original set of questions?"

"Yup . . . go!"

"I've never spied on you. If I had to resort to that, you wouldn't be worth it."

Wow . . . "So, whatever happened with you and *juice girl*?"

Christian chuckled as he shook his head. "She has a name, you know."

"*Fake letter girl* . . . I'm sorry. I know you told me, but I forgot."

"Sacha and I weren't in a serious relationship."

Isabella frowned. "What do you consider a serious relationship?"

"Long-term."

"Did you have sex with her?"

Christian shifted uncomfortably in his seat. "Yes."

"And that wasn't serious?"

He picked up his drink. Now he looked frustrated. "It wasn't supposed to happen."

Isabella shrugged. "Hey, this is your game."

"You think this is a game? Seriously? Listen, it's a long story."

"Good thing you have this place booked all night, huh?"

"Excuse me." He rose from the table for the first time since they'd arrived. She noticed him run his fingers through his hair as he paced. A waiter walked up to him, *perhaps to help him sit down,* she thought, sarcastically.

He came back shortly after. "Okay, you got me. This thing was my idea and I have to play by the rules."

"Yes, you do," Isabella said. "Why do you react to your relationship with Sacha that way? You make it look like it was more serious than you claim."

Christian stared at her with his hand over his mouth and chin—calculating. "When I broke up with Kathy, I made a vow never to have sex with a woman again until I got married. It wasn't supposed to happen, but it did, and I don't know how. Is that enough to stop questions related to this? I should allow for a free pass."

"No. No free passes. Fair is fair."

"You're right again. It's just that I don't want you to think I was leading her on; I'm sure that's what it sounds like, but the truth is, I just wanted company, and I made it clear to her that I didn't want anything else . . . definitely nothing physical. I never led her on, ever."

He looked and sounded sincere but his explanation left her even more confused and quite dissatisfied. It also created more questions—like why was she naked in the hot tub with him, bumping into both of them at the staircase, and that day Sacha wore the shirt she bought for him. Something more happened that he was probably ashamed of and though he'd said she could ask him anything, she didn't feel he was ready, let alone, forthcoming.

"No further questions, your honor," Isabella said with a smile.

"I thought your next question would ask how many women I had slept with."

Isabella shook her head. "No need to, I heard about your reputation."

"You can ask me what you want to know or you can depend on the rumors."

"Oh? But it doesn't seem as though you want to share that part right now. You seem quite defensive."

"Listen, Isabella, I don't sleep around. I've been around a few times but I've always been faithful to whoever I was with. Sacha was a mistake, and it just happened once with her."

"Didn't you want us to lay off Sacha?"

"You know what, I change my mind. I'll tell you everything."

"Chris, don't. I believe you. You don't have to."

"No," Christian said sternly, sitting up in his chair. "I was having a great time with you and Rachel, until I started to develop stronger feelings for you. I didn't think Rachel would approve, so I tried to get you out of my head, and that was when I took on Olivia's offer to meet someone— nothing serious. I had absolutely no romantic feelings for her whatsoever."

"Chris—"

"Let me finish. I couldn't get you out of my head, and it didn't help that you were always in my house. That was why my attitude toward you changed. Then there were the letters that Sacha concocted, convincing me you had someone else; it threw me into a depression for weeks."

Isabella gasped, placing her hand over her mouth. She couldn't tell whether he was about to have a breakdown, but it was clear she had just stepped on a mine.

"Then, I don't know what happened. One minute I felt nothing for her, and the next moment we were in bed, and I couldn't remember how, and I've never been able to forgive myself for breaking my vow."

She reached over and squeezed his hand, but Christian shrugged, appearing upset. "Based on your questions, I'm guessing that my past is what matters to you the most?"

"No, I just let curiosity get the best of me." *Perhaps, motivated by immaturity*, he probably thought.

"Hmm," Christian said, nodding.

"Does my past mean a lot to you?" she asked.

"As a matter of fact, it doesn't." He frowned. "Do you have any more questions for me?"

"For now, no." Her last question would have to wait until he cooled off.

"Okay, I'll go then. This shouldn't be long."

"You're not upset with me, are you?"

"Why should I be, it's just a game, right?" Christian smiled.

"Well, I made you go to a place of hurt."

"Actually, I'm glad I told you, I feel much better." He took her hands in his and stared into her eyes, his gray eyes still glistening with emotion. "Are things completely over between you and Antonio?"

"Anthony—that was his full name. I told you already, he dumped me."

Christian released her hands so quickly that she looked down to inspect them.

"Is everything okay?" Isabella asked, looking around confused. Christian remained silent.

"Something I said?"

"I'm not asking about your exchange boyfriend; I'm talking about the guy you met at the nightclub—the night I took you home."

Isabella frowned, recollecting her thoughts. "Oh, wait, the guy Olivia introduced me to?"

"Yes."

"Seriously?" She chuckled. "I don't even remember what he looks like."

"What's so funny?"

"That you should even ask. What made you think we were together?"

He remained silent.

Isabella sat up in her seat. "Nothing happened. I met him at the club that night, sat at his table for a minute, and then you threw me out."

Christian surprised her by laughing. "I did *not*."

"You know you did." She smiled, glad to see him lighten up.

"Are you currently involved with anyone right now?"

"Nope," she said, folding the edges of her sheet neatly.

"What are your views on infidelity and monogamy?"

"Well, infidelity is plain wrong, and I honor monogamy. It goes without saying."

Christian scoffed. "You'd be surprised. We live in a time where it's not as common."

She made a face. "Creepy."

"So when did you realize you were in love with me?" he asked.

Isabella hoped for a hint of mockery in his eyes, but he kept a straight face. "Excuse me? I didn't say—"

"Answer carefully to avoid follow-up questions."

Isabella looked away. "That's not fair."

"What isn't? We can ask whatever, right? It's not too late for you to ask me anything; we have all night. I may be a grouch about it, but I'll cooperate."

She looked down. "The first time you shook my hand—Aunt Pattie's garden."

He smiled. "Now, that wasn't so hard, was it?"

"I thought you said you only had two questions."

"Ah, you're in the hot seat now. Well, yes, I did, but I also said we could make up some as we go. In case you didn't notice, that was my fourth. You never seemed to have a problem with the third."

"Then we'll probably be here all night," she griped.

His lips formed into a crooked grin. "And we are booked for as long as needed. *Touché?*"

She crossed her arms grudgingly, "So I guess this is where you ask me about my sexual history."

"Nope," Christian said, casually folding his arms, watching her.

"Why not?"

He shrugged. "Some things are obvious," he said, signaling the waiter over for more drinks.

"And some things are assumed," Isabella replied, with a devious smile.

Her response caught Christian off-guard, but because she played her cards well, he couldn't seem to read her anymore. He was at least grateful that she confirmed his hypothesis that Antonio somehow tried to retaliate by finding out where he lived and pulling a stunt to get him suspicious of Isabella. If that was all he got from this date, it was plenty. Perhaps he could have saved himself the heartache if he had asked her out sooner.

As soon as the waiter walked away, Isabella said, "You know, you set up this date. Now would be a good time to ask me anything to put your heart at ease."

"Is there something you wanna say, Isabella?"

She chuckled. "Why, are you nervous, Christian?"

"I guess the most important thing for me to know is whether we are on the same page from here on out. I asked about Antonio because I had reason to believe your relationship was unresolved."

"But don't I need to have been in a relationship in order to have it unresolved?"

"Exactly, and you've told me that you never were, and I'm taking your word for it. Perhaps I'm old-fashioned, but I do take people's words extremely seriously."

"And what if I had been with this guy?" Isabella asked, shrugging. "Would it be so bad?"

His laugh was nervous. "It wouldn't matter. Your past doesn't matter to me. As long as it's over. But your point here is that it never started so it doesn't even matter to start off with, correct?"

"Where's this going anyway?" Isabella asked, brow furrowed.

"What? The conversation or us?"

"Us."

"Where do you want it to go?" he asked, and Isabella looked away.

Christian took hold of her hand. "I want whatever you want," he said, hoping to make eye contact.

"And what if I don't want anything?"

"I won't believe you, but I wouldn't want anything you didn't want. It's a choice."

"Thank you." She smiled. "That means a lot to me."

"Have you ever been hurt by a man before, Isabella?"

"No."

The band began to play a slow song, and he asked her for a dance. She agreed. They slow danced in silence for about two minutes, before he asked, "Tell me something; why is a girl like you still single?"

"I don't know; maybe I'm the kind of girl that guys would rather use?"

He threw his head back, laughing, holding on to her hand with one hand while the other rested on her lower back. "I doubt that."

"Oh yeah? Tell me then . . . why then do you think I'm still single?"

He stopped moving and cocked his head as he looked into her eyes. He took her by the other hand. "Come with me." They walked out to the enormous water fountain located outside the restaurant.

"I'll tell you a story," he said. "There was a very common hiking trail that saw hundreds of hikers each day. One day, a young man went hiking on this trail and came across a very precious stone. Upon seeing it, he picked it up and guarded it as his very own because . . . finders keepers, right?"

Isabella nodded.

"Well, over time he became anxious that he would lose his precious stone. People told him he was paranoid—to just enjoy his finding that was appraised for millions of dollars by some of the most trusted appraisers. But he never quite felt at peace. He feared someone would steal it from him. He trusted no one with the stone, not even the safety deposit box at the bank. Eventually, he began to feel cursed. Every day he would check for it. There it lay, under his bed—the same place he'd carefully placed it every night."

Christian fell silent, staring into the water fountain.

"So what happened next?" Isabella prompted.

He turned to her and smiled. "Oh, I'm glad I have your interest. So the skeptic hiker—let's call him that—still under the impression that his finding was too good to be true, took the precious stone to yet another appraiser. However, this time, he wasn't so fortunate—the appraiser looked at him and said, 'I'm sorry to tell you . . . this is a fake. You didn't think you had the real thing, did you? No, son, stones of such sort don't exist—this is just a very good fake.'

"Rather than question the appraiser or search for another opinion, the skeptic hiker not only agreed with him, but he left the precious stone in the hands of this fraud. He was content with the news and finally felt free again. He walked away and never looked back."

Christian turned around to see Isabella staring at him with tears trickling down her face.

"Are you okay?" he asked, pulling her close.

"That's not how the story ends."

"Yeah, it is." He laughed. "I actually just made it up."

"Yeah, you did, straight from your subconscious. I'll tell you what, that skeptic hiker is foolish."

"Hey, hold up, it's just a story. I just wanted to tell you—"

"I know what you were trying to tell me! He felt he couldn't protect this precious stone from the many people who wished they had it, so he secretly hoped it wasn't as precious as they all told him it was, and he got what he hoped for because you know why? He was lazy. He couldn't fight for what he believed. It was easier just to let it go. That explains why he never looked back. Probably explains why I'm still single."

When she saw him slightly frown, she asked, "So tell me, do you feel like the skeptic hiker?"

He ran his fingers through his hair. "I gotta admit that I have no idea where that came from. I sure hope it wasn't my subconscious speaking."

It had the markings of his Genius—only thing was, it came out straight from his own mouth without a single thought. *Hmm*, he pondered, *could Genius have changed his modus operandi?*

"I hope so, too. Don't be a skeptic—don't let go of what you think is precious. Nothing's ever too good to be true. No one is perfect. So don't ever think you're not good enough, or that someone else is too good for you. I always need to remind myself of that."

"So, can you see yourself spending the rest of your life with someone like me?"

"Of course," she said, smiling.

He held her close as they resumed their slow dance—this time, to no music.

Rachel heard the front door open and rushed down the stairs to meet him. "What happened?"

Christian laughed. "Slow it, Jill, before you come tumbling down." He leaned over to kiss her on the cheek and Rachel frowned as the door shut. "Where is she?"

"Oh, she asked us to drop her off at her place."

Rachel smiled. "Oh yeah . . . she did say that—to feel like a real date."

"That's cute."

"Yeah, she's a hopeless romantic."

Christian smiled. "Oh, is she?"

"So . . . how did it go?" she demanded, tugging on his arm as they walked up the stairs.

Christian grinned. "It was actually pretty good."

"Yeah?"

Christian nodded. "It was great. Unforgettable."

"So you pulled it off, huh? Your non-date date."

"Mmhmm." Christian grinned.

"Another invention from Christian Cervello—my genius brother."

"I just happen to be blessed with a wild imagination. I can't take credit for that."

"I thank God then. So what's next?" Rachel asked, rubbing her hands, giddy.

"I need to meet her parents."

"You mean business."

"I don't play around, Rach. You of all people should know that."

"Wow . . . when, how?"

"Well, I plan to help David and Denise with immigration in a couple of weeks. I'll look into going to Brazil from there. Listen, I know you both are close, but you are not to tell her."

"Ooh, can I come too? They already know me. *Please*?"

"No, kid. I need you here to help plan the engagement party and make sure she doesn't suspect a thing. This has to be airtight because she likes surprises, and I just happen to specialize in that."

"Okay, but you can't just show up at her parent's house. Have you at least spoken to them?"

"I'll get her to introduce me to them over the phone sometime before I leave. I hear her mom is tough, so if it's possible, I would like for Mom and Dad to accompany me. What do you think?"

"Sounds like you have it all planned out." She pouted. "And you don't even need me."

Christian ruffled her hair. "Of course I do. I need your help with the ring."

Rachel squealed as Christian covered his ears and headed to his bedroom. "Get some sleep, kiddo," he yelled. "We've got work to do tomorrow."

CHAPTER TWENTY-TWO

Commitment

IN CHRISTIAN'S Miami office the next day, Rachel spun around in his leather swivel chair. "Come on Chris, I'm starved," she whined.

"Soon Rach—by the way, the appointment isn't until 12:30 so . . . "

"Did you seriously have to get someone cross-country? What happened to just going to the store?"

"He came highly recommended." Christian grinned. "So . . . Isabella—she's not seeing anyone, right?"

"Come on, are we still at this?"

He stared out the window. "There's just something about her. I can't wrap my head around it. She's too good not to be snatched up by now."

Rachel wrinkled her brow. "Oh please, no one is perfect—but funny enough, she *has* gotten that from guys in the past. They find her intimidating for some reason. Either that or they assume she is already involved."

Christian turned to face Rachel. "Hmm, you know her so well. I remember how you fought for her, too. I thought it would destroy us."

"But it didn't," Rachel said, spinning in his seat.

Christian chuckled as he kept a keen eye on Rachel. In her playful mood, he expected her to slip and give away something. "You couldn't stand not having her at the house, could you? Exactly how much do you love her?"

"I'd do anything for her," Rachel said, as her spinning stopped. From the crease between her brows, he could tell she was dead serious. "Whoa!" Christian remarked, watching as Rachel scribbled Isabella's name on her coffee napkin.

"She's seen me through some tough times," Rachel said. "I'm not saying you haven't but . . . "

"I know; I've been busy."

"And for good cause," she assured. "Besides, you've been there for me through the worst."

"So um, you would lie for her?"

"In a heartbeat," Rachel said without hesitation in a grave tone.

"Should I be concerned or my goodness . . . jealous?"

"You shouldn't be. It's a different kind of love. Did I ever stop you from pursuing her?"

"You nearly did." He stared at her name scribble, which now had two hearts surrounding it.

"No. That was in your head. Listen, there's absolutely nothing to worry about with Isa. I know her more than she knows herself, how's that?"

Christian crossed his arms over his chest. "Ha!"

"For instance, I knew she fell in love with you in the garden the first day she met you—she probably didn't know that for herself back then."

"She told you that?"

"Oh, she doesn't have to, but I'm sure she can confirm it." Rachel rose from the chair and paced. "And every time she was glad for the few minutes she had to speak to you alone . . . she has me to thank for that. Have I ever been wrong about my hunches?"

"Well, I know about your dream interpretations."

"And my hunches."

"Come on, Rach. I know you two are close, but you can't possibly know everything about her."

"True. I'm not God, but I do know a lot about Isabella Marie Montes. Listen, if you're second guessing, you really should consider slowing things down. I know you have trust issues and all, but has it ever occurred to you that maybe, just maybe, some girls are simple—unlike your usual complicated type?"

"You don't know everything about her. She's not as timid as you think." He smirked.

"If you are referring to that night at the club . . . "

His eyes widened. "She told you?"

Rachel waved. "Please . . . she tells me everything. Look at you, spending the night at her house."

"Ah, impressive—very impressive."

An announcement came through the intercom from Christian's executive assistant, Erica. "Mr. Cervello, a Mr. Goldstein from Custom Jewelry House is here to see you."

"Thanks, Erica. Send him in."

A suited, middle-aged man with eyeglasses suspended by a brown leather cord walked in, holding a briefcase. "Mr. Cervello? I am Mr. Goldstein."

Christian walked up to him, and they shook hands. "Yes, Mr. Goldstein, it's nice to finally meet you."

"The honor is mine, sir."

"This is my sister, Rachel." Rachel smiled as she shook hands with the jeweler.

"Ah, the young lady's friend," he said.

"Yes." Christian said. "Please have a seat."

"Thank you, sir. I have the samples you selected."

Rachel lifted an inquisitive brow at Chris and asked, "Selected?" Christian winked at her.

"May I?" Mr. Goldstein asked, before setting his briefcase on the desk. Rachel pulled up a chair between both men as Christian cleared his throat. "Rach, what can you tell us about Isabella's taste in jewelry?"

"*Now* you ask?"

"Well it *was* kind of fun winging it for the past few weeks."

"Are we talking rings or jewelry in general?" Rachel asked.

"Both."

"Let's see, she adores pearls, but she'd absolutely hate them on a ring."

The jeweler smiled as he began to pull out individually wrapped velvet satchels from his case. "You did say that was her birthstone, didn't you, Mr. Cervello?"

"Yeah, June."

"Good. I actually second the young lady's opinion. Here are some sketches we had come up with."

"Hmm," Christian said with a disapproving gaze at the variations of the pearl and diamond ring.

"Yeah." Rachel shook her head at the drawings. "I guess they're okay, but Isa wouldn't like them."

"The other designers and I thought as much. Here are some samples we have come up with."

"That's it!" Rachel pointed to a three-stone ring laid out on the desk among two other rings. "When I was looking up engagement rings for myself, she came across something very similar to this, and I remember her saying that was her dream engagement ring. The stones were much smaller but it had the same set of three, with a diamond in between two sapphires. I wondered why she would want a birthstone different from hers on her ring. She was so into birthstones—she sounded like some expert."

"Well, now she can get her dream combination—her birthstone with the diamond."

Rachel brows furrowed at him. "But . . . "

"These are not sapphires," the jeweler said. "They are called alexandrite, and it just happens to be another birthstone for the month of June."

"No way! You think that was what she showed me?"

"Perhaps if she's an expert in birthstones like you said, she probably knows she has an alternative to the pearl. Then again, it could have been a sapphire, as you assumed. Do you remember if it was a deep blue?"

"No, I wish I paid more attention. Then again, it was on a website. All I know is that it looked similar. Wow, I never even knew June had another birthstone."

"Neither did I," Christian replied. "I just happened to like the sketch he sent me and assumed it was some random stone." He inspected the ring with the jeweler's magnifying glass. "Wait a minute, did the color just change?"

"I know." Rachel laughed. "I thought it was my imagination."

"It wasn't your imagination," the jeweler said. "I'll show you something." When Christian handed over the ring, the jeweler tucked it inside its velvet encasement and placed the bag in his hand along with a penlight and they marveled at the color change. The jeweler continued, "In fact, you'd be surprised to know that there are *three* stones for the month of June. The alexandrite, however, is extremely special because of its amazing ability to change color. They are bluish-green in daylight, but in artificial or incandescent light, they turn to a purplish-red. The particular ones in this ring originate from a mine in Brazil."

"No kidding!" Rachel exclaimed, taking the ring from Christian. "Did you know she's Brazilian?"

"No," the jeweler replied, appearing genuinely surprised. "That *is* very interesting."

"Interesting indeed." Christian nodded. "Tell me more about this piece."

"Definitely, sir. This platinum engagement ring features a flawless, five-carat, modern, round, brilliant, cut diamond surrounded by one carat of natural alexandrite on each side."

Rachel handed the ring back to Christian. He slid in his chair to the window to inspect it further.

The man continued. "It's definitely a rare and mysterious gemstone— certainly meant for an extraordinary young lady. Is this Isabella?" he asked, pointing to a picture frame on Christian's desk. It was a group picture they had taken on Christian's birthday.

"Yes," Rachel said. "That's my Isa."

"She's a very beautiful young lady."

"Thank you," Christian replied, swiveling back to his desk.

"Wow, I wonder if Isa knew all this about her birthstone," Rachel said. "I'm sold, that's definitely the one she'll like. She's simple, but at the same time, she likes to be set apart."

Christian grinned. "I thought along those lines when he emailed it to me last week."

"Now if you can keep the wedding ring really simple," Rachel added.

"Definitely," the jeweler replied. "Thank you for bringing that up. We suggest a thin wedding band—preferably, an eternity-type ring."

"What's that?" Christian asked.

"Eternity rings symbolize everlasting love. It's basically a continuous train of equally cut stones—in her case, it can consist only of tiny, white diamonds or alexandrite all around."

"Diamonds!" Christian and Rachel chimed at the same time. Rachel laughed. "Oh, and she would want her husband's name engraved on the back along with the wedding date, so I guess you will have to hold off on the wedding ring for now."

Both men laughed. "We can definitely have that arranged," the jeweler replied, putting on his glasses to take notes. "I'm sure the lucky lady is proud to have someone who knows her so well."

"They're practically twins," Christian joked.

"If I may add for the groom, you did *say* that your birth month was in April, yes?"

"Yeah," Christian said, handing the ring back to Rachel.

"Have you noticed your birthstone is the diamond? I must say it's the perfect combination for both your birthstones."

"Ah, I never knew that. Good to know." Christian grinned.

"That's right; I keep forgetting diamonds are birthstones, too," Rachel said. "Chris, did you decide what you want for your wedding band?"

"I'll let Isabella choose that." He said to Rachel, before turning to the man. "You should definitely hold off on the wedding band, because she may wanna select that for herself."

"Sure, we'll focus on the engagement ring. I understand you want to embed your device in it, correct?"

"Oh, yes, I have the nondisclosure forms for you to sign right here. Please take your time and read them carefully. A Private-I engineer should be in contact with you sometime today. We were actually on our way out, but my assistant, Erica, will show you to a lounge and ensure there is staff at your service while you are here. Let her know if you require lunch or a ride back to the airport."

"Thank you very much, sir." The man smiled. "It was a pleasure meeting you."

Although Christian had spoken to Isabella on the phone a couple of times since their first date, it had been two weeks since he had actually seen her, having missed their weekly Bible study. Knowing how bright she was, he would have it no other way. The closer they got through mere phone conversations, the easier it was for her to read him, and the harder it was for him to hide things from her. Therefore, this distance was necessary to limit any suspicions on her end. The hardest part was over—his mother and father had contacted her parents and officially introduced him to them as their son and Isabella's love interest. They made their intentions known to her parents and informed them that Christian would love to meet them personally before he proposed to her.

The restaurant for the surprise event was ready to go. The finished engagement ring was hand-delivered by the jeweler the day before, and Christian's jet was set to leave that evening for London. His plan was to meet up with his lawyer on David and Denise's behalf for the employer sponsorship, and possibly return with them and Isabella's parents. A lot was riding on this one trip, and he really depended on Rachel to ensure that she was his right arm in Florida.

On route to the airport, he had Julio make a stop at Isabella's place. She welcomed him with a kiss on the cheek, still dressed in her pajamas. "Hey!"

"Hey," he said, sniffing and stroking her hair. "Mmm, that smell."

"Come in," she smiled, pulling on his hand.

"I can't stay."

"No? But I haven't seen you since our date," she said. "I thought it was something I said or did."

"No, nothing of that sort—I've actually missed you."

"I missed you too," she replied in a near inaudible voice.

"What?" he teased, holding up his hand to his ear. "I can't hear you!"

"I missed you, Christian." She looked down.

He drew her close, and slipping a finger under her chin, he softly brushed his lips against hers.

"I leave for London in a couple of hours."

Isabella sighed, resting her head against his chest. "I know." Her voice was muffled against his shirt.

She pulled away slightly to look at his face. "Are you coming back with them?"

"That's the plan. I hope it goes well. The lawyer is confident about our petition, but I don't know. He thinks we can expedite the process somehow. I need to prove that I need David here like ASAP to fill that position. It's actually true; Human Resources says that we couldn't find anyone with his skills to fill it for nearly a year. Apparently, they've spent lots of money on advertising and hiring temporary contractors that can't do nearly half what he can, and that department is suffering."

"Wow."

"Yeah, I plan to expand in that area, so I need someone permanent. There are very sensitive projects involved, and it isn't wise to keep hiring different vendors." Christian sighed. "I need him to train others as well. He should fit right in on Day One. It's a very specialized field that is very similar to what he did for us in London."

"I'm sure it'll work out then. You must be thrilled, your best friend living in Florida. I can't imagine being away from Rachel."

"I bet. You're so close. How did you girls do it when she was in New York and you were in Indiana?"

"It was brutal. We just buried ourselves in schoolwork, and then on every break we hooked up."

"No wonder she graduated cum laude—Rachel was never that focused in school."

Isabella laughed. "I'm telling!"

Christian pulled her close again. "You actually bring out the best in her."

"We bring out the best in each other—I love that girl."

"Well, I just came to see you before I leave, and yeah, drop off a gift. One second." He ran back to the car and returned with a wrapped parcel. "Here." He smiled, panting slightly.

She laughed when she saw a DVD of the movie he interrupted weeks ago. "You're so romantic."

He shrugged. "I just wanted you to finish what you started."

"And finish I will. *Obrigada*," she said, squeezing him.

"You are welcome. See? I secretly started to learn Portuguese," Christian said with a cheesy grin.

"Nice."

"I don't think I told you but David is fluent in Portuguese."

"No way!" Isabella said, eyes widening. "But he's South African, right?"

"Yup, his entire family consider themselves that, although they are part Italian, and part Portuguese. I'm just glad he can't speak Italian; come on, the guy can't have it all."

"Jealous!" Isabella teased. "Hey, since we're in gift-giving mode, I have something for you, too."

"Didn't Rachel tell you I can invent whatever I need?"

"I insist." She smirked. "Wait right here." She returned with a plastic bag. "Sorry, it's not wrapped."

Christian retrieved a shirt from the bag. It was his theme-park shirt—only newer.

"I thought you might need a replacement," Isabella said.

"Why?" he asked, bemused.

"Well, *juice girl* had it on when your mom kicked her out. I figured you never got it back."

"She was wearing the shirt you got me?"

"You didn't know?"

Christian shook his head. "I'm so sorry; I had no idea."

"It's okay, now you have a new one."

Christian drew her close and kissed her passionately. When he let go of her, he saw tears in her eyes.

"Thank you," he said, his voice deep and smooth, as he stroked the sides of her face with his thumbs.

Isabella nodded. "When do you return?"

"A little over a week, we already have a set appointment with immigration, but if all goes well, they'll still need to pack. I'll call as soon as I get there, and I'll be back before you know it."

The immigration interview was a success, and despite some start-date conflict with Denise's observership program in regards to immigration, she was able to obtain her visa as David's dependent under his work visa. Things couldn't get any better for Christian, but just when the excitement would wear down, worry and obsessions began to creep in. Things appeared too good to be true, and he expected something to go wrong.

Brazil was their next stop. *All will go well,* he declared, imagining Genius grinning. He had missed Genius. The more positive he was, the less he heard from him. He and his mother now had Isabella's diligence in the recent weeks to thank for teaching them to work on their negative thoughts. Although it was harder for his mother to catch on, her thinking had improved a great deal.

With the immigration process complete, Christian's focus shifted to the engagement party in Florida. However, he worked hard to refocus on Brazil instead—their next stop. He told himself that no matter how much he obsessed about Florida, the fact was that the ball was now in Rachel's court—to make the engagement ceremony appear to be a decadent celebration hosted by a notoriously wealthy family in Miami Beach. Rachel convinced him that with him being out of town, she had the perfect cover.

On the morning of their departure to Brazil, Christian woke up shaken from a bad dream. All he could remember was that Olivia and Isabella were in it. It frustrated him that he couldn't recall the details but his gut told him it was bad. He picked up the phone and called Rachel.

"Hey, you," Rachel greeted.

"Hey, kid. Did Mom and Dad leave yet?"

"First . . . congratulations on your success—I got your email." He heard her applaud.

"Oh, yeah, we are all pretty excited."

"I bet. Well, I'm taking them to the airport in a few. Don't worry, lover boy, we've got you. I'm just wrapping up a few last-minute invites."

Christian cringed slightly at that title. Only Olivia called him that, and he hated it because she always used it in a sexual context.

"You're not done? Come on, Rach. It's in less than a week. People need advance notice."

"I know, I'm trying my best Chris—you'll be proud of me, I promise. It's mostly just close friends left."

"Which reminds me, are you inviting Olivia?"

"Um—yeah. Why?"

When Christian did not reply, she persisted, "Is there a problem?"

"I'm guessing you sent hers out already."

"Actually, I haven't, it's right here."

"You don't suppose we can leave her out?"

"Chris, she's like family."

"But she's not!" he replied sternly. "All right, do what you must, just seat her far from our table and don't, under any circumstances tell her what's really going on."

"Okay, okay," Rachel replied.

"Did you tell her already? Tell me the truth." He knew Rachel had a habit of telling business that wasn't hers. Since her parents' death, she hadn't been as forthcoming with her personal details, and he wasn't ignorant of the fact that she seemed to know way more about Isabella than Isabella knew of her. Most of Isabella's knowledge of Rachel seemed to stem from the aftermath of the 1997 accident, while the most Christian knew of Rachel stemmed prior to it. Together, he and Isabella had concluded that if they joined forces, they should have at least seventy-percent knowledge of their beloved Rachel. If Thomas joined, it would be a higher percentage. But Christian doubted Thomas was the type to open up about such things. They made an intriguing pair—as open and playful as they both seemed, they kept their personal lives private.

"No, but I was gonna. So it's good you called."

"Promise me, Rachel."

"I promise. Hey, if I pull this off, will you let me plan the wedding?"

"That's between you and Isabella."

Soft music played in the background as Isabella and Rachel got dressed. Rachel's intention for Isabella's outfit was for her to stand out from the crowd. Before his departure, Christian had arranged for a stylist to assist with finding the perfect gown for Isabella. His intention was to offer the stylist a full-time job as Isabella's personal shopper, provided Isabella liked the outcome of her looks. The result was a sleeveless, sheer, stone, mesh dress with a high neckline, fitted bodice, and fit-and-flare bottom. It had a plunging back, and the nude-mesh bodice had white crystal embellishments scattered throughout, sparkling in the light.

Isabella had instantly fallen in love with the dress upon seeing it, but she hesitated in trying it on because she felt intimidated by its glamor. That was Rachel's sign that it was the dress, and she insisted on Isabella selecting it. For her makeup, Isabella had chosen a bronze blush with a bit of shimmer over her cheeks, for her eyes, a coat of mascara. She completed her look by layering some lip gloss over pale pink lipstick. It had been a while since Isabella last wore her hair up, and when she tried to, Rachel quickly talked her into having it down—with an excuse that it would cover her bare back, so she enhanced the volume of her curls, and wore her hair long and loose.

By the time Isabella stared at her final appearance in the mirror, Rachel was grateful that Julio had arrived for them, before Isabella found a reason to change into something else. "I look like a celebrity," Isabella said, bashfully. "Now I'm really nervous from all this stuff you said about this family."

Rachel shrugged as she reached for her purse. "They're just filthy rich, nothing to be nervous about. Besides, it can't top your date with waiters in tuxedos."

"Nothing can top that," Isabella said, giggling.

"Let's just go and have a great time."

"Easy for you to say, it's couple seating only and you'll have Thomas."

"Guess what?" Rachel grinned. "Gracie's coming and she agreed to sit with Thomas."

"You did that for me?"

"Yes, silly."

"Oh, Rach, I feel so much better."

"Glad to hear that. Let's go."

Julio pulled up at the restaurant, and when the girls got out of the car, Isabella instantly recognized the place. When she saw the double "S" initials in cursive, she was certain it was *Sogno Stravagante. Lord, is this the sign?* she murmured. "That's strange," she said with a nervous laugh. "This is where we had our date. There's the marble water fountain." Her head spun with nostalgia.

"He went all out for you, hon. This place is expensive."

"Well, he actually reserved the other end. It was really fancy, but this tops that."

Rachel's reply was hasty, almost shaky. "Remember what I told you about this family . . . ha!"

After her date with Christian, Isabella had finally gathered the courage to ask the Lord to reveal whether Christian was her life mate. After months of praying him away and seeing that he wasn't going anywhere, she'd left the whole situation concerning Christian up to God's will the night she came home from the date. It took everything in her to let him go, asking the Lord to only return him with a clear sign that he was the one. That was why she was slightly worried when she hadn't seen him since their date before his trip. Just after he left for London, the Lord had impressed it upon her heart that she already knew the answer to her pressing question. The problem was she didn't think she did, and she had become frustrated in the past week. Because even though she was hearing more clearly from God by each day, His undeniable reply never changed, *You already know the answer to that question, Isabella.* As of last night, she decided that she would accept nothing but a sign so very clear to her face—even if God had to write it in the clouds. "I wish Chris were here to see me now. Can you take a picture of me so I can show him?"

Rachel sighed. "Isa, hon, they're gonna be taking professional pictures inside; can it wait?"

"I guess so."

They were ushered into the extremely dimly lit room. Apart from the fancy table lamps on each round table, which barely glowed, the room was pitch black, and each guest had to be ushered in by uniformed attendants with small flashlights. The closer they got to their seats, the more impossible it was to make out the faces of those around them.

Rachel and Isabella took their seats quietly as they watched silhouettes around them do the same.

"I feel bad for Frank, being away from Gracie the whole length of the party," Isabella whispered. "Who's sitting with him?"

"Okay, don't laugh."

Isabella laughed anyway.

"Julio."

Isabella covered her mouth with her hands. "Oh, no!"

"They'll survive," Rachel said, looking above Isabella's head. "My, my, my, look who could join us."

Isabella whipped around, and before she could scream, Rachel signaled, "Shh."

Both ladies instantly stood up. "Oh, Rachel, thanks for keeping me company but—"

"User!" Rachel teased, squeezing Christian's hand before walking away.

Isabella hugged Christian so tightly that he pretended to gasp for air.

"I'm so glad you could make it," she said, pulling away. "Hope I didn't wrinkle your suit."

Christian stared her down. "You're dazzling."

"You think so?"

"Of course. Do you realize with that dress, you light up the entire room? Sit, I wanna see your face under the light." He pulled out her chair, and she sat.

"You look handsome yourself," she said, blushing under the dim light.

"*Merci beaucoup, mademoiselle.* I can't have you looking this way. I rather you stay in pajamas."

She smiled. "How was your flight?"

A waiter walked up to their table. "It would be my pleasure to get you drinks this evening."

"Some Chardonnay, please."

Isabella giggled. "You're gonna drink?"

"Yup."

"And you, madam?" the waiter asked, smiling at Isabella.

"I'll have the same thing," she said.

"Thank you. I'll be back shortly."

"Did you hear about the hosts?" Isabella snickered.

"Very high maintenance, I hear and see," he said, glancing around.

"Check out these menus," Isabella said.

"Ah, lights—nice. Did you recognize the restaurant?"

"Yes! I was just saying that to Rachel. Ha, ha, we beat them to it."

He didn't laugh, but his eyes smiled. She wondered if she was talking too much. "So how *was* your trip? I can't wait to finally meet David and Denise."

"They can't wait to meet you too. They're here somewhere; it's just too dark to see anyone."

"And it's a good thing, because everyone is probably dressed so decadently."

"They're probably saying the same about you."

"I would hope so. This cost a fortune, but Rachel said it was my belated birthday gift. To think these people dress like this regularly is intimidating." This time he laughed, and she was glad.

"You're actually very funny," he said. "I like this side of you, so relaxed and chatty."

Isabella squeezed his hand. "You being here really helped get me this way. I'm so glad you made it."

"It means a lot to you, huh? Don't worry about your wardrobe; I'll take care of that."

"No—" she started to say.

"I actually think this sort of clothing suits you. We should go out more."

The waiter walked up to their table with their drinks.

"I'll have the salmon dish, thank you," Isabella said, adding in a whisper, "I'm starving."

"Hmm, that sounds good—I'll have what she's having," Christian said, gaze fixed on Isabella.

She chuckled. "We're copying off of each other tonight."

"We are becoming one."

Could that be the sign? she thought. "I almost made it through without fidgeting around you."

"I notice you get that way when I look into your eyes."

"Do you have to do that?"

"Would you like for me not to?"

"No, I actually like it." She looked away with a sheepish grin. "I can't believe I just said that."

Soon after the waiters arrived with their meal, Isabella's nerves competed with her hunger for which made her the most uncomfortable. Her nerves were winning. This fairytale was too much; she just needed to know because she didn't want to waste any more time if he wasn't the one, and God's message was stuck on replay.

"Chris?"

"Yeah?" He looked up from his plate.

"Do we still have a no-questions barred policy?"

"Ah, yes," he laughed, placing down his fork and knife. "Speaking of that, I meant to ask you . . . I noticed you only asked me five questions but you had six."

"You don't miss a beat do you?"

"Nope, go!"

"Um, what was it?" she muttered. "Aha! I was gonna ask what frustrates you the most."

It must have caught him by surprise because his laugh was loud. "Oh, my Isabella."

"What?"

"No, no, that's a fantastic question. It's the response I'm not sure you are ready for."

"Try me."

"When my Big Red gum runs out of flavor."

"What?" Isabella asked with a mix of amusement and shock.

"Absolutely drives me nuts."

"You are the weirdest . . . "

"I know."

Isabella shook her head as he continued to laugh. He was weird but she loved him anyway.

"I'm glad I put a smile on your pretty face. So, you were gonna ask?"

Isabella sighed. "Remember how you asked me if I could see myself with you forever?"

"Yeah, and you said no."

"No, I didn't!" she exclaimed.

"Just messing with you."

"Well . . . how about you?"

"What *about* me?" Christian asked, his tone suddenly grave.

"Well, um . . . I probably should have asked you the same question that day but since you said we can ask whenever." She shrugged. "Can you see yourself with someone like me, forever?"

"Bella dear, let's not ruin our dinner," he said without looking up.

Isabella's heart dropped. She was perplexed at the idea that the conversation could ruin dinner. The only way she figured it could happen was if his response was *no*. When he had continued to eat without interruption, she chose to remain silent, and it was deafening. The shame from rejection was deep. Thankfully, the dimly lit room hid her tears.

"You've hardly touched your food," Christian said.

"I'm not hungry," she replied, nearly choking with emotion as she shifted her vegetables around.

"But earlier you were starving."

Christian hesitated before switching on the second table lamp. When he saw her tears, he took her hand, and when she tried to pull away, he held on tight. "You already know the answer to that question, Isabella."

"No, I don't, but just forget I asked, okay? The timing was wrong," she said, reaching for her fork. "Wow, I'm hungry again."

Suddenly, the classical music stopped and the song they first danced to on their first date started to play. Christian walked up to her and got down on one knee. "What are you doing?" Isabella whispered, looking around.

"Officially giving you a response to the question you asked."

"You don't have to. Get up."

"But I came prepared to," he said, reaching into his inner suit pocket.

Isabella started to hyperventilate, then began to bawl before Christian could get another word out. While still kneeling, he cradled her face in his hands. "You asked me a question. The answer is yes, Bella. I can only see myself married to you." Then taking hold of both her hands, he said in a soft voice, "Isabella Marie Montes, I am in love with you and would love to spend the rest of my life with you. Will you spend your entire life with me—as my wife?"

She gasped, then screamed, "Don't you ever do that to me again!" she said, slapping his chest.

"Shh . . . "

"You scared me!"

"You're causing a scene, and you haven't answered my question."

"Yes, I want to be your wife. Don't you ever—"

"Hey, you almost ruined my surprise. I wasn't having it. We were supposed to eat first, and you made me turn on the light, and that queued the DJ to—"

She stopped him with a kiss. Soon after, he slipped the ring on her finger.

"It's so beautiful—how . . . ?" she gasped.

"I'm glad you like it."

"I absolutely love it!" she yelled, inspecting the ring under the lamp.

"Shh. . . "

"Oops. . . " The dark room made her feel they were alone.

When the music stopped, he turned around and yelled into the dark. "She said yes!"

The crowd erupted in a thunderous applause as the overhead lights came on one by one. As her eyes adjusted to the bright ballroom light, she was shocked to find all the tables around them had retreated to the back. She guessed it was some unique floor technology, placing their table at the very center of the room.

With her feet glued to the ground and her hand over her mouth, she noticed her loved ones surrounding her—even her parents and cousins. Apparently, they had been sitting next to them the entire time.

"See . . . now you ruined your makeup," Christian said, wiping her face with his handkerchief. Just then, her mother ran to her in tears of joy, screaming in Portuguese, "*Filha, eu não acredito que você guardou este segredo de mim. Justo eu! . . . sua mãe.*"

"English, Ma!" Isabella said, laughing as she hugged her mother tight. Then turning to Christian, she said, "She thinks I kept this a secret from her."

"Oh no, she had no idea at all," Christian assured Ana, before excusing himself to speak to a guest.

Ana continued. "How didn't I realize it the day you introduced him to us on the phone?"

Isabella played with her ring, grinning. "Knowing *you*, Mom, I'm glad we were all in the dark till now."

Ana embraced her again. "Ohh, Isa, *minha filha, estou tão feliz por você.*"

"I'm happy too, Mom, and please speak English around them, okay? Chris is still learning."

"Okay, okay . . . "

"I believe this belongs to you," Rachel said, holding up Isabella's gold pretend wedding ring.

"Ahh . . . I'm gonna kill you. Thief—I was looking all over for it."

"Why, you left it on my dresser when you were getting dressed for your date. It just came in handy for Christian when the jeweler needed to confirm your size. You know he's gonna wanna tie the knot soon, right?"

"That'd be great." Isabella grinned. "I don't like long engagements. Did you help him with this? Look at the size!"

"Oh, that's a story for later," Rachel said before yelling out, "Liv! Here, Isa . . . some guests are lining up for you. I'll be right back, I wanna catch Olivia."

"Hey, I see you, Liv," Rachel yelled. "Why are you leaving so soon? There's an after-party."

Olivia frowned slightly. "Yeah, I have an early morning with the makeup line thingy. Hey, how come you didn't tell me what this was really about? I thought I was family."

"Of course, you are," Rachel said. "It was supposed to be a pleasant surprise for everyone, along with the bride-to-be. Hey . . . at least see them before you leave."

"Nah, they look busy; I probably shouldn't."

"Oh please, never too busy for you. Go congratulate them and let them know you are leaving."

CHAPTER TWENTY-THREE

Greed

TWO DAYS after the engagement party, Isabella's parents were ready to head back to Brazil on an evening flight. They usually riddled her with questions about when she would get married, or would provide unsolicited news about her mates having babies. Now, she was relieved that they would have a different story to tell when they got back home. She was only sad that her favorite aunt and biggest supporter, Febe, couldn't make it to the party, although her two sons did.

It gave Isabella great joy that her parents were proud of her. Her mother was pleased that she had *chosen well*. She'd expressed shock in Christian's decision not only to travel across the world to ask them for their daughter's hand in marriage, but to fly them on his private jet to Miami for the event. Her father, on the other hand, admitted that he actually took to Christian upon meeting him in São Paulo—citing that he was extremely *well mannered*. According to him, he could tell that Christian was crazy about her by the look in his eyes when he expressed his feelings. No one had known just how terrified she was of a follow-up phone call to her mother after she first introduced Christian to her on a three-way call weeks ago. Her mother, who usually had negative things to say about American-raised children, had absolutely nothing against Christian, and Isabella could only credit God for such a divine connection.

Upon driving off from the airport, Isabella called Rachel to remind her of their gym appointment. Although she didn't think she needed the extreme workout—especially now that she didn't have to compete with supermodel Sacha, Rachel had insisted on it, and had arranged for the trainer to assess their individual needs for both their weddings. When Rachel didn't pick up, Isabella left a voice message: "Hey, hon, I'm just leaving the airport . . . on my way for our two o'clock appointment." After Isabella's session with the trainer, she became slightly concerned when Rachel still hadn't arrived, let alone, return her call. She left yet another message, then decided to pass time on the treadmill. Within seconds of starting, the same sound she had heard from her SecureWatch during her assessment with the trainer went off—prompting her to change the settings again to exercise mode. With practice, she would eventually get used to changing the settings without prompting, as she had seen Rachel do so many times with hers. *She has to be sleeping*, she thought. She hadn't heard from her all morning, and was too busy helping her mother pack to check in.

The events leading up to the engagement party went through Isabella's mind. She couldn't believe Rachel and Christian actually pulled off an occasion of that magnitude without her even suspecting a thing. *Decadent family affair, my foot!* She smiled to herself. She was a hopeless romantic, and somehow Christian could read that and had the means to do the impossible things of which she dreamt. She couldn't decide which was more shocking—them pulling off the engagement under her nose or *her* actually completing the major decorations at Christian's new house without her even knowing it. For the past three weeks, she'd assisted Rachel with ideas under the pretense that she was helping them renovate Casa Cervello.

Twenty minutes into her workout, she decided she would give Christian a call to check on Rachel. As soon as the treadmill slowed to a stop, she called his line, only to get his voicemail. Deciding to head over to Casa Cervello, she grabbed her belongings and headed out of the gym. The breeze felt nice and cool over her damp skin, and as her heart rate came down, she considered how great it felt to work out. Rachel was right—she needed this discipline because she took her figure for granted. Just as she reached her parked Jeep, a shrieking sound from her SecureWatch went off. *Argh*, she mumbled, startled by its reminder to restore the settings to rest mode. As soon as she pressed the rest button, she noticed the door to a black van with tinted windows open, and the last thing she saw before the darkness were two masked men.

Christian was heading to his four-thirty appointment when his secure phone sent out an emergency alert. Seconds apart, the security alert in his Range Rover went off via an automated voice: "Isabella Montes: Emergency four-o-five p.m." Just before Christian could process what he'd heard, an incoming call from the police department came through on his secure phone. "This is Detective Marvin Sanders from Key Biscayne PD."

"I know," Christian said.

"We're tracking them right now, and we know exactly where she is."

Christian quietly stared at his tracking device via the GPS portal—they were on the move.

"The voice signal is weak, but we wonder if you could recognize the voices of any of the perpetrators."

"Mr. Cervello? Are you there?"

"I'm sorry . . . yes. I'll be right there."

As Christian headed toward the Key Biscayne PD station, he struggled to put things into perspective. He had always been confident about his devices, but for the first time the SecureWatch would face a real-life test, and he hated that Isabella was the guinea pig. Even though the device would make it almost impossible for an extortionist to collect, he was willing to break all the rules just to have her back. Who could have been behind this, and what did they want from her or him? Money meant nothing because Isabella was priceless.

Upon arriving at the police station, a police officer escorted Christian to the situation room, where Detective Sanders approached him and shook his hand. There were several officers gathered around the tracking screen he had donated to the department years ago. He could make out a male voice, but it wasn't clear. When he couldn't hear Isabella's voice or cries, it only added to his nerves. He had to remind himself that she was indeed alive because the watch was actively picking up her pulse rate.

"Would you like some coffee or tea?" Sanders asked.

This isn't happening to me. Christian shook his head. He was the one that the family came to in times of crisis because he had an uncanny way of making everyone feel calm. According to them, he handled stress very well. His mother often said that wasn't always the case and credited his calm demeanor to some silly tea that she failed to realize he did without when he lived overseas. What they didn't know, or failed to care about, was that he was dying inside, but never showed it. What he needed now was someone to comfort him—not tea.

"You don't need us anymore; give us our cut so we can be on our way," came a clearer voice.

Christian frowned at Sanders as he shook his head. He knew Isabella had to be in the same room with them because the watch radius could only go so far.

"Those must have been the guys we saw on camera," Detective Sanders said.

"What camera?"

"The gym parking lot camera. She was abducted at a local gym."

Gym? She never went to the gym, Christian pondered. "It's interesting you got footage that quick. Unfortunately, I can't recognize that voice."

"Who do you think had motive?" Sanders asked.

Christian ran his hand through his hair. "Frankly, I can't think of anyone who would want to hurt her."

"Can you think of anything else that could have happened recently?"

"Well, we got engaged two days ago; there was a party afterward."

"Congrats," Sanders said, pulling out his pen. "Where at?"

"Sogno Stravagante."

"Oh, that new waterfront restaurant that just opened up on Merrimount?"

"Yeah."

"Do you have the list of the guests who attended?"

"My sister has it."

"We're gonna need that."

"Sure, if you could just excuse me," Christian said as he reached for his phone. "Hey, Rach? Were you asleep?"

"Yeah, what time is it?" Rachel asked, yawning.

"Four forty."

"Don't tell me I slept all day."

"I won't."

"Thomas and I were out late. I actually came in at . . . oh shoot, I was supposed to meet Isa at the gym. I'm just seeing her missed calls. Did she call you—do you know if she ended up going?"

"She called me once, but I was on a call. Listen, could you send me the list of all the guests who attended the engagement party?"

"Sure, why? Sending thank you cards already?"

"Nah, I'll tell you later. Please email it to me now if you can. Oh, and don't answer your calls after this, even if it's from me."

"Why?"

"Just don't. I'll be home soon."

"Okay, Chris, you're freaking me out. What if Isa calls?"

"Just don't, okay? Trust me."

Christian walked over to Sanders. "I should get the list soon."

"Okay, good. By the way, we just got word that the two men were dropped off at the coffee shop near Martha's Grove. Our men should have a hold on them soon."

Christian nodded. "Impressive."

"Hey, this wouldn't have been possible without your technology. You have any idea how many negotiators you would put out of business with this?"

"Glad to help."

"Are you always this calm in an emergency?"

Christian smiled and sighed.

"So, what's the contingency plan in an event of a ransom?" Sanders asked.

"You think that's what this is?"

"From my experience, yeah."

"All phones get shut down, so no one is able to get *the* call. So, by the time the kidnapper gets to make a threat to an actual person on the phone, the authorities are able to locate the victim via GPS. It's basically set up as a way to buy time."

The detective nodded. "Hmm."

"So, what's the plan now?" Christian asked.

"Well, they're still on the move, and we're trailing them."

"Okay." Christian's phone beeped. "Excuse me, that's the email. Where do you want it sent?"

The detective handed over his card. "Use this email."

"So you think it could be someone from the engagement party?" Christian asked.

"We can't be sure. We won't contact anyone if there's no need to. I'll destroy the list when we're done."

"I would appreciate that. Well, if you don't need me, I'll head back home; I need to see my sister."

"Okay, what number can we reach you at if we need you? The same one?"

"Yup, the one that's flashing on the screen next to her name; it's my secure phone—the only phone that's on. No one has that number except for me—and your department, of course. The number is only good for as long as the case is active. It changes with each case for security."

"I see."

Christian's secure phone rang as he drove through the Casa Cervello gate. It was Sanders. "They made their way to Motel Larva off Route 95," the detective said. "We are staked out around the entire area."

"Just make sure Isabella is safe," Christian replied. "If this isn't a good idea, the money isn't a thing."

"I understand. Listen, I want you to consider what I'm about to say."

"Go on."

"We'll get these guys, but when we do, we can only hold them for kidnapping."

"Isn't that enough?"

"Well, it could be more if we added ransom."

"So what are you suggesting?"

"I'm suggesting that you break protocol and authorize all phone lines, including yours, to be reopened. Shutting them off is perfect up until the police are able to locate them. If you reopen them now, you create an access to the threat—which we want in this case."

"Isn't that risky? They're gonna be on guard after the threat."

"Exactly, but they won't anticipate our sudden arrival seconds after the call. Listen, in Miami, it could get tricky fighting kidnapping. So far, we can safely assume they have her against her will, and from the parking lot video, they forced her into the vehicle. Now we need to consider bodily harm and a possible ransom. Those will require proof in court. What we know could change the case entirely. We could be dealing with a simple kidnapping or an aggravated one."

"Okay, I'll arrange for it. Then what?"

"If they have already, I suspect they'll try again to call once they settle in. When they do, we'll make the move as soon as you call us."

"Okay, sounds good."

"Can you get in touch with your attorney?"

"He's out of the country."

"Not a problem. I'll tell our boys to stand back for now."

Christian did as the detective requested before heading for Rachel's room. As he contemplated how to break the news to her, he watched her through the crack in her door, clipping her toenails. "Rach?" He called out, before walking in.

Rachel looked up. "Chris, what's going on?"

"Promise me you won't freak out?"

"It's Isa, isn't it?"

"You didn't promise me yet."

"Stop playing games, Chris. Where's Isa?"

Christian held both her arms. "She was kidnapped."

"No, no, no! What . . . where, when? We were supposed to be at the gym today. It's all my fault; I should have been there with her."

"Calm down, she'll expect us to be calm. The police are on it, and they know exactly where she is. Listen, I need you to turn your phone back on."

"But you said . . . "

"I know; it's complicated."

She reached for her phone and handed it over to him.

"It's unlikely that you'll get the call because the perps may not know you, but I need to make sure it's hooked to a recording device just in case. I just wonder why I'm not getting any tracing from her ring."

"That's probably because she didn't wear it. She told me she didn't feel comfortable wearing it to the gym. She was afraid it would fall off. Besides, she didn't want to attract attention, and I agreed."

"Why?" Christian frowned.

"I mean, it could get lost with exercise when we get sweaty and stuff."

"But it's insured."

"But still—"

"So, why did I bother putting a GPS in it if she's not gonna wear it? Do you realize that we could possibly get Isabella back today just because she had on her watch? What if she decided not to wear the watch because it didn't go with an outfit? Like on our date night?"

"Come on, Chris, you're being paranoid."

"Am I, Rach? Tell me, where's Isabella? Am I dreaming this nightmare up? She's bound up somewhere, miles away from us in some dingy motel."

Rachel gasped. "Don't say that!"

"Besides, that ring isn't just about security, Rach. It's her engagement ring. I want it on her finger. It's not a fashion accessory. Listen, I don't want you encouraging her to take off that ring under any circumstance, and I'll let her know when she comes home."

Rachel nodded.

"One question, what in the world are you guys doing signing up at some gym?"

"What's wrong with getting in shape?" Rachel argued, shrugging.

"You couldn't do that here?"

"We wanted a trainer—besides we need someone to show us how to use half the stuff in our gym."

"Was this Isabella's idea or yours?"

Tears began to roll down Rachel's face.

"I'll have Erica arrange for a trainer to come here instead."

When Christian went up to his study, Rachel silently prayed as she paced the hallway. Suddenly, it occurred to her that exactly sixteen years ago today, she had met Isabella for the first time.

It was September 1997—a week after Labor Day. A twelve-year-old Rachel sat in the back of the car. As Tadd drove, Pattie sat beside Rachel,

holding her hand to ease her anxiety on her first day at the new school—
Nautilus Middle School. It was also the first time she had been out of the
Casa Cervello grounds since her parents' funeral months prior. She had already missed a week of school, and that Monday morning she had surprised
everyone by getting up early and getting dressed a whole hour before anyone woke up.

Tadd hugged and kissed her goodbye, then Pattie walked her inside. After a brief update, Pattie handed her over to the teacher, who assured her
that everything would be okay. Minutes later, all eyes were on Rachel as she
walked into her new class. The teacher formally introduced her to the class,
and she sat down.

At lunchtime, while the rest of the kids left the room, Rachel remained
seated—lost in her thoughts. With her head down on her desk, she drifted
away.

Her parents walked into the class. They were very loud and lively—
unlike their usual quiet selves. She raised her head and stared at them in
awe. "Hey, hey, hey, there's my little girl," her father, Carlos, said as he
picked up a piece of chalk and began to draw on the board. He went about
it with the same ease he had when he taught her seventh-grade math class in
Key Biscayne K-8. Rachel knew she had to be dreaming, but when she
glanced at the window, she could see her classmates still outside.

Her mother, Elizabeth, walked over to her desk, and with concern in her
eyes she asked, "Hey, Nena, how come you don't want to go out and hang
out with the other kids?"

Before Rachel could answer, her father said, "There you go." He wrote
the words *best friends*, over two stick figures holding hands. He turned
around and smiled. "I'm no Michelangelo but that's for you, *anjo*." He
placed the chalk down and walked over to them. "You've got a great school,
kiddo; you'll make great friends here, and Lord knows you could use a good
friend now that Chris is leaving."

Rachel cried out, "Mom . . . Dad, I'm so sorry."

"It's okay, honey," Elizabeth replied, "We're happy here. Aunt Pattie is
your mom now. Listen to her."

Rachel felt someone stroke her hair and raised her head swiftly to see
eleven-year-old Isabella standing above her. "You're going to be okay," Isabella said softly as she nodded.

Rachel panted. "Where did they go?"

"Our classmates? They're on lunch."

As Rachel stared at Isabella in fright, tears rolled down her eyes when she
realized it was all a dream.

"It was so real," Rachel whispered.

Isabella embraced her as she wept bitterly, and that marked the first day of Rachel's recovery from her deep depressive state. When they'd gotten closer, Rachel had told her about the dream, and Isabella convinced her that the dream was God's way of telling her to move on—citing her parent's message to her: *We're happy here.* Rachel came to believe that, and having Isabella around helped her get better by each day.

Christian called David's extension at the Private-I head office to notify him of the change in protocol. He felt for his friend—as it was his first day on the job, and he was still getting acquainted with the new office. He didn't need this drama on Day One, but because part of his responsibility involved overseeing the entire department of emergency systems, Christian was glad that he was present to ensure that all emergency tracking devices worked the way they were designed to.

"Hey, Chris, is everything okay? We lost all emergency contact a while ago, and then it all came back up some minutes ago. I thought it was a drill, but we never got a notification, and I see we're not even scheduled for one for another month."

"I know," Christian calmly said.

"Well, is it really a client in distress? Because I can actually hear voices on this end but nothing adds up—no names, just vitals. I'm kind of in the dark here. I tried calling you but your cell phone was off, too."

"David, Isabella was kidnapped."

"What? I'm coming over."

"No, I actually need you there to keep things in order. You said all phones are up and running again?"

"Yeah, HR was the last to come on. Wait a minute, how come we never saw her name?"

"The system is set up that way for now. There'd been no one to cover that project before you came, so I was doing it remotely. Only the police and I have access to the details, but now that you are here, you will have all those details. Listen, I need you to have all phone tracings on and ready in case a ransom call comes in."

"But, doesn't that go against protocol if she's still captured?"

"Yes, but it's a police request, and they had good reason—let's try it their way."

"Okay, I'm on it. Listen, everything's gonna be okay."

"Thanks, Dave, I need to believe that. Um, can you be the one to um . . . " he gulped. "Handle the call? I need someone I can trust on that call. Offer whatever they ask for, don't negotiate."

"Okay."

"Thanks."

"Hey," David said. "About these voices . . . I mean, the sound is perfect from this end. Are the police getting this stuff?"

"Really? No, as a matter of fact, they have a pretty poor reception."

"This is extremely clear. I thought these were actors for a drill. Don't you have your screen open?"

"I actually hadn't . . . shoot!" Christian said, running over to his screen.

"Do you have sound?"

"Hold on; I'm setting it up."

"Press the orange button, if you have one on your end, to activate—"

"Yeah, thanks. I can't believe I had it off. What did I miss?"

"Don't worry; I was recording the entire thing just in case. I haven't heard Isa's voice yet, but she's gotta be okay because if these vitals are hers, they're strong. But, right before you called, I heard a male voice talking to someone. It sounded like he was on the phone."

"Hold on," Christian said. "I hear something."

There was a sound of a door, then a voice asked, "Are you okay?" followed by a muffled response.

The sound coming from his surveillance audio was crystal clear. In a matter of seconds, Christian was certain that he could recognize the voice of his childhood friend, Kevin. His heart raced as faint memories flashed in his mind. Genius was absent. *Yes,* he thought, *this was definitely Kevin.* He had a very distinctive voice. It was high-pitched and scratchy on the edge. In middle school, he'd been bullied and teased for sounding whiny, and Christian had taken it upon himself to stand up to his bullies. Although Kevin grew out of the scratchy sound, Christian remembered how high his pitch would still rise, especially when nervous.

"That's Kevin," Christian whispered into the phone.

"Hendricks? From the London office?"

"Yes."

"*Your* Kevin?"

"I gotta go," Christian said.

Kevin continued. "Here, let's get this off so you can be comfortable." Christian heard what sounded like tape peeling off. Then he heard Isabella panting as though trying to catch her breath. When she began to cough violently, he couldn't make out what Kevin was saying in between her episodes. Then it sounded as though she was praying in Portuguese in between sharp breaths.

"Your lips are beautiful," Kevin said. "I wish I could see your face. Chris has always been a lucky bastard."

"Kevin?" Isabella asked.

"Who's that?" Kevin asked. From his tone, Christian knew he was nervous—Isabella was on to him.

Christian reached for Detective Sanders number. "Detective, I know who it is. It's Kevin Hendricks. We used to be best friends."

"What? Whoa, best friends?"

"Yes, it appears that I can get a better reception now from here, so I'm recording it for you guys."

"Okay, good. Has he called yet?"

"No, I'm still waiting; all lines are open and hooked up to record."

"Good. As soon as he makes the call, we'll go in."

"Hold on," Christian said. "I hear something."

"I don't wanna hurt you," Kevin said. "I promise it won't hurt. Just don't scream, okay?"

Isabella began to scream.

"Shh, see . . . " Kevin hissed. "Now I have no choice but to put that back on your pretty lips because you won't stop screaming, sweetie."

Isabella's voice became a muffle again.

Christian clenched his fist tight. "Tell your men to go in now."

"But he hasn't made the call."

"It sounds like he's about to rape her."

"Okay, brother just added on another charge."

"What? Whoa, whoa, wait . . . I don't want to wait until it becomes a charge. Go in now!"

"Please calm down, Mr. Cervello."

"Don't tell me to calm down; that's my fiancée in there!" He frantically ran his fingers through his hair as he muttered under his breath, "Kevin, don't do it. Don't do it Kevin. God, please stop him."

Christian grabbed his other phone and dialed the number he knew by heart. Disconnected. That was when he remembered that he hadn't actually spoken to Kevin since he caught him in bed with Kathy.

Kevin continued, "Stop fighting or I can't keep my promise not to hurt you."

Christian jumped at the sound of a phone ringing. It was Rachel's phone.

"Hold on, detective, I think that's him. There's a blocked call on Rachel's line. Rachel!"

Rachel was leaning by his study door. "I'm here."

"Quick . . . your phone." It had to be Kevin because he no longer heard his voice over the screen. However, he wondered if he were brash enough to be calling to speak to Rachel with his own voice.

"Hello," Rachel answered.

"I believe I have something you want," the caller said in a disguised voice.

"Who is this?" Rachel demanded.

"It doesn't matter. What matters is that I have Isabella, and she's still alive. So listen to me carefully, and you may want to grab a pen."

"Hold on," Rachel replied.

When Christian heard Kevin's voice once again over the screen, he realized he wasn't the one making the call to Rachel. Christian went out to the balcony and spoke into the phone to the detective. "Kevin is not acting alone; someone else is making the call. Hold on."

"I'm ready," Rachel said into the phone.

"I want three million dollars cash in one hour at Gateway Cemetery. Call the cops and she dies."

The caller was gone but Rachel was still stuck on *Gateway Cemetery*. She froze, repeating the name.

"Okay, she's off the phone. Go in," Christian said to the detective.

Rachel felt Christian's warm embrace as she went in and out of flashbacks of a cold and rainy day at Gateway Cemetery, when her younger self cried hysterically over her parents' caskets, before men in black suits lowered them into the ground.

Kevin's voice came again, "Now that wasn't that bad, was it? Now, I'm about to carry you to the bed."

Christian said to himself, *any minute now.*

Rachel looked at Christian in horror. "That sounds like Kevin."

Then, through the audio came the sound of a loud boom followed by multiple calls to freeze.

A few minutes later, Christian's phone rang.

"We got him," Detective Sanders announced. "We're searching for the other suspect—the one that made the call. There's a possibility the caller was in the next room. Our men are searching the neighboring rooms as we speak. The guy at the front desk confirmed that he booked two rooms for the same person, a "Mr. Ajax." The most important thing is that your fiancée is safe and on her way to the station."

"We'll be over there as soon as possible," Christian said.

Christian smiled at Rachel, "Let's go get our Isa."

Rachel smiled back through her tears. "Really?"

They hugged each other tight.

"I can't believe Kevin," Rachel said, shaking her head. "I just can't believe that bastard. How much pain must he subject us to? First my parents, then me, then you and Kathy, and now Isa? He is a heartless bastard."

Christian shook his head. "And Gateway Cemetery of all places."

They got into the vehicle, and Rachel flashed Christian a warm smile. He'd always made her feel safe. She was so grateful to have him as a brother. She shuddered to think of what the outcome of this tragedy would have been if not for Christian's invention and his love for them. He had handled himself so well; knowing how much he loved Isabella, it was a wonder how he'd kept his composure.

"Have I ever told you exactly how Isa and I met?" Rachel asked.

Christian said with a twinkle in his eye, "No, but I'm all ears."

CHAPTER TWENTY-FOUR

Keeping Enemies Close

STILL REELING from her nightmare from the day before, Isabella took things easy. Apart from minimal communication with the police, she hardly spoke about the ordeal. She had spent the night and morning meditating—asking the Lord what this all meant and how she was to conduct herself. Despite Christian and Rachel's concern, she felt stronger than ever. She woke up with a boldness that she knew could only have come from the Lord.

Their mutual decision was to keep the news from her parents, who had recently returned to Brazil. It would be best to tell them in person, and with the wedding set for next month, they should be back soon. There was no need to cause them to worry over what could have been. Isabella was certainly glad that Pattie and Tadd were also away. Knowing Pattie, she would probably have her constrained to the house until the wedding. She could just hear her stressing: "I can't afford to tell your parents stories about their only child."

Isabella's hair dripped dry as she stood in her robe, staring out of Rachel's window. The same limpkin bird she and Pattie had repeatedly shooed away was back. When they had caught it with a snail in its mouth, they had solved the mystery of the left-behind shells around the backyard. Why it roamed the compound, far away from the dock, baffled her. Perhaps it lost its family.

"Did you get any of their names?" Olivia asked over Isabella's shoulder, stroking her damp hair.

Isabella shook her head.

"Hmm, and you don't know what they looked or sounded like?" she persisted.

"Enough, Olivia!" Rachel snapped. "She was blindfolded; she told you already."

"Relax," Olivia said. Then turning back to Isabella, she said, "I'm so sorry I didn't come sooner."

"Yeah, you never seem to be around when we need you," Rachel muttered.

"That's not fair, Rach. I was stuck at the airport," she snapped back. "Come on, Isa, talk to us. It helps to."

"Just leave her alone, Liv. Geez . . . let her breathe."

"It's okay, Rach," Isabella said. "She's just concerned. Guys, I just wanna go and take a bath, okay?" At that point, it seemed it would take more than the baths to get rid of the nauseating feel of Kevin's hand over her bare skin.

"Didn't you just take a bath?" Olivia asked, enraged.

"So what?" Rachel replied getting up from the bed. "If she wants to live in the bathroom, it's her choice. For goodness' sake, let her be. Come on Isa," Rachel said softly. "I'll run your bathwater for you."

Olivia took Isabella's hand. "I'm sorry if I'm being so pushy."

"It's okay," Isabella replied. "Everyone's handling this differently, I understand. I just don't wanna talk about it right now."

"Okay."

Olivia's phone rang and she went out to the balcony to take the call. "Hello?"

"Liv, it's Kevin."

Olivia whispered in outrage, "What are you doing calling me?"

"We agreed to be there for each other if . . . "

"What? What in the world are you talking about? I heard what you did to that poor girl, you monster."

"Oh, so now you're gonna act like you don't know, huh? I see how we're playing this game."

"What game, where are you?" Olivia asked.

"Stop the nonsense, Olivia! You know exactly where I am. If you think they're recording this, they're not. It's a pay phone, so you can stop pretending. Just don't forget I can bring you down."

"Don't you dare threaten me. I never said I didn't have your back."

"Good to know . . . so what happens now?"

"What happens is you wait. You were stupid enough to get caught, so you have to wait."

"*Stupid?*"

"I told you to leave that stupid girl and come with me when I saw the cops outside the window."

"Yeah, after you convinced me to have my way with her."

"But, I changed my mind when the cops came. Listen, tomorrow I'll have a lawyer for you over there."

Rachel walked out to the balcony. "Over where?"

Olivia stuttered into the phone. "I um . . . you . . . listen to me carefully, if they're not gonna honor our contract, they will answer to my lawyer. I gotta go. Come over tonight for the makeup samples, okay?"

Rachel asked, "You're leaving?"

"Yeah," Olivia said as she hung up. "Something came up. I would love to come back tomorrow—if that's okay, of course."

"Of course. I won't be here for most of the day, but Chris will. Just lay off Isa with the questions, okay? She's getting enough from the police department."

"I hear you, but I really don't get what the big deal is," Olivia shrugged. "It's not as if she was raped or anything."

"Oh, you gotta be freaking kidding me, Olivia. Do you even hear yourself? You . . . "

"What?" Olivia snapped. "Huh, Rachel . . . tell me? You're mad at me because I show concern for *your* friend. Why are you making me out to be a—"

"*Concern* for her?" Rachel scoffed. "So now all of a sudden, you care about Isa? Give me a freaking break. Since when?"

"Yeah, Liv . . . since when?" Christian asked, standing at the balcony entrance.

Olivia turned around with a nervous laugh. "Oh I see how this is going down—everyone against Liv."

"Hey, I was wondering—did you know Hendricks was in town?" Christian asked.

"No . . . did *you*?"

"Nope. It's kind of strange that he's been here since March, and no one has bumped into him."

"You know what, I'm outta here." Olivia grabbed her bag.

"Why the hurry?" Christian asked, folding his arms across his chest.

"Sorry to burst your little investigative bubble, but I already told your cousin that I had to go before you got here."

"My investigative bubble? I like that." Christian laughed. "But if I may ask, am I missing something?"

"You think I don't know you guys suspect I have something to do with this?"

"Whoa." Rachel looked at Christian. "To do with . . . you know what? I'm not even comfortable having you here tomorrow anymore."

"All right then, fine!" Olivia screamed in Rachel's face. "I won't come!"

Rachel screamed back. "Good!"

"Paranoid freaks," Olivia said under her breath as she grabbed her shoes.

"Olivia, you need to calm down," Christian said. "You're actually the one who's really starting to sound paranoid. No one accused you of anything. It's not like you could've had anything to do with a scheme *that* clever," he said, sarcasm in his tone.

"Exactly," Olivia said through her teeth. "Now if you would excuse me." She walked out, slamming the door.

Christian sighed. "Where's Isabella?"

"Taking a bath," Rachel said.

"For as long as this investigation continues, you are not to trust Olivia with any information."

"Well, I can see that," Rachel said shaking her head.

"I'm serious."

"Come on, Chris. Liv can be obnoxious, but she can't harm a fly."

Christian held both Rachel's shoulders. "Just be careful. I'll be upstairs if you girls need me."

Just when Olivia thought the past four days couldn't get any worse, she received a text message from Kathy requesting to see her immediately; otherwise, *all bets are off.* Here she was, arguing with Christian and Rachel over Isabella, being contacted by Kevin from jail—of all places—receiving daily nags from Antonio, and now ultimatums from Kathy. For the first time in her adult life, she was drowning. Perhaps she was getting too old for this hustle. *Maybe Christian was right,* she thought. *Maybe I should have settled for a conventional job.* She shuddered at the idea; the thought of a nine-to-five, locked in a small box, terrified her. Maybe her greed had gotten the best of her.

The sad truth was she couldn't help but acknowledge the fact that Christian was worth more to her in pain than in love. What was she supposed to say to him? "Um, I'm sorry I had to sabotage your relationship with Kathy because I needed to get back on your payroll?" That would mean she would have to tell Kevin that she made up everything she said about Kathy wanting him. While she was coming clean, she would also have to tell Kathy that she lied about Kevin having a majority of the shares. Heck, while the confessions were rolling, she might as well tell all three of them that she was the one who set up their chance encounter with Christian that steamy night. The truth was that she had everything to do with all the pain around her. Now, because of her greed, Christian was engaged to Isabella and madly in love with her, Kevin was behind bars and likely to turn her in, and Kathy had the audacity to give her ultimatums. In hindsight, she could have just left Christian alone to Kathy and hooked Isabella up with Antonio for a cool million. If she hadn't been so intimidated by Isabella's values, she would have introduced her to Antonio long ago—after Rachel pulled out on Isabella's watch. Thinking back, it would have been sweet to have gotten paid while making Isabella and Rachel fall apart over the same guy. Christian probably thought Antonio was a monster, but she didn't see anything wrong with Antonio's desire to be with a woman he had never been with. She had come to know that rich people did stupid things, so to her, this was simply a challenge that he had set for himself. It wasn't her place to judge what turned people on. It was merely her job to deliver.

By the time Olivia pulled up at Kathy's hotel parking lot, it was pouring rain outside. She didn't have an umbrella and dreaded ruining her fresh hairdo. *My hair,* she snickered. *As if I'll have to be worrying about that if Kevin opens his big mouth.* The longer Olivia sat in the car with the pouring rain beating against her window, the more she felt trapped. "I won't let it!" she screamed. "I won't go to jail. No, I can't, I won't. I gotta think positive like Christian used to tell me and Kev," Olivia assured herself, breathing fast and hard as she wiped off the tears from her face with the back of her hand. "Damn it, why didn't I just leave Kev to go ahead with his plan to apologize to Chris? Why?" The fierce thunder that rumbled drowned the sound of Olivia's cries. Within minutes, she drifted off to sleep.

By the time she awoke, the rain had settled to a drizzle, with lightning that flashed every other minute. *Play it cool, Liv,* she said to herself, as she stepped out of her car and made a dash for the hotel lobby. When the elevator door opened, a little girl screamed in horror upon seeing Olivia. Her mother apologized to Olivia, as she pulled her visibly shaken daughter out of the elevator.

Stupid kids, Olivia muttered under her breath. As the mirrored doors closed, her flustered and disheveled reflection stared back. If she had bothered to look in the car mirror, she would have seen that her mascara had run down her face, and her red lipstick had found its way to her left cheek and forehead. She attempted to fix herself as the doors opened.

"Okay . . . " Kathy said raising a brow as she let Olivia in.

"Listen, Kathy, I'm gonna need more time," she said, making her way in hurriedly. "I've got this under control."

"Would you like to use the restroom to straighten yourself out before we get into this?"

"I'm fine. What does my appearance have to do with this?"

"I'm just having a hard time taking you serious looking like that," Kathy giggled.

When Olivia gave her a blank stare, she shrugged. "I'm sorry, Liv, but I'm going to need something more than that request. If I may remind you, I've already advanced you a little over fifty grand, and you know that comes from what's left from Chris. Once my money is done, so am I—unless I sell off the ring he gave me. I'm not with Private-I any longer."

"Really?" Olivia asked, surprised.

"I left," Kathy said, taking a seat at the edge of the bed. "I couldn't stand the humiliation."

"What's with all you guys leaving a high-paying job because of shame?" Olivia scoffed.

"Everything isn't about money, Liv," Kathy said with a sad smile. "I used to be like you; that's what got me into this mess. I had a job to die for, and a great man . . . but I fell so low. Climbing into his best friend's bed because I believed the fortune really belonged to him."

Then turning to Olivia, she said, "Listen, I'm gonna need something more, hon. What's this other plan you were working on? I can't be in the dark anymore."

Olivia sighed as she sat on a chair. "Okay, listen, what I'm about to tell you is high-profile police stuff, so I'm not even supposed to be saying anything."

Kathy slowly nodded as she rose from the bed. "Okay, hold on; I'll get us a drink."

"Listen, Kathy, I wanna be sober when I say this, okay?"

"Okay . . . no drinks," Kathy said with a smirk, as she pulled up a chair next to Olivia.

"What do you wanna know?" Olivia asked.

"For starters, I want to know why you refused to go with my plan when we already had the first phase done months ago—besides I'm still waiting for the evidence, mind you. In fact, I'm beginning to suspect you never went through with it."

"I did, Kat. It's just not—"

"You keep saying you have something better. What was so much better than my original plan? I mean, do you realize it's more difficult to get them apart now that they're engaged?"

"Yes, but . . . okay listen," Olivia said. "Your plan was solid—yes, and it would have definitely broken them apart. But he wouldn't have come back to you with that."

Kathy threw her hands up. "Heck, at this point, I don't think he even wants to hear my name after that restaurant scene. So yeah, if I can't have him, let the plan at least stop her from having him, too."

Olivia frowned. "Is that what you're paying me to do? I mean, did you change the plan? Because your original request was for me to get him back to you. And you know how I do that? By planting seeds that take time to grow. That was the preferred plan, Kathy, to get him coming back to you, and you alone. Make him believe he was wrong for doubting you in the first place."

"Okay. I mean, I love the sound of that, but how come he's engaged?"

"Okay, listen," Olivia said, as she got up and walked around the room, nervously looking around.

Kathy followed Olivia closely as she hesitantly continued, "The plan involved kidnapping Isa."

"What?" Kathy asked with a mix of amusement and outrage.

"Yes, Kevin kidnapped her, and I convinced him to try to rape her."

"Wait, what? You were part of this?"

Olivia stuttered, "Well, not really."

"Liv . . . "

"Okay, okay, yes, but it was Kevin's idea, and she wasn't supposed to get hurt."

Kathy raised a brow. "Was she?"

"No."

"Please don't tell me this was all just so my silly excuse of being raped by Kevin could make sense. It doesn't, *Liv*. There had to be something else, something bigger. What was in store for you two? How much?"

Olivia ran her fingers through her disheveled hair. "Three million."

"Whoa . . . you go big, huh?"

"It wasn't my plan!"

Kathy said with a nonchalant shrug, "Yeah, of course, it was Kevin's. So . . . did he rape her?"

"No, the good news is that he attempted it before the cops came. They came so quick . . . "

"Wait, what?" Kathy's eyes widened. "Cops? My goodness, Olivia! Are you on the run?"

Olivia scoffed. "Don't be ridiculous."

"And Kevin? I can't believe . . . "

"Listen, he's a fool. I tried to get him out, but he didn't listen. I don't even know how they knew. It hadn't even been up to two minutes since I made the call for the money."

Kathy stepped up even closer to Olivia. "Ah . . . so *you* made the call? Hmm, brazen. So, exactly when do you make the connection to me?"

"Well, I was over at Chris' place to plant more seeds. The plan was to convince him that it all happened as you said."

"Wow, wait a minute, Olivia. This is all so bizarre to me. Have you somehow forgotten that Kevin is your friend? I mean, even if you guys weren't caught for ransom, you had to have known that Christian would have him arrested for rape."

"I was working on the fact that Kevin already implicated himself by allowing himself to get caught."

"No, I'm not a child, Olivia, you made it clear that your original plan was to make Chris think that Kevin raped me by convincing him to do the same to her."

Olivia remained silent.

"Listen, I am not judging you, I just wanna know exactly who I'm dealing with here."

"Well, you didn't seem concerned when you destroyed Kevin's life."

Kathy raised her voice. "Don't you try to twist this around. No one was supposed to get hurt then. I have no idea why Christian came back that day, but he did. This is not about me, or the past. It's about you and the fact that you just admitted to having his fiancée kidnapped and coercing his best friend into raping her.

"Why do I feel like it's so easy for you to hurt Christian? Isn't he supposed to be like your brother? Just the other day, you took me to your million-dollar pad and bragged about how Chris has you living there for free, now this? My goodness, Olivia . . . if you could do this to Chris, what would you do to me?"

"So much for not judging me," Olivia muttered, turning to leave.

"Come on, Liv, I'm sorry. I don't know what came over me." Kathy sighed. "What were you saying?"

"I'm done." Olivia grabbed her bag.

"Okay, let's just end this now. I need my money back."

"I forgot where I was," Olivia relented. "You keep interrupting me."

"You were gonna tell Chris . . . "

"So, I was just gonna tell Chris . . . you know . . . talk about how Kevin did the same thing to you that he could have done to Isa, but then I had to leave because Rachel thought I was coming on too strong to Isabella."

Kathy shook her head. "Yeah, you can't appear desperate—dead giveaway."

"Well, I'm trying, but I'm getting pressured on all ends—you, Kevin, Antonio, even Rana. Gosh, everyone wants someone."

Kathy frowned. "Who's Rana?"

Olivia turned away. "Some girl who wants Chris. It's not what you think."

"Hmm," Kathy nodded. "So, tell me, Olivia, exactly who *are you* working for?"

"I'm working for you and Antonio."

"So that same Antonio guy still wants her?" Kathy asked.

"More than ever, now that he found out she's engaged—he loves the extra challenge."

"And this Rana . . . she wants Chris. And I'm the fool paying you to get them together?"

Olivia grabbed Kathy's arm. "Rana doesn't matter. She's a non-paying sidepiece for my game—a stupid little pawn."

"Oh, yeah? How does she fit in?"

Thinking quick, Olivia said, "She's the piece we need for Plan A—your plan, remember?"

"Ahh, so you have all the players now?"

Relieved to be off the hook, Olivia said with a nervous grin, "Looks like it."

Kathy winked. "We must drink to this, Olivia."

When Kathy went to get drinks, Olivia sighed, knowing she had dodged a bullet.

Kathy poured some champagne in two glasses and walked back to Olivia with the drinks. "Well, thanks for confiding in me," Kathy said, handing Olivia a glass. "I gotta tell you, that was a horrible operation."

"Yeah?"

Kathy nodded. "And I'll tell you why." She sat down on the chair. "For one, Chris' business is all about preventing such crimes. You probably wouldn't know because he said you never took interest in his art, but Kevin of all people should have known—we both worked for him." Kathy shrugged as she continued. "Chris probably had her hooked up with some kind of tracking device. Ever wondered why the cops arrived so quickly? Think about it."

Olivia sat back down, "Yeah, I've been wondering about that."

Kathy smiled and stood back up. "Yeah, he was working on perfecting his latest tracking device when we started dating. That's probably what saved his little girlfriend." Kathy laughed. "Man, that guy is good at what he does."

"How could you be so sure, though?" Olivia asked.

"My goodness," Kathy said. "Come to think of it, that's why it was such a foolish plan. You know what would have been a better plan for Kevin if he wanted some money?"

"What?" Olivia asked.

"Return to Chris and ask for forgiveness. Chris will always have a soft spot for Kevin. Heck, he would forgive him before he forgives me."

Olivia looked away. "I tried to convince him to do that."

"Oh? What did he say?"

"Well, obviously he refused to listen," Olivia scoffed and she stood up and walked to the window. Kathy followed her promptly and stood behind Olivia without a word.

Olivia looked over her shoulder. "What?"

Looking intently at Olivia, Kathy said, "Hmm . . . nothing. Just thinking that was foolish of Kevin. Chris sees him like the brother he never had, a stupid one—but still a brother. I'm the one he won't forgive. You see, my dear, I learned a valuable lesson about Christian Cervello—he can forgive just about anything. But infidelity from the woman he loves? No, he just won't share. Come on, Liv, you two grew up together . . . you probably know a thing or two about him when it comes to sharing, perhaps his toys?"

When both women laughed, Olivia was grateful that the tension in the room lifted.

"Aren't you afraid that Kevin will expose you?" Kathy asked in a soft tone, stepping closer to Olivia.

"Well, I've been thinking about it, but I'm putting together a plan. I figure if it comes to that, it'll be his word against mine. After all, I had asked him to lay low since he arrived about six months ago. In fact, no one has seen us together."

"No one else involved, huh?"

"Kat, can you back up just a little; you keep following me close—it's making me nervous."

"Oh, I'm sorry—bad habit."

"It's okay—just two guys, and they never got to see me. They dealt with Kev. And here's what I just remembered," Olivia said, her countenance suddenly bright. "Kev booked both rooms himself."

"Good," Kathy nodded. "Nothing that a good lawyer can't take care of. Hey, did Chris ever find out you were the one who forged those letters with that other girl . . . what's her name again—the blonde? . . . "

Olivia chuckled. "Sacha. No, I don't think so. Then again, he and I haven't exactly been on the best of terms since then, and he keeps things to himself. I would say he definitely hasn't confronted her about it because she would have brought it up by now."

"You both still talk?"

"Kind of—she's nursing her wounds about losing such a catch. He gave her everything." Olivia shook her head. "Yeah, Christian is very generous with just about anything, but he is picky with his women."

Kathy sighed. "This hurts to say, but did you know that Chris doesn't believe in prenuptials?"

Olivia's eyes widened. "No way!"

"Seriously," Kathy continued as she paced the room. "One day . . . that's all it took. If I hadn't been with Kevin that night."

"What do you mean?"

"I forgot that Chris and I had long ago set up an appointment to meet with his lawyer. The meeting was supposed to take place the day after he caught me with Kevin. So that day arrived, and the lawyer showed up at our condo. When we got to talking, he spoke of how lucky I was and how he typically convinces his wealthy clients to protect themselves, but Christian was stubborn and totally against it."

When Kathy paused, Olivia pressed, "So what happened?"

"He kept wondering when Christian was gonna show up because he was already late for the meeting, and it was unlike Chris to be late. Then his phone rang . . . it was Chris, calling to cancel the appointment. The lawyer packed up his papers, and before he walked out the door, he said, 'Sorry for your loss.' That's how I found out it was really over. Chris never came back to pick up his stuff. Next I knew, he was in Florida."

"Oh my." Olivia gasped.

"I know, just one day." Kathy muttered, staring into blank space.

A few minutes of silence went by before Kathy said with a sad smile, "Come to think of it, I don't think I'll ever get him back. So, go ahead and plant all the seeds in your little garden. When they don't grow, come back so we can finish up Plan A. I can live without Chris as long as he's alone."

Nearly a week after the kidnapping incident, Isabella had slowly managed to get the ordeal past her. The experience had drawn her closer than ever to God, and their premarital sessions with Pastor Bernard helped keep her focused on what mattered most. It did concern her that Christian and Rachel both seemed convinced that she wouldn't have been hurt at all—knowing it was Kevin behind the operation. Because of this strange trust in their oldest friend, they seemed eager to push the incident aside.

Their loyalty to even toxic friendships only reminded Isabella of Rosa's warning about the curse involving trust and how people closest to them were hurting them. Although she was grateful that Christian's lawyers were going forward with all possible charges against Kevin, she really needed him to see the deeper implications—a spiritual connection. Her pastor advised her to let go of the worrying and stop using her strength to get Christian to see things, but rather trust God to get him to look beyond the surface.

"Tada!" Rachel waved Isabella's completed wedding list in the air.

Isabella nonchalantly grabbed the pedicure basket and sat on the floor without a word.

"What's wrong? You're supposed to be elated. We've been working on it nonstop for nearly a week."

"Olivia doesn't like me," Isabella said, filing her toenails.

"Why do you say that?"

"Oh, I know; I'm not stupid," she said with a sarcastic smirk. "She hates my guts; she always has. Please don't insult my intelligence by playing dumb, Rach."

"I wouldn't put it that way," Rachel said. "It's more like jealousy because you and I got closer."

"Nah, it's more than that," she said, shaking her head. "I don't know what it is, but I'm aware that she doesn't like me. So I would prefer she didn't come."

Rachel got up from the bed and went to sit by Isabella on the floor. "Are you serious?"

"I'm dead serious. You see, on your wedding day you would want well-wishers there with you, right?"

Rachel said, "I mean, Olivia's got her issues, but I thought that . . . you guys speak to each other, don't you?"

Isabella laughed. "Come on, Rach, speaking to someone doesn't make you friends with them. You're actually the only reason Olivia is in my life."

"No, I don't believe that."

Isabella frowned. "You know what, Rachel, you're bent on inviting her, so just put her down. I love you, and as long as you're okay, I'm good."

"Oh no, this is not about me, love. It's your big day. You know, the last time people went out of their way to please me when I was fighting for a friend, they lost their lives."

"Rach, I didn't mean for us to go there."

Worry lines appeared on Rachel's face. "Oh no, it's okay; I need the wake–up call."

Isabella smiled. "You know what? Just put her down; it won't hurt."

"She was at the engagement ceremony, right?" Rachel asked, hopeful.

Isabella's smirk returned. "Oh yeah, she sure was."

"What? Why did you say it like that? How was it?"

"Well, let's just say it was very awkward."

"How so?" Rachel persisted.

"I can't believe I never told you. Well, you know how she couldn't make it to the after-party?"

"Yeah, something about doing the makeup line the next day."

"Okay . . . well, she came over to me at the restaurant to say goodnight, not *congrats*, but goodnight."

Rachel gasped.

Isabella continued with a smile. "Anyway, while she was talking, they announced it was time for the toast. When she and I toasted, my glass shattered."

"It what?"

Isabella blinked and looked away, attempting to push back the tears that were forming. "Yeah, it did. Hers didn't, but mine did. I don't know, Rach . . . I don't know if that's a sign, but you should have seen the smug look on her face when she said, 'Your glass is weak.'"

"That's what she said? That's crazy. What does that even mean? Boy, that girl has gotten weird."

"Evil is the word, pure evil."

Isabella got up from the floor and went to wash her hands. "Rachel, I know evil when I see it. Olivia . . . I know she's your friend and all, but that girl is evil. I don't have any proof, and I may just be speculating, but something's not right with her, and all I can wonder is how in the world you two were once so close."

CHAPTER TWENTY-FIVE

Memory Lane

❧

TWO DAYS before the wedding, more close friends and family had settled into Casa Cervello. Isabella's parents had been in her Florida home for the past week—helping with last-minute arrangements, and her uncle Miguel arrived earlier that day with his two sons. That evening, they all joined the Cervellos, Thomas, Denise, and David in the family room to acquaint with one another and share old stories. In honor of Elizabeth's memory, Pattie whipped out some old albums she had guarded over the years—some of which she hadn't even shared with her kids.

Not long after the crowd looked through Pattie's pictures, the questions regarding her twin's passing started, and Pattie's response that she had died in a car accident along with her husband left an eerie feeling in the room. The most awkward moment came when Isabella's mother, Ana, inquired about her other relatives. Hearing that her entire family was gone stunned Ana, and at one point, it seemed as though no one had the courage to speak. The crowd came alive once again when Tadd changed the subject to soccer. Isabella's father, Felix, along with her two cousins, rooted for the Brazilian soccer team, while David, Tadd, Christian, and Miguel defended the Italian team. Isabella's heart went out to Pattie, but she was glad to see that she appeared more relaxed after Tadd's rescue. She had noticed Pattie's disposition begin to sadden since her bridal shower the night before. Rachel had suspected that the party reminded Pattie of the bridal shower she threw for her deceased twin years ago, and Rachel wondered if she could feel her presence in the house.

As the soccer arguments continued, Isabella noticed that Thomas was the only one who continued looking through the albums—perhaps getting to know more about the family he would be marrying into. At that moment, as though reading her mind, he looked at her with his brows creased. He looked back down at the album and up at her again. "Hey," he said, nudging Rachel. "Isn't this Isa?"

Rachel inspected the photo. "Wait a minute, I have this." She pointed to a framed picture on the mantel. "But it was just Isa and our parents." Then beckoning to Isa, Rachel asked, "Isa, don't you have something like this in your living room, too?"

"Yeah but—" Isabella said, looking closely at their high school graduation photo, a group picture of both their families. Christian's attention was still on soccer when Isabella motioned him over. "Have you seen this?"

"Yeah, I have one with Rachel and . . . " Abruptly stopping, Christian looked at Isabella with a puzzled expression. "We met in 2003?"

"But when exactly *did we* take this?" Rachel asked. "Mom?"

"The date is right there, baby, *May 20, 2003*," Thomas said.

Suddenly, the room fell silent with questioning stares.

Rachel said, "I know but—"

Thomas made a scary face and exclaimed, "Da daa daa!" He then explained the strange case to the others.

"Seriously, mom, did you even know you had a picture of Isa and Chris all along?" Rachel asked.

Pattie shook her head. "No, I don't think I've opened that album since your high school graduation."

"That's weird," David said, inspecting the picture.

"Let me see," Denise took it from him. Then she cleared her throat with a smirk. "Okay."

"What?" Isa asked, appearing timid.

Thomas gave Denise a high-five. "I know, you don't even have to say it—I bet you she had a crush on him way back then."

"No I didn't," Isabella said. "I was a good girl—I wasn't thinking of boys."

David laughed. "Yeah right, that's hard to believe. Chris, you must have found her attractive back then. I mean, look at her."

"Oh, please, like she would have wanted Chris," Rachel chuckled.

"Seriously, guys, it's not what you think," Christian said. Then to Isabella, "No offense, love, but I don't even remember taking a picture with you. As far as I am concerned, we met in February."

Isabella's younger cousin, Junior, teased. "I'm with them—Isa definitely had a crush on him."

"I don't remember meeting him," Isabella argued.

"No, no seriously," Rachel said. "Isa's right, I would have known if she had a crush on him. Listen, this girl hardly ever talked about boys. She was the one that kept me grounded."

Tadd looked at Isabella's parents. "You both did such a great job with her."

Isabella blushed. Feeling Christian's burning gaze on her but she dared not look his way.

"Rachel, you all but lived with us at a time," Felix said. "I can't believe we never met your brother."

"It sounds strange, but if you think about it, it's possible," Tadd replied. "Remember, you guys met Rachel shortly after her parents died. Well, Christian started college that fall."

"Yeah, but he went from home, Dad," Rachel said.

"Yes, but he was busy. Besides, you also started the new school around that time, and when you kicked it off with Isa, you spent most of your time at her place. Didn't Mom used to drop you off during the week and pick you up on weekends?"

"Oh, yeah, I remember," Rachel's eyes lit up with excitement. "Come to think of it, every time Isa was here, Chris was gone, and when she was in Notre Dame, he was here."

"It was for the best," Felix said. "That's probably why they both did well in school—no distractions."

"That's assuming I would have wanted her then," Christian muttered.

"Ooooh," Thomas teased.

Denise asked Tadd, "Didn't Isa ever spend nights at your place?"

When the parents looked at each other and laughed, Thomas asked, "What's funny about that?"

Ana replied in a strong accent, "Because we never let her spend nights in anyone's home."

Miguel excused himself. It was his devotion time with the Lord. About the same time, Pattie excused herself and quietly slipped away, leaving an awkward silence before Felix continued. "We had our reasons," he defended. "We had just arrived in Florida earlier that year and didn't know anyone. It took some time, but eventually when the girls got to senior high, Isa spent nights over here."

"Okay, wait," Denise said, "What year did all this happen—when she started spending nights here?"

"It had to be between 2002 and 2003. Because soon after their high school graduation, Ana and I left for Brazil. Isa practically lived here before she left for Indiana."

"And how come she never met Chris?" Thomas asked.

"Probably because I was at MIT between 2002 and 2004," Christian replied.

"No vacations?" Denise persisted.

"I came back quite a bit." Christian shrugged. "I guess she was in school."

"But seriously," Felix said to Tadd, "I have to thank you for taking care of her when we left."

Tadd replied, "I had no choice. She was like my very own daughter. Isa leaves you no choice but to love her. Besides, we could never pay you back for blessing us with her company when Rachel needed a friend in that new school. Rachel went to Nautilus right from your home in Miami. She was hardly speaking to any of us then. Isa brought her back out of her shell." The two men exchanged a hug. Rachel and Isabella followed suit.

"Okay, okay, enough with the mushiness," said Isabella's older cousin, Ivan, as he boldly held up the picture. "There's still no explanation for this. Look at how he's holding her," he said, referring to Christian's arm around Isabella's shoulder.

"You gotta be—" Christian muttered. "You guys are impossible."

Ana shook her head. "But it's still so strange that we never met Christian—not even once."

Tadd sat up in his recliner. "Okay, son, come help me out with the timeline. So, when the girls met, you were in your first year of under-grad, yes?"

"Yup . . . '97," Christian replied.

"By the time you graduated, they were in junior high, and Felix still didn't let Isa spend nights here."

"I guess," Christian said, shrugging.

"So what are we up to?" Tadd asked.

"2002—I wrapped up my internship with KBPD and left for MIT in September."

"There . . . when you were off to Massachusetts, Isa started spending nights here. Then, by that picture in 2003, you came home for their gradu-ation and the mystery remains how neither of you remember meeting that day. Let's skip that for a second. Isa went off to Notre Dame later that year—for how long?"

"Five years," Isabella said.

"Okay, Chris was between MIT, Florida, and Canada around that time. Then by the time Isa returned to Florida, where were you, son?"

"Still in Vancouver," Chris said. "Then I moved to London in 2009, and back here in 2013."

"Okay, so there you go," Tadd concluded.

"Well, at least we know they did in fact meet in 2003," Thomas said looking down at the timeline he had diligently taken on his phone as Tadd spoke. "Whether they remember it or not, that was a decade ago."

"Geez . . . when you put it like that," Rachel pondered aloud.

Felix laughed. "I know your timeline makes sense, but all I see is a bunch of kids that can't stay put."

Everyone laughed until Pattie walked back into the room with a videotape in her hand.

"What's that?" Christian asked.

"I need you to play it."

"Mom, it's like 2013, what's in it anyway?"

"I'm not telling," Pattie teased.

"Then I'm not playing it."

"Come on, Chris," she persisted.

"Okay, everyone, would you care to join us downstairs?" Christian asked. "Mom wants us to watch something on a VCR and there's one down in the entertainment room."

Everyone gathered on the main floor.

As Isabella sat in the front row with Rachel and Ana, her heart pounded. She wasn't sure she could take any more surprises for the night. Pattie sat directly behind them with Tadd and Felix next to her. Christian stood by the side of the screen with the remote control in hand as Thomas helped set up the VCR.

As soon as the video started rolling, Pattie's voice filled the speakers. The date on the screen was 1/21/98. A younger Pattie handled the video camera without focus, clearly fiddling with the settings.

"Christian!"

"Yeah, Ma?"

"Here, can you figure out how to get this started? I'm not sure if it's even working."

When a nineteen-year-old Christian made funny faces into the camera, the crowd in the entertainment room laughed. Christian covered his face in embarrassment.

"You want me to record, Mom?" Christian asked on the tape.

"Oh, I'd really appreciate that. I still have so much to do—Tara can help you."

"*Good, there's a whole bunch of kids out there, and I don't know how to keep 'em entertained.*"

Christian focused the camera on himself. "*Okay, I'm coming to you live from Casa C on Rachel's thirteenth birthday party. I'm your host, Chris C, and this is my lovely girlfriend, Tara M. Say what's up Tara!*"

A shorthaired blonde came into view, waving frantically.

"*Okay, so as you can see, the guests are dressed to impress and the music . . . is too slow. DJ! Something up-tempo, please!*"

Tara giggled in reply.

Christian continued. "*Okay, we've got some brave young ladies from Nautilus Middle School starting to boogie down but a few others are still seated. So here's what we're gonna do, we're gonna give them a chance to leave a birthday message to the birthday girl, Rach . . . my best friend, I love you, kid.*"

"*Rach!*" he yelled out.

A thirteen-year-old Rachel with black, shoulder-length hair came into view and grinned. "*It's my birthday,*" she said shyly. "*Wait, I gotta change my shoes—my feet hurt, be right back.*"

"*Okay, guys,*" Christian announced. "*That was the birthday girl. Now, on to the guests. Let's start here.*"

A young lady sat idly blowing bubbles with her gum. She blushed when the camera got to her.

Rachel and Isabella laughed. "Oh, my . . . Tiny T," Rachel said. "She's married now with a kid."

"*Hello, young lady, I'm Chris, Rachel's cousin. I'm just going around making sure you're all having a great time and also to give you a chance to leave a message for our shining star. So we'll start with your name?*"

The girl stared blankly, trying to suppress a giggle. Tara asked, "*What's your name?*"

"*Oh . . . Tanya.*"

"*And how old are you, Tanya?*" Christian asked.

"*Twelve.*"

"*Okay, Tanya, do you have a wish for Rachel?*"

"*Um, that she, um . . . gets many gifts.*"

"*Okay,*" Christian said. "*I have a feeling that wish is gonna come true. Thanks a lot, Tanya, and hit the dance floor, will ya?*"

"*Okay, that was fun,*" Tara teased.

"*Hey, Liv!*" Christian yelled over the music. "*Come leave a message for Rach.*"

A sixteen-year-old Olivia stuck her tongue out. "*Here's to getting a raise on that allowance.*"

"Olivia!" Tara said, covering her mouth in amusement.

"Olivia was always a grouch," Rachel said to Isabella.

"Here, wait," Tara said. "Let's go to this one. She's too cute with her little flower in her hair."

Isabella's heart pounded when she realized that the little girl in the pink, A-line dress and white jasmine flower was her. Looking back, she seemed overly dressed for the party compared to the rest of the kids.

Rachel laughed. "Look at Isa . . . oh shoot, I remember, *Mom?*" Rachel turned back to look at Pattie before Isabella hushed her, "Shh."

"Oh yeah . . . sorry," Rachel said. They began whispering back and forth with their mothers.

Christian rewound the tape.

"Yeah, quite the lady," Christian replied to Tara.

As the camera approached Isabella, Tara whispered, "She's gorgeous, look at her. I'll interview her."

"Hey, girl," Tara said. "Don't you look pretty . . . what's your name?"

"My name is Isabella Montes."

"Aww . . . look at those braces," Tara whispered. "She has a nice little accent, too."

Christian laughed. "And complete sentences—that's a first."

Tara continued. "Oh, honey, you look nervous, are you okay?"

"Yes, I am fine—thank you," Isabella replied.

"How old are you, Isabella?" Tara asked.

"I am eleven years old."

"And . . . oops, what else are we asking them?" Tara whispered to Christian.

"Birthday wish," Christian said, asking Isabella, "Do you have a wish for Rachel?"

"Yes, I'd like to wish Rachel many happy and healthy years to come."

"Oh . . . okay," Christian replied. "That was very well put . . . miss?"

"Isabella Montes."

"Yes . . . of course," Christian said. "Thank you."

Tara whispered, "Talk about an old soul, I love that girl, I wish she were my little sister. Hold on, Chris. Um, Isabella hon, don't you wanna dance—come on with me."

Isabella shook her head. "No, thank you."

"Here, why don't you continue with the interviews?" Christian told Tara. "You're doing a great job."

"All right, pause it right now before I explode!" Thomas yelled, prompting laughter across the room.

"Oh no, the lawyer is about to analyze his case," Denise teased.

"First of all," Thomas said standing. "Why did Isa look tense—like she was shy? Secondly, why did Christian end his recording soon after he interviewed her?"

"Aha!" Junior yelled.

"No, I believe I actually continued with the recording," Christian said. "I remember now—I got around to speaking to all those kids. Now if you would just play it, you'd see."

"Come on, guys," Rachel pleaded. "Let's watch it to the end; this is so much fun."

"No baby, wait," Thomas said to Rachel. "I heard you guys whispering about something—what were the four of you talking about?"

"Nothing," Ana said while Pattie added, "Mind your business, Thomas."

Thomas pointed, "All of you over at this section know what happened that day, and you're not telling, and if you ask me, Isa had a crush on Chris. I rest my case."

"Thomas, man, you are truly twisted," David said, patting him on the back.

Thomas shrugged. "Hey, I call it like I see it."

Denise said, "What I wanna know is exactly how you guys met in 1998 and don't remember."

Later that night, Denise's comment lingered on Christian's mind. He wondered if thinking back would prompt a feeling or a spark that he might have felt even back then. Nothing came to him. He headed back to the entertainment room and seeing Thomas and Rachel fast asleep as the birthday video neared the end for the third time, he nudged at them. "Hey . . . go to bed."

Rachel stretched and nudged at Thomas before stumbling out of the room.

Christian rewound the tape. The more he watched, the more he remembered.

"Ah . . . there you are," Isabella said, at the entrance of the room. Christian paused the video and motioned her over. She chuckled at the sound of Thomas' snore. "He loves sleep as much as his fiancée."

"Did you know all along?" Christian asked.

"Know what?" she asked, sitting next to him.

"That we met years ago?"

"I knew we had to, but this is too much. We can't both have memory issues."

"This video seems to have triggered something." He stood up and paced. "Tiny memories."

"Yeah?" Isabella asked, following him with her gaze.

"Something about a flat tire . . . "

"Wait, there was a time my uncle was visiting, and his rental got a flat. That was *you?*"

"And when I picked you girls up from the train station—you weren't supposed to be on a train."

"Yeah, that was Olivia's fault." Isabella smiled. "I remember it was raining."

"You didn't remember that was me?"

"I always thought that was Uncle Tadd that night."

"Come on, you were young, but you had to know I wasn't my dad. I was with Tara that night."

"She suppressed it, that's why," Thomas said, catching the two of them off guard. "Perhaps she didn't wanna believe the guy she had a crush on had someone else."

"Thomas," Christian's tone warned.

"Come on, guys, admit it . . . you totally had the hots for each other. See this chemistry you two have? It didn't start in February, that I know—everyone knows."

"Shut up, Thomas," Isabella snapped.

"Would you please excuse us?" Christian asked. "Weren't you supposed to be asleep?"

"It's okay, he can stay—I gotta go to bed anyway . . . early start tomorrow."

Pattie and Tadd had convinced Isabella's family to stay at Casa Cervello and later that night, when Isabella visited her parent's guestroom, her favorite aunt, Febe, came to mind.

Febe Martines was married to her mother's only brother, Miguel, and she pastored a church in Rio de Janeiro, where they both lived with their two sons. Isabella had always gotten along with Febe, and she in turn considered her the daughter she never had. So when she hadn't attended the engagement ceremony, it concerned Isabella, especially since Febe was her biggest supporter. When Febe didn't arrive with the rest of the family earlier that day, she began to wonder if she even had her blessing.

"Mom, isn't Tia Febe coming for the wedding? I thought she would be here by now."

"Oh, dear, I forgot to mention, I spoke to her a few minutes ago. She should be here by tomorrow morning. A last-minute engagement came up at the church. Don't worry, she won't miss it for the world."

"Okay, great. I'm excited."

"You know, when I was speaking to Febe earlier, I told her about how Pattie is the last member of her family left. Your aunt was very interested, and when she asked for their last name and the part of Spain they were from, she was shocked when I told her."

"Why?" Her mother was the last one she wanted to confide in about the curse.

"She said if it's the family she has in mind, they may be under a curse. In fact, she reminded me of the stories we heard growing up about that family. It's no secret. We read about them in literature."

"There are books about them?"

"Well, we always just thought it was folklore. We never knew whether it was true, but the story is famous back home—*Tragédia da Família Gomes*."

Isabella grew cold from fright. "What else did Tia Febe say?"

"She was shocked. The more we talked, the more she was sure it was them. But filha, listen, this is very serious, because from what I remember, everyone that was involved with this family also died. As for the family, they're all gone, children, wives, husbands . . . perished. Pattie is all that's left—and her son and niece, of course. I need you to think very seriously about what you are about to do, because I don't want to lose you."

Isabella frowned. "So, what are you saying, Mom?"

Felix returned to the room, and seeing Isabella, he asked Ana, "What did you say to her?"

"Oh, I was just telling her about *The Gomes Family Tragedy*."

"Oh, get off that," Felix said heatedly. "Why instill fear in her? It may not even be the same family."

"No, seriously, Felix, you know as a pastor Febe talks about this in her church service when she discusses curses. It's just that we didn't really know it was actually a true story."

"You still don't know!" Felix snapped.

Isabella stood up and sighed. "This *is* the family. I just don't have all the information yet. But I do know this . . . the person who told me what I know also said that the Lord was going to use me to help them."

Ana's eyes widened. "So you knew all along about this, and you still chose to go ahead with it?"

"Mom—"

"Stop it! Don't be stupid, you're not cut out for this. This is more than us."

"So what are you saying, I'm not supposed to marry Chris because of some kind of curse on his life? Yes, it's bigger than us, but is it bigger than God? You know, it's funny, because you were the one who taught me that there was nothing that was too much for God to fix."

Ana looked away and Isabella continued, "What happened to all that talk about what Jesus can do? I mean . . . where's your faith, Mom? Was it just talk? So I'm supposed to just throw everything you told me out the window because the heat is on?"

"No, filha, what I am saying is that there are some things we're not cut out for, and this is one of them."

Isabella nodded. "I guess I missed that part of your lesson—the part where I was supposed to learn about the things that the blood of Jesus couldn't fix. So this is one of them? Is that what you meant to say? That there's a limit to what Jesus can do? Well, Mom, I remember being the hungriest student in your school of life, and I know that with every lesson comes a test. This is it—we are being tested now."

When Felix looked at Ana, she quickly turned away. Isabella began to pace the room. Then with a frustrated laugh through tears, she shook her head, "I try so hard to understand some Christians. This is exactly why the world laughs at us. We're hypocrites. What happened to salt and light? Now, I am supposed to cower away from the man I love because of some curse that's too much for the blood of Jesus to wash away. So tell me, what should I do? Throw away everything you taught me? It doesn't apply now, right?"

"You know she's right, Ana," Felix said.

Ana slowly nodded. "I'm so sorry; I let my fears get the best of me. You're right about everything—there's nothing that Jesus can't do."

Isabella sighed. "We're not perfect, Mom. I get afraid too. But now more than ever, we have to stick together and lean on the Lord and believe that He'll see us through."

"This is true," Felix said.

"So Mom, since you seem to know so much, are you gonna help us or what?"

"If I'm going to help, we have to do this from back home, because I don't know about these American churches. They don't understand curses. We gotta fight this from back home."

Isabella laughed. "So now God's hand is too short to reach America? Oh yeah, it stops at Brazil."

Ana smiled sheepishly. "You're right, we can do it from here, but it's just that there's this pastor back home I have to tell you about; he'll have good information about this. Febe and I spoke of him earlier. She knows him very well, and she said he has a lot of information on this."

Isabella smiled. "Well, I look forward to meeting him then."

The next day, the amount of guests at Casa Cervello doubled. The last time Christian had seen so many people there was on Isabella's birthday, and before that, during the funeral reception for Elizabeth and Carlos. The trips to the airport continued into the afternoon, and everyone had their share of picking up to do. They expected both Cervello homes and even Isabella's house to reach maximum capacity by the end of the night. Casa Cervello was a first stop for everyone—from there, Tadd decided where each guest would stay, and whoever couldn't find room in any of the three homes had access to hotel rooms that were reserved for special guests.

Febe was the first to arrive that day, and Isabella had the pleasure of personally introducing her to the man she loved right there at the airport. Christian was astonished to learn that Febe was originally from Spain—citing that she looked more like Isabella's side of the family. Febe joked about getting that all the time, especially since she spoke Portuguese so well and made Rio home. Isabella could instantly tell that the two of them had hit it off, and Febe teased them the entire way home. Isabella had never seen Christian laugh so hard and she loved Febe's playful spirit. Her approval meant a lot to her because she considered her a spiritual advisor and confidante.

Soon after Febe met with everyone, Isabella escorted her to her guestroom.

"I'm so glad to hold you again, Nena," Febe said, squeezing Isabella tight. "I missed you so much."

"I know; it was exactly a year last month since we last saw each other."

Febe smiled. "Remember what I told you at the airport then?"

Isabella's eyes widened. "That I'll meet the man I marry within a year . . . Tia Febe!"

"Shh . . . God has a funny sense of humor, huh? Having me meet him at an airport of all places."

"I know!"

"So, Nena . . . he's very good-looking, eh?" Febe said as Isabella blushed. "And I'm the last one to meet him."

"Come on, Tia Febe, you were the first person I told. You even prayed with me back in August."

"I know, but it all happened so fast after that, and I was visiting my parents in Spain when he came to meet Felix and Ana."

"How are they doing?" Isabella asked.

"Are we seriously about to start talking about my folks? And ah, he's very polite, too."

Isabella nodded. "Extremely."

"So, you remember our one deal breaker?"

"Yes, tia, he's a believer."

"Good. That's all that matters; with that, everything else can be fixed."

"So, Mom told me you know something about them."

"Oh, yeah, that."

"So, are you like Mom, too—do you think that I am crazy?"

"Is that what she said?" Febe asked, frowning.

"Well, she didn't actually put it that way, but initially she tried to talk me out of it."

"Oh, no, Nena, pay your mom no mind, you know how your mom gets at times. It's only because she loves you. I told her there was nothing to worry about. There really isn't anything to worry about."

Isabella nodded.

"See, I was thinking about it last night, and it hit me—If the Lord, knowing everything that He knows about the situation, chose my niece of all people to be involved with this family, he knows there's something you can do, something that only you must handle."

"Oh, Tia Febe, you're so understanding." Isabella squeezed her.

"But I'll tell you the truth, we all know about this family. It's no secret, we even read about them."

"Yeah, Mom mentioned that. Are there actually books out there about them?"

"No, not like there are *book* books, just short stories—legends and myths. Sometimes, they had no real names and other times, a couple of real names because no one knew what really happened. We all thought it was an urban legend. I gotta tell you"—Febe's giggle was mischievous—"I couldn't wait to meet a *real* Gomes."

Isabella laughed. "So are you saying we're famous now? I bet a sermon's coming out of this."

"You know me," Febe said, laughing. "But only because I've used them as an example of families who face generational curses. It'll be an honor to help this family find peace. Pattie seems so nice—and finally I got to meet this Rachel—she looks just like her aunt."

"We all refer to her as her daughter. You know they legally adopted her?"

"I see; that's nice of them. It would be nice to give a sermon of a happy ending. Think how creepy this is. What are the chances that you've been building up your faith all these years, and I've been preaching about them back home. Then lo and behold, you meet and fall in love with the son of the last surviving Gomes."

"That *is* creepy," Isabella said, rubbing her arms.

"You know how else I know this is a God setup and not just a coincidence?"

"Uh-uh."

"There's this pastor in São Paulo—a really good friend of mine. He knows a lot about them, and he actually believes that whatever happened started in Brazil. Don't ask me why because I don't know, but this is the guy you need to talk to if you're interested in finding out more."

Isabella went on to tell Febe about the scripture that Elisabeth gave her and of Rosa's final message to them. Febe assured Isabella that she was off to a good start and encouraged her to be excited rather than fearful. But, she cautioned her to be on guard now that she was aware of her role. She warned that the enemy wouldn't make it easy for her, seeing that his attempts to thwart their meeting over the years had failed.

By six o'clock that evening, most of their guests had arrived and were unwinding around the mansion. Rachel and Thomas were the only ones absent. Christian's grandparents had arrived a couple of hours earlier, surprising everyone, as they should have been in Sweden as part of their world trip. After making their rounds, they came out to the family room to join the small group that gathered there.

Back in Pattie's dressing room, Isabella stood in her wedding dress as Ana fixed her hem. She was glad that her mother's seamstress classes were finally paying off. Apparently, it was a passion she sought to develop after offering her service as Isabella's home-school teacher up until the seventh grade. As Ana worked on her final seam, Isabella overheard Pattie and Febe discuss in Spanish that she and Tadd planned to leave the morning after the wedding for Sweden, with Christian's grandparents. She had been in the dressing room with her mother for so long that she had no idea when they arrived. Just as she was pondering, Tadd abruptly called for Isabella to meet his parents before they left for Highland Beach.

Her growing nerves made changing into her regular clothes a challenge. She walked down the hallway in what felt like slow motion, but soon relaxed when she heard Pattie, Ana, and Febe behind her. From afar, she watched as a medium built man swirled a slightly taller woman around to the crowd's cheer. The man had on a green Goofy hat with long floppy ears. Although he didn't quite resemble Tadd and Christian, from Rachel's description of her grandfather, this had to be him—the great and mighty, Carmine Cervello. Isabella stood at the entrance of the family room, watching along with the crowd until the man took a bow. When the applause died down, she made eye contact with him. His brown eyes registered both warmth and humor. He walked up to her with a slight limp in his gait, and cradling her face in both his hands, he spoke in Italian. When the crowd laughed, Isabella gave him a puzzled smile.

"Do you understand Italian?" He asked, this time in English.

"No, Grandpa C," she said.

Placing his hand over his chest, Carmine looked around the room. "A child after my very own heart! You heard what she called me? Please my dear, call me *Nonno* to avoid confusion—my son calls *my* father Grandpa C." Then in a low tone he said to her, "If you ask me, too many of us are still living, so I don't blame you if you can't keep up." When Isabella giggled, he said, "I was saying that you remind me of my little Pattie."

Isabella grinned.

"Not to worry, my grandson will teach you Italian."

"Nonno, check this out!" Christian yelled. "She can speak three languages!"

"Oh yeah?" Carmine's brows rose. "See, you should pick it up quickly since you already know others. You are a beautiful girl," he said, kissing her on the cheeks repeatedly. "Who is responsible for this child?" he asked, looking around. When Isa's parents waved, Carmine walked up to them. "Ah . . . see the mother—no wonder. What is your name, my dear?"

"Ana."

"Beautiful woman." He kissed her and did the same for Felix.

His wife, Maria, also made rounds to greet them. Isabella noticed that Christian's grandmother didn't say much but smiled a lot. Returning to Isabella, Carmine said, "My dear, it's a pleasure to meet you. My parents send their blessings and are sorry they can't make it. You see, they are too weak to travel far now—ninety-three and ninety-one."

"I understand, Nonno," Isabella replied. "I'm glad you and grandma could make it."

He grinned. "*Nonni* for her," he whispered, nodding over to Maria.

Isabella nodded to Maria. "Nonni." She had the killer gray eyes, like her son and grandson. They must have gotten their height from her as well. Although she seemed charming, she had to be the serious one, because her husband was a big kid.

"Guess who came bearing gifts for you from the entire family?" Carmine said with animation. "Some more of us are here for the wedding but visiting friends all around this great state. You shall see them tomorrow—we are a large family." He guided Isabella to a seat next to him. "Now, I have a question for you."

"Oh, no!" Pattie and Tadd yelled simultaneously, prompting Maria to laugh.

Isabella assumed it was an inside family joke, but Christian appeared lost too.

"Okay, here we go, Pa," Tadd said.

Carmine looked at Isabella. "My dear, I heard a rumor that you are from Brazil, is this true?"

"Yes, Nonno," Isabella said, smiling cautiously.

Then raising his hands dramatically, he looked around. "We all know that Brazil is in . . . "

"South America!" Christian's parents yelled.

Isabella's eye lit up with excitement, she still didn't catch on, but Christian seemed to have.

Carmine waited for the room to grow silent. "And where in Brazil do your folks live?"

Felix yelled, "São Paulo!"

"Is that south?" Carmine asked.

"Yes, Nonno," Isabella grinned, finally catching on.

"Good," he said. "Right now, you live in Miami. What part of Florida is that?"

"South."

"And can somebody tell me which part of this great country Florida is located?"

"South!" yelled the crowd.

Isabella laughed. "Oh my, so many souths– I never thought of that."

"No, no, wait a minute, Figlia, I'm not finished. What's this city called again?" he asked, whispering in her ear.

"Key Biscayne," she whispered back.

He yelled out, "Casa Cervello is located in . . . "

"South Florida," Christian replied.

"Good," Carmine said.

"And Christian . . . that new house of yours in Highland Beach, you call it?"

"Yes," Christian said.

"Where's that?" he asked, crossing his fingers and closing his eyes.

"South Florida," Christian said, laughing.

"Ahh, great . . . that one was just a guess," he said with a mischievous laugh that led to a cough.

"Are you okay, Nonno?" Isabella asked, patting his back.

"Yes dear, my throat is a bit dry." When she got up, he held her back and Christian said, "Don't worry, I'll get him some water."

"And my darling Isabella," Carmine continued through his cough. "The family you are about to marry into is originally from Italy. As you know, Italy is located in Southern Europe."

"Yes, Nonno."

Carmine looked at Tadd. "Where in Italy are we from, son?"

"Calabria," Tadd said.

"Yup, that's south," Pattie said.

Isabella smiled as she shook her head. The room quieted down as Christian handed Carmine the glass of water. As he drank, Christian said to Isabella, "Nonno has this belief that everything good is from the south. It's an obsession, pay him no mind."

"Excuse me?" Carmine frowned, returning the glass to Christian. "My father and I, and even your own father all married women from the south of Spain and when I decided to purchase property overseas, I went with just that—south, and it landed me in Florida." He turned to Isabella and said, "The south has always been good to my father. He was the one that started the trend, and I simply followed. It's never failed us. We have successful restaurants in the south of Italy and Spain and it's all because of that one philosophy."

With a gleam of mischief, Carmine sat up in his chair and Pattie yelled, "oh-oh, here it comes!"

"Welcome to the Cervello family. And remember, when you go south . . . "

"You never lose your route!" The family members yelled in unison.

Just then, the front door opened, and everyone grew silent again. Rachel yelled, "Anybody home?"

Thomas laughed coming up the stairs directly behind her. "You mean who *isn't* home?"

When they reached the top of the stairs, Rachel dropped the bags in her hand and screamed in delight when she saw her grandparents standing at the doorway to the family room.

"Rachel, my child, you arrived just in time for our toast," Carmine said to a hysterical Rachel as they embraced. "But first, I never officially told you that this home couldn't go into better hands, and I especially thank

Christian for his generosity." As Rachel wept, he held her tight. "I heard you renamed it," Carmine said.

"Yes, Nonno," she said through sniffs.

"Our trip wasn't just for the wedding, you know. It was also to bless your home and Christian's new home for future generations." Then, turning to Christian, he said, "Son, go bring that package."

Christian disappeared and returned with a box. His grandfather unveiled a name plaque specially designed in Sicily with the words *"Casa Del Amor"* engraved on it. Rachel jumped up and down, screaming.

Carmine said, "I must say, I love the name. Initially we had it engraved in Italian but your mom said you specifically wanted it in Spanish to honor your maternal family. As for how we knew the exact design, you can blame Christian for stealing it and sending it to us." Rachel scowled at Christian. Tadd handed Carmine a glass, which he held up ceremoniously. "Now we must toast."

At a quarter to nine that evening, Christian's father and grandparents set out for his Highland Beach home with David, Thomas, and Junior. Ivan, on the other hand, opted to ride back with Christian. Ever since Ivan had met Isabella's Notre Dame friend, Abigail, earlier that day, the two had been inseparable. Christian motioned Isabella over. "Come walk with me to the gate. Ivan could use some extra time with your girl."

Isabella chuckled.

Christian shrugged. "Something about this house, I tell you. Rachel is right about renaming it. Do you realize that two of the guests from your party who met here are still together?"

"I'm not surprised." Isabella watched him rummage through tools. "What's going on at the gate?"

"Taking my sign down and putting Rachel's up."

"It couldn't wait?" she asked with a bemused smile. "Here, I'll hold something." She reached for the flashlight.

"I guess she doesn't think we'll be coming back anytime soon."

They walked side by side down the long trail that led up to the gate. Lighting the way were the light poles that lined the entire trail. Isabella could feel his burning gaze on her and looked up right before he said, "So, where it all started for us."

"Yeah."

"Excited or nervous?"

"Both."

"*Isabella Montes,*" he teased in a high-pitched voice.

"Stop."

"So, we *did* meet each other a long time ago. I remember feeling something when I met you back in February; maybe that's what it was."

"So weird," Isabella said, shaking her head slowly.

Upon their arrival at the gate, the motion sensor lights lit up. Christian placed the toolbox and Rachel's plaque on the ground and pulled Isabella close, wrapping his arms around her. "Soon you'll be Isabella Marie Cervello—a coincidence for your firm's acronym or destiny."

"That's what it looks like, but it's actually a combination of all our initials—my colleagues and I."

"Interesting. By the way, thanks for taking my name—I know you didn't have to."

He lifted a hand and softly stroked back the baby hairs from her temples.

"Are you kidding me? I would love to be a Cervello."

His palms rested on her cheeks as he slowly stroked each side with his thumbs. "It's like God put a veil over our eyes all those years," Christian said. "He knew we had a whole lot of growing up to do. You being here all along just gives me the chills." Isabella closed her eyes and rested the side of her face into his palm, pushing it into her shoulder. Christian kissed her forehead. "I can't get over that video, and those braces!"

She giggled, shyly breaking away from his embrace. "That's what I get for sucking my thumb."

"No way! I didn't know that."

"Till I was seven. I started wearing braces soon after we got to America; I still remember that day."

"Now you've got perfect teeth."

"You think so?" she asked, flashing her grin for him to inspect.

"Look at that, a night before our wedding and we're still learning about each other."

"Hey—your girlfriend, Tara . . . What happened to her?"

"Cool girl, huh?" Christian crossed his arms across his chest.

"She looks like fun."

"I'm sure she'd be glad to see what became of you. Of course, we would have to remind her with the video. Well, anyhow, she dumped me."

Isabella laughed. "Why?"

"I told her I was no longer interested in law school."

"That can't be why. *Seriously?*"

"Seriously. She actually told me she didn't think I'd amount to much. Who could blame her?"

"Aww, Chris, I'm so sorry."

Christian pulled her waist close again. "I would expect you to be thrilled."

"Well . . . yeah, I like her even more for making you available for me, but—"

"No buts. Besides, who's to say we would've been together still."

Isabella locked her fingers around his waist as he planted a small kiss on her lips.

"Did you ever regret not going to law school?" She asked.

"No. Law was my dad's passion for me. I guess he wanted me to follow his footsteps. It was a pretty big deal because he was the first Cervello to attend university."

"Really?"

"Yup. My passion was to be a detective."

"Aunt Pattie told me, and I always wondered why."

"Well, let's see," Christian said, gently releasing hold of her. "It all started when I was a young teen. I started to grow curious about my mom's family after a family tree assignment in junior high. That was when it really hit me that the rest of her family was gone. It was terrifying. I became paranoid and overly protective—especially of Mom, Aunt Liz, and Rach. I thought people were after us. Dad traveled a lot then, and Mom couldn't join him because I was young. Then, because I felt Uncle Carlos was so laid back, I took it upon myself to try to protect everyone. I strongly believed that some group wanted the Gomes family eliminated because I heard they were a powerful family."

"You mean like you felt some sort of mafia was after them?"

"Exactly. It was bad. At some point my brain was playing so many tricks on me that my family thought I had some sort of disorder and even had me evaluated. In fact, Aunt Liz was the only one who didn't think I was nuts. We were very close."

Isabella frowned. "What did they find from the test?"

"That I was fine, but shortly after that, I told them I wanted to be a detective. Mom was terrified because I was her only child. Dad told her she was overreacting because I was still young, and it was probably a phase I was going through. But she eventually got so ill from worry that I promised her I wouldn't be a cop. So I followed dad's footsteps for law and got accepted into college."

"Notre Dame." Isabella nodded.

"Then when Aunt Liz and Uncle Carlos died soon after my high school graduation, the desire to be a cop came flooding back. It consumed me— the thought that this group did it again. I knew I needed to be strong for Rach, but no one knew what I was going through inside."

Isabella interrupted. "Yeah, I always wondered what exactly happened that night. Rachel doesn't talk about it."

Christian ran his hand through his hair and released a heavy sigh. "That's because she blames herself for it."

"I figured that much out from what she said to Rosa, but why?"

"You see, Kevin never really took the fact that I was graduating without him well. People said he was jealous but I chose not to believe that. But as it would seem, he wasn't himself and was driving reckless with a suspended license on the day of my graduation. He says he wasn't drunk but . . . "

"Did anyone get hurt?" Isabella asked clutching her chest.

"No, thank God, no. He got pulled over before he could cause any damage. They probably thought he was just some rich kid pulling stunts with his flashy car. I mean, he had lots of money then."

Christian heaved a sigh before he continued. "Apparently he tried to reach me and my parents to bail him out but we were still at the after party and didn't know any of this."

"How about his parents?"

Christian shook his head. "They weren't involved in his life; we were all he had."

"That is sad."

"Tell me about it . . . A rich kid with no parental guidance. It was a disaster waiting to happen and it happened to my aunt Liz and Uncle Carlos. They got the call. They always thought Kevin was irresponsible and didn't want any part of it but Rachel pleaded with them to go. Kevin had told Rachel he was terrified. I know Kevin, I know he had to have been terrified, he's not that strong.

"So her parents tried to reach us and couldn't so they eventually buckled. But check this out, right before aunt Liz walked out the door, she told Rachel that her friends would be the death of her."

Isabella gasped.

"That's why," Christian said, nodding slowly. "She was in a depression for months until she met you."

"So that was why you never went to Notre Dame?"

Christian nodded.

"But why blame Kevin?"

"I think she does that for two reasons. One, if he wasn't so irresponsible, he wouldn't have been in that predicament. But the one that gets her is the fact that he never called her since that day—not to even offer a condolence."

"You're kidding!"

"Nope. I think it was a huge misunderstanding, though. You see, since they never made it to the jail, and he had no one else to call, he stayed there for nearly a week before Rachel had opened her mouth to say why her parents left in the first place. That was how we figured Kevin was still locked up. By the time we got to him, he was so tormented, he hated us all for neglecting him."

"Did you guys tell him what happened then?"

"Not right away, but yeah. You need to have seen him when we found him. He wasn't in the right frame of mind to tell him anything."

Isabella watched frightfully, as Christian's gaze trailed off to the open space. She had to find a way to stop this.

"Something happened to him in there," Christian said in a near whisper. "He wouldn't say it, but I know it. I just know it."

"Um, Chris, I."

"But the accident itself was strange," Christian said, his tone, suddenly normal. "Especially when the investigation showed it to be mysterious. No one else was involved in the crash but them. It was so absurd; their bodies revealed no drugs and no alcohol. The road and weather conditions were great, and traffic was light. It just made no sense. I thought someone set them up, perhaps messed with their brakes or something."

"Did they have any enemies?" Isabella asked, suddenly glad that the conversation had shifted from Kevin. She didn't want to imagine what had happened to him in jail.

"None that we knew of. They would take the shirt off their backs for anyone. My aunt and uncle were such grateful folks. Since they had stayed with us for free, they kept paying the kindness forward."

"So . . . " Isabella prompted.

"So I chose to stay close to Rach during her depression and I managed to go on to University of Miami to . . . "

"That's when you met Tara," Isabella interrupted.

"Yeah, first semester of freshman year. We both majored in criminology to prepare for law school. I have to tell you, it was tempting. I aced all my courses and seriously considered going to grad school for criminal justice, but it was my promise to my mom that kept my future sights on law, at least up until graduation. Still, it didn't stop me from getting so many ideas for catching criminals and stopping crimes before it happened. I shared my ideas with Dad, who encouraged me and helped patent my work. Before we knew it, I had close to twenty registered patents, even before I graduated. Then in 2002, I was off to grad school to specialize in engineering—to focus on my growing patents. In 2005, Private-I was born."

Isabella's mouth silently formed an "O."

Christian smiled. "I know. It's true that God works in mysterious ways because, as you see, I get to use my detective brain without ever being in the field."

"You're right! That's amazing."

"Oh, and check this out, I still ended up having some sort of experience working with cops because I interned at Key Biscayne PD for a year, and I also gave body language courses at the police academy. Miami-Dade police is like my family. I love my job."

"I *see* that, and you still got to keep your promise to your mom." Isabella's mind wanted her to return to the phrase he just used, body language, but she refused to dwell on the frightening confirmation that he'd read her from Day One.

"Yup. As for my dad, he couldn't be more proud, and at least now he has another lawyer in the family to follow in his footsteps."

"Who?"

"Thomas." They both chuckled. "Hey, speaking of Thomas, tell me something . . . "

"Yeah?"

"Was he right about what he said?"

"About what?" Isabella asked, pretending not to know where this was going.

"Did you really have a crush on me back then? Is that what you guys were whispering about?"

"That's just nasty." Isabella playfully jabbed him. "I was eleven—gross!"

Christian wasn't amused. "Then what were you all giggling about, and why did you look so tense in the video? I need to know."

"No, you don't."

"Please?" he pleaded, his features softening.

"Okay, I know you won't let this go so . . . believe it or not, that day in your house, I got my period for the first time, and I was sitting there thinking, 'oh my goodness.' "

Christian laughed. "No way!"

"Yup, it all happened before the taping. You should have seen Aunt Pattie running around like a chicken looking for pads, and my mom was beaming so proud, like she had something to do with it. Then there was Rachel teasing me like she was a big girl already. Her birthday turned into a session for that talk. Aunt Pattie and my mom were just so happy about me becoming a woman. So . . . nosy, here's what you saw in that clip—I wasn't used to pads, and I was afraid that I might have stained my pretty dress. By the time you two came over with your camera, all I was thinking of was how I was no longer 'daddy's girl.' "

"Aww," Christian drew her close again.

"Then your girlfriend came asking why I wasn't dancing. I thought she was gonna force me to dance. I was so miserable. I just wanted to go home."

"Oh, honey, I'm sorry I made you go over all that grossness. Now I really wanna see the video again."

Isabella rolled her eyes. "Whatever."

"Well, see it this way, this place has housed many milestones for you. You started your period here, we met here, we had our first fight here—then our first kiss, and you left from here for our first date."

"And I'm leaving from here to get married."

"Ah, the most important of all. Well, since we're on the subject of firsts, after the wedding, this could be . . . "

"Uh-uh." Isabella frowned.

"Why not?"

"In Aunt Pattie's house? Then Rachel and . . . no way. It's just gross."

"Highland Beach is far, I don't think I can drive a whole hour to be with you."

"You waited *this* long. Besides, that's why we have a suite at the hotel."

"*Oh*? I didn't know that."

"Rachel took care of it." His arms tensed around her waist, and his deep and silent gaze made her feel slightly uneasy. "Um, you should probably get working on that sign." Isabella said. "It's getting late."

"Right." He let go of her and opened his toolbox.

Isabella watched him select his tools—placing a couple in his back pocket. She had never seen him in this capacity, and it reminded her of just how handy Rachel and Pattie said he'd been around the house. Before she could reach out to help him with the ladder, he'd moved it swiftly from the pedestrian gate with one hand.

"Was that there the whole time?" she asked.

"No, Julio let me borrow it. He dropped it off earlier."

Even though she didn't think he needed it, holding up the flashlight for him gave her a sense of duty.

After some failed prodding, he pulled out a wrench from his back pocket, and his relentless pursuit at the screw continued. She had the pleasurable advantage of watching his arm muscles tense from his steady movements and felt her heart race with anticipation of tomorrow night. "Before I forget, I have good news."

"Bring it!" he replied enthusiastically, dusting off the wrought iron *Casa Cervello* plaque and handing it to her. "Careful it's kind of . . . "

"Whoa! This is heavy."

"I know; it doesn't look like it from up here, huh?"

"Did you install it?"

"Nope. It's been here since I was born—I guess, and it took some effort to get it out."

A loud beep went off at the gate, startling Isabella. "What's that?"

"Shoot! I forgot to disable the security. Give me a second." He retrieved his phone from his pocket and touched some numbers on the keypad. Pattie's voice came in through the gate intercom. "Hello!"

"It's okay, Mom, it's just me, installing the new sign."

"Oh, okay, is Isa with you?"

"Yeah, do you need her?"

"She needs to get some sleep."

"I'll be there in a few, Aunt Pattie—we're almost done," Isabella said.

"Okay," she replied. Then the sound died.

"Isn't the ceremony still starting at four thirty?" Christian asked.

"Yeah, but she's probably panicking because we gotta get a suit for Ivan in the morning."

"Oh, he didn't bring any?"

"He was hoping to get one here. He never could find a good suit back home because of his long arms."

"I had that problem when I was younger. I grew into mine. Could you pass me Rachel's sign?"

"Oh, yeah?" Isabella handed over the new sign. It wasn't as heavy, yet looked solid all the same.

"Well, that shouldn't be a problem." Christian continued. "I can have my tailor take care of him. Besides, he promises to be at my beck and call the entire day. That ought to give him a challenge."

His side smile was irresistible. "It must be nice to have people at your beck and call."

Christian said, "I heard the debate earlier—did you guys finally decide he was joining the wedding party?"

"Yeah, he made such a fuss about wanting to be part of it, but he wasn't responsible enough to take the time to make it to the store to get a suit. Abby's got him hooked."

"But didn't you say we were supposed to have three couples on each side?"

"Uh huh."

"So it works out perfectly with him and Abby, right?"

"Exactly!" She said, grinning to herself. "So, I see you're all done. I love this new sign."

"You want Nonno to make one for us like this?"

She loved the sound of "us" in one sentence. "Nah, I love ours just the way it is."

"You don't sound convincing."

Isabella giggled, as he made his way down the ladder.

"You were gonna say something—what were we talking about before the sign?"

"Ivan . . . "

"Yeah, but even before that."

Isabella searched her brain before Christian interrupted. "It'll come to you. Speaking of Ivan, shouldn't we be getting him a tux instead of a suit? My dad, Tom and Dave are all wearing one."

"Yeah that makes sense. I don't know what uncle Miguel has, though."

"Don't worry, the tailor can take care of both of them. Your uncle should be leaving with us to the church anyway, so I can send Julio for him in the morning. Come, let's get back in so I can talk to him before I head home."

He replaced the ladder while Isabella closed the toolbox. "Head home?" Isabella smiled. "You like the ring of that?"

"Not till you move in," he said, smiling. "That's it! You said you had good news." They began to make their way back.

"Ah yes, thanks. Remember how Rosa said your aunt was obsessed with going to Spain to research?"

"Mmhmm."

"Well, it looks like she may have been barking up the wrong tree."

"How so?" he asked.

"Well, according to my mom and my aunt, Febe, the Gomes family curse is well known in Brazil. It actually has a name in Portuguese that translates to *The Gomes Family Tragedy*."

"*No way,*" Christian said, stopping in his tracks and running his hands through his hair.

"Yeah, and they think it started there." Isabella felt goose bumps begin to creep over her arms. "Come on, let's keep walking—this is creepy stuff."

"Hmm, I don't recall my mother's family ever going to Brazil for anything."

"Exactly. We should ask her about that after the wedding." She exhaled deeply. "The plot thickens."

"Wow. That *is* good news," Christian said. "Because at least we know where to start. Are you thinking what I'm thinking?"

Isabella frowned. "I'm not going to Brazil for my honeymoon."

"Come on, I've never—well, apart from meeting your parents."

"That's enough for now."

Christian lifted a suggestive brow.

"Stop Chris, it's awkward for me to go back home for my honeymoon. Besides, we're already booked for Hawaii."

"We are?" he frowned.

"Chris!"

He planted kisses on her forehead and cheeks as he pried the toolbox from her fingers. "I'm just messing with you." He walked over to his car and placed the sign and toolbox in the trunk, then strolled back to Isabella. "I meant to ask if you ever got around to opening that envelope from Rosa."

"She made me promise not to for three months. Thanks for reminding me, I need to check the date."

Isabella opened the front door and called out, "Tia Febe, is Uncle Miguel free?"

"No, Nena, it's his devotion time. Is everything okay?"

"Just tell her it's okay." Christian said. "Call me later and let me know what he decides."

Isabella nodded. "Yeah, tia, I'll be up in a sec!" He squeezed her close and tight for the last time. "Hey, go get your beauty rest Ms. Montes." Then reaching down, he brushed his lips gently over hers and whispered, "I love you so much."

"I love you too, and just so you know, it's tradition for me to arrive a little late, so no worrying."

"Good to know," he winked.

CHAPTER TWENTY-SIX

Bull's-Eye!

THE NEXT morning, Isabella woke up to the shrill ring of Rachel's alarm clock. *Rachel doesn't have an alarm clock,* she mused, her drowsy eyes squinting at the square archaic box. Either she was dreaming this or Rachel was going through one of her many phases, and from the look of the clock, she had them all back to the '40s.

Stranger than the design was the fact that it didn't tell time, just the date. OCTOBER FIFTH stood out in bold white, and beneath it was an image of a hen that shook its head from side to side to a ticktock sound. Bizarre as it all was, her wedding date was accurate, so she couldn't possibly be dreaming, especially since Rachel and Denise lay next to her in bed, soundly asleep.

Isabella held back a chuckle at Denise's unusual sleep position—a crouch-like pose but on her belly. Although she didn't look it yet, Isabella had taken bets with Rachel earlier that week that Denise was pregnant, but neither had the guts to ask—in respect of the three-month rule. Besides, they had all hung out enough times that if she'd wanted to tell them, she would have by now—like when she threw up in Christian's boat, rather than have them all assume she was seasick.

Just as Isabella gathered her tousled hair into a ponytail, she felt chunks of it missing, with some scattered bald patches. Her sudden squeal woke Rachel. "Shh . . . you'll wake Denise up, she doesn't feel good."

Isabella struggled to catch her breath as Rachel ushered her to the restroom. She didn't have the heart to look at herself so she kept her head down while Rachel closed scarlet red drapes over the mirror. Rachel's assurance seemed far away as Isabella focused on the bold drapes—wondering why she'd never noticed them and what they were doing against the mirror in the first place. In a matter of seconds, Christian hurried into the restroom with a large, red bag and she leaped to embrace him. "Chris! You'll never believe . . . "

Without making eye contact with her, he carefully pulled her away.

"What are you doing?" Rachel asked. "This is the stylist."

Isabella screamed, "Chris!" However, there was no sound from her mouth.

The man quickly went to work, unpacking his goods from the bag. There had to be over a hundred wigs in there. Isabella nodded mechanically, counting them one by one in her head as he retrieved each piece. She momentarily tore her gaze to search Rachel's face for some reassurance. None came. Rather, Denise walked in, holding a *now* visibly swollen belly. "Can I steal Isabella for a minute?" she asked.

Isabella followed Denise back to the bedroom, and they both sat on the edge of the bed.

"I'm sorry I woke you," Isabella started.

"Don't be ridiculous, you didn't." Denise smiled. "I wanted to tell you that I am pregnant."

Isabella frowned. *It was obvious she was pregnant now. Why would she be telling me this when I can see it for myself? This is absurd; I must be dreaming.*

"Did you hear me?" Denise asked. There was a warmth in her eyes.

"Yes," she replied as she reached for Denise's belly.

"I want you to be the godmother," she said, caressing Isabella's hand.

"Are you trying to cheer me up because of my hair?"

Denise frowned. "There's nothing wrong with your hair. It's gorgeous."

Isabella ran her fingers through her hair. Nothing had changed. It was still in patches.

"We must go now," said the male stylist. He stood by the door with his gaze still averted. Isabella reached over to kiss Denise on the cheek before standing to leave.

"Wait!" Denise exclaimed, holding back Isabella's arm. "What are they doing to you?"

"They are going to fix my hair, can't you see?"

"See what?" In Denise's hand suddenly appeared a mirror in the shape of an inverted triangle. "Look, your hair is fine."

Isabella marveled at the sight of her hair. Her golden tresses were back. "How did you do that, Dee?"

"Don't let anyone deceive you," Denise cautioned, concern in her eyes. "You are just fine, and you will make a beautiful bride. But listen, you must give this to Chris."

"The mirror?" Isabella asked, perplexed.

"No, the triangle."

Her eyes widened as the mirror in Denise's hand became an orange, yield traffic sign. "What . . . "

"Take it," Denise whispered. "There are two messages, one on each side. The first is he must give up fighting with his own strength and let God fight his battles."

"Wait, I'll grab a pen."

"No! You have no time. Besides, you'll remember. Just listen—they're coming for you."

Before Isabella could reply, Rachel and the hairstylist ushered her back to the dressing room.

"He'll have to shave off your whole head," Rachel said in a flat tone as she prepared to pull back the drapes over the mirror. "Is that okay?"

"But my hair is fine," Isabella argued.

Rachel turned her chin to face the mirror and Isabella gasped at the sight of her hair. *Why would Denise lie to me?* She chanted under her breath, *don't let anyone deceive you.* She forced her eye to remain on the glorious face of the man she would marry in a matter of hours. *Why isn't he speaking to me?* He seemed to go out of his way to avoid eye contact with her even through the mirror. After he had leveled her hair, he began fitting her with a white-blonde wig. Sacha immediately came to mind. *It's not even my hair color.* Tears streamed down Isabella's face, and she opened her mouth to argue, but words betrayed her. Just then, Rachel's eyes met hers in the mirror.

"Come on, Isa," she pleaded, wiping Isabella's tears. "No one will even notice; just say it's yours."

"But I can't, because it's not mine," Isabella said, certain that her reply was a wasted effort.

"Yes, you can! Just say it's yours. No one has to know. We need to move on from this, Isa . . . just say it's yours, and let it go. No one is perfect. Chris will understand. Besides, he likes blondes."

Isabella's lips parted to cry, but there was no sound. The yield sign she was carrying began to weigh heavily upon her thighs, but when she went to move it, there were worms in its place, forming a perfect triangle until her legs shifted in fright—sending some of the insects to the ground. Filled with terror, her mouth widened, but the screams only reverberated in her head.

Isabella's eyes flung open at the sound of her own screams. Throwing the quilt to the floor, she obsessively dusted herself off and eventually pulled down her blue silk pajama bottoms to inspect her thighs. Instead of worms, there were goose bumps. Her trembling fingers hesitantly lifted to her hair—it was all there. There was no alarm clock on the nightstand—just her cell phone, and it was 9:33 a.m. on October Fifth.

Fortunately, her scream hadn't budged Denise, who was still fast asleep on her side, facing Isabella. But, there was no sign of Rachel. She leaped from the bed, nearly stumbling upon Abby—who lay asleep on the floor, wrapped securely like a mummy, clutching her cell phone. *No wonder I didn't see her in my dream*, Isabella mused, stepping over her and into the restroom.

"Good morning, sunshine!" Rachel greeted through a mouthful of toothpaste.

"Argh! You scared me." Isabella clutched her chest.

"Who scared who?"

"Rach, is it possible that you and I could have the same dream?"

Rachel spit. "About what?"

"The one you had last year of me losing my hair."

She giggled as she rinsed out her mouth and spit again. "Symptoms of cold feet. Just so you know, Chris gave me permission to drag you to the altar if I have to. Come on, let's get you in the shower before the girls wake up. The hair and makeup team will be here shortly."

"Did Denise ever throw up in Chris' boat?"

"What?" Rachel frowned. "Of course not. I don't even think she's been in his boat."

"She told me she was pregnant."

"Really? When?"

"In my dream."

Rachel sighed impatiently. "Was your dream about hair or pregnancy?"

"Both."

"Well, tell me quick, perhaps I can interpret it for you."

"Wait, did you hear that?" Isabella whispered.

"What? You're freaking me out, Isa."

"Shh . . . hold on." Isabella rushed out the door and into the hallway.

She looked down the staircase to see Pattie shooing away at something with a wooden spoon. Then running down the stairs to meet her, she giggled. "Good morning, my darling mother-in-law-to-be."

"Nena, here," Pattie said, handing her a black garment bag. "Take Chris' dry cleaning to his bedroom. It was just delivered."

Leave it to Chris to have his dry cleaning delivered, Isabella pondered, holding up a small plastic pouch. "What's this?"

"Oh, just stuff he must have forgotten in his pockets. The ring came off while I was chasing this stubborn . . . I said shoo!" she yelled.

Isabella smiled, finally realizing Pattie was on to that same limpkin bird that had invaded their compound. "Um, am I supposed to be in there?"

"In where?" Pattie asked, half-distracted.

"His room."

Pattie turned sharply and stared incredulously at her. Isabella took an involuntary step back. She was giving her the kind of look her own mother gave her as a kid when she held a wooden spoon to scold her.

"Are you telling me you've never been in Christian's room?"

"Does his study count?" Isabella asked cautiously, lifting her fingertips to her mouth.

Pattie smiled and shook her head. "What?" Isabella was suddenly embarrassed. She realized she was dangerously stumbling upon a subject she was sure to dread.

"Nothing," Pattie said. "Can you seriously believe this bird? You should have seen it standing behind the dry cleaner—you would think they came together—the creepiest thing."

"I bet," Isabella said, chuckling a little harder than warranted, relieved that Pattie had dropped the room subject. "The sound it makes gives me the chills."

"Check this out—so I ran to get this spoon, and when I got back, there were two doves standing beside it like they were all talking to each other."

"This sounds like a wild dream, Aunt Pattie. I also had a crazy dream."

"No, it wasn't a dream. I grabbed my phone to take a picture, and all I got was this one in it. Tell me I'm not going crazy."

It was hard to take Pattie seriously with white facial paste, a wooden spoon and an oversize white robe that must have been Tadd's. "You probably scared the doves away, looking like that. They're messengers, you know."

"Hmm, I was wondering about that. Isn't it supposed to be a good omen for your wedding?"

"The doves, yeah; the limpkin, no clue. Are you sure you're not mistaking white pigeons for doves?"

"See, I knew no one would believe me," Pattie mumbled as she picked up snail shells from the base of the manicured shrubs by the front entrance.

"Isa!" Rachel cried out over the staircase, "There you are—there's a delivery coming through the gate for you. And can you please shower already, the stylists are on their way."

"Okay!"

"What's little missy's rush?" Pattie said, "Don't we have till four thirty?"

The delivery van pulled up to the front entrance, and a woman dressed in overalls and a baseball cap got out and strolled up to them. "Isabella Montes?" she asked.

Isabella froze at the sight of the blue orchid bouquet in the woman's hand, but what surprised her were the three white flowers that lay across the blue bunch. "That's her," Pattie said, fastening her robe. "I'll sign, her hands are full. What do we have here?"

"Twelve blue orchids, three Ghost Orchids, and a card for the lady."

Pattie frowned as she stroked the white flower. "Running short on supply, huh?"

The lady laughed. "No ma'am, these are extremely rare. Their kind is nearly extinct."

Isabella didn't miss the woman's quick appraisal of her. From her name-tag, she was Jennifer.

"He apologizes for the amount but figured it was better to go with something."

"And by 'he,' I'm guessing these are from him," Pattie said, raising one eyebrow at Isabella as she signed for the delivery.

"I gotta say, you raised him right," Isabella replied.

"Tell that to your father-in-law, he always takes the credit." Returning the pen to Jennifer, Pattie said, "Would have loved to tip, but I have no cash."

"It's okay, ma'am, he covered it with the order. Congratulations on your big day."

Isabella raised a brow. "*Thanks?*" It came out more like a question.

"Oh, I only know because my boss is attending—Maria Echavez, Julio's wife."

Isabella grinned. "Julio's your boss? I never knew he had a floral shop."

"Well, his wife does."

"I see; send our greetings."

"Will do," Jennifer replied, promptly walking to the van and driving off.

Isabella couldn't wait to get her hands on the white beauty. She doubted Pattie knew of its value from the way she handled it.

"Well, looks like you got yourself something blue," Pattie said.

It just had to be a coincidence because Christian knew she wasn't follow-ing that tradition, but for anyone bent on it, it didn't hurt to have that, and of course, Pattie's shoes for something borrowed.

"Did you pack for Sweden yet?" Isabella asked as Pattie sniffed the white flower and analyzed the roots. Knowing her, she was probably thinking of how to grow them in her own garden. Pattie didn't seem to be paying atten-tion to her. She glanced over the card with a smirk. Although it was sealed,

Isabella cringed at the thought of having to read the content in front of her. Before meeting her son, such talk was their pastime; now, it was downright awkward.

"Halfway," Pattie replied. "Febe kept me company late into the night, and we ended up talking about anything and everything. God knows I need friends like her; she's down-to-earth. I didn't expect that from a female preacher."

Isabella smiled. "You must not know Joyce Meyer. Tia Febe's role model."

"Oh yeah? She sounds familiar."

"Well, I'm glad you two like each other." Isabella stared off into the distance. She reminisced on Febe and Christian's first meeting. She never did get to witness Febe's first meeting with Pattie—it was hard to do with everyone running in and out for airport runs. Nevertheless, she was glad that the families were getting along quite well. When Isabella's eyes drifted back to Pattie, it took her a few seconds to gather why she'd gone quiet. "I'll go put these away, thank you," Isabella said sternly, gently prying her Ghost Orchids from Pattie's grip.

"Come on Isa, just one," Pattie said.

"Didn't you and Rach plant orchids in June?"

"I know but—"

"Besides, you don't plant these that way—they grow over trees!"

"*Get out!*" Pattie's eyes lit up.

"Yeah, these are endangered species. I don't even wanna think of how Chris got these." Perhaps that was the wrong response, because Pattie's eyes lit up the more. "You know it's going down in history that you tended to your garden on my wedding day."

"I'm sorry," Pattie sulked. "I don't know what came over me."

"You need help, Aunt Pattie. I would say you have an addiction, but it's more of a timing issue."

"Hey, you should use them for your hair," Pattie said.

"I was just thinking that," she grinned. "It's probably best because I have absolutely no idea how to care for these—they are so delicate."

"As long as they last for your pictures, that's fine. Let your stylist figure out how much you need on your hair—then you should probably have one of the girls hold on to the rest for backup in case you lose one. It's probably the best use you can get out of them. What better way than your wedding day, right? They'll be in your pictures forever."

Isabella's eyes lit up. Pattie was right. She wanted Christian to see how she'd used them. Hair seemed to mean more to him than it did for her. She'd planned on an updo style, but when Rachel said Christian's must-have request was for his bride to wear her hair down, she decided to compromise with a half up, half down style.

Isabella hesitated outside of Christian's bedroom. When her semi-free hand rested on the doorknob, she noticed it was slightly trembling. *This is crazy, it's just a room.* A rush came over her as she slowly made her way in. *Wow!* She said to herself, as she took every inch of it into memory. For all she knew, his equally magnificent study could have been his room because he'd regularly entertained her there. For whatever reason, he never invited her into this room, and she never asked why, but with all that talk about Tara for the past two days, all she could imagine was the two of them there. Granted, the room had to be different sixteen years ago.

She had always imagined this room as dark and mysterious—much like her initial perception of its owner, but to her surprise, it was extremely bright. If she hadn't seen Pattie and Tadd's room, she would've assumed this was the master bedroom just from the size of it; then again, all the rooms in the house were enormous.

Having a corner room at the end gave him an unfair advantage. With a view of Biscayne Bay on both sides—this outlook was even better than his study—and she didn't think anything could surpass that. The open drapes revealed windows that went from wall to wall, and on the other wall was a double door that opened to a large walkout porch, at a distance, his boat at the dock. She had to be giddier than a kid in a candy store at the amount of high-tech gadgets around her. Surely, those women he brought here had to be impressed. Above his end coffee table was an elaborate sketch sloppily taped to the wall—perhaps a patent. On the table were two value pack rolls of Big Red gum. *He's nuts,* she giggled quietly.

An intermittent blink from a large screen at a far section of the room caught her eye, and she froze at the notion that he may have been surveying the room remotely. She walked up to the large screen—the images on it split into many sections of the house. There was a view of just about every major corner. How he could sleep with all that distraction confounded her. He must have known every time she'd visited—perhaps most of their run-ins weren't as coincidental as she thought. The blink came from the screen that recorded Pattie. Isabella smiled as she watched Pattie on camera trying to lure the poor bird down to the dock—she was obsessed with the thing. She quickly went back to the porch to look out and sure enough, it was real time. *Oh, my cuckoo bird mom-in-law.*

Christian's bed was impeccable—the first chore he told her he had to master as a child before moving on to bigger chores around the house. Isabella couldn't bring herself to look at it without imagining things. This time, it was Sacha she saw laying there. She placed the dry cleaning on the bed before quickly turning away. Then on second thought, she turned around and placed one single Ghost Orchid stem on the bed before walking away. It made no sense why her heart raced. Out in the hallway, she sat on the floor and opened the envelope. The card was blank but the letter inside read:

> October 4, 2013
> My darling Isabella,
>   I never told you how grateful I am to you for opening my eyes to so many new possibilities. You literally continue to give me something new to focus on. Ever since I knew you loved orchids, it's become an obsession for me. I never realized just how many there were. Hence, the challenge. My florist says blue orchids are a rarity, but I found that Ghost orchids just might be the rarest, like you. I went through great lengths to find what has been in Florida all along. I know you hate it when I sound pessimistic, but I still keep thinking I'll wake up from this dream and find myself waiting for my London flight to Florida. I guess if you make it out today, I can finally bury this hatchet I've held onto for years. What do you say? I'm practically bribing you with these flowers to make it to the altar. No cold feet, please!
> Love,
> Chris
> PS: When I came through the gate that February afternoon, I'd made a last-minute decision to move back to Vancouver the next day. Apparently, it never crossed my mind again until Dad reminded me of an email I had sent him minutes before I met you.

He stayed back just for me, she gasped.

"There you are!" Rachel cried, snapping her back to reality. "Good thing I'm not officially your maid of honor because you're getting on my last nerve!"

"What?" Isabella asked, her voice cracking.

"What happened, are you crying?"

Isabella quickly rose to her feet. "Nothing, it's just Christian's note."

"Well, did he dump you?"

"*No*," Isabella said, frowning.

"Good. Now get in the shower while I go get the door for the stylists."

With all the anticipation, it was a wonder how Christian even slept at all. He was the first one up at his Highland Beach home—he awoke to Julio's call to inform him that he was on his way with Isabella's uncle, Miguel. He would have to wake Ivan up to get ready for his fitting—but first . . . a quick call to Julio's wife. The delivery to Isabella was a success. If only he could have seen the look on her face as she held the flowers or read the note. He loved surprises, and Isabella was the only one he'd been with that shared his zeal.

He began his search for Ivan upstairs at the topmost floor. Perhaps designating rooms to everyone might have made it easier to locate them. As he navigated through the top floor, he started to lose patience when each new room turned up empty. He wasn't used to all this space and wondered how Kathy ever convinced him otherwise. The last time he'd spent a night there was before the engagement party. Still, walking down the hallway without passing Rachel's room or the kitchen felt awkward. With time, he and Isabella would make a home out of it as well as new memories.

He headed back down to the second floor, and one by one, he found his men in the next few rooms. Something about the way they'd sprawled out to sleep, wearing the same clothes from the night before, was a lot like the morning after a bachelor party. Only thing was they didn't have one because he had specifically told David not to throw one. He felt less guilty about his decision knowing that David and Thomas were committed to their mates and could care less about being entertained by the half-naked women Olivia desperately tried to convince Thomas to have. No one had even mentioned the word—as if they knew of his secret struggles with promiscuity.

He still couldn't find Ivan, so he headed to the main floor. Even though Ivan's mother was a pastor, he seemed like the kind who would want a wild party, and he was at that age too—twenty-seven. However, as fate would have it, his love connection with Abby seemed to be the only thing on his mind—he'd even texted her their entire drive to Highland Beach last night. As for Junior—who he just found sleeping innocently in his pajamas—he was too young to even think about such things. Excuses aside, Christian knew quite well that a bachelor party wouldn't have been a wise move for him. He'd done too well to mess up now. If it hadn't been for that fateful night with Sacha—a night he couldn't even remember—he would have been a little over eight month's celibate. Still, this was a long way from where he used to be, and for that he was proud.

He heard a slight cough from behind the sofa in Junior's room. "Ivan?" Christian called out blindly.

Ivan stuck his head out from behind the furniture—his eyes bright like the sun. "Hey Chris, *Bom Dia!*"

A sound from Ivan's phone took his eyes off Christian, and what followed were lightning-speed fingers typing away at his phone.

"Did you ever sleep?" Christian asked.

"Um," Ivan stuttered, without missing a beat at texting. "I, um."

"I probably shouldn't know. You need to get in the shower. The tailor's on his way."

"Oh, shoot! I forgot, Chris. I'll be out in a minute—so sorry."

Christian headed back upstairs. The truth was, he knew exactly what Ivan was going through, and if he'd had access to Isabella from day one, he probably would have done the same thing, even at thirty-four.

At four fifteen, the wedding photographers at Casa Cervello got their shots of the female bridal party as the limo driver helped the ladies in one by one. Once Isabella settled in, Rachel handed over her vivid white Cattleya Orchid bouquet as she carefully arranged the train of Isabella's dress. Weddings were Rachel's most blogged about topic, and although it was her wish to plan one, she never quite wanted the first to be hers. When Isabella and Christian were gracious enough to offer themselves as her guinea pigs, not only was she stunned that they trusted her with the task, but she marveled at how easy it had been to serve them in that capacity. Some had warned her not to do it, citing that it might damage their relationship, as brides showed their true colors when it came to their weddings. But, Isabella proved them all wrong. She was as simple as they came.

For her dress, she insisted on having it plain but elegant. Rachel had always envisioned her in the dress they had featured in their magazine last summer, and all it took for Isabella was one look to fall in love with it. She was stunning in the white, A-line, silk, organza, tiered, ruffle gown. Rachel had its original sweetheart neckline altered to a bateau at Isabella's request, but couldn't help thinking she may have created a problem because ever since she had introduced her to that neckline, it'd become quite an obsession for her. Rachel had her reservations about Isabella's dressing. She knew her friend was fashion savvy, but it was getting her to wear the clothes, let alone experiment with new things, that was a problem. No doubt, the neckline suited Isabella's narrow shoulders and slender neck. Behind the fitted bodice were several pearl buttons descending into the layered train, giving way to ruffles beginning from her mid-thigh in a fit-and-flare fashion.

When it came to finding her shoes, Isabella could care less as long as she could walk and dance. She even joked about the desire to wear tennis shoes if Christian weren't so tall. She ended up wearing Pattie's comfortable pearl-studded pumps, which Pattie had bought during their summer trip to Sicily. Rachel admired Isabella's confidence in her natural beauty. In fact, working that close to her inspired her latest blog—*SkInToIt*—for women who were comfortable in their own skin. She loved how her friend never felt pressure to measure up to anyone and didn't follow the unending fashion trends that Rachel bombarded her with.

Isabella wasn't the only one who caught Rachel by surprise. Her fashion-forward brother, Christian, not only consented to her handling the wedding plans, but hired her as his stylist. While Pattie called him crazy for doing that, he simply shrugged off the idea, citing he was willing to wear a sack if it meant marrying Isabella. Rachel played it safe with Christian—placing him in a black, designer tuxedo—of course, working closely with his personal tailor. This didn't exactly make her feel like an authentic stylist, but it was better to be safe than sorry.

Isabella shocked her with her request for the venue. For as long as Rachel knew her, Crandon Park beach had been her dream destination. Rachel had attended so many of Isabella's imaginary weddings there, overlooking those palm trees and beach waves. However, when it came down to the real deal, she was adamant on exchanging her vows at Faith House Church. As far as must-haves went, Isabella wanted orchids as the main décor, and Christian wanted Isabella's hair down. *Talk about strange*, Rachel muttered as she prepared to take her seat at the end of the limo next to Denise and Abby. Poor Abby—for whatever reason, she looked exhausted. Her job was to carry the last Ghost Orchid—and carry she did—like a newborn baby, she cradled that thing. Denise, on the other hand, looked like she could use some fresh air, so Rachel gladly traded her spot by the door—perhaps she *was* pregnant, like Isa dreamt.

Isa, my darling Isa, Rachel thought. *Never once did I consider pairing you with Christian, and this is why I can't take credit for any of this. It was fated.* Rachel watched the older women fuss over whether Isabella's hair would look better with one or two Ghost orchids. Isabella's hair alone was a work of art. When she'd settled for an up and down do, the stylist suggested the curly waterfall braid with fresh orchids.

Isabella remained quiet the whole time the women bickered. Rachel was positive that her best friend was nervous—but she glowed all the same. She wanted to look simple, but nothing about her looked it. Something about marriage made women look more glorious.

Ana won the hair flower debate, and she beckoned Abby over for the last one. Rachel smiled to herself as she watched Ana snicker in Portuguese, carefully fixing the flower into Isabella's hair.

"English, Mom!" Isabella said.

The white Bentley limousine carrying the women came to a stop far from the main church entrance, as the driver waited for the traffic attendant with a sign to guide some guest cars through.

Isabella appreciated Febe's timely hand squeeze. She couldn't shake the feeling that this marriage was happening for a bigger purpose. Perhaps it tied into breaking the Gomes' family curse. She didn't know, but the scripture of a sheep led to the slaughter stuck out—that and the counsel from Elisabeth, Rosa, and even Febe.

Why can't I just have a normal marriage, Lord? She knew God appreciated her honesty—yet, she still couldn't help feeling selfish for asking. The limousine started to move again. Ana warned, "Now you better not mess up your makeup, filha."

Febe rolled her eyes at Ana, and with a smile, she whispered to Isabella, "I've got a hanky if you do."

When Pattie winked at Isabella, she turned away because she felt the tears coming.

"Isa!" Abby cried. "Are you gonna have those Brazilian cake thingys? I love those!"

"What's that?" Denise asked, checking her makeup in the mirror.

"I don't know—it's like a little cake sandwich that . . . mm, Isa?"

"Yeah," Isabella replied. "They're called *Bem Casados*, Denise. They are part of the wedding favors."

"Now you've got me craving this thing, Abby," Denise grunted.

"Are you sure the hotel will let the caterers bring them in?" Febe asked Ana, appearing concerned.

Ana replied sarcastically in Portuguese, "I would think so, they're the ones making it."

Her reply set off an entire squabble about whether American caterers would get the recipe right. Isabella didn't think it was an issue. She and her mom had met with the wedding director a week ago to discuss the menu, and they seemed competent. Apparently, the delicacy wasn't foreign to the staff that specialized in customized catering. Febe tried to convince Ana to give the caterers the benefit of the doubt. Leave it to her mother to start prophesying doom and gloom even though *she* made the final arrangements. She didn't remember her being this critical about everything.

Pattie sat quietly as the two women debated in Portuguese. Granted, she would have joined in if she hadn't been at a disadvantage. Isabella couldn't blame Febe—she could only hold out for so long when Ana insisted on replying in her native language. Isabella knew it was rude, but she was tired of reminding her mother to speak in English around everyone else.

Their limousine pulled to a final stop behind a white *Corvette* limousine.

"Oooh, they came in that?" Rachel gushed, nudging Denise to unwind the window. "We gotta make sure they . . . Hey!" Rachel yelled out to the traffic attendant. "We can't have them see us!"

"They're already inside." The attendant replied. "The driver just needs to remain there for a quick exit."

"Oh, I see," Rachel said, nodding.

What Isabella saw was the sign the attendant waved around in his hand—a *yield* sign. Goosebumps formed on her skin as she recalled the message from Denise in her dream, and it just occurred to her that she never did get the other message.

"Okay, Nena, here comes your dad," Febe said as the driver opened the door. "We'll see you up front."

Isabella turned to Febe. "Tia Febe, I forgot to tell you my dream, I think it's important."

"We have no time for that, filha," Ana said.

"Didn't I ask you to tell me that dream, Isa?" Rachel chimed in.

"Can it wait?" Febe asked. "We're already later than we expected to be. You don't want him anxious."

Isabella nodded.

"Pray for her, Febe," Ana said.

After a quick prayer, and then a bear squeeze from Pattie, the women headed out, and Denise whispered, "Don't entertain fear, Isa." Before Isabella could respond, Denise was gone, and her father was standing before her.

Isabella spotted David and suspected Christian wouldn't be far away. "Oh no, the guys are outside!"

"Yeah, they have to make an entrance. Just stay put. Chris is about to walk down with his mom."

"Are they arguing over there?" Isabella frowned at a distance. There seemed to be a confrontation with three men; two appeared to be security guards, and another was a guest.

"Hold on, I'll go check it out," her father replied.

Isabella stared into the mirror. She had done well with keeping her tears in check, but it was getting harder by the minute. Her father strolled back to her. "David took care of it. Apparently, someone tried to deliver something and was giving security a hard time. Listen, your groom is up there with everyone else now. The world is waiting on you, my love." He held out his hand. She could tell he was fighting back tears. Just last night she overheard him telling her mother that he hadn't spent her adult years with her, and now he was giving her away. She'd never seen it that way. "Promise me you won't cry till you say your vows."

"I can't, Dad. Not with you looking like that."

"Try, Bella."

That opened the floodgates, and it was just a matter of time for the first tear to drop.

"What?" he asked in a panic, "What did I say?"

"You called me, Bella, Dad. How come you stopped calling me that?"

Felix frowned. "I didn't realize I stopped, honey—I'm sorry. I'll make sure to call you that more. Please stop crying. Take this . . . " he handed her a handkerchief. "Oh, *meu Deus*! Your mother will kill me."

"No, Dad, you don't need to anymore. Chris wants to call me that now."

He nodded, his spirit appearing crushed. "Oh Dad, I'm so sorry. He's not replacing you. He just—"

"It's okay, *filha*. I understand."

She nodded as she took her father's hand and stepped down. A few steps in, she saw that the walkway was laced with lavender and white orchid petals. When her father insisted she walk on it, she focused on fighting back a roll of new tears. There were photographers and videographers around them as they made their entrance.

They paused at the inner entrance doors, and a male usher asked, "Ready?"

When Isabella nodded, Felix reached over and kissed her forehead before covering her face with the veil.

The usher opened the double doors and she developed tunnel vision for Christian. She wasn't certain of what reminded her of the hairstylist in her dream, but it caused her to tense up. She felt her father's hand squeeze, and one by one, she dismissed the fears that came through—her hair loss, the triangle, the worms, and even the limpkin. *The Lord will cause everything to work for our good,* she said under her breath. It was a good thing they had both decided to stick to the standard vows because her memory would have probably failed her. Besides, even if given an entire year to make one, she couldn't put into words how she felt about the man she was about to call her own.

Isabella and her father reached the altar in one piece, and she made it without adding any fresh tears to the Bella tears she'd cried. But, it was Christian who surprised her. He couldn't possibly be crying. His smile was crooked, but his eyes glistened with emotion. Pattie and Rachel joked about him never crying except for Pattie's hair story when he was a little boy. *Okay, don't think hair.* She formed a smile, which was probably hopeless since he couldn't see it beneath the veil. She wasn't quite sure why he mouthed 'thank you' to her, but she was touched. The past two months had revealed a sense of insecurity in him that he must have concealed when they first met.

It took quite some effort to pry away from his kiss when they were pronounced husband and wife. It felt more passionate. His gaze froze her momentarily—though it felt longer. This look was different—more intense—and she wondered whether her parents and pastor would notice. It was quite embarrassing to think that the people she respected and loved would be imagining what she and Chris would be up to later that night. Heart now pounding, she tried not to focus on the way his lips had felt against hers and on the message in his eyes, but on Pastor Bernard's earlier pronouncement of them as husband and wife. *It worked!* she thought. Her excited gaze met with Febe's as she winked in reply to Isabella's silent message. The applause and cheers in the sanctuary pumped Isabella's heart the more, and it took everything in her to keep from doing cartwheels at the altar.

It wasn't until they were exiting that she noticed just how packed the main sanctuary was. There had to be close to three hundred guests. She blamed her earlier tunnel vision for now noticing the final decorations Rachel had worked so hard on. It was exquisite. The overhead of the entire aisle walkway rained white and lavender orchids along with several stringed crystal beads. She hadn't expected this much from the church decorations because Pastor Bernard had already warned against serious alterations to the sanctuary. Somehow, Rachel had worked her charm on him. Fresh lavender orchid petals lined both ends of the aisle and every other aisle chair had a tall hurricane vase with a white Dendrobium orchid stem in each vase. On every seat, adorned in a white satin chair cover, hung alternating colors of white and lavender flower balls held in place by a ribbon. It was clear that Rachel had tried her best to fit orchids every chance she got.

Outside the church, Rachel beamed. "I hope you're impressed."

"Are you kidding me? I'm speechless!" In hindsight, it was a crazy idea to allow Rachel to talk her into not seeing the decorations until the day of the wedding.

"Well, expect many more flowers at the Ritz. Your husband ordered a ton. We just may have enough to give each guest a bouquet."

"No way!" Isabella giggled mischievously.

"It's ask and receive with Chris—he's a tad bit obsessive. Hey um, I don't mean to ruin your mood, but you'll never guess who just arrived."

Isabella replied, "Olivia isn't exactly high on my priority list today."

"I mean, we can't expect everyone to show up early, but for goodness' sake, at least—"

"At least what? Go on and say it."

"Show up for your friend."

"Good. Well, she's not my friend."

"But she's your husband's friend."

"We'll see about that—come on, let's go; I can't wait to see what you did with the reception."

For the next hour and a half, the bridal party belonged to the photographers while the guests settled in at the Ritz-Carlton around the corner from Casa Cervello. Perhaps starting the wedding so late wasn't such a great idea because they were practically chasing the sun toward the end.

Well into the reception, Christian's eyes followed his bride as she gracefully made rounds around the Ritz-Carlton ballroom in her new dress. The first dance, toast, and cutting of the cake were complete, yet the party had no end in sight. Unlike her birthday party, where he easily had the DJ announce closing time, this wasn't that simple because most of their guests had traveled across the world for this—some of whom were paternal cousins, aunts and uncles who were meeting Isabella for the first time. He decided that his best chance was to kidnap his bride, because if left to his family, they would be there all night with Nonno's endless tales.

With his attention divided, he wasn't doing such a good job himself at greeting the guests that approached him. He watched at a distance as his uncle swirled Isabella around to a samba beat on the dance floor. The skirt of her dress swayed effortlessly, and the opening behind exposed her delicate back. His eyes started to undress her. He smiled slightly to himself. As beautiful as her wedding dress had been, he knew he lacked the patience to deal with what seemed like a hundred tiny buttons. He would have to thank Rachel for this new dress. *Just one—small—zip*, he said, carefully isolating each word under his breath. The more he stared at her from across the room, the more he craved her. Strangely he'd never thought of her in this light before. It felt as though an "on" button switched—sending the strongest sexual desire for her. His gaze fixed on her every move as His Mind calculated subtle ways to steal her away from the crowd. She was too vibrant for her disappearance to go unnoticed, so this would have to take great skill from Genius.

With both their phones in Rachel's care, and Rachel out of sight, all he had was his imagination of the next couple of hours alone with Isabella. His eyes flew open when an MIT classmate and his wife brought him out of his trance. He plastered on a smile and tried his best to be polite as the wife gushed over the decorations. He got a whiff of Isabella's scent before he heard her angelic whisper from behind. "I'll be upstairs." She apologized to the guests for interrupting, and with a smile that drove him temporally insane, she disappeared into the crowd. In his insanity, he robotically started after her, without excusing himself.

Just as he reached for her arm, someone pulled on his other arm.

It was Olivia, and she was holding David's hand. "Hey, handsome, you never officially introduced me to your friend."

"You sure have impeccable timing, Liv." He watched Isabella at a distance as she walked out the door.

"Well, you know what they say, a stitch in time . . . " Olivia replied with a side smirk.

Christian caught David's bemused look and said, "That's Olivia for you, our metaphorical princess."

David released a low chuckle.

Christian gestured. "David—Olivia, Olivia—David. Now if you would excuse me."

"I guess you're retiring for the night, huh?" Olivia said. "No time for a quick chat with an old friend?"

"Can we talk and walk?" Christian said, starting for the exit.

Olivia and David trailed behind him as he reached the elevator. Seeing Olivia texting, he frowned and cleared his throat. "Who needs to chat with old friends when old friends have got cell phones?"

Olivia appeared embarrassed. "I'm sorry, my date was wondering where I was." The elevator opened.

"That's fine," Christian said. "I guess we can chat another time. David . . . " Christian nodded as he entered the elevator.

"Yeah, I remember—no calls," David assured.

"Come on, Chris, I said I was sorry." Olivia begged. "What's your rush? I don't even have your honeymoon plans."

David frowned. "Come on, Olivia, be reasonable."

"Oh, shoot!" Christian said patting his pockets.

"What's wrong?" David asked.

"I need the key to access my floor and Rach has it . . . Damn!"

"I'll go get her," David said.

"No—you stay," Olivia said. "I know where to find her."

Christian ran his hand through his hair and caught David's grin. "Don't start—it's not a crime to be up there with her, is it?"

"Oh, of course not. Congratulations, by the way. We never really had time to talk."

"Thanks for everything, Dave, I just can't think straight now."

"I bet." They both looked eagerly at the elevator signals above.

"Can you call Rach from your phone? I can't trust Olivia to remember why she went in."

David laughed as he reached for his phone. "Sure." Then he looked nervously at him. "Sorry man, it went straight to voicemail."

"Great," Christian said. "The only thing keeping me from my wife is a stupid key."

Just then, a man walked up to them, holding a black box wrapped with a red bow.

"Mr. Cervello?" the man asked, looking at both men, as though he didn't know his intended recipient.

David frowned. "Who wants to know?"

Christian glanced impatiently at the elevator and muttered, *ridiculous*.

"I have a gift from a special guest who was unable to attend."

Christian turned his attention to the man with a raised brow.

"Weren't you the same guy who tried to deliver this earlier at the church?" David asked.

"Yes, sir."

"Hmm, must be some gift, huh?" Christian asked sarcastically.

"It requires a signature, please," the man said as he handed the parcel to David along with a pen. David signed for it and handed the pen back to the man, who promptly walked away.

David's expression was grave. "Come on, let's see if we can get you a new key at the front desk."

"I doubt it—the security is tight."

"We could try. You're the groom, for goodness' sake."

"Are you kidding me? I gotta see this," Christian said, rubbing his hands together in anticipation.

David shook his head. "I don't know, man—maybe you shouldn't open it now. I'll keep it safe for you. Come on, let's try for the key, Isa's waiting."

"Oh, lighten up. What, you think it might be an explosive?" He grabbed the package from David and ripped it open to find a tablet. He flashed David a wary look. The tablet was already on, and all it took was a swipe to reveal a video. He looked at David again, and with a frown, he tapped the play button.

A lean, shirtless man in boxer shorts came into the camera's view. *"Okay, here we go. Recording sweet memories. Antonio here! My beautiful girlfriend Isabella has decided to record her first experience."* He held up the camera to Isabella, who quickly covered herself with a bedspread, blushing.

"So Isa, what will this mean for you?"

Isabella appearing bashful, smiled nervously as she responded, "I think it'll be great because it'll get me in touch with my feminine side, you know, feel whole as a woman should," she said, flirting with her hair.

Antonio whispered into the camera, "That's right, and I'm the lucky guy." *He then angled the camera for the bed and climbed on top. "I won't hurt you; I promise I'll make it special."*

Christian turned away, hyperventilating, while David turned off the video.

Christian heard ringing in his ears. The lobby spun around him, and the guests at a distance seemed to walk in slow motion. A blurry image of a couple came over to greet him—they also spoke in slow motion.

He heard David's voice. It was the only clear sound. "Sorry, he can't talk right now." Then grabbing him by the arm, David swiftly moved him into an empty room close by.

"What just happened?" Christian asked, bewildered.

"Now listen, it's probably some ex-boyfriend that wants to hurt her with a sex tape."

He muttered without looking at David, "She never had anyone that serious."

"How would you know, you never asked her, remember? You assumed because she broke up with the exchange student that . . . forget it. You don't even know what she was talking about when she said he wanted something more because you never asked her."

"Okay, fine, you're right, I didn't ask. But this isn't about her past; this was after we met."

David frowned. "What are you talking about? How would you know when it was filmed?"

"Do you recognize the watch on her wrist?" he said with a smirk.

David slid the controls on the tablet. "Oh man, it's the watch!"

"Exactly, and do you know when I gave it to her? It sure wasn't in her past. And that's not some guy from her past, that's Antonio—the same guy from the club I told you about. She sat there and lied through her teeth about him."

"You asked her about him?"

"Yes. I had reason to believe something more happened between them so I asked."

David grabbed his shoulder. "Okay, listen. She probably dated this dude and dumped him for you, and he's pissed and trying to get back at her. That explains the urgency. That's still the past. Anything after your date with her was the past. Why is this even a debate?"

"Is it?" Christian asked, seething. "So, how do we know this film didn't come after our date? And, even if it was before then, why lie about it? My question to her was 'what became of you and that guy' and her reply was, 'nothing.' Let me remind you that I was there the first night they met, and I gave her that watch long after that."

"Stop it, you're confusing me!" David yelled. "I don't know what came first or last. Just hear me out, anything before today—your wedding day—was the past. Let it go, you're married now."

"Am I?" Christian yelled, tugging at his wedding band, with tears in his eyes.

"Chris? No. Chris . . . don't!" David said, stopping him from removing it.

"As far as I am concerned, I have no idea who I just married. I refuse to touch her, and if I don't, we never consummate the marriage. This is all grounds for an annulment."

David rubbed his face nervously. "Oh, my . . . come on! Tell me I'm dreaming. Stop overreacting—like all the girls you've ever been with were virgins. That's what this is about, isn't it?"

"I could care less if she was—heck, I'm not one myself and I NEVER asked her that question on our date. Why? Because it doesn't matter. What matters is the fact that she lied to me about ever being with him." Christian stormed out of the room.

He stood at a corner outside the hotel, silently watching guests stroll in and out. If he stayed outside long enough, the cool breeze would wake him up from this nightmare. Perhaps Olivia was right—this was his punishment for living recklessly in his past. What did he think? He could just turn a new leaf without facing the consequences of his actions? He'd been too hard on Olivia—she may have lacked tact but she was right. He tried to turn away when he saw Julio approach the door, but it was too late.

"Christian . . . is that you?" Julio asked, peering closely. "Are you okay?"

"Yeah, Julio. You're not leaving, are you?" His gaze fell on the jacket in Julio's hand.

"Nah, the wife was cold, so I went to grab this from the car. What are you doing alone out here? Where's our blushing bride?" Christian scoffed against his will and Julio frowned. "Christian!"

A group of guests who'd recognized Christian rushed over to request pictures with him. Accepting their request, Christian put on a smile. In less than a minute, Julio announced, "Okay, guys, that's enough for now, he needs to go." He ushered Christian to his car, parked nearby. "What's going on?" Julio asked.

After he'd told Julio what happened, Christian relaxed into the back seat and loosened his tie.

"I'll go get you a new room," Julio said, exiting the car.

The elevator doors opened, and as Christian stepped out, he mumbled, *finally.* He hesitated at his and Isabella's door before tapping twice. Isabella opened the door with a beautiful smile. She was dressed in her original gown with its hundreds of tiny buttons—perhaps to punish him. The flowers in her hair were gone and he frowned at the sight of her hair—up in a tight neat bun. Still, she was beautiful. How could something this beautiful be so deceptive? He should have known better, nothing this good could possibly be true. "Hey what took you so long?" she asked, going to embrace him. He held back his embrace. As soon as she released him, he walked past her— into the room and straight to the window. A brick wall replaced the ocean view.

"Honey, are you okay?" Isabella asked, walking toward him and proceeding to hold him from behind.

"Why were you waiting for me?" he asked, in a flat tone.

Isabella laughed. "What do you mean *why?* It's our wedding night, silly."

Without another word, Christian began to take off his clothes; first, struggling with his buttons on his shirt.

"What's wrong?" she asked in a high-pitched tone.

He saw tears in her eyes. "Come on, let's go," he said.

Isabella frowned. "What?"

"It's our wedding night, right? Come on," he repeated, grabbing her arm.

"Don't touch me!" Isabella cried, snatching her arm away. Christian ran his hand through his hair and said through tears, "Oh, yeah, I'm sorry, that's not romantic enough." He then carried her up and dropped her carelessly onto the bed.

"Christian—Christian!" Julio yelled. Christian opened his eyes and looked around frantically.

"I've got you a new room," Julio said. "Let's go. I won't even ask what that was about."

"Where's Isabella?" Christian demanded.

Julio scoffed. "In a safe place."

David bumped into Rachel at the lobby, and leaning forward with his hands on both knees, panting, he asked, "Did you see Christian?"

She frowned. "No, but he's probably with Isa; are you okay?"

"No, he's not," David said, struggling to catch his breath. "At least I hope not. Come here." He took her by the hand and in seconds led her into an open elevator. "Take me to their room floor," David demanded.

Rachel lifted a brow. "Are you gonna tell me what's going on?"

"Just do it, Rachel!"

"Okay—Okay!" She fumbled in her purse for the key card and swiped it.

"I just ran through this entire hotel structure looking for him. I tried to get to their room, but the receptionist couldn't give out that information. I gotta show you something—but before I do, I need you to head straight to their room and find out if he's in there. I'll be waiting in the corner."

The elevator doors opened. "Why?" Rachel asked. "What's going on?"

"Just do it!"

Rachel robotically knocked on the door to the wedding suite. She didn't like feeling that something was wrong.

The door opened slightly—Isabella had on a silk white robe over the little white lingerie they had both picked out for this night. Rachel stuck her head to peer into the room. She could hear music in the background. "Are you gonna let me in?"

Isabella took a step back as Rachel made her way in, smiling as she casually strolled past the lit candles.

"Are you okay?" Isabella asked. "You look flustered."

"Yeah," Rachel said, heading to the connecting room. "I take it Chris isn't here?"

"No, not yet, I was too nervous to notice. Still practicing how I'm supposed to be. Silly, right?"

"Listen, I'll be right back. Lock the door, okay?"

"Okay."

Rachel went over to David, who stood by the corner, as promised. "He's not there, now can you please tell me what's going on?"

"Watch!" David said, playing the film.

Rachel frowned when the strange man spoke, but as soon as Isabella came up on the screen, she gasped.

"I know," David said.

"No, you don't, Isa's been framed."

"What—by whom?"

"Olivia. This clip was from Isabella's pool party—on her birthday, for goodness' sake. I can't . . . Olivia is the devil incarnate. She had the camera and the interview all planned out. This definitely had to be edited."

"What?"

"I gotta find Chris before he does something stupid," Rachel said.

"No, you stay here and make sure he doesn't get to her first. I'll go ask your parents if they've seen him—I hate to scare them, but it's time to let them know he's missing."

"They left already for Highland Beach. They leave for Sweden first thing in the morning with Nonno and Nonni."

David sighed. "Okay, just stay with her and don't say anything to her unless you absolutely have to. There's no sense ruining her night."

Rachel nodded. "Here, you're gonna need the key to get back up here."

David left while Rachel headed back to Isabella's door. "Who is it?" Isabella asked.

"It's me again—Rachel."

Isabella opened the door, appearing concerned this time. "What's going on Rach, Is Chris okay?"

"Of course, don't be silly, he's probably trying to get away from those guests. Did you see how many were out there? It's a miracle you made it in here. Exactly how did you do it?" Rachel watched Isabella from the corner of her eye as she turned the music off. Up until then, she'd had her favorite song, "La La La," on repeat and now that it was off, Rachel knew she would have to say something to fill the silence.

She sent David a text, requesting an update.

Isabella walked to the edge of the bed and sat down.

With a cautious smile, Rachel asked, "Nervous?"

Isabella sighed, and got back up. "Do you realize that you asked me that question like three times already? That's it; I'm going to find Chris."

Rachel went after her. "Come Isa, he's probably coming up to you on the elevator right now. What if you miss each other, then he'd be the one waiting for you because you're stuck down there with all the guests?"

She relented. "You're right."

"I can keep you company until he gets here, no?"

"Nah, he won't be expecting you. Are you heading back home tonight?"

"Yeah, we only have rooms for you both and a few guests."

Isabella nodded and opened her arms for an embrace. "Come here."

Rachel came forward and they both embraced. "I can't thank you enough, Rach."

"Oh, please, it's nothing. You know I love you."

Isabella nodded.

"Um, can I use your restroom for a minute?"

"Sure."

When Rachel got to the restroom, she smiled sadly at the sight of extra flowers. This had to be Isabella's doing because she couldn't remember arranging for any flowers there. Surely orchid dreams or nightmares would follow tonight. She dialed David's line. "Hey! What's going on?" She whispered into the phone. "I can't stay here anymore, she wants me out."

"It's okay, Rach, we found him. I bumped into Julio's wife—she told me he put Chris in a new room."

Rachel sighed. "Phew, thank God! So? Did you tell him?"

"No."

"What do you mean, *no*? Okay, would it be better if I told him, maybe he'll believe me since I was . . . "

"He's wasted, Rach."

"That makes no sense, Christian doesn't drink."

"I know; that's probably why he's wasted. Apparently, he asked the concierge for something to knock him out. I have no idea what he drank. There are bottles all over and shattered glass. It's like a war zone. Have you ever seen him this way?"

"Never. He's usually even calmer in a crisis. Why would Julio let him get to that?"

"He's sorry that he did. He didn't know what to do when Chris kept crying. He said he got scared."

"Wait a minute, Chris cried?"

"Listen, your brother has been with several women, but based on what I know of him, I seriously doubt he ever reacted this way for any of them—I know for a fact that he didn't with Kathy. This really got to him."

"But, we are gonna tell him the truth."

"Rach, I heard what you said, but I really don't know how he's gonna take that—come on, how can you explain Isabella on tape? That *was* her."

"Just the beginning was. David you gotta believe me."

"Well, we're gonna have to tell her ourselves because nothing is happening between them tonight."

Rachel panicked. "No, don't say that Dave, what am I . . . how can I? Isa's waiting, she's so . . . "

"Don't worry, just wait until I get there. We're putting him in another room, and Thomas will stay with him and make sure he stays put because Julio needs to take his wife home."

"Why another room?" Rachel asked. "Didn't you say . . . "

"He trashed this one. That's what I meant when I said war zone. You should see glass all over here."

"Oh my goodness, it's worse than I thought, this is all my fault."

"Don't be ridiculous."

"No, really. . . Isa, Chris, and even Thomas tried to warn me about Olivia. I should have been on to her schemes."

"Just stay put; I'll be up in a minute. I'm coming with Denise; is that alright?"

"Sure, I'll be in the restroom until you get here."

About ten minutes later, there was a knock on the door and Rachel emerged from the restroom in time to see Isabella's nervous smile. "That's him," she whispered with a twinkle in her eyes. "Now get going."

Rachel grabbed a bathrobe from the closet and handed it to Isabella. "No, it's not. Put this on."

Trying hard not to focus on Isabella's dropped jaw, Rachel let David and Denise in before turning back to help a dazed Isabella into her robe.

"Okay, what is going on and where in the world is Chris?" Isabella said, struggling to breathe.

David closed the door and took her by the hand. "First of all, Isa, I promise you, Chris is alive and well, and he is in this building, but we need you to sit down so we can show you something."

Isabella burst into tears before they could even present her with the tablet. She felt sick to her stomach, but managed to sit down. Rachel and Denise sat on both sides of her as David pulled up an ottoman and sat in front of her. "I was speaking with Christian when someone delivered this to him." Isabella looked at him and then at the tablet, and with a trembling index finger, she tapped the play button. It started as a blur to her—*Why am I watching a video of a half-naked stranger?* Then she heard him say her name. She clutched the robe over her chest. *Wait a minute, that's me.* She shook her head vigorously, and then released a scream that sent the tablet crashing to the ground. "Oliviaaaaaaaa!" Rachel and Denise held her down on both sides as her body shook. The video continued on as it lay on the floor, but no one paid attention to it. Isabella stared at the wall but did not speak.

"Isa?" David asked with concern as he shook her. "Are you okay? Isa?" He let her go when she began to shake. Her eyes rolled back. "Does she have a history of seizures?" Denise asked, as she tightened her grip on Isabella's arm.

"No, never. I've never seen her like this," Rachel replied.

Isabella could hear the commotion around her, but it seemed distant. Her eyes blinked continuously, and she was certain she was back to her dream when she heard Denise's distorted voice ask in slow motion, *"What are they doing to you?"*

Rachel rushed to the restroom to get a glass of water. "Should I call 911?" Rachel yelled.

"No," Denise replied. "She's in shock. Grab me the waste bin; it's coming."

"What's coming?" Rachel yelled.

David made a leap for the nearest bin by the bed—just in time for Isabella to vomit into it.

"Yeah, you're right, Dee," David said. "She's just in shock. She'll be okay, Rachel."

In Christian's new room, he talked to himself the entire time as he pranced around intoxicated and bleeding on his foot from shards of glass. There was a knock on the door, and Thomas went for it.

As David walked in, Christian smiled. "Ah! My best man . . . good! You are just in time; I was about to tell my soon-to-be-brother-in-law a story. Hey Dave, did I tell you?"

"Tell me what?" David asked as he dropped Christian's duffel bag on the bed.

Christian walked up close to David's face and whispered excitedly, "Our family is cursed. Yup, we are, and you see . . . my mom's side of the family is all gone. My Patkey is all that's left." Then turning to Thomas, he said, "Oh yeah, Rachel's dad went with the last one of us who died, so you may wanna reconsider involvement with us. You know, this is actually good for Isabella, because she probably would have died too."

"Shut up, Chris!" Thomas said.

Christian continued on like a broken record. "Then I lost my best friend Kevin, then Kathy . . . to Kevin, of course. Fate had to make sure it was twisted and close enough to hurt me. Hmm, what else . . . " Christian asked as he brought out his fingers to count. "More close friends . . . Aha! Olivia uses me for money, Okay, I already said Kevin, right? Oh, then the kidnapping—Kevin, my own best friend kidnapped my woman for money." Christian scoffed, "Imagine that, *my* woman . . . she never really was mine, was she? Got her own agenda. They all do." Christian yelled to David's face, "What's next huh! What?"

Without a word, David wiped his face and walked away from him. Then after taking off his tie and shirt, he sat on the bed and began his own count with his fingers, "Well for one, you have Rachel, Thomas, me and Dee, your parents and Isa, your wife!" David said at the top of his voice.

Christian scoffed again. "Isa . . . ha! All the other men probably have her too. Imagine Julio calling her *blushing bride* . . . ha, ha, blushing my foot."

"Excuse me?" David scowled.

"What was I thinking marrying her? She was too perfect; they all want her and I can't compete."

"No one's perfect."

Christian nodded with a sly smirk. "Yeah, you know what?" he asked, rubbing his nose as he walked towards David with a crooked gait, "You're right." Then screaming, he added, "She's no different from slutty Sacha! You know what, I'm gonna call Sacha." Christian picked up the hotel phone. David snatched the phone from him. "What are you doing—have you lost your mind? And stop yelling in my face, I'm not deaf!"

Christian threw himself at David and wept bitterly into his chest. "Where did I go wrong in my life? I'm probably the next to die."

David held him close. "You won't die. You'll live a long life, my friend."

"Yeah? Probably alone with no wife and kids," Christian sobbed.

"You won't be alone; you'll be with Isa, and you'll both have lots of kids. Come get some sleep."

Kathy stepped out of a taxi parked outside the hotel and slipped into the back seat of a black car parked near the hotel entrance.

"I've been up like a hawk watching for signs of Christian or news of some catastrophe," Kathy said. "Am I missing something? Are you sure your guy was up to any good?"

"Let me worry about my business," Olivia said from the shadows. "Antonio should be here with her jacket soon."

Kathy snickered. "You gotta be kidding me—a jacket? What would that do?"

"It's not that farfetched, Kathy . . . it *is* hers, after all. Listen, if you were expecting something else, don't hold your breath. They haven't allowed me anywhere near her since the investigation, so this is all we've got."

"And what if Antonio never bumps into Chris tonight? Or if security doesn't allow him to get close—like they did to the delivery man earlier at the church."

"Don't worry about it, he's prepared to wait all night. He is coming with his men to keep tabs on Chris. As soon as they see him alone, they'll page Tony's room. Besides, we didn't know about security being at the wedding until this morning—apparently, it was David's idea."

"Fine. But if he has seen the video, why haven't I seen him walk out of this hotel?"

Olivia looked at Kathy's face for the first time. "And what makes you think he'd walk out on her? Have you thought of the possibility that he might forgive her?"

Kathy scoffed. "Forgive isn't in Christian's vocabulary when another man has had his woman."

"Well, he and Isabella may just be a stronger couple."

"And your point?" Kathy fumed.

"Listen, here's the receipt to prove the package was delivered and signed for, okay? Now, as for him walking out, that wasn't part of the bargain."

Kathy inspected the sheet and sneered, "You stupid good-for-nothing fool. What can you do right?"

"*Excuse me?*" Olivia asked in disbelief.

"Excuse you? Look at the freaking signature!"

Above the line was the name, *David.* "Now, how in the world was I supposed to—"

"Shut up!" Kathy yelled. "Did you at least give your guy a description of the groom? For all we know, David could have intercepted the video. Shit, I knew it! Chris never got it, because he would have been out by now."

"You know what? I won't take this nonsense," Olivia said. "I am done. Take your money." She pulled out a wad of cash, and flinging it at Kathy, she said, "I'll write you a check for the rest."

"How dare you?" Kathy seethed.

Olivia reached for the door handle, but before she could get out, her own voice filled the car—it was her confession to the kidnapping on tape. She smiled as she relaxed back into the seat, remembering how strange she'd felt that day in Kathy's hotel room. She'd even scanned the room with her eyes for a recording device. She must have had it on her—explaining why she followed her around like a dog.

Kathy released a loud wicked laugh. "And oh, it goes into how you forged the letters too—just in case he thinks it was blondie's idea." Kathy's vibrating laugh went on for several seconds and came to an abrupt end. Then she threatened, "Step out that door, and I'll destroy you."

Olivia snickered. "I'm glad that you can use that brain in other creative ways. But just don't think for a second that I don't have anything on you, honey."

"Humph!" Kathy grunted.

"Yeah, interesting how you never wanted me to bring Chris' camera in when you were editing the final footage. You think I'm a child that you could tell to switch it off and I'll listen? Who do you think you are?"

"What are you talking about?" Kathy asked, frowning.

"Don't you think Chris should know the role we both played?"

"Who played? I'm supposed to be in London—cut off by him."

"Shut up!" Olivia yelled. "I had it recording the whole time it was on my neck. Yeah, honey, the proof of your glorious directing and editing is on camera. I cover my ass pretty good. Now you can lift your jaw up off the floor."

"Good," Kathy said in a shaky voice. "Now I'm sure you see just how valuable we are to each other."

Catching Kathy off guard, Olivia attempted to snatch the device from her hand, but a struggle ensued, sending the device to the backseat floor. The struggle for it continued until Kathy pulled out a silver revolver from her purse and pointed it at Olivia. Then stepping over the device, Kathy slid it close to herself. "You're not done till I say it's done, and don't be foolish enough to think this is the only copy I have."

"If it isn't, how come you're ready to shoot me over it?" Olivia's nervous gaze met the driver's in the mirror. "Take that shit out my face!" she said, livid.

Kathy laughed. "Make me, you sorry piece of shit."

Olivia's anger turned into sarcasm. "I'm sorry; the pot is calling the kettle black. If you had it so good, why aren't you Mrs. Cervello right now? Why wasn't it you saying your vows today and moving into that huge house you planned from the start? You got greedy. Dirty loser. Imagine how rich you would have been with no prenup signed. But no, you had to screw his best friend."

Kathy smacked Olivia's mouth with the gun, and Olivia screamed. "Shut up!" Kathy yelled, unlocking the gun with her thumb. "I should just finish you off now and call it self-defense—no one will miss you. I knew you were a no-good to Christian when you planned all this against him, when all he did was love you, and it was *you* who told me that Kevin had the private-I shares."

"*It was you who told me Kevin had the Private-I shares,*" Olivia mocked Kathy in a British accent. "And you were stupid enough to believe me, you fool, even though you worked closely with him. Shit! Talk about who can't do anything right."

"So, you knew all along?" Kathy asked in shock, as Olivia laughed uncontrollably.

"Okay ladies, enough!" the driver said, stepping out of the car.

Olivia looked down to her lap to see blood from her mouth splattered across her skirt. She punched Kathy, and another fight ensued. Merely seconds before the driver opened the back door, a shot went off.

CHAPTER TWENTY-SEVEN

Letting Go

CHRISTIAN OPENED his eyes yet again—this time to the slow-moving blades of the ceiling fan. It nearly hypnotized him back to sleep. He counted backward in his head from ten to one—the entire time his eyes fluttered as he struggled to keep his heavy lids open. When he was done, he noticed that his heart was racing. *Deep breaths*, he whispered to himself. Genius was mute now, after having nagged him in his dream about doing right by Isabella. Perhaps he was upset that he'd been ignored, or perhaps he had died—if so, good riddance. He wasn't going to beg him to stay.

Christian reached for Isabella but she wasn't there. But there was a shadow against the window—and in seconds . . . bright light. He growled at the sight of it and then little men with drums lodged in his temples and began practicing a new tune. The room went dark again. There had to be someone else there because he heard typing. "Bella?" he asked blindly, his mouth terribly dry.

Thomas rose slightly from the floor—at the foot of the bed. "Well, look who's up!"

"Oh, no!" Christian groaned. "Please tell me I was dreaming, tell me I was wrong," he said, pressing in his temples. David handed him a glass of water and two pills.

"Well, yes and no," Thomas said, sitting back down and continuing to type.

Christian stared at David, confused.

David said, "what Thomas is saying is, no you weren't dreaming—but yes, you were wrong."

Christian winced as he grabbed his head. "Okay, now I'm confused."

"Take it," David said, nodding to Christian's palm and sitting next to him.

He made a face as he gulped down the pills.

"Well you see, Chris, we saw a video with Isabella in it but she was framed."

Chris frowned. "I know what I saw."

"Exactly!" Thomas said, closing his laptop and sitting up on the sofa. "It was a pretty good edit but—"

"Has she seen it?" Christian interrupted.

Thomas replied, "Yeah, they both did."

"Both who?"

"Isa and Rach. They were both in the room the day Olivia shot the original footage on Isabella's birthday party."

"Wait, what? *Olivia?*"

Thomas nodded. "Come to think of it, I remember that you two argued that day."

"Where is she now?" Christian demanded. "I gotta see her."

Thomas frowned. "Who cares where she is; how are we supposed to know?"

David said, "When last we saw her she was supposed to be getting the access key, remember?"

"This is ridiculous." Christian rushed out of the bed. "None of you have seen Isabella?"

"Oh, Isabella! Of course we have," Thomas said echoing David's response. "She's with Rach and Denise, we thought you meant Olivia."

David pulled Christian back as he approached the door. "Not so soon, you stink."

"I'll go freshen up. Get her . . . please?"

Rachel mumbled into her phone, "Hello."

"Hey Rachel," David said. "Did I wake you?"

"Mmhmm, it's okay."

"He wants to see her."

"Uh-uh. Did you guys talk to him yet?"

"Yeah, it's okay now."

"Good." She sighed. "Well, it looks like she's taking a shower now, so just give us a minute."

"Okay, no rush."

Christian paced the room after a failed search for the tablet. He wasn't sure why David would keep it from him if it was a fake, as he'd said. Perhaps he had made much more of it than was warranted in his drunken stupor. Still, it was a struggle to replace the thoughts that crept up over that video. Although they had discussed renewing the mind in their most recent Bible study, rather than meditate on scriptures, he enjoyed the feel of having his mind blank for a change. However, the peace didn't last five minutes before a new negative thought crept up. Each time, he stopped the thoughts with the words, *she didn't do it.*

He jumped at the knock on the door and soon sighed heavily upon seeing David and Thomas return from the hotel restaurant.

"I take it they're not here yet," David said, amused.

"Where's that video?" Christian asked, breathing sharp and fast.

"I told you no! Why do you want it? We told you it was fake, didn't we? Just forget all about it."

Christian ran his fingers through his hair before going back to pace the room. How could he know if he made much of nothing if he wasn't even allowed to see the video.

"I thought you were going to freshen up," David said, raising his voice slightly.

"I brushed my teeth and washed my face, why?"

"Come on, all this time you've been pacing you could have taken a shower by now. Look at you!"

There was a knock on the door.

"Ha! Too late now," Christian said with a half-smile as he rushed to answer it. He greeted Rachel and Denise with a kiss. Isabella was the last to follow. As she made her way in, he took her by the hand and closed the door behind her. He figured this would be harder than he thought because she wasn't even making eye contact.

The room grew silent when he pulled her close. He sniffed her hair—it smelled like fresh flowers.

"Mmm, what's that in your hair?"

"Jasmine shampoo," she replied. "They had it in our room."

"I like it."

Isabella pulled away to look into his face. She smiled slightly but it didn't reach her eyes. "They said you were drunk," she said softly.

"Yeah," Christian said with a wry smirk. "Can you believe it? My first beer."

"Beer did that to you?" David asked, surprised. "Just how many *did* you have?"

"No clue, I just remember one, though."

"Julio said you had more than that," Thomas said. "And whatever else the concierge brought in."

"Well, there you have it!" Christian shrugged, smiling at Isabella. "I just remember one beer and it sure was nasty. I don't know how Tom and Dave do it."

"I hear it's an acquired taste," Isabella said. Her smile was sad.

"And might I add, he was talking a load of crap, too," Thomas added.

"Hmm . . . " Isabella pursed her lips.

Christian flushed. "Well, I was drunk, so I didn't mean any of it, Thomas."

Isabella shrugged. "You know what they say . . . alcohol frees you to say what you really think."

"Hey, Denise!" Rachel called out. "Weren't you craving a beer last night?"

"That's because . . . " Christian said, stopping himself when he realized he'd probably said too much.

Denise held up an index finger. "One second!" she looked through her phone and in seconds yelled, "Yup, exactly three months yesterday!"

Rachel and Thomas looked at each other, confused.

"We're pregnant!" David confirmed.

The room broke into a cheer. Thomas and Rachel reached over to embrace the couple. "No way," Rachel gasped. "Where are you carrying a three-month load?"

"I don't think it should show this soon," Denise said, giggling.

The chatter continued in the room as Christian felt Isabella's body tense up in his arms.

"Are you okay?" he asked in a whisper. Before she could respond, Rachel yelled, "Isa! Didn't you dream that Denise was pregnant and threw up in Chris' boat?"

Christian's brows creased at Isabella. "You did?"

She nodded.

"That's strange, she threw up in the car last week."

Isabella released herself from his hold and went to embrace Denise. "Congrats, Denise."

"Thanks—you're not upset that I didn't say anything, were you? We typically wait three months."

"It's okay, most people do." Isabella smiled.

"Isa and Chris are next!" Rachel cried with delight.

Denise cleared her throat. "Did you guys hear about the shooting outside the hotel last night?"

"What shooting?" David asked.

"Someone just told us in the elevator."

"Did anyone die?" Thomas asked.

"Thank God, no," Rachel said. "But it's horrible to have happened on . . ."

The room grew quiet again as Christian noticed all eyes on Isabella. He went up to her. "Can we talk alone for a minute?"

Isabella nodded.

He led her out to the balcony. "I'm sorry our night was ruined," he said, his voice thick with emotion.

"So am I," she replied.

"When do we leave for Hawaii?"

"Tomorrow evening."

"Good, we have some time to catch up."

She nodded.

"I feel like we should have been somewhere today," he said, brows creasing slightly.

"Thanksgiving service with pastor in the boardroom."

"Oh." Christian slapped his forehead. "That's not good."

"It's okay, I spoke to him when he called Rachel's phone. He met with Tia Febe and my parents."

"Does he know?"

"I just told him we overslept. Which was true—I mean, you just woke up, didn't you?"

Christian nodded as he watched her intently. "Did you sleep?"

Isabella's smile was lost in a scoff. Even though she seemed slightly disconnected, she still glowed. She was so much more beautiful without makeup. She had on a pair of sweats and a white T-shirt and she wore her hair down to her back—just the way he liked it. He had intended on kissing those full soft lips the minute she walked in. Perhaps it had to do with the way she smacked them together on the video. He didn't mean to replay the video image in his mind. He had to remember that it wasn't her, as David said.

"Excuse me, Chris?" David interrupted by the entrance of the balcony. "Someone is at the door—a Detective Sanders. Were you expecting him?"

Christian's shook his head. "He was at the wedding, let him in."

Christian and Isabella followed David back into the room.

"Detective Sanders!" Christian greeted as he extended his hand. "What brings you here?"

Christian had come to learn about the man known for his knack of closing forgotten cases when he saw them through the kidnap incident last month. He had great respect for the high-ranking African-American detective who had risen through the ranks at Key Biscayne PD. He had handled their case with such ease and never failed to keep the family in the loop in the aftermath. Therefore, having him as a wedding guest was a great honor.

Detective Sanders looked surprised as he shook his hand. "I wasn't expecting to see *you* here."

"No?"

"Well, the room isn't exactly booked in your name, but a *Julio Echavez*. We actually got a tip about suspicious activity last night. This room was booked minutes of another being trashed and shortly after, a gunshot went off outside the hotel."

"Oh, no, it's a misunderstanding. Julio is my driver and he didn't spend the night at the hotel. He booked both rooms for me. It's a long story, but I trashed the first one." Christian could tell from the look on the detective's face that he wasn't buying it. "The hotel knows we will take care of everything," Christian affirmed.

"And the shooting?" the detective asked with a raised brow.

"Oh, no, we have nothing to do with that."

"So you are telling me that they are two isolated incidences."

"They must be—honestly, I was so messed up last night that I'll have to ask my friends if they can piece what's missing." Christian looked back as Thomas and David approached.

"Detective Marvin Sanders," the detective said, as he shook their hands. "I take it you all heard about the shooting," he said in a deep commanding voice, his eyes scanning the room.

"The girls mentioned it when they came in," David said. "Someone in the elevator told them."

The detective explained. "Apparently two people were involved and an ambulance got to them before the police did because one was already on the premises for an unrelated case. The cabbie who witnessed the shooting was under the impression that his call to 911 went through but it didn't. Turns out his emergency system was broken."

"Sounds like a scary movie," Rachel said, clutching her chest.

"It sure does, but it would seem the victim is lucky to be alive because she lost quite a bit of blood, I hear. Key Biscayne PD should apprehend the suspect soon. I hear the suspect needed treatment also."

"Were these our guests?" Christian asked.

"No idea—I should be getting their names any moment now and the suspect should be ready for discharge soon. I am actually here because the cabbie mentioned there was a third person involved in a scheme they were planning and that person is probably here in the hotel."

"Oh, no!" Denise said, holding her belly. "Is the hotel on lockdown?"

"Oh, there's nothing to worry about. It's business as usual. Police are on the premises as a precaution. The investigation is discreet until we get a better lead from the two individuals who we *know* were involved."

"Sounds good," Thomas nodded.

The detective's eyes scanned everyone. "I actually had to leave the reception early. Did any of you notice anything out of the ordinary well into the party and afterward?"

Christian looked at Isabella as he replied. "Well, we all had a pretty rough night—especially the girls."

"Hmm," Detective Sanders said, casting a glance at Isabella.

"Where are our manners? Please have a seat, Detective," Christian said.

After the detective took down as much notes as he could about each person's account of the reception, he stood up to leave. "Okay, guys, I can't say this will help any, but it looks like my work here is done for now."

"Um, Detective," Christian hesitated. "There's something I would like to show you." He then beckoned David over and whispered, "I need that video."

"No," David replied sternly.

"At least show it to the detective!" Christian reasoned.

David hesitantly handed the tablet to the detective and played it for him. Within a minute of watching, Detective Sanders glanced at Christian and then at a flushed Isabella. Then with a bewildered expression, he stuttered, "Um . . . what's this, a sex tape?"

"She was framed," Christian said.

Detective Sanders sighed and sat back down.

"Our friend Olivia did this to Chris and Isa," Rachel explained. "We're not exactly sure why but—"

Christian interrupted. "I was wondering if there was anything that can be done."

"You mean in terms of pressing charges?" the detective asked.

"Yes."

"More and more of these sorts of things are popping up," he said. Christian watched him closely as his gaze shifted to Isabella when he added, "And they are getting harder and harder to prove." Isabella flinched as the detective continued. "It's tough because you would have to establish she didn't give consent."

"Detective," Christian felt his heart rate pick up speed as he interrupted. "I said she was framed."

"I'm sorry—this isn't you, Ms. Montes?" he asked Isabella.

She did not look up, let alone respond. When no one spoke, the detective looked around. Christian had made his way over the detective's shoulder to steal a glance of the video. Of course, it *was* Isabella. Christian scowled at David, who gave him a fierce stare in return.

"*Mrs.* Cervello," Christian corrected, his jaw beginning to tense.

"Yes, of course. Oh dear, I got used to your old name from the last case."

"It's okay," Isabella nodded, still looking down.

"Like Rachel said," Christian continued. "Our friend Olivia did this but—"

"Is there something else you want to say?" the detective asked, twisting around to face Christian.

Christian sighed. "It's just that Olivia is usually forward about things." With Genius missing, he didn't realize that he was thinking aloud and before he could hear himself, Isabella spoke.

"What are you saying?" It was a near whisper.

Christian's eyes closed. "I didn't—listen, I just mean it's unlike her, that's all. Besides, she could never edit that well. That was flawless from the beginning to the end, right down to the watch," he said, eyes burning into Isabella's.

Isabella nodded slowly and repeatedly—her expression blank.

"You—have got—SOME nerve, Christian Cervello!" Rachel roared. "Why don't you just dig a hole and drop Isa in there?"

"Rach, just hear me out, I'm not—"

Ignoring Christian, Rachel turned her attention to the detective. "The original footage was an interview Isa did for Olivia and I was there when it happened, period!"

Rachel yelled into the awkward silence. "It was about lipstick, for goodness' sake!"

After a long silence, the detective spoke. "In that case, we need to prove it was indeed a setup and not Mrs. Cervello. As you can see, the recording starts off with her, so it's tricky."

Christian felt heat run through his skin.

"Have you talked to this friend?" Sanders asked. "Maybe it was her sick idea of a joke. Getting a confession or the original footage may be easier." When no one spoke, he added. "I'll look into this. What's her name?"

"Olivia Saunders," Rachel said.

Detective Sanders frowned. "Sanders?"

"Close, Saunders with a u."

"Humph! Too close for comfort." The detective stood up to leave. "Wow! Another friend, huh? I tell you, with friends like these, you don't need enemies."

The detective closed the door behind him and there was just silence. Isabella pondered his last words. Deep down, she trusted that he would get to the bottom of the video—she felt it. He'd taken care of her during the kidnap case and she knew he hadn't meant to refer to her by her maiden name, but it hurt all the same. She wasn't sure what to make of Christian and where he stood, but she didn't want to overthink the matter.

She quickly searched for an excuse to accompany her next comment: "I'll be right back." As it turned out, she didn't need one because the party seemed to have grown mute and Christian made no intention to come after her. As nausea crept up, she wobbled her way to the elevator. Bits of the nightmare she had on the morning of her wedding flashed in her memory. *God please, please*—the doors to the elevator opened and she was grateful it was empty. Now if she could make it to her suite without vomiting all over the fancy flooring, get a hold of Febe and . . . God no, *I can't be losing my marriage already*.

Once inside her suite, she found where Rachel had laid out their phones last night—hers and Christian's. Out of the twenty-six missed calls, Febe's was sure to be there somewhere. Her fingers shook as she found Febe's number but her heart fell as the call went straight to voicemail. She hadn't spoken with her earlier when the pastor called and now she just couldn't recall when her flight back to Rio was. Her calls to Abby and Ivan also proved fruitless. She couldn't even remember seeing the two of them during the reception, but she remembered Abby mentioning having to work tomorrow.

Her phone vibrated. The call came from her house line. She picked up to her father, calling to check on her and mention that Julio had taken not only Febe's family to the airport, but also Abby. She ended her call feeling worse. Nothing was right. So many loved ones who had labored for her were gone and she'd never gotten the chance to thank them—let alone say good-bye. She scrolled through her missed calls and sure enough, Abby had called a couple of times and had texted too. Too heartbroken to check her messages, she tucked her phone into her pocket and went to pour water over her face. At least the nausea had subsided.

As the afternoon went on in the other room, Isabella watched as the rest of the party chatted away as though everything was okay—but nothing was. For one, she couldn't help but notice that Christian had grown increasingly distant since the detective left. They never did resume their balcony talk; rather, he excused himself and left the room several minutes at a time, and when he did interact with her, he did so only as a group. She felt invisible—as though outside her body watching everyone. There was laughter, but Olivia's actions were no laughing matter to her and she wasn't ready to let go of this without confronting her. Growing up, she'd always had her suspicions about Olivia but she never quite knew how to address it without seeming troublesome; especially since Olivia had been in the Cervellos' lives longer than she had been.

Later that evening, the group settled for a game of poker. Into the game, Christian noticed Isabella had been unusually quiet for most of the day. He couldn't bring himself to speak to her, but it seemed that no one else could either. The silence in between plays wasn't good for him because he was still fighting back flashbacks of the video. He thought back to his first meeting with Antonio at the club. It was obvious he wanted her back then.

Her awkward behavior didn't help matters. She had gone out of her way to avoid him, and when he'd invited her out with the group for a swim she'd refused it for a nap. Now, there was absolutely no eye contact between them. It was happening again. His Mind was out of control. He'd been free of doubt for a while. Why then were his thoughts getting out of hand, especially after months of his getting them in control? Maybe he wasn't crazy this time. Perhaps, it was God's way of warning him not to be naïve regarding the video. It had to be real because no one had an explanation for the sex scene.

The more he considered Isabella's quiet demeanor, the more he found that he couldn't trust her—she had a secret, and the same part of him that hadn't called Olivia yet didn't care to know what that secret was. Why would Olivia go to such lengths to do this? Especially since she had boldly told him that Antonio even wanted Rachel at a time. After all, Isabella went to the club by herself that night—half-naked—looking to hook up with someone. Not to mention, she went without her so-called *taken* ring. Olivia had her faults, but boldness wasn't a crime. Supposing Olivia denied this and could actually prove Isabella and Antonio had a relationship? That would mean . . . *Could Rachel be covering for Isabella?* he thought. He glanced at Rachel. For the first time in his life, he didn't think he could trust her. They were too close—even closer than he had been with Rachel once. Something had changed in their relationship; perhaps it had to do with being away from her for so long, but her loyalty definitely seemed to lie with Isabella and not him. She said it herself, she'd lie for Isabella in a heartbeat.

"Christian! Hello!" Rachel yelled.

"Earth to Christian," Thomas said in a robotic voice.

"Yeah," Christian replied, attempting to refocus.

David frowned. "Where did you go? We've been calling you—it's your turn."

Christian grabbed the tablet and excused himself from the game. Back in the restroom, he replayed portions of the twenty-minute clip; rewinding when necessary to focus on the two people in bed. The watch he'd given her was on her wrist the entire time. He despised the idea that Rachel would cover for Isabella at his expense.

"Are you okay?" came Isabella's voice. It was soft. He sighed deeply, realizing he'd forgotten to lock the door. When he turned around to face her, their eyes met. "I will be," he replied, returning the tablet to the case. Without making further eye contact, he asked, "Is there something you'd like to tell me?"

"No," she said, taking more steps toward him.

"Remember our no-questions-barred policy?"

She leaned against the sink. "Yeah."

"Well, do you have any questions for me?"

"No," Isabella said, crossing her arms. "Do you? Wait, let me guess, the answer is *yes and no,* isn't it? And concerning the no-questions-barred policy, what you really mean is no volunteered-information-barred, don't you?"

Christian snapped around. "What in the world are you talking about?"

"Oh, you know exactly what I'm talking about, Christian. I am talking about something about you that I've noticed. You avoid hot-button issues if it has to do with the perfect preconceived notions you've created for yourself. So what do you do? You avoid asking direct questions and if you ask questions, they're shallow because the truth is, you really don't want to know, do you? You don't want to mess up that fantasy—that I'm perfect or that Olivia can do no wrong to you because she's like your sister. That's why you haven't asked me if that was me and that's why you haven't even called Olivia. Yet she hurt me, Christian. I'm your wife!"

Christian sighed and shifted uncomfortably as Isabella continued. "So you secretly hope that information is volunteered to you and if it is, it better be what *you* want to hear. And when someone doesn't volunteer information, you make assumptions."

He looked in the mirror and eyed her reflection suspiciously.

"You know what the problem with that is, Chris? The problem is that the fact remains that you have a pressing question to ask, but because I can't read your mind, I can't volunteer the information even if I wanted to. And because I don't volunteer, you assume. Unfortunately, the problem with assumptions is that they could be wrong, but when you finally muster up the nerve to ask the question you should have asked in the first place, it's too late!"

Smiling slightly into the mirror, he applauded. "Well, I'm glad you know me so well because, yes, I've got so many questions for you, but they're all jumbled up in my head. I can't seem to think straight right now, so I'll get back to you on that."

Isabella walked up close to him. "My goodness, you're actually upset with me," she said, searching his face. "You know, the irony of the whole thing is that no matter how much I tell you that wasn't me, you've already condemned me."

"I need some fresh air," Christian muttered.

"Fine!" Isabella mumbled in reply, staring at the open door, long after he left.

Christian arrived at the lobby and just as he approached the doors, he realized it was pouring rain outside. So he paced the lobby instead, until he recognized the man approaching him was the infamous Antonio.

"What the hell are you doing here?" Christian asked, broadening his shoulders and fuming.

"Listen, I swear I had no idea you two were together," Antonio replied.

"Like hell you did!"

"I didn't come here to cause trouble. I just wanted to return this, she forgot it at my place."

Christian's gaze shifted to the familiar red jacket resting on his arm. Then with a frustrated laugh, he said, "Yeah, wait till she's married to return a stupid jacket . . . nice."

"I just—"

"Just cut the crap. You're here about your sex tape."

"My what?" Antonio asked, eyes widening. "What do you know about that?"

Christian didn't know whether to be amused or angry over his charade. "Oh yeah, you're good."

"Oh, no!" Antonio gasped. "Someone must be trying to frame us."

"*Us?*" Christian chuckled, outraged. "Nice. I see you have unfinished business with my wife."

"It's over, no hard feelings, I just came to—"

"No, why don't you give it to her yourself?" Christian reached into his pocket. "Damn! I'll have her paged. You stay right there." He had the front desk page the room and by the time David picked up the room phone and Christian looked back, Antonio was gone. *Coward*, Christian muttered.

"Is everything okay?" David asked.

"Listen, can you get the access key from her and meet me down at the lobby?"

"Chris, I—" David started to say. But Christian returned the phone to the attendant.

"Excuse me, sir," came a voice from behind him. A bellhop held up the jacket. "A gentleman just informed me that this belongs to you."

Christian smiled. "Yes, thank you."

"No problem, sir."

Christian waited in front of the elevator, trying hard not to focus on the fact that his marriage was over. This was just the confirmation he needed— it stung but it was necessary. The elevator doors opened, and Christian smiled when he saw David. "We meet again, David—exactly where the nightmare began." The elevator ride was quiet. Christian sniffed the jacket. All traces of her were gone and he couldn't remember the original scent.

The elevator doors opened but Christian stood frozen in his line of thought.

"Chris, are you okay?"

How could I forget? He was at my place, looking for her, he thought.

David ushered him out of the elevator. "You look like you saw a ghost."

Christian remained silent as David unlocked the door. "Wow, this place is amazing," David said, making his way into the room. "Check out that view. It looked smaller last night with all the commotion." David walked around the suite while Christian quietly retrieved his laptop. As the computer loaded, he spotted his phone and placed it in his pocket.

"What's going on, Chris?" David asked.

"I'm as clueless as you are, David," he replied, typing away.

"Are we back to that stupid video again? Please don't tell me you don't believe Isa."

"Do *you*?" Christian smiled. He picked up the room phone and dialed. "You saw the video too, right? You even tried to keep it away from me."

"Yeah and, yes, it looked legit, but it's hers and Rachel's word against Olivia's."

Christian held up a finger, signaling David to hold on.

Rachel answered the room phone. "It's for you, Isa."

Isabella was on the phone for seconds and hung up.

"Well . . . what?" Rachel asked.

"He wants me to come up to our room," Isabella said, feeling an uneasy twinge in her stomach at the lack of emotion she'd heard in his tone.

"I'm coming with you," Rachel insisted.

"What if he gets upset?"

"I don't care; I'm not leaving you alone. Come on, I've still got the other access card."

"Hey, Dave . . . do me a favor and find out who this is registered to," Christian asked, handing over the tablet containing the video. There was a knock on the door. As David went to get it, Christian joked, "I bet you she brings her partner-in-crime." When Isabella and Rachel walked in, Christian turned from his laptop and chuckled. "What did I say—she brought her sidekick."

Rachel rolled her eyes at Christian. "Whatever!"

"Nah, it's okay, Rach," he replied. "You should probably be here anyway."

Isabella rubbed her palms on her sweatpants as Christian walked up to her.

"Sweaty palms?" he smiled. She smiled back nervously.

"Isabella," Christian said, followed by a long pause.

She broke down. He took a step back and cocked his head to the side as he analyzed her. *Hmm . . . sweaty palms, and sudden outburst.* His guilty list was just about complete. "I didn't even ask you a question yet," Christian said. "You sure you don't wanna speak first?"

She shook her head rigorously as she cried with her head down. *Shame?* he pondered.

"So, I have the question. But I want to start by acknowledging a few things," Christian said, taking another step back, before beginning to pace the room. "So, some months ago, I was at a club and that was where you met a guy named Antonio."

"Yes," Isabella said, sniffing.

Christian nodded. "That's a good start. So, this guy is, at least I think . . . a good-looking guy. In fact," he said, looking at David, "you should have seen the girls flock to him, Dave. I heard he settles for nothing but the best," Christian said, emphasizing with a sarcastic bow before Isabella.

"Then, my beautiful Isabella walked into the club and Antonio was hooked."

"She wasn't yours then!" Rachel blurted.

David nodded in agreement. "She's right. Where are you going with this, Chris?"

Christian ignored both of them. "The same evil Olivia helped, of course, and back then, you didn't seem to mind her help. In fact, you promptly followed this *stranger* back to his table.

"Then lo and behold, the big bad wolf . . . me, came over, snatched you up, and took you home."

Isabella nodded.

"Okay, so fast forward to our wedding day. I get a cruel wedding gift—a video of a guy and *someone* that looks just like you. Oh wait, pardon me for never asking, do you have a twin?"

"Christian," David's tone warned.

"Well, you admit the beginning is you but I guess someone else did all the hard work."

"Bastard!" Rachel hissed. "Come on, let's go, Isa." But Isabella was frozen.

Christian carried on. "I see the video and I think, wait, I've seen this guy before. But David talks me into thinking this is your past but . . . " Christian stalled for a few seconds. "But then I see the watch I gave you and I know, it couldn't be your past, right?" he asked, voice now thick with emotion. "But okay, everything's okay, because you, Dave, and Rach admit the video is a fake, although it appears very real, right?"

"Yes," Isabella replied, choking up.

"I believed that. I really did, but a lot of things still don't add up. So here's where my question for you comes in. During that month I was depressed, this Antonio guy came to my house looking for you."

Isabella stared wide-eyed at an equally surprised Rachel and David.

"Yes, I know you're all hearing this for the first time." Christian said. "I wasn't going to let what I believed was some revenge on his part get in the way of what we had going on. But now I wonder if I made a mistake by assuming it was a prank."

Isabella frowned as he continued. "You know, I just can't understand how in the world a man you don't know knew to look for you at my house. My address isn't even listed, Isabella."

"There's gotta be a mix-up somewhere," Rachel said. "Are you sure it was the same guy?"

Christian nodded.

"That can't be," David said. "Who told you that?"

"Oh, don't worry, no one did," Christian said smiling slightly. "I opened the door and spoke to him myself." Then looking directly at Isabella, he said, "Now would be a good time to say something."

Isabella's tears blinded her. Flashbacks of the broken champagne glass came to mind. *Olivia won*, she thought. *It's over between us.* He wasn't saying it, but she knew. Her cell phone vibrated in her pocket.

"I don't know that man," Isabella said in a near whisper. "I met him once—that night, I told you."

Then, reaching for her jacket, Christian said, "Oh, pardon me, that wasn't a question. Bear with me while I get better at asking *direct* questions. My question is, is this yours?"

"My jacket!" Isabella exclaimed. "Where did you find it? I've been—"

"Well this guy you don't know felt the need to come all the way to our hotel this evening to drop it off because you somehow forgot it at his place. How did he get a hold of your property, Isabella?"

"I have no idea, the last time I saw that jacket was at the club!"

Christian laughed. "Well, that's funny, because the last time *I* saw it was the morning after the club when Julio picked it up for you. I held this jacket in my hand and reminded Julio to drop it off and if Julio didn't, tell me why he would give it to Antonio?"

"I don't know—I never got it," Isabella said in a withered voice.

"Someone call Julio!" Rachel yelled.

"It's going to voicemail," David said, fumbling with his phone.

"Forget the stupid jacket!" Christian snapped. "What was he doing in my house? Let me guess, Julio gave him a ride too, and opened the gate for him. Listen, I'm not sure why you just won't admit that something went on with you two. There's nothing to be ashamed of. We all have a past. I just wish you didn't think I was too stupid to put it all together."

"Are you asking me to admit to something I didn't do?" Isabella asked. Her phone's buzz was now persistent.

"I'm asking you to be honest so we can move past this," Christian said, clearly livid. "This guy was at my home looking for you and he was here—at our wedding hotel, for goodness' sake! How do I know he won't be back in our lives again in the future? Don't you see, Isabella? There's no closure with you and this guy. He probably still wants you. You need closure!" Christian yelled.

There was silence.

Then in a calm voice, he said, "You know what, forget it. How can you possibly get closure from a relationship you claim never existed. I'm beating a dead horse." As he turned to leave, Isabella held on to him, but he gently pried her hands off and kissed them, his hot tears dropping onto her fingers. He walked away.

Before going after Christian, David said to Rachel, "Take care of her."

Rachel walked up to Isabella and handed her the phone. "Your parents have been calling my phone. I hope they're all right. Please call them back now."

Isabella blinked and more tears came rolling down. The phone conversation took less than a minute.

"Are they okay?" Rachel asked.

Isabella nodded. "I forgot that my dad wanted me to check their flight in for them."

"Oh that's right, they leave tonight."

Isabella searched through her belongings for a folder that contained her parent's flight information and went over to the laptop to begin the check-in process. As she navigated through the main screen, she noticed that Christian had been searching for information on the process of an annulment. She screamed.

Rachel rushed up to her. "What's that?"

"Look!" Isabella said through tears, pointing at the screen, her other hand covering her mouth.

"Oh, no! Isa listen, Christian is very forgiving. Just tell him the truth. Tell me what really happened and Mom and I will talk to him."

"Oh my . . . you don't believe me either." Her wedding nightmare came true. With a frustrated laugh mixed with tears, she got up and began to frantically throw all the belongings she could grasp into her suitcase, shouting, "Oh, Olivia, Olivia, yeah . . . you won! Yeah!" As she zipped up her suitcase, Rachel pleaded. "I didn't say I don't believe you, Isa! What are you doing? Come on Isa, don't you have to check your parents in?"

"Nope, we'll do it from the airport." She sniffed as she went through her phone. She ripped off a piece of paper from the hotel notepad and wrote a number on it. She swiftly pulled off her rings and watch, and placed them in a hotel room courtesy bag, and handed it to Rachel with the piece of paper. "Here! Give these to your brother, he can send the annulment papers to that number or to the address." She walked past a dumbfounded Rachel.

Isabella arrived at the lobby hoping to request a taxi. The lady at the front desk seemed to recognize her from the wedding but simply smiled before asking how she could be of service to her. Rather, Isabella heard the lady conclude by saying, *"You shouldn't have gotten involved with this family in the first place; you knew they're cursed—now you're messed up like them. Run now, run as fast as your feet can carry you and don't look back."*

Isabella screamed to the lady, "Stop it! Just stop it, Get behind me, Satan!"

The lady asked, "Are you okay, Ms.?"

A bellhop held her up, seeing that she was about to fall over. Snapping back into reality, she realized that a sizable crowd at the lobby had gathered around her. "I'm sorry," she said, shaking. "I was just thinking aloud."

"Isabella?" came a warm familiar voice.

"Pastor?" She whipped around and ran to embrace him.

Pastor Bernard nodded to the receptionist. "I'll see to it that she's okay." Then he whisked her away. "What is the matter, my child?" he asked, with deep concern in his eyes.

"I thought you'd left."

"I left after the meeting with your family, but I had to come back for my notes." He held up his tablet. "What happened out there, Isabella?"

"I just needed a cab and then I got attacked spiritually."

She noticed his gaze drop to her hand. "Where's your husband?" She looked down without a word. "Come, I'll take you home."

Having argued the entire way, Christian and David pulled up to Casa Cervello.

"My problem isn't when it happened, but the fact that she would lie about any involvement at all," Christian said. "All I needed for her to do was 'fess up. If she can't even do that, what else can she lie about in the future? I should have paid attention to my gut—she just seemed too good to be true."

"Isa's your wife now," David snapped, slamming the passenger door. "What happened to trust?"

"Of course, I wanna trust her. But that's a little hard to do watching a video of the two of them."

"She said it wasn't her. She even had an alibi—your own sister! What, you can't trust her either?"

"Listen, David, it's not like I didn't initially trust either one of them; I did. I mean, it was a stretch but I still gave them the benefit of the doubt. But tell me, what can I say when the guy himself shows up at the hotel looking for her? Or my house, for that matter."

"Did it ever occur to you that he could have followed you home that night from the club?"

"But he didn't," Christian said, closing the front door behind him.

"And you know this because?"

Christian paused with a cynical smile in front of the staircase. "Because I didn't go home that night, Dave. Julio and I went straight to Isabella's place from the club, so there." He climbed up the stairs. It was dead silent. To think just two nights ago, Thomas had likened it to the United Nations, but with his parents off to Sweden, an empty house was exactly what he needed.

David was sending a text message at the kitchen table when Christian headed for the fridge. His eye caught Isabella's high school picture, which he had tacked onto it days ago. "My goodness, she's always been so beautiful," Christian said. "I wonder what it would have been like to make love to her."

"It's not too late to find out," David replied, without looking up from his phone.

Christian scoffed. "I don't wanna see her, Dave."

David placed his phone on the table and sighed. "Okay, I know you both need time to cool off and I'm telling you, as soon as you do, you need to head back to the hotel or send for her."

Christian stared at the picture. "I knew it wouldn't work out. She's too perfect."

"*Perfect?*" David scoffed. "Listen to yourself. Didn't you just accuse her of cheating?"

"Listen, it's not as if I think she cheated on me. I don't really think she did anything wrong. They had an affair before we got serious and they probably recorded that video before our date."

"Okay, then what's all this fuss about?" David asked, his voice going up an octave. "What happened in the hotel room earlier? Please tell me because I'm completely lost!"

"What this is about is the present and the future, Dave. If something happened between her and this guy in the past, and I know it did, that's fine, especially since I had hurt her around the time she met him—so it'd be justified. I just need to know it's resolved now. But how can it be resolved if she says it never happened? And how could it have never happened if he has the nerve to keep popping up in my private space?"

"Have you thought that perhaps Olivia could have had a hand in that, too? Why does it seem like you trust her over your own wife?"

"No, I saw the look in his eyes," Christian said shaking his head. "He still wants her. Where else is he gonna show up? In Highland Beach? Then we blame Olivia? She doesn't even know where the house is. You see, we can keep blaming Olivia for everything, but at some point we must start believing there's a fire with so much smoke in our face. All this can't be Olivia; she's not that clever."

"See, that's your problem," David said. "You underestimate the people you should be wary of and you accuse the people you should trust."

"I won't compete with him, Dave. I'm not sharing her. It's gotta be him or me. Forget the stupid water," he muttered, as he slammed the fridge door and walked down the hallway to his room.

"Wait one second," David grunted after him. "So that's what this is about, huh? Stupid insecurities. You know what, I'd rather go back to believing that you really thought she did something wrong than have to listen to this nonsense. You're willing to hurt a nice girl, on her honeymoon, for that matter, just because of your insecurities? What does she even have to do with that? You know what? I'm going to check on Isa. You, my friend, are a moron!"

Christian slammed his room door and as he closed the drapes, David barged in. "I need the key!" Christian reached into his pocket and threw the car key to David. "So this is how you deal, huh?" David said. "No food, water, dark room."

"Yup."

"So that's it, you don't even care where Isa is?"

"Oh, she's probably thinking of a way to confess. I'll be here when she's ready or you never know, she'll probably bump into her old lover at the lobby, who cares."

"Have you even prayed about this?"

"I have no strength left to pray."

"No kidding. You have no strength to pray but you have the strength to daydream and worry?"

"Then pray for me, Dave, please!" Christian moved a garment bag laying on his bed to the nearby sofa and pulled back the sheets. Something fell to the floor and when he went to pick it up, he realized it was one of the Ghost Orchids. They looked more mysterious in person. His heart raced as he analyzed it. "So fragile . . . Dave, do you realize just how scarce this flower is?" He looked up, but David was gone.

"I should have known something was wrong when you didn't show up for service this morning," Pastor Bernard told a despondent Isabella. For nearly an hour, they had sat in his car, outside her home. "It will take more effort if you expect your marriage to survive."

"What difference does it make if I want to fight but he doesn't? You should have seen his face."

"Let me talk to Christian."

"The odds are against me—even Rachel doesn't believe me. I just have to leave; at least for now, until the truth comes out."

"Are you going to run every time you face conflict?"

"But I never thought of leaving until I saw he'd been looking for ways to annul our marriage. It's too embarrassing; I won't force him to stay."

"What do you plan to do while you're there?"

Isabella ran her fingers through her hair and gathered it into a bun. "I have no idea now. After my parents kill me and raise me back from the dead, I could probably look into some mission work. Their church organizes great programs around this time of the year in the countryside. I have always wanted to be part of that since I was little," she said. "I'm completely blindsided. I am supposed to be getting ready to leave for Hawaii. I just want to wake up from this nightmare, Pastor."

He held her hand. "Give me some time. When do you plan to leave?"

"We should be heading out within the next hour. My parents have an 11:30 p.m. flight. I'll book mine when I get to the airport."

He glanced at his watch. "I'm sure I can get a hold of Christian before then. Just promise me you'll wait. I'll call you as soon as I get him."

"I promise that if you get in touch with him while I'm at the airport and he wants to see me, I will come back—even if I've checked in."

"Fair enough."

CHAPTER TWENTY-EIGHT

Revelations

❧

LATE INTO the next morning, Christian slept as His Mind played back its favorite scenes with Isabella.

David barged into his room. "Rise and shine! Up, up, up!" he yelled, opening up the shades.

"Why, David, why?" Christian shrieked, pulling the silk covers over his face. "I was just with her."

"You're sick!" David yelled back. "Why see her in your dreams when you can see her in real life? You are married to the woman, for goodness' sake. Listen, we're not going over this craziness again. Detective Sanders called and wants to see you as soon as possible."

"Ugh, not again, Can't you just go for me? I have a splitting headache."

"Look at this!" David uncovered some nearby food in a tray. "I see you didn't eat the food I brought you last night. You know why you have a headache? You haven't eaten in two days. The last thing you had in your system was alcohol and you haven't shaved or showered since your wedding day. Chris, have you seen yourself? You're still in your wedding clothes!"

"Then handle the detective for me, so I can freshen up," Christian said, throwing a pillow at David.

"Remember the shooting outside the hotel?" David asked.

Christian mumbled with a pillow over his face. "Can you close the blinds please?"

"That was Olivia!"

Tossing the pillow away, Christian asked, horrified. "Olivia got shot?"

"No, Chris, Olivia shot someone. The detective remembered it was her from the name we gave him."

"Could Isabella have been—?"

"There you go blaming Isa again. Do you ever give her the benefit of the doubt?"

"No, I meant her target."

"I don't have details, but you need to go in. Go shower now. I'll grab you a bite to eat on our way."

After Christian had showered, he ripped opened the garment bag and pulled out a white polo shirt and a pair of faded blue jeans. He then emptied the contents of the small laundry bag containing his pocket extras on the coffee table. *Well, I'll be . . .* He had all but forgotten about the small bag of colorful pills he had found in Sacha's tablet case over the summer. The pills were still intact and seeing them took him back to their night together. Genius started humming—he was hard at work as Christian laced his white tennis shoes.

"Hey, you ready?" David asked, tapping the key on the door.

"Hey, Dave, I wanna show you something." He threw the bag to David, who caught it high up.

"What's this?" David frowned.

"Beats me . . . I found it in Sacha's stuff."

"Sacha?"

"Months ago. I meant to give it back to her but I forgot it in my pocket."

"These are a lot of pills. Was she sick?"

Christian felt blood leave his face. "I sure hope not."

"Wait, I never asked—" David's voice went down a notch "—did you use protection?"

"Of course!" he snapped. "I always do. It's just . . . I can't remember being with her."

"At all?" David asked, disturbed.

Christian shook his head as he stared at David in confused horror. "At least I hope I used one."

"Well, I mean, these could be vitamins," David said. "But if they're not, we are left with two options."

Christian froze as he thought, *Either she's sick or on drugs. She drugged you,* Genius concluded. The humming had stopped.

"You know who'll know? Dee. I'll send her a picture."

The drive to the police station was gravely quiet. Not even Genius had anything to say.

"Denise still hasn't replied?" Christian asked.

"Soon, my friend. Come on, I'm sure you used protection . . . but hey, didn't you and Isa get tested?"

"We did."

"Okay . . . then why are you worried?"

"Well, excuse me if I'm feeling a little vulnerable right now for possibly having been taken advantage of. What if she's somewhere pregnant?"

David chuckled. "Why, you don't want a new year baby?"

"It's not funny, Dave. Give me your phone."

"Patience. Well, apart from the pill issue, you look more relaxed. The shower or the sleep?"

Christian sighed. "I finally made love to my wife."

David shook his head. "I'm worried about you."

"What? It was good, though."

"Oh, yeah?" David laughed. "You sure you didn't hurt her?"

"Me? Never. When thoughts of her and Antonio crept up, I just redirected them. It was awesome. I wish you could see what goes on in my head, it's like a game."

David marveled. "You see that?"

"What?"

"You have a genius mind and your crazy imaginations have made you rich. Listen to yourself, you just said you successfully managed to redirect your unconscious thoughts in your dreams yet, you can't seem to get it stirred in the right direction in reality."

Did he just call my name? Genius asked. *He's a keeper.*

Christian considered David's words as David pulled up in front of the police station and parked.

"Oh shoot, I forgot to get you breakfast. Will you survive?"

"I did for two days."

Inside the station, an office assistant escorted them to Detective Sanders office. The detective waved them in as he wrapped up a phone call.

"Hello, detective," Christian said as they shook hands. "David said you needed to see me."

"Yes, please have a seat. Is there anything we can offer you to drink?"

"No, thank you, sir," Christian replied, turning to David. "You?" David shook his head.

Detective Sanders sat down and swiveled his seat up to his desk. "You've done so much for this agency. We can never repay you."

"I should thank *you*," Christian said. "You did great with the kidnapping case—I appreciate it."

"It wouldn't have been possible without your technology. Speaking of that case, it's one of the reasons I needed to see you. But first, as I mentioned to David, we found out that your friend Olivia Saunders was in fact the shooter that night."

Christian frowned. "I can't believe it. Who did she shoot?"

"A lady by the name of Kathy Giles."

Christian's eyes widened as he and David echoed. "*Kathy?*"

"You both know her?"

Christian stuttered. "She's my ex-fiancée."

"Man . . . you can't catch a break, can you?" Sanders said.

"Is she—"

"Oh, she's alive," the detective clarified.

Christian stood up and began to pace the room as the detective continued. "We don't have much on her, though; no history in Florida at all."

"She's British—from London. We met at MIT but she returned to London soon after we graduated."

"Oh, that explains it."

"Where is she now?" Christian asked.

"Well, she suffered a gunshot wound to her femur from the struggle that ensued between her and Ms. Saunders in the car. She didn't lose as much blood as she should have for a typical femur fracture because the ambulance was on site. She had a TSF fixator attached to correct the displacement. With that and the sciatic nerve damage to her upper thigh, the doctor said she is looking at about six months of recovery time."

"Do you think Olivia tried to kill her?"

"At this point, we don't even think she attempted to hurt her. She's not talking now but her story to both the EMS attendant and the arresting officer has been consistent. Allegedly, she was trying to take the gun from Ms. Giles when it went off. Ms. Giles says otherwise; she may be pushing for attempted murder."

Christian gasped.

"Yeah, Ms. Saunders hasn't said anything more. She is awaiting her lawyer, who is out of state at the moment. She's gonna need a good lawyer because she'll be fighting a number of charges."

"In addition to the shooting?" David asked, frowning.

"Well, we know the gun isn't hers—it was reported stolen and had both their prints on it," The detective opened a file. "As far as charges, she may be looking at check fraud, a prostitution ring case that went cold but we are considering reopening, possible attempted murder, assault, ransom, and kidnapping."

Christian's brow furrowed as the detective stood up and approached him. "Yes, we found a match for the DNA we obtained from the kidnapping scene—her hair and saliva was on a jumpsuit and voice disguise device dumped in the trash of the neighboring hotel room. It matched perfectly with the DNA obtained from her blood in the car on the day of the shooting."

"But wouldn't that have been Kathy's blood?" Christian asked.

"There were two samples of blood. The reports show that Ms. Saunders was bleeding profusely from her lips when the ambulance arrived. That should at least help her case to prove a struggle."

Christian sat back down and held his heaving chest.

"It appears that your friend Olivia was the mastermind of the kidnapping. Your boy, Kevin, was left in the cold because she didn't want to implicate herself. But this all comes before his court date so—"

"Did she confess to this?" David asked.

"At this point, she doesn't need to. We have her DNA. We can't question her in regard to an alibi without her lawyer but there is something even more damaging—a confession to the kidnapping during a taped conversation between her and the shooting victim a month ago. It appears that Ms. Giles threatened her with the recording prior to the shooting. The driver gave us the device—apparently, they were struggling over it.

"Having said that, Ms. Saunders' lawyer is not needed to prove her innocence; she needs the lawyer to try to lessen her sentence. I gotta tell you, her lawyer's got her work cut out for her. The driver is our prime witness and has been cooperative. He's provided us with a voice recording from his phone and a video recording from his car. The case is tight."

Christian shook his head slowly.

"This is good news, Mr. Cervello," the detective said. "It's not every day we get to solve concurrent cases. At least now, you can rest easy, knowing we've found the other person involved in the kidnapping. We knew Mr. Hendricks didn't make the ransom call and now we know who did."

"That's how she knew about the cemetery," Christian muttered.

"I know you said she was your friend, but she'll be away for quite some time."

"I should be happy, but this girl has been more than a friend . . . a sister."

"I bet—I look at how you and your sister turned out and can't help but wonder what exactly goes wrong to cause people that grew up so close to drift so far apart. Listen, this is tough—take all the time you need." The detective left the room.

Christian sat with his head in his hands. Neither he nor David spoke.

Some minutes later, Detective Sanders returned with a gift box in hand.

David stood up. "Detective, we thank you so much. Chris will be in the Miami area in case you need him—let us know. We must get going now; he doesn't look too good."

"Sure, I understand."

Christian quickly stood up to shake the detective's hand and nearly fell over from that single movement. He quickly smiled to avoid drawing attention to himself.

The detective smiled back. "Well, for your wedding, I've been cracking my brain thinking of what I could possibly get a man that has everything and can invent whatever he doesn't have."

Christian managed a small smile. "It's okay, Detective. The solved case is the best gift I could ask for. I just wish it didn't involve another friend, but at least there's closure."

"I figured I may not be able to give you material things, but peace of mind is priceless," Detective Sanders said, pressing the wrapped box into Christian's hand. "I just hope it isn't too late."

Christian shook the box. "What's this?"

The detective grinned. "Icing on the cake."

David's cell phone beeped and, as he looked through it, he frowned.

"Was that her?" Christian asked.

David nodded and handed Christian the phone.

The message read:

> Hey babe, the picture wasn't so clear but a couple of those are definitely date rape drugs—bring the actual bag so I can see 'em up close. Oh, and could you grab me some peanut butter? The crunchy kind in Chris' house—he's out of it . . . Pulleeeease!

"Is everything okay?" the detective asked.

"You got the bag with you?" Christian asked David.

David pulled out the pills from his pocket and Christian handed it over to the detective. "A girl I was with months ago forgot this in my house. I didn't know what they were till now."

"These are roofies," the detective said. "Do you think it was used on you?"

"I can't remember being with her or anything leading up to it, but I know we were together."

"Most likely she drugged you, then. I'm gonna have to confiscate these."

Christian nodded.

"Can't she face anything for this?" David asked.

"I hate to tell you, but it's your word against hers. These drugs don't last more than a few hours in your bloodstream and we are talking months ago."

"Can men be—?" David started.

The detective smirked. "It's used on both women and men." He patted Christian on the back. "Wow, you're getting the whole ton of bricks thrown at you. You gotta be careful who you let into your space."

"I just have so many questions and she was Olivia's friend. Olivia's here, right? Can I see her?"

Detective Sanders shook his head. "Go live your life." Then he turned to David and said in a low tone. "Christian is a good man. Take care of him for me."

David nodded. "Will do."

David walked ahead to the car, while Christian lagged behind in a daze. The scorching heat against his skin stung. In the face of turmoil, the silence was equally painful. He wasn't ignorant of the fact that Genius hadn't engaged him in any active thinking dialogues since he walked out on Isabella. The most he did was throw out one-liners every now and then or hum. He was responsible for Genius feeling ignored, but this was unlike him, and Christian suspected he was punishing him with the silent treatment to force him to reflect on where he had gone wrong.

"Can we get something to eat now?" Christian said squinting from the sun's glare as he entered the car. "I'm dizzy."

"Sure, you know a good place around here?"

"Yeah, just go straight on and make the first right after the Village Green intersection. Next time we are around here, I'll show you where I went to grade school; it's around the corner."

"You sound horrible," David said as the car slowed at the stop sign. "Okay, what is going on there?" he asked, looking ahead into the one-way street. "Perhaps we should turn here so we don't get stuck?"

Tell him yes . . . turn right, Genius urged. Rather Christian said, "Just stay, it's a short strip to Crandon Boulevard."

David continued on the one-way street and soon found that the cars ahead of him no longer moved. With the left turning lane closed for construction and two more vehicles now behind them, they were in a real bind. A police officer walked back to the Village Green intersection to prohibit cars from backing up into the active traffic.

David sighed. "I should have just turned at that stop sign. Will you survive?"

Christian had no strength to speak and he didn't want to, especially since he'd ignored Genius again.

"You gonna open that?" David nodded to the package on Christian's lap.

Christian shook his head and handed it to him before leaning on the door panel and closing his eyes. Even thoughts of Isabella couldn't suffice now. Running away looked like a better option. He'd look into that as soon as he had something to eat or drink. He wasn't sure what was worse, the hunger or the thirst. His tongue felt stuck to the roof of his mouth and he kicked himself for refusing the detective's offer of a drink. He heard David tinkle with the DVD player and in seconds . . . Olivia's voice.

"Testing—Testing!" Olivia said into the camera, grinning.

"Here's the birthday girl," Olivia said.

"That's a really nice camera, Olivia," Isabella said.

"Hey, Chris has one just like that," Rachel said, from behind Olivia.

"I know, it's his. He let me borrow it for a project I'm working on."

"Yeah? what project?" Rachel asked.

"I'll tell you later, this is rolling."

"Now or never."

"Okay, it's for a makeup ad."

"Really?" Isabella exclaimed.

(There was a knock on the door and Rachel disappeared.)

Olivia cleared her throat. "Oh, Isa, I was wondering if you could help me with a sound bite for the ad."

"Really? That's big! Sure, I'd love to help."

"Great, it means a lot to me. Here, I'll just fix you up a little," Olivia said, running her fingers through Isabella's hair. "Just a slight tousle here."

"I'll go change into my clothes."

"No, you're perfect the way you are. It's just your face anyway. Prop this pillow under your elbow."

"Like this?" Isabella motioned.

"Atta girl. Look relaxed but don't smile too much—look sultry."

"Don't you wanna pause it until we're ready?" Isabella asked.

"Oh, I can edit it."

The door closed and Rachel returned. "Hey chicas, what did I miss?"

"Let me guess . . . that was your little pit bull making sure you're safe from big bad Liv."

"I'm going to ignore that," Rachel replied.

"I'm Olivia's face model for the night," Isabella said bashfully.

Rachel chuckled. "Oh yeah, that. A makeup ad? Please Olivia . . . the day you find a job, I'll—"

"Why not? I got a contract."

"Are you serious?" Rachel sounded outraged.

Ignoring her, Olivia spoke right into the camera. "Okay, today is June twenty-second, 2013 . This is Olivia recording live from the coolest pool party at Casa Cervello."

Rachel yelled. "Casa Del Amor!"

"Oh yeah, missy here is changing it to Casa Del Amor," Olivia said. "So, my girls and I are relaxing in the room right now. Say hello, girls!" Olivia turned the camera on them.

"Hello!" Rachel yelled, waving and blowing kisses as the camera focused on her.

Olivia snickered. "Okay, okay, that's enough," she said, turning the camera to Isabella.

"Wait, not yet!" Isabella cried, covering up her bathing suit.

"Oh please, Isabella, it's just a bathing suit. You're such a prude."

"Whatever."

Rachel yelled, "Hey! Get me! I've got a song to sing!" She struck a pose, and with her brush, sang out.

Olivia snapped. "Spare us, Rach! This is for the birthday girl."

"So, here's the gorgeous Isabella—the birthday girl. Happy birthday!"

Isabella waved one hand as the other clutched the white bedspread over her bathing suit. Olivia continued. "So, she's ready for her audition for Florida's top model. No, just kidding, she agreed to try on a lipstick from our intimate line, so here goes . . . " Olivia handed Isabella the lipstick and Isabella put some on and smacked her lips together as Olivia flashed the mirror at her, prompting a smile.

"So Isabella, you just tried on the lipstick from our latest line of cosmetics. Please tell us what you think about it so far," Olivia whispered, "Flirt with your hair a little when you speak."

Rachel giggled. "Is that part of your interview?"

"Shut up, I'm gonna edit it."

Rachel laughed so hard in the background that Isabella struggled to keep a straight face. "Shh, I'm trying to focus, Rach."

"Olivia and a lipstick line . . . that's something to blog about," Rachel teased.

Olivia whispered. "Shh—Stop!"

Isabella smiled as she flirted with her hair in the camera, "Well, I think it's great because . . . um . . . I um . . . " she giggled.

Rachel snickered. "Liv is about to explode."

"David, move!" Christian said, nodding to the road, as it cleared a whole two car spaces.

"I'm so sorry, Liv," Isabella said, "I don't want you to think I'm not taking this serious; it's just that Rach keeps making me laugh."

"Okay, okay," Rachel struggled to contain her laughter. "I'll leave, make it snappy!"

Isabella mouthed, "I'm sorry."

"Don't worry, I'll have it edited," Olivia said.

"I don't know what else to say." Isabella pouted. "Probably I should say something about the moisturizing effect and say I'll definitely use it again."

"No, that won't sell. Say something about how it'll make you feel as a woman; make it, you know . . . intimate. It's from our intimate line so bring out that side. I'm sure you have it in you, Isa."

"Okay, ask me the question again," Isabella said confidently.

"Don't worry about it, I don't have much time, I told you I can edit it—just answer."

"Okay, I think it'll be great because it'll get me in touch with my feminine side, you know, feel whole as a woman should."

"Perfect!" Olivia said.

"I heard that!" Rachel yelled, laughing. "'Whole as a woman?' you must be kidding me. Get the camera on me, I have something better."

The video went blank and both men sat in silence. The traffic hadn't cleared again.

"I think I should head off on foot and get you something to eat," David said.

A shuffling sound came from the DVD and to Christian's surprise, another footage followed. It was unsteady but it showed a man he recognized as Antonio in bed with a woman they referred to as Rana. The small bright-lit room was complete with a set of makeup artists and stylists and during the shoot, they coached this Rana on how to pose.

"You did good," Antonio said, "she does look like her."

"You can thank him for that. I never saw the resemblance till she told me he called her Isabella."

Christian knew this was his cue to think but nothing came and there was no humming. He squinted at the screen and asked, "Is that Private-I editing equipment?"

"I was wondering the same thing," David said. "Did you lend it to her?"

"No," Christian said, looking down at his hands, which were visibly shaking.

"Here, take my spot and just sit behind the wheel while I get you something."

"I'll be fine." *It's just a panic attack*, he thought, heart now racing. *It's more than that*, Genius said.

They inched closer to the police officer who was directing traffic. "I gotta see if he could make a way out for us, this is crazy. See the next holdup around Crandon? It's worse than I thought."

Christian's eyes fell back to the screen and he was staring right at . . .

"Wait a minute, is that Kathy?" David asked, outraged.

Christian knew he was going in and out of consciousness but he could still hear David frantically call out to the police officer. The voices from the video now faint.

"That's the watch I was talking about," Kathy said. *"He probably used it to trace you guys."*

Olivia grunted. *"What a waste—I wish I had shown you the video before we planned it."*

"I've got a replica for . . . "

Everything went black.

Christian opened his eyes to a blur of bright light and distant chatter. It reeked of iodine and other forms of antiseptic and the bed was uncomfortable. After a few blinks, his gaze focused in on his right arm—connected to an IV. It had to be a hospital but he was too frightened to turn just yet, so he closed back his eyes. *Did we crash?* He pondered. Someone laughed in the background. It sounded like Rachel. He couldn't be badly hurt because she would have been crying. He whipped his head around and their eyes met. Her mouth formed an "o" and Denise grinned in the chair next to him, crunching on ice cubes from a Styrofoam cup.

"Guys, he's back!" Rachel cried. David came running in with Thomas and Pastor Bernard. Christian knew he was smiling, even if his face couldn't register it with motion. He fixed his eye on the door but no one else came through. "Where's Isabella?" His voice was weak.

"Don't worry about that now," Thomas said reaching for his arm. "Do you know why you are here? You were severely dehydrated."

"Where is she, Thomas?"

"I told you, Chris—"

"He needs to know!" Rachel interrupted.

"Not now, Rach," Thomas argued.

"When? You tell me." Rachel turned to Chris. "Isa is gone. She left with her parents."

Without a word, Christian turned his gaze back to the IV. The drip-drop was painfully slow and loud.

Rachel fumbled in her purse, "Here, she wanted you to have this."

Thomas clenched his teeth, "Rach!"

Ignoring him, Rachel handed the bag to Christian.

He tossed the contents onto the bed, and seeing the watch and rings, he gulped. That too sounded loud.

"Give me your phone," Christian said, frowning at a piece of paper.

When Rachel complied, he unsteadily dialed the numbers with his left hand.

"It's a fax," he mumbled, as he desperately redialed the number.

"She wanted you to fax the annulment papers there."

"Annulment?" he asked, confused. He turned to David. "You told her?"

"Oh, he didn't have to," Rachel continued. "She saw it on your laptop."

Christian shouted. "Oh, no . . . NO! NO! NO!"

His nurse came in and requested some visitors leave, citing his need for rest. Pastor Bernard remained.

"She couldn't have gone," Christian mumbled. "No, she wouldn't do that."

Pastor Bernard sat next to him. "Son, listen, Isabella left last night. She left me a message before she boarded. She waited for you to send for her until the last minute. I called your cell and home phones to no avail. Rachel's phone was dead, and I didn't have David's number. I waited outside your home for about two hours before David arrived with the rest. Apparently, they had all gone looking for her at the airport, but it was too late and she had left her message."

"What did it say?"

Pastor Bernard played Isabella's voicemail for Christian:

> Um, Pastor, it's Isa. I'm still at the airport. I waited just as you asked me to, but I actually just went through security a minute ago—I was the last to go. We should board soon and I . . . I want to thank you for your support. We don't have answers but God knows everything. I promise to call you as soon as I get home. Oh, that was my row; we're boarding now. Please pray for me for strength. Good-bye.

The phone went dead and Christian remained silent as Pastor Bernard spoke. "I still called her, hoping I could get her out of the plane. It went straight to voicemail."

There were no tears on Christian's face but his heart was drenched.

"I tried to convince her to stay," he continued. "She was very hurt and alone. She's terrified of seeing her family now but she also needs them. Therefore, I understand why she had to go. Do I agree with it? No, but I understand. Before you make a move in her direction, I will urge you to deal with whatever trust issues you have.

"I believe that you love each other and I attribute whatever went wrong to pure wickedness. Nevertheless, this wickedness has exposed a weakness that you must deal with. That's one good thing that has come from this tragedy. I don't know exactly what we're dealing with here, but it appears to be more than it seems. The roots are very deep.

"The reason you are hurting is because the enemy of your soul is using everything close to you to hurt you. Your friends, ex-fiancée, your kindness and generosity. David told me about how they used your own work equipment and video camera against you. Now, I'm afraid that the enemy is even using you . . . yourself."

Christian looked up at him, eyes glazed with bewilderment.

"Yes, through your mind. I sense a battle going on within you. You seem split—one part jumps to erroneous conclusions and the other tells you the way you ought to go but you don't seem to think much of yourself to believe that any good can come to you. So you self-sabotage. The enemy will use anything or anyone for his bidding; and they let him by way of their weaknesses—open doors. With your friends, it's jealousy, love for money, lust, greed, power and pride. For you, it's fear—shut that door before it's too late!"

There was a tap on the door. Detective Sanders nodded. "I met your sister downstairs in the lobby."

"Come on in," Pastor Bernard said, standing. "I was on my way out."

Shortly after the detective left, the doctor cleared Christian for discharge.

"I'll go pull up the car," Julio said.

"Um, Julio, can you just take David home?" Christian asked. "I still have some business to take care of. We have the Range here, don't we Dave?"

"Yeah, here's the tag—it's valet-parked."

"Thanks. See you guys later."

"Are you going to see Kathy?" David asked. "I heard the detective say she was here."

"Yeah," Christian said.

"Want me to come with you?"

"I need to do this alone."

David tapped him on the shoulder and walked away.

Out in the orthopedic wing, Christian stood outside Kathy's room, silently watching as she balanced her body in an impossible position. She had a pillow under the foot of the affected leg and it was intimidating to see the massive metal device around her upper thigh. His heart warmed to her the more he observed her pitiful state. He tapped his key on the doorpost and she looked up with a blank facial expression.

"Kathy Giles! My MIT wiz," he said as he strolled in uninvited. "Always the best at what you did."

Kathy cocked her head with a smirk. "That's why you hired me."

Christian nodded. "You're right. One of Private-I's finest. You never did disappoint, did you?"

Kathy shrugged.

"Tell me, Kat, when exactly did good meet evil?"

"Don't you blame me for your bad friends, you chose them."

Christian laughed. "So you're gonna pin this all on Olivia, just like Kevin sexually assaulted you."

"Oh they influenced me all right. That's what bad friends do, influence. Who do you think set up your little girlfriend's kidnapping? That wasn't me, Chris—those were your friends. Not mine."

"Yeah, they're so bad but you kept in touch with them long after we were done. Oh wait, I guess that was part of their influence. Now we know they're capable of influencing, what did they influence you to do?"

"To make a mistake."

"Even mistakes have consequences."

"Well, obviously, they do," Kathy said, pointing to her leg. "And consequences should be forgiven."

"Are you going to forgive Olivia?"

"Olivia can go to hell, for all I care. She'll be in hell when my lawyer is through with her."

Christian shook his head. "I understand the pain is making you talk like this."

"You don't understand a thing!" Kathy snapped. "This pain is nothing compared to the pain you left me with, having to cancel an entire wedding in Spain and London—I faced that shame alone."

"Shame?" Christian snickered, outraged as he ran his fingers through his hair. "Well, excuse me if I had to leave London for the shame *you* caused me by sleeping with my employee and best friend!"

"Oh, that's what this is about, isn't it?" Kathy said with a frustrated laugh. "You can't stand another man having your woman. Well, if it's any consolation, he was no good in the sack. You were the best I ever had."

"Oh, so now he didn't rape you? You know what, cut this nonsense! You really have no idea what you did to us, do you?"

"Yes, I made a mistake, but we should have been able to work through that."

Christian paced the room. "And why does Isabella get punished in all this?"

"This is not about your little girlfriend."

"She's my wife!"

Kathy scoffed. "Whatever . . . It wasn't about her. I've been trying to get your attention and now it seems like I finally got it because you're here. Listen, this is all a waste of my time and money, isn't it, Christian? Even if I said that you were a hundred times better than Kevin, that wouldn't help, would it? That's because you're a jealous bastard. You can't stand another man wanting your woman.

"What, Chris? Did you have problems with sharing in kindergarten?" she mocked. "Even Kevin said he couldn't stand your ass; getting all the attention, the girls, acceptances into the Ivy League schools, intellectual and real properties, businesses . . . now, the trophy wife. Just who the hell do you think you are? You need to take out your frustration on Kevin, not me.

"You know what Christian, if I must say so myself, your little wife is stunning. Yeah, I saw her. If I were you, I would keep an eye on her, because there are lots of men who would love to get a piece of that. How's that for your jealous ego? Oh wait, rumor has it she isn't with you, is she? Your jealousy drove her away already. It's all over the news, Chris! You can have all the good things thrown at you, but you will NEVER be able to keep them."

Kathy laughed as she threw the morning paper to him. "Everyone's talking about how she went crazy at the glitzy hotel lobby. Imagine that. Rumor has it you slept in different rooms on your wedding night and don't think I don't know the press followed her from her house to the airport—alone! What a shame. So much for trust, She's all alone and available now. Like you and me."

A nurse walked in. "Is everything okay in here, Ms. Giles?"

"Mr. Cervello was on his way out," Kathy replied coldly.

As Christian left the hospital, he thought about how Kathy had spoken to him. That wasn't the Kathy he'd known. What Pastor Bernard had said about the enemy resounded—this had to be the devil himself speaking to him through her. He remembered the chills that ran through his entire body as she'd spoken and how he'd tried to speak but his mouth couldn't move.

CHAPTER TWENTY-NINE

Timing

❧

OCTOBER 7, 2013. SÃO PAULO, BRAZIL, 10 P.M.
(7 P.M. MIAMI TIME)

"FATHER, PLEASE, vindicate me just as you promised you would," Isabella said as sleep took her. Before she knew it, she was back in her Miami room—praying in bed in her same pajamas, so she knew it had to be a dream. Moreover, her prayer request was different: "Lord, would you reveal the second message Denise had for me?"

There was a knock on her bedroom door and, before she could speak, her father, Felix, walked in dressed in the same clothes he'd worn for school the day before. "What did I tell you, filha," he cried. "He came back for you!"

Isabella jumped out of the bed to embrace him and as soon as she pulled away, he'd turned into David, and in his hand was that same yield sign. "Denise wanted me to give this to you," David said, pointing to the top. "She said he needs to put God right here. I don't know, but she said you'd understand."

Her eyes flew open and she reached for her notepad. It was two minutes past three in the morning and she'd been asleep for five hours. She praised God for the next few minutes, for having finally received the last message and the meaning of the two signs to that triangle. The inverted side called for Christian to yield his struggles to God, while the regular side called for him to put God first—even above her. Isabella drew a triangle shape and put names where they belonged. The journalist in Rachel would probably disagree about the placement of the most important information, but this was different—it wasn't about what was inside the triangle, but out. Come to think of it, during marriage counseling, Pastor Bernard had warned them about the dangers of putting each other above God when he discussed God's protectiveness over each of them as individuals. He had described it as God's jealousy and she had never heard it explained so beautifully. To know that God was crazy about them individually and would want each of them to put Him first, assured that He would not set them up with anyone who would hurt them or be a threat to Him being their head. Her pastor had told them that God could trust such an individual to carry on that love jointly with their spouse and He in turn would bless that marriage, all provided they both kept Him first.

She knew what it was like to obsess over Christian. She had done it for that entire spring and most of summer and it had strained her relationship with God to the point of him taking God's place in her life. She saw first-hand how easy it was to make an idol out of someone. She'd taken the issue of addiction for granted for so long, not knowing that all it took to fall prey was the right kind of drug. In her case, it was Christian. At one time, he'd had so much power over her that it began to affect her mind and work and eventually led her to seek therapy to deal with the emptiness she felt without him. Febe had told her that no man should ever make her feel empty and the minute she felt she needed a human being to fulfill her, she would know that the balance was off. She understood it now, but she feared that Christian hadn't. Her next prayer would be just that. To get Christian to understand she wasn't God and that, without her, life still went on.

OCTOBER 7, 2013. MIAMI, FLORIDA, 7:20 P.M.
(*10:20 P.M. SÃO PAULO TIME*)

Before Christian reached the top of the stairs, he heard the loud chatter in the family room come to a halt. The group of four had assembled there. He nodded a greeting before continuing to his bedroom—the one room that least reminded him of Isabella. However, the first thing he'd spotted was the Ghost Orchid he'd placed on the coffee table. It was withered now, just like his marriage. He hadn't heard from Genius since he passed out. That meant that all he had were his usual negative and fearful thoughts. Before he could conjure any up, he headed back to the family room for safety. Once again, there was loud chatter down the hallway and upon arriving at the entrance of the family room, he saw they were watching the DVD from Key Biscayne PD.

When Christian cleared his throat, Denise nearly fell off the edge of the sofa she had been leaning on. Rachel leaped to stop the DVD and the men appeared flustered. "Um . . . we were just—" Thomas stuttered.

"Do you mind if I watch with you?" Christian asked.

"Of course not," Thomas replied. "We just started."

Rachel resumed the video as Christian took a seat. Memories of Isabella grabbing hold of him as he walked away crept up. As the video rolled on, he got up and went out to the balcony to get some air.

"You want us to pause it?" Rachel yelled.

Christian turned around. "Oh, no, I saw that part already."

David walked out to the balcony. At this point, Rachel and Isabella's laugh from the birthday party footage filled the room.

"Are you sure you can handle this now?" David asked.

"I'm okay—I just got dizzy. The doctor said I might feel like that for some hours. Come on, let's go."

The group watched intently until the raw footage from Olivia's recording started. Christian sat up and squinted. Kathy's final work intrigued him. He knew Olivia couldn't have pulled it off alone.

It was then that he recalled who Isabella's stand-in was. The girl from the hotel room who he called 'Isabella.' David was right; he didn't give Olivia enough credit. Her plan was airtight—right down to the white bikini Isabella had on that day.

"Sure feels better to play the victim, doesn't it?" David said.

"Yup."

"It wasn't your fault; Olivia and Kathy had a good plan. You're only guilty of not trusting Isa."

"That's bad enough."

"But you had good reason, Chris. Even Rachel and I had a hard time believing when it came to the jacket and him showing up at your house. It's been hard on Rachel, too. We all failed Isa."

Christian sighed. "I don't wanna sound like a jerk, but I'm still curious about how he got her jacket."

"Oh, that's right, I didn't tell you yet. Julio told me everything on our drive here. Remember how Isa said the last time she saw it was the club night, and you said Julio picked it up?"

"Yeah?"

"Well, Julio said he had the jacket in the car and then it mysteriously went missing before he could give it to her. He said he'd asked her assistant to tell her about the mix-up—he'd suspected that one of the girls had mistakenly taken it and when he asked Olivia, she confirmed that she took it and was gonna give it to Isa."

"You gotta be kidding me. I had no idea that Olivia was with Sacha that day."

"She must have been plotting against Isa the entire time," David said. "But what I wanna know is how he got through the gate if you hadn't let him in."

"Humph, let me know when you find out."

"Rachel says Olivia has always had the code to this place. The only way to be certain is to check the security footage of that day."

Christian shook his head. "I already tried."

"Really? When?"

"Ha, soon after he left. Apparently it's the last thing I remember before Sacha got to me."

David looked lost.

"What? I said I checked the gate surveillance footage. Why are you staring at me like that?"

"Well, what did you find?"

"Nothing. It was off."

"That's absurd. You didn't design it to shut off unless . . . "

"Manually, I know."

"So *you* turned it off?"

"It wouldn't have been deliberate. Earlier that day, Sacha was buzzing at the gate and I suspect that when I went to silence it, I must have touched something."

David shook his head vigorously. "Still doesn't explain it. Give me access."

Christian escorted him to his bedroom. David rolled up his sleeves and pulled up the desk chair. "What day was that?"

Christian laughed. "How would I know?"

"Well try to think, for goodness' sake!"

Christian sighed as he paced. "Um, okay I had been in bed for over a week . . . Sacha was here."

"A calendar would be nice," David said. "Were your folks in?"

"That's it! Mom and Rachel had just returned from Italy and . . . Rachel!" he called out into the hallway.

Rachel ran into the room. "What's up?"

"When did you guys get back from Bianca's wedding?"

His heart pounded as Rachel went through her phone. "June Seventh."

"And you both came into my room the next afternoon. So, check the day after, Dave."

"I'll be right back," said Rachel, leaving the room as David searched through the archives.

"Okay, I see your mom and Rach come through—skip. Okay, this is them leaving. There goes Julio!"

Christian pulled up an ottoman and sat, peering into the screen.

"Wait a minute. Who's that? Someone standing at the gate."

"Oh, that's Sacha."

"That's the notorious Sacha?"

"Yeah," Christian said with a smirk. "Why?"

"Hmm—I just imagined her different. Okay, Julio's leaving. Were you in the car?"

"No, I sent him away. The recording should end there because I silenced the gate buzz around . . . "

"Nope . . . Watch!"

Sacha crept through into the gate as it closed. David paused the recording. "Did you know this?"

"Yeah, she told me."

"You need the motion sensor package—so it can send out an alarm next time that happens."

Christian laughed. "You sound more paranoid than I do. I'm pleased."

"Seriously, this is unacceptable." David resumed the skipping. "Okay now, who's this?"

"That's Liv's car."

"Do you remember her coming that day?"

"Yeah. It's weird, I thought for sure all this would be gone because I . . . "

"You keep saying you think you touched the wrong button but the two buttons are on opposite ends—even the remote pad is set up that way. So it's quite impossible. Here, I'll show you." David stood up, pointing to the far end of the screen; he explained button functions in detail. Although Christian was the brain behind the security, David had knowledge about how it all came together—the intricate details.

"Oops, I forgot to pause it," David said.

By the time they returned to the tapes, it was footage of Christian's room.

"Wait a minute, what the hell is this?" David asked.

"That's my room!" Christian peered into the screen.

"You gotta be kidding me—you record yourself?" David looked around the room. "There's a camera here? Are you just self-absorbed or what?"

"Stop it, Dave! I didn't. That only happens when the gate security is manually switched off. It's been happening by default. Remember I told you I had that problem?"

"But why do you have a camera in here in the first place? You know what . . . I don't wanna know."

"Will you stop it?" Christian said impatiently. "I was experimenting with the surveillance system."

David raised a brow.

"That's all, I promise. Now can you rewind the tape? So this proves what I said earlier, if it recorded my room, that means I manually switched it off."

David rewound the tape.

"Stop!" Christian wailed.

The surveillance showed someone walk out of the room.

David paused the video and looked at Christian with fright in his eyes. "No way!"

"It goes further—it's an instant record. Go back some more."

The tape showed Olivia's image from four angles, including her face. She removed her hands from the settings and walked away.

"Why would Olivia switch off the surveillance?"

"To set me up. Watch as she looks around. I must have been in the shower. That explains why there's no footage of him. She had to have let him in that day."

"Man, I am so sorry," David said, shaking his head. "You've got some pretty twisted friends."

"Careful . . . You're supposed to be one of them."

"Don't joke like that, Chris."

"I'm not laughing."

"So now you're gonna look over your shoulder at the rest of us. This teaches us to be careful of who we trust. You're going to have to trust someone but the question is who. You can't go one treating the right ones like you did Isa."

"What do I do?" Christian asked, running both hands through his hair. "Dave, I'm terrified. How many other secrets must I uncover? I just miss her so much. I've called both her cell and home numbers incessantly— nothing. I called her assistant—no answer. It's almost like she never existed."

"Isa loves you too much to disappear," Rachel said, suddenly back in the room.

"Yeah, but no one's ever hurt her but me—"

"She'll forgive," David replied.

"So, what did I miss?" Rachel asked.

Later that night, Christian's guilt kept him awake in bed. His eyes burned from weariness, yet sleep eluded him. He thought of Isabella by the fountain on their date night, pleading for him not to become the *skeptic hiker*. In hindsight, he knew the story had to have been Genius' idea—perhaps a public plea for salvation from himself. Isabella knew it.

There was a knock on his door. He smiled as Rachel let herself in and sat on the bed. It took everything in him to keep from crying.

"I wanna let you know that you're not alone in this," she said. "I betrayed her trust, too. She was so hurt when she knew I was skeptical." Rachel threw her face into her palms and cried aloud.

Christian sat up and embraced her. He felt a release—something told him it was okay to let it out. Their embrace took him back to how they consoled one another when Rachel's parents died.

She pulled away and cradled his face, stroking a tear away. "They're right, you *do* have tears!"

Christian laughed. "Don't be ridiculous. I'm human, Rach." She didn't look convinced that he was; or perhaps she wasn't ready to accept her superhero cried, so he straightened up. "You saw her on the night of the wedding, didn't you?"

Rachel smiled through her tears as her gaze trailed off into the distance. "Yes, I did."

Christian stood up from the bed and walked to the window. The wind looked turbulent—at least from the waves it caused. "How did she look? Please tell me."

"You should have seen her—she was an angel—so beautiful. She had candles all over. It was like she dreamed it since eleventh grade. I was amazed. You would have loved it. The room smelled so sweet and was warm and cozy with her favorite song playing."

He turned around swiftly. "'La La La'?"

"Yup," Rachel laughed. "She had it on repeat."

Rachel continued with laughing through tears. "She wanted me out of there so bad, said you wouldn't want me there. While I sat there in a panic, thinking of how to tell her the news, she kept fixing her hair. She wanted everything to be perfect." Rachel paused and looked at Christian. He turned around. "Why did you stop?"

"I have something for you, just wait." She returned with a plastic bag with the hotel name on it.

He pulled out a white lingerie and smiled. "That's what she had on?"

Rachel nodded. "She forgot it in the room. Keep it safe for her. I know she'll come back soon."

OCTOBER 8, 2013. SÃO PAULO, BRAZIL, 6 A.M.
(*3 A.M. MIAMI TIME*)

By daybreak, a deep sense of despair replaced Isabella's earlier high from the dream. She was back to being bitter and felt helpless. She despised Christian and Olivia for what they had done to her and even loathed them the more for making it impossible for her to express the pain. She had no control over even expressing herself. The only person she wanted to speak to was Febe; however, she was on a mission trip to Venezuela and wasn't expected to return for another week. Her mother nagged her about going to the salon—"it'd make you feel better," she had said. Perhaps feeling better inside would reflect on her face. That morning marked two days since her return to Brazil and last night was her longest sleep since the day before her wedding. The sleep was kind to the bags under her eyes. After she'd showered and prepared breakfast for her parents, she brushed her hair thoroughly and put it into a neat bun. She then drove her father's Volkswagen Tiguan straight to the hair salon that she and her mom had frequented since she was a little girl.

When she walked in, the salon owner, Marisa, quickly went to embrace her. Isabella sighed as she hugged her tight—nostalgia hit as she took the scent of various hair sprays. Marisa had always taken pride in Isabella's hair. She had used her as a poster child for her expertise. Pictures of Isabella throughout the years even adorned the walls. Marisa's excitement was confirmation that Isabella's bad misfortune had not reached São Paulo yet and she was glad. After Isabella took her seat at the station, Marisa looked at her in the mirror. "Are you okay, baby?"

"Yes, Tia Ma." Isabella had affectionately called Marisa that since she was a child.

She took Isabella's hair out of the bun and grinned as she ran her fingers through it. "Oh my, you'll never hear a hairdresser say this but, those folks in Florida really do a good job taking care of your hair."

"You think I trust anyone to my hair except you?" Isabella said with a half-smile. "I do it myself." *Except for on my wedding day*, she mused. Marisa squeezed her shoulders. "Ahh, you learned from the best." She rubbed her hands together with a twinkle in her eye. "Okay, I'm glad you are here because I learned a few new styles that I could only do on a hair like yours."

"Yeah?" Isabella asked, eyeing Marisa's reflection in the mirror. "Wanna post them up?"

"You wouldn't mind?" she asked.

"Sure, why not."

For the next three hours, Marisa washed and styled Isabella's hair. It took an hour for Marisa's professional photographer to arrive, and another thirty minutes for him to take the pictures. The entire time, Isabella told herself that the ordeal was a sacrifice for an old friend. Her mother would expect such treatment to cheer her up—and for most women it should, but for her, it was a crude reminder of what she'd lost. It all reminded her of October Fifth—from the hairstylists to the clicks of the professional camera. It was tormenting. No one who knew her would believe that taking beautiful pictures was an ordeal for her usual playful and cheerful self. But today she needed prompting from Marisa just to smile.

When the photographer left, Isabella reached into her purse. "How much do I owe you?"

Marisa scoffed. "Oh please! I owe *you* for all your trouble—it's the least I could do."

Isabella insisted, "It's a very beautiful style and it took you long to do it."

"Stop it, Isa! Look around you; see yourself all over this wall. Have I ever paid you for any of this? No! You and your mom always paid me for all those styles. It's high time I did something free for you. You know my competitor, Ana, down the street?"

"Yeah."

"She has to pay models to get her hair pictures . . . either that or she buys ready-made pictures of hairs she never even styled. And me? I have the most beautiful girl in the city gracing my wall."

Isabella smiled. "Okay, I won't push it then."

"So, what are your plans for the rest of the day, how long will you be in town?"

"Um, Tia Ma," Isabella whispered, looking around the salon. "Can we go to the back room?"

Once there, Isabella said, "I didn't want to cause a stir out there."

Marisa frowned. "Sure, what's the matter?"

"I want you to cut my hair."

"But you don't need a trim."

When Isabella shook her head, Marisa's eyes widened in horror. "What? Is it the style? You don't like it? I'm sorry, I should have asked, I'll do something else, please don't talk like this."

"No, it's not the style, I love the style. I actually came in to cut my hair but I thought it fair to give you one last photo for your wall. I know how much it means to you."

"No, I won't let you."

"Please don't do this." Isabella pleaded. "I wouldn't have come here if I knew how to do it myself."

"What's wrong with you, do you realize how many women want hair like yours?"

"Look, they can have it. I'll give it all to you to donate or make into a wig for someone."

"No, I knew something was wrong with you when you walked in. What happened, who hurt you?"

Isabella sighed. "You leave me no choice but to go to Ana's."

"I'll call her and offer her money not to do it!" Marisa yelled, pulling out her cell phone.

Settling on an entirely different salon, Isabella pulled up into a random shop and asked the hairdresser to cut off her hair. She ensured they washed all the treatment out and blow-dried it first. The hairdresser complimented the pixie cut, but Isabella avoided her reflection.

Out in her car, she still couldn't look at herself but she mourned her loss all the same. Her mid-back length hair was gone—so was the weight, and one of Christian's obsessions. She wept. On her way home, she stopped at Marisa's shop. Before she walked in, she put on her father's baseball cap. She could tell that Marisa had been crying and she hated to remind her. "I didn't go to Ana's," Isabella said, handing her the bag containing her hair before kissing her on the cheek. "I promise to return when it grows back."

OCTOBER 8, 2013. MIAMI, FLORIDA, 3:47 A.M.
(6:47 A.M. SÃO PAULO TIME)

Christian tossed and turned throughout that night. He was extremely exhausted, yet he still could not sleep. It was three forty-seven in the morning and he could hear Isabella's voice in his head; she seemed to have replaced Genius.' He embraced her white lingerie—it still had her scent. As he reached for his stereo remote, he felt the urge to get down on his knees and pray. When he was done, he got up and mechanically, walked into the bathroom. Once he had showered and fully dressed, he packed a small bag. Whatever came over him gave him the strongest urge to leave the city. He peeked into Rachel's room and, seeing that she was fast asleep, he left a note for her and began to head down the steps when he bumped into an equally fully dressed David.

"What are you doing up this early?" Christian asked.

"I could ask you the same question, but I won't because I had the weirdest dream about us in Brazil and Denise thought I should convince you to go bring her back."

Christian's mouth dropped.

"Well, it looks like you don't need any convincing."

"David, I kid you not; I had no idea where I was going. I just had to get out."

"Yeah, you're going to Brazil."

"But the jet is across the world—my parents are en route to Australia."

"Who said anything about the jet? Our next flight out is in less than three hours and there's still a lot of room on that flight. We'll plan our strategy at the airport."

OCTOBER 8, 2013. SÃO PAULO, BRAZIL, 7 P.M.

Isabella hadn't let her mood get in the way of gathering the last-minute necessities for her mission in the outskirts of Araçoiaba da Serra. Signing up gave her a sense of purpose, knowing she would be volunteering math lessons to an up-and-coming school. She would be able to clear her mind and spend quality time with the Lord without her mother nagging her. She still hadn't told her about the possible annulment and her father advised her not to, promising to keep the fax—which would arrive at his office—private. But her mother had her ways of uncovering things, so just in case she did, the distance would be good for them—she didn't think her poor mother could handle another shock after nearly passing out from her haircut. She was clueless of the Lord's next plan for her, but she couldn't help but wonder whether this was part of the grand plan. Of all the places in the world she should have been, it was ironic that she was back in Brazil—the same place she had told Christian she didn't want to be for her honeymoon. Also, the same place that supposedly held the key to the Gomes family tragedy. Until the Lord revealed the next step, she'd put her heart into the church's mission, while waiting patiently for the annulment papers. She knew the Lord would give her strength to deal with that moment when it came.

Close to seven that evening, Isabella had completely packed up for her trip. She would need to be at the church by six the next day and was glad she had packed early and had extra time to spend with her mother. Unfortunately, her father, who was a professor at the University of São Paulo, would be out until late for his final class.

Isabella walked into the kitchen just as her mother, Ana, wrapped up a phone call on her cell phone.

"Mom, did you ever figure out the deal with the home phone?"

"No, I'll have the phone company look into it. You know you can use my cell phone if you need to. In fact, you should use it instead of the one your dad gave you for the mission. I can't use most of the functions on this anyway."

"Oh, ok thanks! Um, yeah, before I forget, remember the pastor you promised to introduce me to?"

Ana grunted. "Don't tell me you're still interested in that."

"I may not be with Christian, but the fact still remains that I was the one that Rosa said will help his family and I intend to keep my promise."

"But filha—"

"No buts, Mom. They've been my family for years. When you and Dad left, they took care of me and regardless of what happened to Chris and I, I still love them. This could mean freedom for them and their next generations—no one else deserves to die tragically."

"And this is your problem because?"

"Are you going to help me or do I have to do this on my own?"

Ana sighed as she picked up her phone. "Grab a pen and paper."

Soon after Isabella took down the information, the gate's bell sounded. When she arrived at the gate, a tall gentleman—nearly Christian's height, grinned through the opening of the wrought-iron gate.

"Good evening," Isabella greeted.

"Good evening, senhorita," he replied, his voice deep and low. "I see you don't remember me?"

"Wait a minute," she said, trying to place his face.

"Olá, Eduardo!" Ana yelled from behind Isabella. "That was fast—we just hung up."

"Olá, mommy, I was in the neighborhood," he replied, eyes steady on Isabella.

Isabella grinned. "Edu? Oh my, it's been ages."

"We were ten," Eduardo said, slowly nodding.

"How are you? Congratulations on your practice. I hear good things."

"Thank you."

"So, what brings you here?"

Ana scolded. "Isabella, have you no manners to have a conversation with our guest at the gate?"

Isabella blushed, stepping back and pulling the gate open toward her. "I'm so sorry."

Eduardo smiled as he walked in. "It's okay, mom told me you relocated."

Isabella scowled at her mom. "Of course she did."

"It's good to have you home," Eduardo said. "You *did* cut your hair."

His provocative stare and the way he moistened his lips made her uncomfortable.

She ran her fingers through her cropped hair, "Yes, I needed a change."

"Change is always good." His lips formed a slight smile. "It shows off your beautiful face."

Isabella looked away. It was obvious he was flirting with her, but what was more disturbing was the fact that it didn't seem to faze her mother. "Come on, Eduardo," Ana said, taking him by the hand and heading back into the house.

Sighing deeply, Isabella closed the gate.

CULMINATION

They pulled up at Isabella's family gate some minutes after 9 p.m. Christian struggled to contain his heart rate as David handed him the bouquet of orchids they had purchased along the way. A man who appeared to be in his mid- to late-twenties approached the gate. His hair was a medium brown wavy shag, cut in uniform layers.

He smiled at Christian and David. "Olá, senhores!"

"Olá!" David replied to the man, before stepping up close to Christian and saying, "Let me handle this."

Christian took a step aside as David and the man conversed in Portuguese.

"How may I help you?" the man asked David, before eyeing the bouquet in Christian's hand.

"I'm David Crenshaw and this is my friend, Christian Cervello. We're here to see his wife, Isabella."

When Christian noticed the man's countenance change, Genius started to hum. He was fully aware that Isabella had no sibling but two male cousins—both of whom he had met.

Ana yelled out in English from behind the man as she approached the gate, "Who's that?"

The man scowled at Christian as he replied in Portuguese with a sarcastic smirk, "*Um típico Americano.*"

Ana arrived, and standing directly behind the man, she said in English, "Isabella is not home."

Christian pleaded, "Mom, please let me explain."

"She's not here!" Ana said, sharply cutting him off. "Explain to her when you see her."

"When will she be back? I can't reach her on her phone and—"

"She traveled to the countryside. Just go, okay?"

Christian glanced at the man, who appeared to be losing his patience. When the man's gaze met his, he said something else in Portuguese, "*Quem você pensa que é?*"

Then, visibly shaken with his hands clenching in and out of a fist position, the man looked directly at David and said in English, "You heard the lady, leave now. You're not welcome here."

Christian watched as the man retreated into the house. "This is going to be harder than I thought," he said. It didn't help that he had no smart ideas from Genius.

At six the next morning, Christian and David parked a few feet away from Isabella's family gate. They planned to sit out in the car until someone emerged and they practically had all day to do this. About an hour into their wait, David had drifted off to sleep right before Christian noticed the gate open. He leaped from the car and ran toward the gate as his father-in-law's car surfaced. Christian flagged him down, yelling out. "Dad!"

The vehicle came to a stop as Christian neared it.

"Chris? Is that you, son?" Felix asked, squinting.

"Yes," Christian said, panting. David lagged behind.

Felix shook his head. "How long have you been out there?"

"We arrived at six. Sorry, I know it's early but we were hoping to catch someone before . . ."

"I can't believe you missed her," Felix said, sadness reflected in his eye. "She left with our church on a mission trip an hour ago. Like five minutes to six. I know because she mentioned having five minutes to get to church. Oh, *meu Deus*, you should have called!"

"But I've been calling her. Her cell phone's voicemail is full and I keep getting a busy signal on the house phone."

"House phone?" Felix asked before retrieving his cell phone and dialing. He soon frowned as he hung up.

Christian continued. "Wait, you said she left this morning, but yesterday Mom said she had already left."

"You spoke to Ana?" Felix's frown deepened.

"We were here last night but—"

"What time?"

Christian looked at David. "A little after nine or so."

"But Isa was . . . Come with me," Felix said as he backed his car into the compound, the gate closing in automatically.

They followed Felix up to the front door, and opted to remain by the foot of the stairs as he went up. A few seconds later, they heard yelling in Portuguese coming from upstairs. When Christian began to speak, David whispered, "Shh, wait!"

Christian set his SecureWatch to record the conversation. He was certain he would get a near-perfect transcription as their voices were extremely loud. They couldn't have been far away, and he thought for sure that Ana would surface at any moment. After no more than ten minutes, Christian heard Ana break down as Felix returned downstairs. He escorted them outside. "I'm very sorry, son; Isabella was home when you came last night but she didn't know."

Christian gulped as Felix put his hand over his shoulder. "You must understand. Ana is very hurt. Isabella is her only child and it was an embarrassment to have her newly wedded daughter return to her parents' home. Ana felt like a laughingstock among her peers."

"I can see how. I am very sorry for what I've done. I would want nothing more than to talk to her and apologize myself."

"Not now, son. She is very emotional. Still, that doesn't excuse her behavior and I'm sorry."

Christian lowered his head. There was no mask for him, the pain was unbearable and Felix must have seen it because he grabbed him close as Christian wept into his chest. "What do I do now?"

"Listen, I don't want you to think this trip was a wasted effort. You actually did the right thing by coming. She didn't know you'd come back for her and that's why she made a commitment to the mission."

Christian sniffed. "Do you think I can go see her at this place she's going to?"

"Oh, no, son, they'll be heading deep into the rural areas. In fact, she probably won't have cell phone service there. But I expect her to call as soon as she gets service or at least a landline—I promise to let her know you were here; she will be happy."

Christian and David both nodded.

Felix asked, "This issue between you two, is it resolved?"

"Yes."

"Okay. Go back to Florida and take good care of yourself. I'll take good care of Isa for you."

"Thanks, Dad."

They said their good-byes, and just as Christian and David arrived at the gate, Felix's phone rang. "Chris!" Felix yelled, signaling them to return. He then handed Christian the phone, whispering, "That's her!"

Christian stuttered into the phone, "Baby, I don't—" The tears flooded back. He'd rehearsed the conversation so many times, yet the moment had arrived and words failed him. He wept into the phone.

"Please don't cry," Isabella said. "I have forgiven you."

"But I haven't even told you everything that happened, I was . . . "

"It doesn't matter." She waited for his cries to settle before adding, "I just have one request."

"Anything." He sniffed.

"Try to find it in your heart to forgive Olivia and Kevin."

Christian hyperventilated. "I don't know if I can do that." It came out in a near whisper. Then he shrieked, "I trusted them."

"Do you remember what Rosa said about friends hurting you?"

He literally couldn't speak when his mouth opened. Crying as an adult was awkward and it hurt in his chest and throat.

"That was them. Release them so you can move on. I'm not asking you to be as close, but forgiving them will release your pain so it won't lead to resentment."

"They have to face time. Can you believe she was even behind the kidnapping?"

Isabella's sigh was deep. "We all have to face the consequences of our actions. Look at me; who would believe that forgetting my jacket at a nightclub would land me here on my honeymoon. If I dwelled on my mistakes that day, I'd go crazy. Yet, God still protected me from something worse by having you there that night. But even though He loves me, I still had to face the consequences of not listening to all the warnings that day. And remember how I told you the SecureWatch's beep was annoying?"

He smiled through tears. "Yeah."

"Well, if it hadn't been, only God knows if I would have been alive today. I would be facing that consequence too."

He cringed at the thought.

"Listen, I am not saying they shouldn't face time for whatever they did; they should. All I'm asking is that you don't neglect them entirely. Pray for them, because when God opens their eyes, they'll be shocked to see just how much the enemy used them."

"I'll try my best."

"God will help you. One last thing. I think Kevin is in trouble. I'm dreaming more now, and just before I woke up this morning, I dreamed that I pulled off the blindfold he had over my eyes and saw marks on both his wrists."

Christian gasped.

"I know," Isabella said.

"Wait, but you never saw his face. How would you know that was him?"

"I still don't know what he looks like—I never got to see his face, just his wrists. But in the dream, it was supposed to be him. You just know that in a dream. Besides his voice was the same."

"I bet."

She said in a near whisper. "I don't think I could forget that voice. He said something before I pulled off the mask, I just don't remember what now. Just promise me that you will check on him or at least alert Detective Sanders about it. Maybe he will know what to do or have the guards check-in on him or something."

"I promise," Christian said, before he heard a loud noise in the background.

"Thank you. Listen, they just announced that we are heading out of Sorocaba in a few minutes. I don't have much time before we lose the connection. Dad said you came with David. Could you put him on the phone?"

"I can't see you?" Christian asked.

"Soon. I gave them my word. Just know that I love you."

His voice broke as he replied. "I love you, too."

Disheartened, he held the phone out to David. "She wants to speak to you."

David took the phone. "Isa, how are you doing?"

"I'm good, how's Denise?"

"We're all waiting for you to come home, Isa. We're so—"

"Dave, listen, I'll lose the connection soon," she said sternly. "I need you to speak in Portuguese now."

"Okay."

"I need you to promise me that you'll keep what I have to say private until I release you to tell."

David hesitated.

"Listen, it's nothing that'll harm your friend, I promise."

"Okay."

"Promise me," she insisted.

"I promise," David said in Portuguese, looking at Christian.

"Do you remember when Pastor Bernard asked you and Denise to join us for our last premarital class?"

"Yes."

"Remember what you said your concern was?"

"Yes"

"You were right. The Lord showed it to me."

"Really?" David asked.

"Yes, he needs to get his priorities in order. He's put me where God needs to be and it's not right."

"What can I do?" David asked.

"There's nothing either one of us can do but pray. He needs to see it for himself; otherwise his walk with Christ will never be authentic. That's why I need you to keep this quiet. I trust that the Lord will show Him as He did for me. You may not believe it, but I was in the same place and it took pain to see that I placed too much of my joy in Chris."

"What is she saying?" Christian whispered to David.

David shook his head and held up a finger.

"He enjoys the Bible studies and I pray he continues to attend even in my absence. You and Denise are welcome to join. Pastor Bernard knows about all this. I spoke to him yesterday so you can work with him on it. You're free to discuss this with Denise because she's your wife, but ensure she keeps it confidential. I am begging the two of you to pray for Chris and I. Things are beginning to unfold. This is nothing compared to what we will have to face and if we expect to survive this marriage or solve the mystery of the curse, he needs to be spiritually stronger than he is now.

"Take care of him for me. As you can see, he has issues with friends, but he trusts you. He said you kept him out of trouble in the past. I need you to keep doing that to the best of your ability. God will give you wisdom. Don't go far even if he pushes you away. He tends to do that and I don't know why. Just love him."

"Oh boy, he keeps staring at me. He'll be eager to hear something after we are done. What do I say?"

"Tell him I love him," Isabella said. "That's all he needs to know. I love him very much."

"When are you coming home?"

"This trip is for three months. I don't know what God has in store for me after that. I do know that God honors marriage, so He won't keep me away from Christian for long. This church mission was my doing. I just needed to get away, but since I gave my word, I must honor it. I signed up when I thought our marriage was over. I take it there are no annulment papers?"

"No."

"I'm glad because I really want this marriage, but it's toxic now and it has to change. I must go."

"I'll do as you said. Take care, Isa; we love you."

"I love you all, too. Tell Rachel to stop beating herself up."

"I will. Do you think you. . . " David started to say. He then handed the phone to Felix. "We lost the connection."

"I'm just glad she got to speak to you both," Felix replied.

Christian cleared his throat. "Um . . . Dad, there was a man in your house when we came last night."

"A young man—slightly long hair?"

"Yeah."

"Oh, that was Dr. Eduardo Lopes. He was still there when I got home," he said, shaking his head. "Her mother had pushed for them to marry long before. I wouldn't worry about him, son." He patted Christian's back.

Christian slowly nodded. "Will you all be okay? Is there anything I can provide?"

"That's thoughtful of you, son," Felix said with an appreciative gleam. "We're okay. Thanks for asking. But until I get our home phone back on, reach me on my mobile phone. I will write down Ana's number on the back—that's the phone Isa is using right now." He scribbled the number on the back of his business card. "I doubt you'll reach her, though, because there will be little to no connection. But she intends to call me from time to time when she can get away to the nearest working phone. I'll keep you posted."

"I appreciate this," Christian said, now hopeful.

After David had translated the fight between Isabella's parents, the rest of the drive back to the hotel was agonizingly quiet. Christian figured that speaking would silence the new breed of negative thoughts.

"Wow, for her to even disconnect the house phone." Christian shook his head. "He's right. I embarrassed them all."

"Oh, don't you worry about that," David said. "There's a lot more of that to go around on your end."

"What do you mean?"

"We *are* going back to Florida, aren't we? Well, you're gonna have lots of explaining to do when people start wondering where your new bride is."

Christian shook his head. He had never thought of that.

"Tell me something, were you serious about wanting an annulment?"

"No, I was just so angry. The minute I read what it was about, I thought it was insane. I love her too much. I just can't believe I forgot to close the stupid browser. Now I have to deal with some young doctor. The nerve of that coward to call me *entitled*. He should have spoken in English so I could punch him."

"Oh, *you're* jealous? He sounded like the jealous one when he asked, *Who do you think you are?*"

Christian fumed over the thought that he could lose her to someone else. This time there was a real threat—someone her own mother was fond of.

"You're going to have to stop obsessing over Isa. She would expect you to stay focused on the Gomes project."

"You think she'll still do that after what I put her through?" Christian scoffed.

"That's something else you gotta watch—give her more credit. From the little I know about her, she's probably working on it as we speak."

"I can't believe I missed her by just five minutes," Christian said, shaking his head. "Just when fate finally had us bumping into each other, we're back to missing each other again."

David sighed. "Now we're stuck on five minutes, great."

A chime went off on Christian's phone. He read the transcription, then closed his eyes—breathing deeply.

"Are you okay?" David asked.

"Why didn't you tell me Isabella cut her hair?"

"How did . . . ?" David looked down at his phone. "Don't tell me . . . Chris! That's got to be illegal."

"Not when it involves me, it's not. I was the only one there at a disadvantage."

"Then wait for me to translate!"

"You did . . . and left out that detail!"

"I only told you what was relevant."

Christian scoffed. "Relevant? You don't think my wife chopping off her hair is relevant? Do you realize how this messes up my head right now—I've been picturing her the same way I saw her last."

"What difference does it make, you didn't marry her hair! Listen, I'm not arguing while I'm driving!"

Christian sighed. "Are you gonna tell me what she said to you on the phone?"

"She said she loves you very much."

"And I'm supposed to believe that it takes those many words in Portuguese to say I love you."

"Believe whatever you want."

Epilogue

❧

Their bus had finally ventured out of the city of Sorocaba and Isabella was glad that she had gotten to speak to Christian before she had lost the connection. She replayed the phone conversation in her mind. Hearing the pain in his cry broke her heart and that was all she needed to know that everything that had happened had to be tied to the curse. The bus ride had progressively become bumpy and she decided it might be a good idea to roll up the chart she had been working on. Up until the phone call, she had begun tracing over some of the now faint characters plotted on the Gomes family tree, as Rosa had advised her to do. The chart even contained drawings. One of them was the charm necklace; another, what looked like a mountain or heap, and strangely, the drawing of men in hard hats surrounded by ladders. They had instruments in their hands—perhaps it was a farmland. There was no way that Liz could have drawn something that elaborate unless she was an artist.

As she began to roll up the chart, she stopped to peer closely at a name that was scribbled below the drawing. It very well could have been the name of the artist, as it was located at the bottom right corner of what was starting to look more and more like a mine. *Farmers wouldn't wear hard hats*, she mused. It was nearly impossible to make out the full penciled name although the first was clearer: 'Joseph.' The last name was illegible. Now intrigued, she unrolled the rest of the map and headed back to the map legend. She saw where Liz had traced the drawing back to a name in print—Joseph J. Gomes. Next to this name was the word 'waiting.' This had to be the same, *Joseph* listed under the drawing.

She hadn't heard the latest announcement from the bus driver but someone tapped her on the back to ask if she had a map. As she searched through her binder for one, she came across the sealed envelope from Rosa containing Liz's final dream. It was eerie remembering how Rosa scribbled the July Fifth date on it. *I still can't believe she's gone,* Isabella said under her breath, frightened at the thought of hearing the deceased woman's voice again from the July recording. Eventually, she would have to, because most of her notes were there.

Seeing that she was well justified by the date to open the letter, she carefully peeled back the edges of the envelope. The note inside seemed to have been sloppily ripped off from a page in Liz's journal. The message was written in Spanish, in the form of a conversation between the writer and God. There that name was again, Joseph Gomes, this time, with a middle name: Juan and it was next to the word 'Who.' Under it was the word, 'Arocoba d Cere' and next to *that* was: 'Where it all started.' A chill came over Isabella as she read further:

> Father, I know the 'Who' is Joseph Juan Gomes, and I know
> 'Where' it started, but I need to know what exactly happened
> and why. Also, I need to know when we will be free and how.
> Thank you, Lord.

The chatter around her seemed to grow silent as she read the answers given to Liz in a dream dated May 17, 1997.

> **What:** He who holds the what, dwells in your household.
> **Why:** He who holds the why, holds the What.
> **When:** A marriage unconsummated for seven months.
> **How:** You will need three things—Isabella will know.

Isabella jumped when the passenger behind her tapped on her back once again and asked if she had found the map, saying she needed to know how far they were from Araçoiaba da Serra. It was then that it occurred to her that although Elizabeth didn't have the right spelling, Isabella's group was heading to the city where it all started.

Acknowledgments

The Lord sent people along my way to ensure the perfection of DF. They couldn't possibly know what they were getting involved in when I contacted them but they all seemed eager to get to work, as if they knew something I didn't know. Whether these people think they have nothing to do with this book's success is up to them but I am grateful that they were faithful to the call.

A big Thank you, Grazie, Gracias, and Obrigada to:

My critique partners: **Patricia Mwiza and Alda De Sousa.** You both were officially my models for Isabella Montes because you had plenty in common with her. You worked on DF tirelessly and like great detectives, left no stone unturned. Patricia, you proofread and critiqued. Alda, you were our source for everything Brazil; who would have guessed that your critiques would be more brutal than Patricia's in the end—and for a good reason. You both read and re-read EVERY chapter without complaining. DF made you cry, and even think of your own lives. In some instances, you swore the story was speaking to you or highlighted particular life experiences, but in reality, I had not known either one of you long enough to know your individual stories. **Babatope Babajide** (Boon), not only were you a critique partner and proofreader, you were my muse. With your trusty little flashlight, you always found me when I was stuck in Casa Cervello playing counselor to their constant bickering. You had no choice but to live vicariously through the Cervellos day and night. You, my dear, were my counselor. **Donna Zaki,** what didn't you help with between stressing over med-school applications? You listened to my Chris and Isa stories and despised me for that particular scene that got stuck in your head. You picked out Isabella's entire wardrobe and even wanted to design the book cover! **Lourdes Venard**, my professional copyeditor, how fortunate I am to have met you. You walked through DF without leaving a trace of ever being there. The only fear I had working with you was that one day you would wake up and wonder, why in the world am I so vested in this project? Now it makes sense. . . I remember how you said you felt as though you lived in Casa Cervello yourself! It was a delight having someone with vast editing knowledge—you teach the art for goodness sake! It was a bonus having an editor who lived in Miami for nearly three decades! **Nike Babajide,** Even though I am pretty sure you don't remember half the stuff you told me when I was still jotting down the voices in my iPhone, I will let you know that all you said to me in a span of 30 minutes via those international text messages, didn't come from you. You were a vessel, and confirmed many things for me. Do you realize that those messages mysteriously disappeared soon after I read each one? **Ijeoma Opara,** just when I needed to put an actual face to the Isa I saw in my head, you casted the perfect actress; and since that day, it was easier to write about her. My critique partners all agree to your choice; isn't that something? You encouraged me by consistently listening to my DF scenes. Though you loved them, you hated me for fear of spoilers. By the way, did you know I finalized the whole manuscript on that tiny laptop you gave me? Yes, right from my iPhone. You probably didn't realize why you gave it to me. I didn't. It had to be part of the divine plan. **Andrea Douglas,** you took your time to critique the DF website in detail. Your feedback was paramount and I am grateful. **Kelechi Ezeadi,** you encouraged me to write the manuscript when I was bent on just having it as a screenplay. You had faith in DF and said you had never heard such a story before in your years of screenwriting. To all the people—and there were lots—who listened to bits of DF and encouraged me to stay strong . . . I THANK YOU! To my future readers, I thank you for picking up this book. I look forward to hearing the effect DF has on you and/or your close relationships.

Above all, I give the glory to God. If He hadn't given me a story to tell, I wouldn't be writing one. I look forward to celebrating the success of DF with you all. I didn't do this alone.

It took a village!

www.ingramcontent.com/pod-product-compliance
Lightning Source LLC
Chambersburg PA
CBHW030545180626
46816CB00005B/1405